Praise for
Sophie Hannah

"No one writes twisted, suspenseful novels quite like Sophie Hannah. I just love her dry, edgy wit and the way she brings her weirdly wonderful characters to life. *Woman with a Secret* is unpredictable, unputdownable, and unlike anything you've read before."

—Liane Moriarty

"Mesmerizing! Sophie Hannah puts the 'psycho' in psychological suspense with this riveting thriller involving the ultimate closed-door crime scene—and a narrator who is both more and less than what she seems." —Lisa Gardner on *Woman with a Secret*

"Sophie Hannah's books are heart-stopping stuff. They slide into the darkest corners of your mind and just won't leave. . . . Like watching a nightmare come to life." —Tana French

"Her plots are ingenious—she's a writer in complete command of her material. . . . She keeps you puzzled and intrigued, right until the end." —*New York Times Book Review* on *Woman with a Secret*

"[Sophie Hannah] has clearly mastered the psychological methodology deployed to exciting ends by Gillian Flynn or Tana French."

—NPR

A Game for
All the Family

A Game for
All the Family

SOPHIE HANNAH

WM

WILLIAM MORROW

An Imprint of HarperCollins*Publishers*

HarperCollins
PUBLISHERS
—— Since 1817 ——

This book was originally published in Great Britain in 2015 by Hodder & Stoughton, a division of Hodder Headline.

P.S.™ is a trademark of HarperCollins Publishers.

HarperCollins books may be purchased for educational, business, or sales promotional use. For information please e-mail the Special Markets Department at SPsales@harpercollins.com.

A hardcover edition of this book was published in 2016 by William Morrow, an imprint of HarperCollins Publishers.

FIRST WILLIAM MORROW PAPERBACK EDITION PUBLISHED 2017.

Library of Congress Cataloging-in-Publication Data has been applied for.

ISBN 978-0-06-238830-8

17 18 19 20 21   OV/LSC   10 9 8 7 6 5 4 3 2 1

*For Karen Geary—thank you for looking after
my books so brilliantly for a decade!*

A Game for
All the Family

The people I'm about to meet in my new life, if they're anything like the ones I'm leaving behind, will ask as soon as they can get away with it. In my fantasy, they don't have faces or names, only voices—raised, but not excessively so; determinedly casual.

What do you do?

Does anyone still add "for a living" to the end of that question? It sounds stupidly old-fashioned.

I hope they miss out the "living" bit, because this has nothing to do with how I plan to fund my smoked-salmon-for-breakfast habit. I want my faceless new acquaintances to care only about how I spend my time and define myself—what I believe to be the point of me. That's why I need the question to arrive in its purest form.

I have the perfect answer: one word long, with plenty of space around it.

Nothing.

Everything should be surrounded by as much space as possible: people, houses, words. That's part of the reason for starting a new life. In my old one, there wasn't enough space of any kind.

My name is Justine Merrison and I do Nothing. With a capital N.

Not a single thing. I'll have to try not to throw back my head and laugh after saying it, or sprint a victory lap around whoever was unfortunate enough to ask me. Ideally, the question will come from people who do Something: surveyors, lawyers, supermarket managers—all haggard and harried from a six-month stretch of fourteen-hour working days.

I won't mention what I used to do, or talk about day-to-day chores as if they count as Something. Yes, it's true that I'll have to do some boiling of pasta in my new life, and some throwing of socks into washing machines, but that will be as easy and automatic as breathing. I don't intend to let trivial day-to-day stuff get in the way of my central project, which is to achieve a state of all-embracing inactivity.

"Nothing," I will say boldly and proudly, in the way that another person might say "Neuroradiology." Then I'll smile, as glowing white silence slides in to hug the curved edges of the word. *Nothing.*

"What are you grinning about?" Alex asks. Unlike me, he isn't imagining a calm, soundless state. He is firmly embedded in our real-world surroundings: six lanes of futile horn-beep gripes and suffocating exhaust fumes. "The joys of the A406," he muttered half an hour ago, as we added ourselves to the long line of backed-up traffic.

For me, the congestion is a joy. It reminds me that I don't need to do anything in a hurry. At this rate of travel—approximately four meters per hour, which is unusual even for the North Circular—we won't get to Devon before midnight. *Excellent.* Let it take twenty hours, or thirty. Our new house will still be there tomorrow, and the day after. It doesn't matter when I arrive, as I have nothing pressing to attend to. I won't need to down a quick cup of tea, then immediately start hectoring a telecommunications company about how soon they can hook me up with WiFi. I have no urgent emails to send.

"Hello? Justine?" Alex calls out, in case I didn't hear his question over the noise of Georges Bizet's *Carmen* that's blaring from our car's speakers. A few minutes ago, he and Ellen were singing along, having adapted the words somewhat: "Stuck, stuck in traffic, traffic, stuck, stuck in traffic, traffic, stuck, stuck in traffic, traffic *jam*. Stuck, stuck in traffic, traffic, stuck, stuck in traffic, traffic *jam*, traffic *jam*, traffic *jam* . . ."

"Mum!" Ellen yells behind me. "Dad's talking to you!"

"I think your mother's in a trance, El. Must be the heat."

It would never occur to Alex to turn off music in order to speak. For him, silence is there to be packed as full as possible, like an empty bag. The Something that he does—has for as long as I've known him—is singing. Opera. He travels all over the world, is away for one week in every three, on average, and loves every second of his home-is-where-the-premiere-is existence. Which is lucky. If I didn't know he was idyllically happy with his hectic, spotlit life, I might not be able to enjoy my Nothing to the full. I might feel guilty.

As it is, we'll be able to share our contrasting triumphs without either of us resenting the other. Alex will tell me that he managed to squeeze four important calls into the time between the airline staff telling him to switch off his phone, and them noticing that he'd disobeyed them and telling him again like they really meant it this time. I'll tell him about reading in the bath for hours, topping up with hot water again and again, almost too lazy to twist the tap.

I press the "off" button on the CD player, unwilling to compete with *Carmen*, and tell Alex about my little question-and-answer fantasy. He laughs. Ellen says, "You're a nutter, Mum. You can't say 'Nothing.' You'll scare people."

"Good. They can fear me first, then they can envy me, and wonder if they might take up doing Nothing themselves. Think how many lives I could save."

"No, they'll think you're a depressed housewife who's going to go home and swallow a bottle of pills."

"Abandoned and neglected by her jet-setting husband," Alex adds, wiping sweat from his brow with the sleeve of his shirt.

"No they won't," I say. "Not if I beam blissfully while describing my completely empty schedule."

"Ah, so you *will* say more than 'Nothing'!"

"Say you're a stay-at-home mum," Ellen advises. "Or you're taking a career break after a stressful few years. You're weighing up various options . . ."

"But I'm not. I've already chosen Nothing. Hey." I tap Alex on the arm. "I'm going to buy one of those year-planner wall charts—a really beautiful one—and stick it up in a prominent place, so that I can leave every day's box totally empty. Three hundred and sixty-five empty boxes. It'll be a thing of beauty."

"You're *so annoying*, Mum," Ellen groans. "You keep banging on about this new life and how everything's going to be so different, but it won't be, because . . . you! You're incapable of changing. You're *exactly the same*: still a massive . . . zealot. You were a zealot about working, and now you're going to be one about not working. It'll be so boring for me. And embarrassing."

"Pipe down, pipsqueak," I say in a tone of mock outrage. "Aren't you, like, supposed to be, like, only thirteen?"

"I haven't said 'like' for ages, actually, apart from to express approval," Ellen protests.

"That's true, she hasn't," says Alex. "And she's frighteningly spot-on about her drama-queen mother. Tell me this: if you crave tranquility as you claim to, why are you daydreaming about starting fights with strangers?"

"Good point!" Ellen crows.

"Fights? What fights?"

"Don't feign innocence."

"Not feigning!" I say indignantly.

Alex rolls his eyes. "Aggressively saying, 'Nothing' when people ask you what you do, making them feel uncomfortable by refusing to qualify it at all, or explain . . ."

"Not aggressively. *Happily* saying it. And there's nothing about Nothing to explain."

"Smugly," Alex says. "Which is a form of aggression. Flaunting your pleasurable idleness in the faces of those with oversensitive work ethics and overstuffed diaries. It's sadistic."

"You might have a point," I concede. "I've been particularly looking forward to telling the hardworking, stressed people I meet that I do Nothing. The more relaxed a person looks, the less fun it'll be to boast to them. And it's pointless bragging to the likes of you—you love your overstuffed diary. So I'm just going to have to hope I meet lots of people who hate their demanding jobs but can't escape them. Oh God." I close my eyes. "It's sickeningly obvious, isn't it? It's me I want to taunt. My former self. That's who I'm angry with."

I could have escaped at any time. Could have walked away years earlier, instead of letting work swallow up my whole life.

"I literally cannot believe I have a mother who . . . homilies on in the way you do, Mum," Ellen grumbles. "None of my friends' mothers do it. *None.* They all say normal things, like 'No TV until you've done your homework' and 'Would you like some more lasagna?'"

"Yes, well, your mother can't go ten minutes without having a major, life-changing realization—can you, darling?"

"Fuck off! Oops." I giggle. If I've ever been happier than I am now, I can't remember the occasion.

"Aha! We're on the move again." Alex starts to sing, "End of the traffic, traffic, end of the traffic, traffic, end of the traffic, traffic *jam,*

end of the traffic, traffic, end of the traffic, traffic *jam*, traffic *jam*,
traffic *jam* . . ."

Poor, long-dead Georges Bizet. I'm sure this wasn't the legacy he
had in mind.

"Excuse me while I don't celebrate," says Ellen. "We've still got
another, what, seven hours before we get there? I'm boiling. When
are we going to get a car with air-conditioning that works?"

"I don't believe any car air-conditioning works," I tell her. "It's
like windshield wipers. The other cars want you to think they've got
it figured out, but they're all hot and stuffy on days like today, whatever Jeremy Clarkson might want us to think. They all have wipers
that squeak like bats being garroted."

"Aaand . . . we're at a standstill again," says Alex, shaking his
head. "The golden age of being in transit was short-lived. You're
wrong about the seven hours, though, El. Quite, quite wrong."

"Yeah, it's just doubled to fourteen," Ellen says bitterly.

"Wrong. Mum and I didn't say anything because we wanted to
surprise you, but actually . . . we're very nearly there."

I smile at Ellen in the rearview mirror. She's hiding behind her
thick, dark brown hair, trying to hang on to her disgruntled mood
and not succumb to laughter. Alex is a rotten practical joker. His
ideas are imaginative enough, but he's scuppered every time by his
special prankster voice, instantly recognizable to anyone who has
known him longer than a week.

"Yeah right, Dad. We're still on the North Circular and we're
very nearly in Devon. Of course." Big, beautiful green eyes and
heavy sarcasm: two things I adore about my daughter.

"No, not Devon. There's been a change of plan. We didn't want
to inconvenience you with a long drive, so . . . we've sold Speedwell House and bought that one instead!" Alex points out of the
car window to a squat redbrick 1930s-or-thereabouts semi-detached

house. I know immediately which one he means. It looks ridiculous. It's the one anyone would single out, the last in a row of eight. There are three signs attached to its façade, all too big for such a small building.

My skin feels hot and tingly all of a sudden. Like when I had cellulitis on my leg after getting bitten by a mosquito in Corfu, except this time it's my whole body.

I stare at the house with the signs. Silently, I instruct the traffic not to move so that I can examine it for as long as I need to.

Why do I need to?

Apart from the excessive ornamentation, there is nothing to distinguish this house from any other 1930s redbrick semi. One sign, the largest—in the top right-hand corner, above a bedroom window—says "Panama Row." That must refer to all the houses huddled bravely together, facing six lanes of roaring traffic immediately outside their windows.

The other two signs—one missing a screw and leaning down on one side and the other visibly grime-streaked—are the name and number of the house. I try to make myself look away, but I can't. I read both and have opinions about them, positive and negative.

That's right: number 8. Yes, it's called . . . No. No, that isn't its name.

Pressure is building in my eyes, head, chest. Thrumming.

I wait until the worst of it subsides, then look down at my arms. They look ordinary. No goosebumps. *Impossible. I can feel them: prickly lumps under my skin.*

"Our new house appears to be called 'German,'" says Alex. "Ludicrous name! I mean, er, won't it be fun to live in a house called 'German,' El?"

"No, because we're not going to be living there. As if Mum'd agree to buy a house on a nearly motorway!"

"You know why she agreed? Because, in no more than ten minutes, we'll take a left turn, then another left, and we'll have arrived. No more long journey, just home sweet home. As the old Chinese proverb says, 'He who buys a beautiful house in the countryside far away might never get there, and may as well buy an ugly house on the North Circular and have done with it.'"

"It's not ugly," I manage to say, though my throat is so tight, I can hardly speak.

It's lovely. It's safe. Stop the car.

I'm not looking at number 8 Panama Row anymore. I tore my eyes away, and now I must make sure they stay away. That won't be hard. I'm too scared to look again.

"Mum? What's wrong? You sound weird."

"You look weird," says Alex. "Justine? Are you okay? You're shivering."

"No," I whisper. "I'm not." *Not okay. Yes, shivering. Too hot, but shivering.* I want to clarify, but my tongue is paralyzed.

"What's wrong?"

"I . . ."

"Mum, you're scaring me. What is it?"

"It's not called 'German.' Some of the letters have fallen off." How do I know this? I've never seen 8 Panama Row before in my life. Never heard of it, known about it, been anywhere near it.

"Oh yeah," says Ellen. "She's right, Dad. You can see where the other letters were."

"But I didn't see it. I . . . I *knew* the name wasn't German. It had nothing to do with what I saw."

"Justine, calm down. Nothing to do with what you saw? That makes no sense."

"It's obvious there are letters missing," says Ellen. "There's loads of empty sign left at the end of the name. Who would call a house 'German,' anyway?"

What should I do and say? I'd tell Alex the truth if we were alone.

"Dad? Accelerate? Like, you're holding everyone up. Ugh! I said 'like' again, goddammit."

"Don't say 'goddammit' either," Alex tells her.

"Don't let me watch *The Good Wife*, then. And you two swear *all the time*, hypocrites."

The car creeps forward, then picks up speed. I feel braver as soon as I know it's no longer possible for me to see 8 Panama Row. "That was . . . strange," I say. *The strangest thing that has ever happened to me.* I exhale slowly.

"What, Mum?"

"Yes, tell us, goddammit."

"Dad! Objection! Sustained."

"Overruled, actually. You can't sustain your own objection. Anyway, shush, will you?"

Shush. Shut up, shut up, shut up. It's not funny. Nothing about this is funny.

"Justine, what's the matter with you?" Alex is more patient than I am. I'd be raising my voice by now.

"That house. You pointed, and I looked, and I had this . . . this overwhelmingly strong feeling of *yes*. Yes, that's my house. I wanted to fling open the car door and run to it."

"Except you don't live there, so that's mad. You don't live anywhere at the moment. Until this morning you lived in London, and hopefully by this evening you'll live just outside Kingswear in Devon, but you currently live nowhere."

How appropriate. Do Nothing, live nowhere.

"You certainly don't live in an interwar semi beside the A406, so you can relax." Alex's tone is teasing but not unkind. I'm relieved that he doesn't sound worried. He sounds less concerned now than he did before; the direction of travel reassures me.

"I know I don't live there. I can't explain it. I had a powerful feeling that I belonged in that house. Or belonged *to* it, somehow. By 'powerful,' I mean like a physical assault."

"Lordy McSwordy," Ellen mumbles from the back seat.

"Almost a premonition that I'll live there one day." How can I phrase it to make it sound more rational? "I'm not saying it's true. Now that the feeling's passed, I can hear how daft it sounds, but when I first looked, when you pointed at it, there was no doubt in my mind."

"Justine, nothing in the world could ever induce you to live cheek by jowl with six lanes of traffic," says Alex. "You haven't changed *that* much. Is this a joke?"

"No."

"I know what it is: poverty paranoia. You're worried about you not earning, us taking on a bigger mortgage . . . Have you had nightmares about losing your teeth?"

"My teeth?"

"I read somewhere that teeth-loss dreams mean anxiety about money."

"It isn't that."

"Even poor, you wouldn't live in that house—not unless you were kidnapped and held prisoner there."

"Dad," says Ellen. "Is it time for your daily You're-Not-Helping reminder?"

Alex ignores her. "Have you got something to drink?" he asks me. "You're probably dehydrated. Heatstroke."

"Yes." There's water in my bag, by my feet.

"Drink it, then."

I don't want to. Not yet. As soon as I pull out the bottle and open it, this conversation will be over; Alex will change the subject to something less inexplicable. I can't talk about anything else until I understand what's just happened to me.

"Oh no. Look: roadwork." When Alex starts to sing again, I don't know what's happening at first, even though it's the same tune from *Carmen* and only the words have changed. Ellen joins in. Soon they're singing in unison, "Hard hats and yellow jackets, hard hats and yellow jackets, hard hats and yellow jackets, *boo*. Hard hats and yellow jackets, hard hats and yellow jackets, boo, sod it, boo, sod it, *boo* . . ."

Or I could try to forget about it. With every second that passes, that seems more feasible. I feel almost as I did before Alex pointed at the house. I could maybe convince myself that I imagined the whole thing.

Go on, then. Tell yourself that.

The voice in my head is not quite ready. It's still repeating words from the script I've instructed it to discard:

One day, 8 Panama Row—a house you would not choose in a million years—will be your home, and you won't mind the traffic at all. You'll be so happy and grateful to live there, you won't be able to believe your luck.

FOUR MONTHS LATER

FAMILY TREE

The Ingreys of Speedwell House

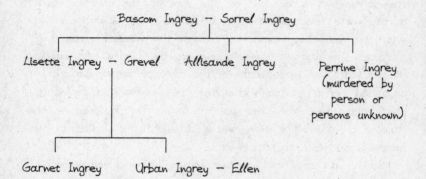

Bascom Ingrey — Sorrel Ingrey

Lisette Ingrey — Grevel   Allisande Ingrey   Perrine Ingrey (murdered by person or persons unknown)

Garnet Ingrey   Urban Ingrey — Ellen

Murder Mystery Story

by Ellen Colley, Class 9G

Chapter 1
~
The Killing of Malachy Dodd

Perrine Ingrey dropped Malachy Dodd out of a window. She wanted to kill him and she succeeded. Later, no one believed her when she screamed, "I didn't do it!" Both of their families, the Ingreys and the Dodds, knew that Perrine and

Malachy had been upstairs in a room together with no one else around.

This was Perrine's bedroom. It had a tiny wooden door (painted mint green, Perrine's favorite color) next to her bed. This little door was the only way of getting from one part of the upstairs of Speedwell House to the other unless you wanted to go back downstairs, through the living room and the library, and then climb up a different lot of stairs, and no one ever wanted to do that. They preferred to bend themselves into a quarter of the size of the shortest dwarf in the world (because that was how tiny the mint-green door was) and squeeze themselves through the minuscule space.

After she dropped Malachy out of the window and watched him fall to his gory death on the terrace below, Perrine squashed herself through the tiny green door and pulled it shut behind her. When her parents found her huddled on the landing on the other side, she exclaimed, "But I wasn't even in the room when it happened!"

Nobody was convinced. Perrine hadn't been clever enough to move a decent distance away from the door, so it was obvious she had just come through it. Her second mistake was to yell, "He fell out by accident!" For one thing Malachy was not tall enough to fall out of the window accidentally (all the adults agreed later that his center of gravity was too low) and for another, if Perrine wasn't in the room when it happened, how did she know that he fell by accident?

A third big clue was that every single other person who might have murdered Malachy was downstairs in the dining room at the time of his hideous death. All of the Dodds were there, and all the Ingreys apart from Perrine. Her two older sisters, Lisette and Allisande, were sitting in chairs facing the three sets of French doors that were open onto the terrace where Malachy fell, splattering his red and gray blood and brains on the ground beside the fountain.

It felt as if his falling shook the whole house, especially the French "purple crystals" chandelier above Lisette and Allisande's heads, but that must have been an illusion.

Lisette and Allisande definitely saw Malachy fall and smash, however, and, what's more, they heard a loud, triumphant "Ha!" floating down from above. Both of them recognized the voice of their younger sister, Perrine.

So, if all the other possible suspects were in the dining room, who else apart from Perrine Ingrey could have been responsible for Malachy landing in a heap on the paving slabs? I'll tell you who: nobody.

There was no doubt that Perrine killed him, however much she wailed that she was innocent. (The death of Malachy Dodd is not the murder mystery in this story. The mystery is who murdered Perrine Ingrey, because she went on to get murdered too, but that comes later.)

No, there was nothing mysterious about the cruel killing of Malachy. Both of the families, the Ingreys and the Dodds, knew the truth, and soon everybody in Kingswear and the surrounding towns and villages knew it too. You cannot keep anything quiet in a place like Devon, where the main hobby is spreading cream and jam onto scones and gossiping about everything you've heard that day.

It came as a surprise to absolutely nobody that one of the Ingreys had committed a murder, because they were such a weird family—the weirdest that Kingswear and its environs had ever known. But there was one big shock for everyone when they heard the news. People should have realized that the most bizarre family for miles around would do the opposite of what you'd expect, or else they would have no right to retain their title of weirdest family. And what most of the nearby town and village folk would have expected was that if 1) there was a murder and 2) the killer was one of the three Ingrey sisters, it was bound to be either

Lisette, the eldest, or Allisande, the middle sister. Certainly not Perrine, the youngest, who was the only one who had had what you might call a properly balanced upbringing.

You see, unlike most parents, especially so long ago, Bascom and Sorrel Ingrey couldn't

1

"Ellen?" I knock on her bedroom door, even though it's ajar and I can see her sitting on her bed. When she doesn't respond, I walk in. "What's this?" I hold up the papers.

She doesn't look at me, but continues to stare out of the window. I can't help looking too. I still haven't gotten used to the beauty of where we live. Ellen's room and the kitchen directly beneath it have the best views in the house: the fountain and gazebo to the left, and, straight ahead, the gentle downward curve of the grass bank that stretches all the way from our front door to the River Dart, studded with rhododendrons, magnolia trees, camellias. When we first came to see Speedwell House in April, there were bluebells, primroses, cyclamen and periwinkles in bloom, poking out of ground ivy and grass: little bursts of brightness interrupting the lush green. I can't wait for those spots of color to reappear next spring.

In the distance, the water sparkles in the bright light like a flowing liquid diamond. On the other side of the river, there's wooded hillside with a few wooden boathouses down at the bottom, and, above them, a scattering of pink, yellow and white cottages protruding from the greenery. From this distance, it looks as if someone has dropped pick-and-mix sweets from the window of an airplane and they've landed among the trees.

Since we moved here, Alex has said at least three times, "It's a funny thing about the English coastline: the land just stops. It's like the interior of the country, and then it suddenly plunges into the sea without any interim bit. I mean, look." At this point he always nods across the river. "That could be in the middle of the Peak District."

I don't know what he means. Maybe I'm shallow, but I don't much care about understanding the scenery. If it looks gorgeous, that's good enough for me.

Boats drift past: sailing dinghies, small yachts, pleasure boats and the occasional schooner. There's one passing now that looks like a child's sketch of a boat: wooden, with a mast and a red sail. Most have less elegant outlines and would be fiddlier to draw.

These are the things I can see out of Ellen's window. Can she see any of them? She's looking out, but there's a shut-off air about her, as if she's not really present in the room with me.

"El. What's this?" I say again, waving the pieces of paper at her. I don't like what I've read. I don't like it at all, however imaginative and accomplished a piece of writing it might be for a fourteen-year-old. It scares me.

"What's what?" Ellen says tonelessly.

"This family tree and beginning of a story about a family called the Ingreys."

"It's for school."

Worst possible answer. Too short, too lacking in attitude. The Ellen I know—the Ellen I desperately miss—would have said, "Um, it's a family tree? And a story about a family called the Ingreys? The answer's kind of contained in the question." How long has it been since she last yelled "Objection!" swiftly followed by "Sustained!"? At least a month.

Whatever Alex says, there's something wrong with our daughter. He doesn't see it because he doesn't want it to be true. When he's home, she makes a special effort to be normal in front of him. She knows that if she can fool him, he'll do his best to persuade me that I'm wrong, that this is standard teenage behavior.

I know it's not true. I know my daughter, and this isn't her. This isn't how even the most alarming teenage version of her would behave.

Bascom and Sorrel Ingrey. It's Ellen's handwriting, but I don't believe she would have made up those names. Allisande, Malachy Dodd, Garnet and Urban . . . Could she have copied it out from somewhere?

I'm trying to work out how I can tactfully ask what prompted her to invent the alarming Perrine Ingrey, whom I resent for splattering my lovely terrace with blood and brains and celebrating with a "Ha!," when the phone starts to ring downstairs. I would leave it, but it might be Alex. As I run to get it, I remind myself that I must call about having some more telephone points put in.

Must. I hate that word. In my old life, it meant "Move fast! Panic! Prepare for catastrophe! Turn it into success by the end of the day! Keep two people happy who want incompatible outcomes! Be brilliant or lose everything!" Fifty times a day, "must" could have signified any of those things, or all of them simultaneously.

I stop at the bottom of the stairs, out of breath. I refuse to hurry. *There is no urgency about anything. Calm down. Remember your mission and purpose. If you're fretting, you're not doing Nothing.*

I'm not going to worry about missing Alex's call. And if it isn't him on the phone, I'm not going to wonder why he hasn't called today. I know he's fine—being fawned over by acolytes in Berlin. Discussing the Ellen situation with him can wait.

Worries are pack animals as well as cowards: too flimsy and

insubstantial to do much damage alone, they signal for backup. Pretty soon there's a whole gang of them circling you and you can't push your way out. *Stuff the lot of them*, I think as I cross the wide black and white tiled hall on my way to the kitchen. I'm lucky to be happy and to have this amazing new life. I don't have much to be anxious about, certainly not compared to most people. There are only two points of concern in my current existence: Ellen's odd behavior, and—though I'm ashamed to be obsessing about it still—the house by the side of the North Circular. 8 Panama Row.

I've dreamed about it often since the day we moved, dreamed of trying to get there—on foot, by car, by train—but never quite making it. The closest I got was in a taxi. The driver pulled up, and I climbed out and stood on the pavement. The front door of the house opened, and then I woke up.

I pick up the phone and say, "Hello?," remembering Alex's pretending-to-be-serious insistence that we must all from now on greet anyone who calls with the words "Speedwell House, good morning/afternoon/evening." "That's how people who live in big country piles answer their phones," he said. "I saw it on . . . something, I'm sure."

Our new house's solitary phone is not portable. It's next to the kitchen window, attached to the wall by a curly wire that makes a plasticky squeaking sound when pulled. Finally at the age of forty-three I have a big, comfy sofa in a kitchen that isn't too small, and I'm unable to reach it to sit down when I make or answer a phone call. I have to stand and look at it instead, while imagining my legs are aching more than they are. My mobile can't help me; there's no reception inside the house yet. Coverage seems only to start at the end of our drive.

"Hello," I say again.

"It's me."

Not Alex. A woman whose voice I don't recognize. Someone arrogant enough to think that she and I are on "It's me" terms when we aren't. It should be easy enough to work out who, once she's said a few more words. I know lots of arrogant women, or at least I did in London. Arrogant men, too. I hoped never to hear from any of them again.

"Sorry, it's a terrible line," I lie. "I can hardly hear you." How embarrassing. *Come on, brain, tell me who this is before I'm forced to reveal how little this person matters to me.* Alex's mum? No. My stepmother? Definitely not.

"It's me. I can hear you perfectly."

A woman, for sure. With a voice as hard as granite and a slight . . . not quite lisp, but something similar. As if her tongue is impeded by her teeth, or she's speaking while trying to stop a piece of chewing gum from falling out of her mouth. Is she disguising her voice? Why would she do that if she wants me to recognize her?

"I'm sorry, this line is appalling. I honestly have no idea who I'm speaking to," I say.

Silence. Then a sigh, and a weary "I think we're beyond lying by now, aren't we? I know you came here to scare me, but it won't work."

I hold the phone away from my ear and stare at it. This is absurd. I've never heard this woman's voice before. She is nobody I know.

"This is a misunderstanding. I don't know who you think you're speaking to—"

"Oh, I know *exactly* who I'm speaking to."

"Well . . . lucky you. I wish I did. I don't recognize your voice. If I know you, you're going to have to remind me. And I've no idea what you mean, but I promise you, I didn't come here to scare you or anyone else."

"I've been frightened of you for too long. I'm not running away again."

I lean my forehead against the kitchen wall. "Look, shall we sort this out? It shouldn't take long. Who are you, and who do you think I am? Because whoever you think I am, I'm not. You're going to have to give your speech again to someone else." I should have hung up on her by now, but I'm holding out for a logical resolution. I want to hear her say, "Oh my God, I'm so sorry. I thought you were my abusive ex-boyfriend / delinquent child / tyrannical religious cult leader."

"I know who you are," says my anonymous caller. "And you know who I am."

"No, you evidently don't, and no I don't. My name is Justine Merrison. You're delivering your message to the wrong person."

"I'm not going to be intimidated by you," she says.

Should have hung up. Still should. "Good. Excellent," I say briskly. "Any chance that I could not be intimidated by you either? Like, no more crank calls? Is your No Intimidation policy one-way, or could it be reciprocal?"

I'm making jokes. How bizarre. If someone had asked me before today how I'd feel if an unpleasant-sounding stranger called and threatened me, I would probably have said I'd be frightened, but I'm not. This is too stupid. I'm too preoccupied by other, more important things, and even some unbelievably trivial ones, like the list pinned to the cork board on the wall opposite: tasks Alex has assigned to me. *Musts.* Call a landscape gardener, find a window cleaner, get the car valeted. Alex is trying to insist I use a local firm he found called The Car Men, because of the Bizet connection. He's written "CAR MEN!!" in capitals at the top of the list. The exclamation marks are intended to remind me that our Range Rover is a biohazard on wheels.

No, I'm sorry. Never make me look at a list again. Haven't you heard? I do Nothing.

Apart from when I'm diverted from my chosen path by a phone call from a lunatic. Or, if not a lunatic . . .

My darling husband.

"Is this one of your hilarious stunts, Alex? It doesn't sound like you, but—"

"I won't let you hurt us," the voice hisses.

"What?" All right, so it's not Alex. Menacing isn't his genre. Then who the hell is she and what's she talking about?

"I don't want to have to hurt you either," she says. "So why don't you pack up and go back to Muswell Hill? Then we can all stay safe."

I stumble and nearly lose my balance. Which seems unlikely, given that I thought I was standing still. Many things seem unlikely, and yet here they are in my life and kitchen.

She knows where we lived before.

Now I'm concerned. Until she said "Muswell Hill," I'd assumed her words were not meant for me.

"Please tell me your name and what you want from me," I say. "I swear on my life and everything I hold dear: I haven't a clue who you are. And I'm not prepared to have any kind of conversation with someone who won't identify herself, so . . ." I stop. The line is dead.

I knock on Ellen's door again. Walk straight in when she doesn't answer. She hasn't moved since I left her room. "Where is it?" she asks me.

"Where's what?"

"My . . . thing. For school."

"Thing? Oh." The family tree and story beginning. I took them with me when I ran to answer the phone. "I must have left them in the kitchen. Sorry. I'll bring them up in a minute." I wait, hoping she'll berate me for first reading and then removing them without permission. She says nothing.

"Shall I go and get them now?"

Er, yes? How would you like it if I took some important papers of yours and spread them all over the house in a really inconvenient way?

It's like a haunting: the constant presence in my mind of the Ellen I've lost and wish I could find. A voice in my head supplies the missing dialogue: what she would say, should be saying.

Her real-world counterpart shrugs. She doesn't ask me who was on the phone or what they wanted. I wouldn't have told her. Still, my Ellen would ask.

Who would call me and say those things? Who would imagine I must recognize their voice when I don't? I can't think of a single person. Or a reason why someone might think I want to intimidate or hurt them.

"I can't bear this, El."

"Can't bear what?"

"You, being so . . . uncommunicative. I know something's wrong."

"Oh, not this again." She lies down on her bed and pulls the pillow over her face.

"Please trust me and tell me what's the matter. You won't be in trouble, whatever it is."

"Mum, leave it. I'll be fine."

"Which means you're not fine now." I move the pillow so that I can see her.

She sits up, snatches it back.

"Are you missing London? Is that it?"

She gives me a look that tells me I'm way off the mark.

"Dad, then?"

"*Dad?* Why would I be missing Dad? He'll be back next week, won't he?"

It's as if I'm distracting her from something important by mentioning things she forgot about years ago.

She's not interested in you, or Alex.

Then who? What?

"Can I ask you about your story?" I say.

"If you must."

"Is it homework?"

"Yeah. But Mr. Goodrick couldn't remember when it had to be in, he said."

I sigh. The school here is better than the one in London in almost every way. The one exception is Ellen's form tutor, Craig Goodrick, a failed rock musician who has never managed to get my name right, though he did once get it promisingly wrong: he called me Mrs. Morrison, which isn't that far removed from Ms. Merrison. When I suggested he call me Justine, he winked and said, "Right you are, Justin," and I couldn't tell if he was deliberately winding me up or awkwardly flirting.

"And the homework was what?" I ask Ellen. "To write a story?"

She eyes me suspiciously. "Why are you so interested? I'd hardly be writing a story if I'd been told to draw a pie-chart, would I?"

Hallelujah. "I withdraw the question."

No reaction from Ellen.

Pull that in my courtroom again, I'll have you disbarred, counselor.

How could I explain to anyone who didn't know us that I'm worried about my daughter because she's stopped pretending to be an irascible American judge? They'd think I was insane.

"Does the story have to begin with a family tree?" I ask.

"No. Mum, seriously, stop interrogating me."

I think about saying, *I'm not keen on family trees. In fact, I loathe them.*

No, I'm not going to do that. It would be a bribe—"Chat to me like you used to and I'll tell you a juicy story"—and it wouldn't be fair.

Hardly juicy. A family tree on a child's bedroom wall. With the wrong family on it.

Cut.

That's one useful thing about having worked in television, at least: I have extensive experience of ruthless cutting. If I don't like a scene that's playing in my mind, I can make it disappear as quickly as an axed TV drama.

Usually.

"Where did you get those names from?" I ask Ellen. "Bascom and Sorrel Ingrey—"

"Mum! For God's sake!"

"Garnet, Urban, Allisande . . . they're so strange. And why did you use your own name? Why is there an Ellen in the Ingrey family?"

"I don't know. There just is. Stop inventing things to worry about. It's just a story."

I can hardly tell her that reading it made me feel as if I'd swallowed a lead weight. "Yes, and you've decided to put things in your story for a reason."

"I didn't think about the names." Ellen studies her fingernails, avoiding my eye. "I wanted to make the story sound old-fashioned and sinister, I suppose."

"You succeeded," I tell her. The heavy feeling in the pit of my stomach lifts a little. Maybe there's nothing to worry about after all. "You should add dates. To the family tree—not necessarily to the story. What time period are you in? What year did Perrine Ingrey murder Malachy Dodd?"

"I don't know!" Ellen snaps. "Some time in the past. And don't talk about the characters as if they're real. Ugh, it's embarrassing."

That's her. She's still in there.

"Look, it's only some stupid homework," she says, expressionless again. "It doesn't matter to anyone. Twenty years ago, twenty-five. What do dates matter? It's just a story. Why do you care?"

Am I deliberately trying to enrage her because any reaction would be better than blank withdrawal? She isn't nearly angry enough. The old Ellen would never have tolerated this level of interference or said that any creative project of hers didn't matter. By now I would have been having clothes thrown at me.

"I care, Ellen. Why did you put a murderer in your bedroom?"

"What?" For a fleeting moment, I see my own fear reflected in her eyes. Then it's gone.

"Perrine Ingrey. Her bedroom in the story is this room." I point to the little mint-green door by the side of Ellen's bed. *A quarter of the size of the shortest dwarf in the world.*

"No reason," says Ellen. "Literally, *no* reason. I needed a room, this is a room . . ." She shrugs.

"I wondered if maybe it's going to turn out that Perrine didn't kill Malachy Dodd after all. That someone else did."

"No, because it says more than once that she *did* kill him. That part's not in doubt. You can't have read it very carefully."

"I read it four times. I thought all the stuff about her killing him was protesting too much, and that—"

"*No,* Mother. That would be a cheat. It's in the third person. That wouldn't be an unreliable narrator, it would be me, the author, lying. You can't do that."

I smile. "How do you know the unreliable narrator rules? Not from Mr. Goodrick?" This is a man who regularly cancels proper lessons in favor of impromptu circle-singing sessions. I chose Ellen's school because of its unusual flexibility, then quickly realized that I didn't want it to flex for anyone but me.

A miracle happens. Ellen smiles back. "What do you think?

Mr. Fisher, the Nerd King, gave us a mini-lecture about narrative perspective, including unreliable narrators. It was *so* boring. His class is doing the story homework too. All Mr. Goodrick said was 'Don't use the word "said."' He wants us to use more interesting speech words. That's why everyone in my story exclaims and yelps, in case you didn't notice."

"I didn't. I think I'd yelp if I encountered an Ingrey. And there's nothing wrong with 'said,' *said* your mother."

Too late. Ellen has shut down again. We were starting to talk properly, like we used to, so she had to distance herself.

Mr. Fisher—which one is he? The Scottish hard-blinker with the huge glasses? His first name is something Celtic-sounding. Lorgan? Lechlade?

"Why did you choose a murder mystery story?" I ask Ellen. "And why do the Ingreys have to live in our house? I'm not sure I want to share it with the weirdest family in the whole of Kingswear, even if they are fictional."

Ellen gives me an unfathomable look. "Are you thinking Perrine Ingrey's going to get murdered in my bedroom? She isn't. Don't worry. She doesn't get killed in the house or the grounds."

"Then where?"

"I haven't written it yet."

"Still. It sounds as if you know."

"I'm saying: you don't have to worry about murders in your house." Ellen rolls her eyes. "If you're so addicted to drama, go back to work, for God's sake."

"I'm not addicted to—"

"Really? Then why are you always imagining things that sound like the beginnings of really crap TV movies?"

Happily, I feel no urge to point out that nothing I made was crap. *You are dead to me, old life and former career.* I'm proud of different things these days—proud that this morning I sat on the doorstep for nearly an hour, wrapped in a blanket, watching the boats on the river.

"Like that thing with the house on the North Circular—your weird premonition," Ellen says. "I bet you never bothered to Google it, did you?"

"No. Why? Did you?"

She nods. "You were right, German isn't its name. It's Germander. You must have seen the outlines of the three missing letters. *Germander.* Do you get it now?"

"Germander Speedwell." I know the right answer, but can't immediately work out what conclusion I'm supposed to draw.

It's a plant. I hadn't heard of it until I looked up the name Speedwell, after our first tour with the real estate agent. *Veronica chamaedrys*: an herbaceous perennial plant with hairy stems and leaves. Blue four-lobed flowers. Otherwise known as Germander Speedwell.

"You saw a house called Germander and you connected it with Speedwell House because of the plant name," says Ellen. "That's why you had that weird feeling. That and Dad being an arse and saying, 'Look, there's our new house.' It's so obvious."

"Don't call Dad an arse," I say distractedly.

Is this the resolution of a four-month-old mystery? Can I put up a big "Solved" sign in my head? It bothers me that I'm unable to answer the question definitively. I need to tell Alex, see what he thinks. Did I see the outline of the three missing letters? I don't remember seeing them.

"How long have you known?" I ask Ellen.

"Couple of months."

"Why didn't you tell me as soon as you found out?"

"I didn't know how you'd react. For all I knew, you'd start wif-fling on about the name connection being even more of a sign that you were destined to live there one day."

"Yet you've told me now."

I'm glad she did, even if it doesn't cancel out the strong feeling I had.

"What made you Google that house, months after we drove past it?" I ask.

"Nothing. I don't remember. I was probably bored one day. Have you finished interrogating me now? Because it's getting old."

"Sorry." *No further questions.* "I'll go and get your story."

"No, chuck it," says Ellen. "I've already typed it up. I'm writing the rest on my laptop."

For which I know the four-digit access code.

"Don't waste your time," Ellen says with quiet efficiency. "I've password-protected the file."

Later that night when she's asleep, I sit down to do the online search I probably should have done a long time ago. What did Ellen type into the Google box? "German, 8 Panama Row, London"? I try it. I didn't do it sooner because I didn't think there was any point. What could the internet tell me that would be useful? "This house is famous for provoking spooky feelings of belonging in people who have no connection with it"?

Here it is: Germander, and the correct address. I'm looking at some kind of planning application document. The owner of 8 Panama Row seems to be an Olwen Brawn, or at least that was who wanted to stick a conservatory on the side of the house in June 2012. She might have moved by now, I suppose.

A conservatory? With a lovely view of the six-lane North

Circular? Evidently she decided against it or else permission wasn't granted. There was no side conservatory when I saw the house four months ago.

Olwen Brawn. The name has no effect on me at all, which is a relief.

Could Ellen be right? Was it the first six letters of Germander that did it, and Alex pointing and saying, "There's the house we've bought"? *And the heat, the stress of moving day, the traffic jam . . .*

I'd like to believe that's all it was.

The computer screen in front of me is too tempting. I go back to the Google page and type "Bascom Sorrel Ingrey Speedwell" into the search box. Nothing useful comes up, though I do find a man by the unlikely name of Bascom Sorrell, with two *l*'s, in Nicholas County, Kentucky.

I try "Perrine Ingrey Malachy Dodd." Nothing. "Ingrey Allisande Lisette," "Ingrey Garnet Urban"—nothing.

A full-body shiver makes my skin prickle. *Garnet. Urban.* According to the family tree, they're Lisette Ingrey's children. Their names both sound Victorian English. So do the names Bascom and Sorrel—their grandparents. Lisette, Allisande and Perrine, on the other hand, sound French. Different parents and generations; different tastes in names.

Would a fourteen-year-old think of that?

Yes. Ellen did. That's why it's in her story, and that's all it is: a story.

I'm not convinced. The names seem far too esoteric for even the brightest, most mature teenager to come up with.

As for Ellen password-protecting the file, that's easily explicable: reticence, embarrassment, a defense of privacy against a parent's desire to know everything—all children do it at some point.

I sip my tea, which is now lukewarm and so might as well be freezing cold.

There's no reason to believe that the weirdest family in Kingswear once lived in our house. They're made up. Fictional characters.

There is no Perrine Ingrey. My daughter's bedroom did not once belong to her.

You see, unlike most parents, especially so long ago, Bascom and Sorrel Ingrey couldn't agree on anything. They never had been able to, from the moment they met. They were opposites in every way. It is amazing that they managed to agree to get married, in fact. Ask any of their three daughters and they will tell you (well, apart from Perrine, who got murdered, but before that she would have said so too) that every time Bascom Ingrey expressed an opinion on any topic, his wife quickly spoke up and contradicted him. He did the same to her. And their behavior showed how opposite they were as much as their opinions did.

Bascom Ingrey liked to plan everything in detail because he was a pessimist who believed that disaster would strike if you weren't well prepared. Sorrel Ingrey was not like that at all. She was an optimist and thought that everything would work out fine if you left it to chance. She was very spontaneous and did what felt right at the time, and she enjoyed it when life surprised her (apart from when her youngest daughter became a murderer and was then murdered—but let's not get ahead of ourselves).

Bascom liked to be very early. Sorrel always arrived late. Bascom liked to read but never watched TV. Sorrel liked TV and never read. Bascom always voted Labour, and Sorrel always voted Conservative. Bascom always sat with his back straight and his feet on the floor, even when he was in a comfortable armchair. Sorrel stretched out horizontally, kicked off her shoes and took up a whole sofa. She liked bright colors like turquoise and raspberry pink, which her husband hated. He only liked neutral colors like beige, gray and white. Bascom was obsessively tidy and could not bear it when any of his possessions was not in its proper place. Sorrel was happy for things to be a mess—she hardly noticed. If she needed something urgently and couldn't find it because it was buried under a pile of random jumpers, she didn't care. She would laugh and say, "I'll have to buy a new one."

You're probably thinking that all this disagreement meant that Bascom and Sorrel Ingrey had a terrible relationship, but the opposite is true (which, if you think about it, is predictable for a couple who are so opposite to one another). They were very happily married. This was because they did have an important thing in common: neither of them was the sort of person who agreed with their spouse just because it would be easier to do so. They respected this about each other, and they both learned the art of compromise—an art rarely learned by married people in marriages where one is definitely the boss. Both Bascom and Sorrel became brilliant compromisers.

Their three daughters (well, perhaps not Perrine but definitely Lisette and Allisande) were pleased that both of their parents had strong principles that they stuck to, though they wished they didn't have to listen to so many back-and-forth discussions about whether to go on holiday to a golden sandy beach in a hot country (Sorrel) or to a European city with lots of art

galleries and museums (Bascom), or whether to go swimming as the main activity on a Saturday (Sorrel) or to
the library (Bascom), or whether to fill the house with
cute, furry pets (Sorrel) or have no pets at all, not
even a goldfish (Bascom). When Lisette, Allisande and
Perrine visited their friends' houses, they noticed at
once that there was not always a "No, this / No, that"
debate going on. Many of their friends' parents hardly
spoke at all.

Lisette, Allisande and Perrine had been brought up
very differently from their friends. Bascom and Sorrel
Ingrey couldn't agree about anything, as I have explained above, and this included how to bring up a
child. Bascom firmly believed that children need fixed
routines and strict rules if they are going to grow
up to become civilized people. If you let a child do
what it wants, he thought, it will never learn virtues
like hard work, obedience and self-discipline. Also,
if you let children eat what they want, and sleep when
they want, they will end up exhausted all the time
with greasy spotty faces. Grown-ups, he believed, must
impose their will on children.

Sorrel (you will not be surprised to discover)
strongly disagreed. She thought that parents who insisted on routines and tried to control what their
children did were neurotic loons whose offspring would
probably end up hating them while struggling to shake
off anxiety disorders. Sorrel thought that as long
as you loved your children, fed them (whatever they
want to eat, especially crisps!) and provided a happy
and secure home for them (even a really messy one),

everything would work out okay. But when she tried to say this to Bascom, he always contradicted her and said, "That's all very well if you want to bring up a troop of gamblers and jazz musicians. I'm afraid I don't." Sorrel laughed at him when he said things like that.

Do you remember I mentioned that Bascom and Sorrel Ingrey were brilliant at compromising? Well, this is how they solved the dilemma of how to bring up their children. "Let's have two," Sorrel suggested. "We'll bring up the first one your way. I will help, even though I think your way is crazy. And then we'll bring up the second one my way, and you will participate enthusiastically even though you disapprove."

Bascom agreed, but he made another suggestion too. "What would be really fascinating," he said, "is if we then had a third child, and brought it up using a blend of our two approaches—exactly half and half." Sorrel liked this idea. "It would be so useful to be a family of five instead of a family of four," she said. "Just in case the your-way child always agreed with you about everything, and the my-way child always agreed with me, the both-ways child could have the casting vote." "Only when it's eighteen and old enough to vote," Bascom pointed out. "Oh, don't be so stuffy!" Sorrel teased him. "As soon as he's old enough to voice his wants, he can have a vote."

But the third Ingrey child, as we know, was not a "he." She was Perrine the murderer.

Lisette and Allisande came first, of course. Lisette had a strict timetable, set by Bascom, which she followed from the day she was born. Sleeping, eating, music lessons, reading, homework, physical exercise, helping with housework—Bascom had made a special chart with boxes for all the time slots in the day, and he wrote in each one which activity Lisette was supposed to do between these times. Allisande had no such routine. From the minute she was born, she was allowed to mill around doing whatever she wanted. She could watch TV all day long if she fancied it, and no one ever told her to do her maths homework, practice the piano or finish her green vegetables when all she wanted was a chocolate Mini Roll. Allisande could have crammed a whole packet of Mini Rolls into her mouth while lolling around in her pajamas at six o'clock in the evening if she'd wanted to—neither of her parents would have stopped her.

At this point, I hope you are asking yourself who you would rather be: Lisette Ingrey or Allisande Ingrey. I would much rather be Allisande, because there is nothing more annoying than being bossed around by a parent who thinks they know best.

If Sorrel and Bascom Ingrey hadn't loved her as much as they did, Allisande might have felt neglected, but they did love her, and she knew it. So she was very happy to have so much more independence than most children. Lisette was also happy. She'd had a stimulating and interesting routine to follow since birth, and it was one that allowed her to do everything she wanted to do without worrying about when she was going to do it. There were no decisions to be made, so she could concentrate on enjoying all the activities in the boxes on Bascom's chart without having to arrange them herself. Freedom was something she had never had, so she didn't know she ought to want it. She had no desire to sort out her own life. And Allisande never felt the need to have a full schedule like Lisette's. She liked making her own decisions far more than she would have liked any number of music lessons or gold stars for getting her homework in on time (Allisande never did her homework, always got in trouble, and didn't care), and so she regularly decided to do as little as possible, and she never regretted her decision.

If you're waiting for me to tell you that the two sisters hated and resented each other, prepare to be disappointed. Each one was content with her lot in life, and neither one ever said, "Why aren't I doing what she's doing? Why is it different for me than it is for her?" Don't forget, these two girls grew up in a home that could have been a museum of difference! They were used to seeing their father sitting at the dining-room table eating homemade roast beef with roast potatoes, carrots and peas, while their mother ate pears and wheels of camembert from a horizontal position on the sofa. Lisette and Allisande grew up seeing their parents do everything differently and never envying each other, and so they followed this example. Such was the brilliance of Bascom and Sorrel Ingrey's strange parenting that *each girl believed she had the far better deal!* Imagine that!

The really strange and interesting thing is this: although they were brought up in completely opposite ways, Lisette and Allisande Ingrey were startlingly similar. They did not fill their days with the same activities, but their basic characters were like replicas of one another. They were both happy, polite, nice girls with relaxed temperaments, and everyone who met them liked them. And for years and years and years, they liked and loved each other. Even when trauma and horror struck their family, when their little sister Perrine killed poor, lovely Malachy Dodd, Lisette and Allisande remained close and the best of friends.

It took the murder of Perrine herself to split them apart and tear their sisterly love to tatters.

2

There's a text from Alex on my phone when my alarm goes off in the morning: "Soz I didn't call yest. It's mad my end. Talk later? A ☺"

Lying in our bed, my eyes not yet fully open, I send him a quick reply: "All fine here. Speak tonight. J xx." I don't have the energy for more at the moment, only for the easy white lie: *all fine*. Will Alex continue to believe that even after he's heard everything I need to tell him?

Which is what, exactly? Ellen's too wrapped up in herself? She wrote a story with a family tree in it, and the characters' names were strange? So what?

Nothing is quite significant enough in itself; I have nothing concrete to point to. All my instincts tell me something is wrong and has been since . . . No, not since the day we moved here. My reaction to seeing 8 Panama Row was an aberration. Our first month in Speedwell House was idyllic. Then . . .

Then what?

Something happened, and it changed everything. *To Ellen*. I'm convinced of it. But what? What could that something be?

I climb out of bed and pull on my dressing gown, wondering what time I finally fell asleep. I remember hearing distant church bells at four A.M., so it must have been after that. And now it's six thirty, and I could sleep for nine hours straight, but I have to go and haul Ellen out of bed, which gets harder each school-day morning.

Swallowing a yawn, I head downstairs, thinking about hot water with a slice of lemon and a spoonful of honey in it—my new morning drink now that I have given up coffee, the favored fuel of those with too much to do—and what to put in Ellen's packed lunch. This will be the biggest decision I'll make today: tuna mayonnaise or roast chicken and pesto? Once that's sorted, I'll have the whole day free to do what I want, and, as luck would have it, I don't want to do anything.

The best thing is that whatever choice I make about the sandwich, it won't matter. Ellen won't notice the difference; she eats everything. My decision will affect nothing, which makes me wonder if it counts as a decision at all. Probably not. I find this idea profoundly calming.

I stop in the hall when I see, framed in the kitchen doorway, a cereal bowl on the table with a half-drunk glass of orange juice and a carton of milk next to it. Splashes of milk on the wood: Ellen's trademark.

Impossible. Ellen, awake and finished with breakfast by half past six?

She's curled up on the kitchen sofa, already in her school uniform, typing on her laptop. I walk into the room and she shifts her body around so that I can't see the screen.

This is unheard of. Normally I have to drag her out of bed at seven.

"Story?" I ask.

She nods from behind a curtain of hair. It's not only her creative efforts she's keen to conceal; she doesn't want me to see her eyes, either.

"You've been crying."

"No. I'm just tired. I woke up at five and couldn't get back to sleep."

"Ellen, I've known you all your life. I know what tired looks like, and I know what recent weeping looks like."

I've asked myself more than once if Speedwell House might be the problem. Does Ellen feel lonely here? Is it too isolated, too grand to feel like a proper home? Alex laughed when I put this question to him, and said, "Never say that in front of anyone but me. It sounds like passive-aggressive boasting: 'Oh, it's such a nightmare—my new house is so intimidatingly stunning.'"

But it is. I don't mind being far away from other people—I love it, in fact; people are overrated—but I do sometimes feel as if I'm living inside a rare work of art and don't belong here. I grew up in a redbrick government-owned semi in Manchester with mold on the walls. The house we sold in London was nothing special, though we loved it: it was exactly like every other house on our street—a two-up, two-down Victorian terrace with one bay window at the front.

Is that why I had that strange fantasy about 8 Panama Row when I saw it: because it felt more familiar, looked more like the sort of house someone like me ought to live in?

"Can I have the day off?" Ellen asks. "I don't want to go to school. If I stay here, I can blitz my story and finish it by this evening. Look, I'm being honest—not faking illness, not saying I think I'm coming down with something." She twists her mouth into an exaggerated smile. "If you want me to be happy and not cry, letting me miss school will do the trick."

"Why don't you want to go to school? You've always wanted to before."

"I'm getting really into this." She nods down at her computer. "I don't want to have to stop. I don't believe creative work should be interrupted for the sake of an oppressive work regime that dictates I have to do *this* kind of work, at *this* time, in *this* place."

So this is how she plans to block me in future: with a rat-a-tat-tat of impressive words, devoid of all emotion. There's a new brittleness to her voice that makes me want to howl and smash my fists against the wall. I'm scared that if I can't think of a way to get through to her in the next twenty seconds, I might lose her forever.

"If I let you stay home, will you tell me what's wrong? I've got no plans for the day. We can talk it all through—*really* talk."

Ellen snaps her laptop shut. "Way to make me want to rush to school," she says. "Have you considered a career in truancy prevention? Oh, sorry, you don't want a career, do you?" She pushes past me on her way out of the room. I watch her in the hall as she pulls her bag off the peg by the door, thinking of all the things I absolutely mustn't say. *All right, you fuck off to school, then. I'll just stay here all day and worry about you while you have fun with your friends.*

Does she have any friends at the new school? She's never asked to bring anyone home.

"Ellen, wait . . . Don't . . . Where are you going?"

"School, Mother. I believe we've covered that. If I don't go now, I'll miss the bus."

"Where's your coat?"

She stiffens and stops near the door, as if she's been zapped by invisible rays. "I don't know. Maybe at school."

"Will you have a look for it?"

"Yeah."

"Ellen, wait! Turn around and look at me!" My Strict Mother voice. I haven't needed to use it for well over five years. "I haven't seen your coat for at least a week. I should have spotted it was missing before. Where is it? You need it. It's chilly outside."

"I told you: I'll look at school." Her bag slides off her shoulder, drops to the floor. I see uncertainty in her eyes.

"I get that you're scared of telling me what's going on," I say. "But you're going to because I need to know. If you want something to fear, start being scared of *not* telling me. That's what's going to make me angry. Tell me the truth, and I promise you won't be in trouble."

"I'm going to miss the school bus. Shouldn't I be hurrying to school to track down my missing coat? Isn't that what you want?"

Her callous tone nearly breaks me. It also reminds me of how much I hate to lose any battle.

Burying the hurt I feel, I say, "Tell you what, forget the school bus. I'll drive you in. I've nothing else to do today."

"No. No way! I'm getting the bus. Goodbye." Ellen reaches for the door handle.

Two can play the nasty smirk game. "Fine. I'm going to drive to school anyway. I'll look for your coat on my own, and you can devote your full attention to being oppressed by the regime. How does that sound?"

Her eyes fill with tears. "No."

"Face it, Ellen. You can't stop me from going to school if I'm determined to. What are you going to do, bash me over the head with an umbrella? Knock me unconscious, lock me in the cellar? If I want to wander the corridors asking everyone I pass about your coat—"

"All right." She bursts into tears. "You want to know that much? I'll tell you! See how much you enjoy knowing."

I want to hug her and promise that everything will be okay. I stop myself. It'll be easier for her to talk if I remain impassive. *Please, please, let this be the moment when it all changes. Let this be the beginning of the end of Ellen's pain, whatever its cause.*

"Go ahead," I say. "If you're being bullied, we can tackle it however you want. If you'd like me to go in with all guns blazing, I will. If you want me to find you a different school, I will."

"Bullied?" She blinks, as if the possibility hasn't occurred to her. "No, it's nothing like that. *I'm* fine."

So someone else isn't?

"Then what?" I ask.

Ellen shakes her head and walks past me, back into the house. *Too important a conversation to have in the hall.*

I stand still for a few seconds, then follow her. I find her in the kitchen, filling the kettle with water. Wow. This is a first. Now she's putting a teabag in a mug. Ellen doesn't drink tea or coffee—she thinks both taste disgusting.

She's making me a drink: something that hasn't happened before. I watch in stunned silence as she adds the milk, then squashes the bag against the side of the mug with a teaspoon before throwing it in the bin. It's going to be orange and revolting, but who cares. My daughter has made me a hot drink, unprompted. This is a historic occasion.

She brings the mug over to the table and puts it down where she wants me to sit: opposite her. "My best friend in the whole world was expelled yesterday," she says. Then, rolling her eyes, "To which you're going to reply, 'I didn't know you had a best friend in the world.'"

I didn't. I'm relieved to hear that such a person exists. Unlike most fourteen-year-olds whose parents announce a sudden house move, Ellen was excited about the prospect of leaving her old school and social circle. "I can make new friends," she said, and it was as close to a sigh of relief as words can be. In London, she'd been part of a close-knit gang of four: Ellen, Natasha, Priya and Blessing. Blessing and Priya were lovely, but they were also inseparable, and Ellen found herself, at an early stage in the gang's formation, forced to be the official best friend of Natasha, who was a devious, under-mining backstabber with ultracompetitive parents. "Are you sure you're okay sitting next to me for maths?" Natasha would ask Ellen, all wide eyes and fake concern. "It's just that I know you find it so hard, and I don't, and I don't want you to get upset when I get more answers right than you do." At least three comments of that sort every day, and other nonsense like random periods of withheld eye contact—strenuously denied when pointed out—soon led to Ellen disliking her supposed best friend intensely.

As she regularly explained to me—and indeed, as I remembered from my own school days—you don't get to choose your friends at that age. I suggested booting Natasha out of the gang, but, sadly, Priya and Blessing were both far too nice to authorize anything like that.

Before Ellen started at her new school, I warned her about cliquey groups of girls. "Don't worry," she said in a world-weary drawl, "I'm going to keep my distance from everyone until I've sussed them all out. I'll be bland and smiley and friendly, but I won't be anyone's *friend*. No way."

Since then she's mentioned a few names—Lucy, Madeline, Jessica—but there's been no hint of a change of policy, nothing to herald the arrival on the scene of anyone significant. "So who is this 'best friend in the whole world'?"

"His name's George." Ellen rolls her eyes again. "Yes, he's a boy. Big deal."

"I'm just surprised," I say. "Most people your age pretend to hate the opposite sex, unless they're . . ." *Er, no, let's not take the conversation in that direction, Justine.*

I mustn't ask if there's any element of boyfriend/girlfriend to the friendship. It wouldn't go down well, and it doesn't matter. "What's George's surname?"

Ellen's eyes fix on me. "Why do you want to know?"

"No reason. I wondered, that's all." What have I done wrong? Let me rephrase that, even though no one's hearing it: I've done nothing wrong. So what does Ellen think I've done?

"Donbavand," she mutters, so faintly that I have to ask her to repeat it. And then, because it's an unusual name, I ask her to spell it. This all takes longer than I want it to.

"And . . . George was expelled?"

Ellen nods. Her expression hardens, and I see how furious she is. Anger radiates from her body in waves. "Yesterday. He did *nothing* wrong. I told them that, but no one believed me. They think he stole my coat, but he didn't. I gave it to him—at the end of last week. I said he could keep it. It was . . . like a gift."

"You gave George your coat as a present?"

"Yes. He lost his. It must have been somewhere at school— George doesn't go anywhere else—but he couldn't find it and he was literally white-faced with horror at the thought of going home without one. So I gave him mine—which isn't girly-looking and could easily be a boy's coat," Ellen adds defensively, as if my main issue with this story is likely to revolve around the gendered clothing debate.

"I'm sorry, all right?" she snaps. "I knew you'd buy me another one if I said I'd lost mine."

"Okay. And . . . ?" I wait.

Nothing. The shut-down face.

"I was going to pretend I'd lost it, but then the weather warmed up a bit, so . . . I put off saying anything."

I sip my tea, wondering what and how much she's still withholding. We both know there's a lot more she could tell me. "So . . . I'd buy you a new coat if you lost your old one, but Mrs. Donbavand wouldn't buy another one for George?"

Ellen's mouth sets in a firm line, as if she's trying not to say something. "Mrs. Donbavand isn't Mrs. She's Professor."

"Okay. Well, with her PhD and all, she presumably isn't on the breadline, and knows how to find the coat section of a department store?"

"She—" Ellen stops as the phone on the kitchen wall starts to ring.

I sigh. I'd suggest leaving it, but it might be Alex. I'd like to hear his voice, if only because it will sound jollier than mine at the moment.

"Hello?" I tuck the phone under my ear so that I don't have to hold it in my hand. That's how resentful I am of having to stand in this spot every time I talk on the landline: I'm not willing to make any extra physical effort. Not being able to sit on the sofa is bad enough.

"Are you still pretending you don't know who I am?" says a voice that is—unfortunately—familiar.

"I wasn't pretending. I genuinely don't know who you are. Who are you? Tell me."

"Pack up your possessions and go home."

Possessions? For some reason I picture an elaborately carved wooden trunk full of jewels.

"Nooo," I say, deliberately drawing it out. "You pack up your plan to hound me with threatening phone calls, and fuck off. I *am* at home. This is my home now—not that it's any of your business."

Ellen is mouthing "What?" at me.

"You're trying to scare me, like you always have before, but it won't work this time," says my anonymous caller. "Am I supposed to wonder if you'll destroy me? Is that it? Are you hoping I'll drive myself mad, not knowing when you're going to attack?"

"I'm nowhere near as ambitious as you seem to think," I tell her.

"I'm hoping you'll get off the phone, never call this house again, and have a happy and productive life thereafter. How about that? Does that sound good to you?"

"Get out!" the woman shrieks. It's such a shrill, violent sound that I gasp. Ellen looks startled.

"Don't make me hurt you," stammers the voice, quieter now. "Please don't, because . . . I don't want to have to. I'm a peaceful person."

"Are you sure? That's not the impression I'm getting."

"Go back to your TV executive high life in London. Before it's too late."

"I shouldn't have told her to fuck off," I say for the third time since Ellen and I set off in the car. "Or been sarcastic. I provoked her. Stupid." The drive to school consists almost entirely of quiet country roads overhung by canopies of trees, with bright winter sun dropping patches of light through the leaves; scattered gold on the tarmac. It's like speeding through a series of beautifully illuminated green tunnels. I wish the inside of my head were as lovely and peaceful as what I see all around me.

"Why wasn't I more temperate?" I ask pointlessly. And why didn't I have the gumption to produce a plausible lie to explain the threatening phone call to Ellen? She's unhappy enough already, and now I've added to her burden by telling her about the stranger who has targeted me for persecution. I should have told Alex first. I'm sure the first thing he'll say is, "Let's make sure Ellen doesn't get wind of this." Too late.

As someone who screws up all the time, I know exactly what I have and have not done wrong. I've never tried to scare or intimidate a woman with a funny sort of lisp. Or anybody at all, for that matter.

Yet she expected me to recognize her voice. Who the hell is she?

Go back to your TV executive high life in London. That's too close to be a coincidence. My career—ugh, how I loathe that word now—was in television, though I'd never have described myself as an "executive." This woman knows where I used to live, and she knows what line of work I was in.

"You're never temperate," Ellen says. "You're a zealot. Please don't be a zealot when we get to school. I'm the one who has to go there every day. Can't you just drop me off and then go home?"

"No."

"Mum, *please!*"

"No, Ellen. If this George boy has been expelled for stealing your coat and he didn't do it, we need to sort it out."

"I thought you were determined to do nothing ever again."

"Yes—apart from have fun. I'm going to enjoy getting George unexpelled." It will take my mind off the horrible phone calls.

"It won't work," says Ellen. "Don't you think I've tried? No one wants to listen."

"Well, they're going to listen to me whether they want to or not. I suspect they don't believe you and think you're covering for George: he stole your coat, but he's your best friend, so you're trying to get him off the hook. To be fair to them . . . a coat is a pretty unusual present."

"I'm an unusual person. It's one of my main selling points."

"You are and it is. But it sounds as if George's mum is even more unusual. The professor. Before the lunatic called, you were saying she wouldn't have bought George a new coat—why not?"

"I don't know! Ask her."

"Why are you so angry with me, Ellen?"

"I'm not angry with *you.* I just . . ." Her voice cracks. She turns her face away. I can hear her crying, or trying hard not to. I fantasize about smashing my car into the face of whoever has made her so miserable. Is it George's mother? Mrs. Griffiths, the head? The more the merrier. If they've made my daughter cry, I'll mow them all down—in my dreams, at least.

"It's okay, El. If yelling at me makes you feel better, I don't mind. I won't take it personally."

"George was scared. He was actually frightened! I've never seen anybody look like that apart from in a film, when a murderer or a monster's chasing them."

Great. Thanks to my aversion to any and all censorship, my daughter knows what pure terror looks like. If Alex and I hadn't let her watch so many 18-certificate films, she might still have her coat, and I might be at home, easing myself into another day of pleasurable inactivity. Yesterday I tried meditation for the first time. I'm not sure how well it went. I lay on the chaise longue in the garden room for nearly an hour and a half, but the silent mantra repeating itself in my head was not a peaceful one. The word "fuck" kept cropping up: *fuck your two-page treatments, fuck your series bibles, fuck your show-running and your brainstorming, fuck your greenlights and your BAFTAs—up the arse, actually. Fuck the BBC, fuck ITV, fuck Sky . . .*

Something went wrong, clearly, even though I followed the instructions in my meditation book to the letter. It said, "Don't put any energy into thinking, but if thoughts come into your mind, let them come. Observe them from a distance as they drift in and out. Don't push them away." The book doesn't specify what to do if only a load of fucks turn up.

And now here I am, the very next day, driving to school to cause trouble. Maybe yelling at some teachers for half an hour or so will purge me of all my repressed anger, and my meditations thereafter will be obscenity-free. My life will be a smooth-surfaced pool of tranquility.

"I gave him my coat thinking the worst that would happen was you'd moan at me for losing it," says Ellen. "If I'd known he'd get expelled, I wouldn't have given it to him. And now I'll never see him again."

"Yes, you will."

"I won't. You don't understand."

"None of this is your fault, El. You did a kind thing. But . . . George wasn't scared of going home with a different coat?"

"No. Mine was black and padded; his was a black duffel coat. He said his mum wouldn't notice the difference."

"And his dad? Does he have a dad living with him?"

"Yeah. His dad would notice, he said, but there's no way he'd say anything."

"Right. So the dad's scared of the mum too?"

"I don't know. George didn't say."

"Well, he must be, mustn't he? Unless George is the one he's afraid of. Is George scary?"

"George is the least scary person in the world. George is just . . . amazing." Ellen sighs.

"It's interesting," I say. "A mother who would go ballistic if her son told her he'd lost his coat, but who, at the same time, doesn't notice if he comes home with someone else's."

"She's a weirdo."

"What else do you know about her? What's she a professor of?"

"Assyriology. Which has nothing to do with Syria."

"I know." I didn't, but I see no need to admit to my ignorance. I bet Professor Donbavand doesn't know how many times Peter Florrick had sex with hooker Amber Madison in *The Good Wife*. I do: eighteen times.

We all have our different specialties.

"Her name's Anne," says Ellen. "I *hate* her." She clenches her fists in her lap. "If it weren't for her stupid rules, George could email me and text me."

I hear in her voice how much this boy means to her. Yet she hasn't mentioned his name before today. Why didn't she tell me about him? I must ask Alex if he's heard the name George Donbavand, though I know what the answer will be.

"We could chat on Instagram, FaceTime each other, hang around together outside school," Ellen goes on. "She won't let him do *anything*."

"Don't worry," I say. "George will soon be unexpelled. Does he have brothers and sisters?"

"One sister. Fleur. She's older—first year sixth form."

"Same rules for Fleur?" I ask. "No emails, no texting? Does the mother really not let them visit friends?"

"Really," says Ellen. "She knows most parents let their kids use the internet, and she thinks George and Fleur would see bits of it if they went to other people's houses. And no one can ever go round to their house because she's always working on her *stupid* Assyriology and needs the house to be silent all the time."

"What does George's dad do?"

"Creeps around the house like a mute slave, George says, doing her bidding."

"No, I mean work. What's his job?" I hate myself for wanting to know this. What will the answer tell me? He'll be a lawyer, or an architect, or he'll work in a shoe shop. Whatever work he does, he's an idiot who hasn't realized that doing Nothing is the only way to save your soul.

"He also works at Exeter University," says Ellen. "I don't know what he does there."

"Well, they sound like a screwed-up family." Come to think of it, the Donbavands sound almost too dysfunctional to be true. "Did George tell you all this? Are you sure he's not exaggerating?"

I look at Ellen to see why she's not answering. She's crying again. "And now George hasn't even got school, or me to talk to. It'll be even worse for him that Fleur's still going every day. Though they'll probably expel her next—for dropping a pencil on the floor or something."

I nearly miss the unmarked crossroads ahead and have to brake fast. There's nothing coming at us horizontally, so I drive on. Where is everyone? I've thought that so many times since moving to Devon. Why don't Devonians clog up their roads all day long the way Londoners do? They can't all be confined to their homes by Professor Anne Donbavand.

"Why would school want to expel Fleur?" I ask Ellen.

"Forget it," she murmurs.

"I never forget anything. I'm like an elephant. Why would they?"

"Vindictiveness. Why do they want to expel George, when I've told them over and over that he didn't steal my coat? That phone call, before . . ." She stops suddenly. Starts biting her thumbnail, something she hasn't done for ages.

"The anonymous phone call?" I ask. "What, Ellen? You have to tell me."

"I think it was school. Because of George."

"*School?*" I pull over to the side of the road, cricking my neck in the process. "You think someone at school is threatening me, telling me to go back to London? Who would do that?"

"I don't know who. If I knew, I'd say the person's name and not just 'school,' wouldn't I?"

"But . . . if you're saying it at all, you must have *some* idea." Another unmarked crossroads I wasn't prepared for. It would never have occurred to me in a million years to connect the two creepy phone calls with Ellen's friend being expelled.

What the hell is going on here?

"Ellen, you need to tell me everything you know. This isn't funny."

"I don't *know* anything."

"Then tell me what you suspect."

"I've told you! I think whoever's calling and trying to drive us away is someone from school. One of the teachers."

"And you also think the school wants to be rid of George *and* Fleur, and they'll do whatever it takes to achieve that, even framing them for offenses they haven't committed?"

"Yes," says Ellen with feeling.

I've never heard anything so unlikely in my life. Yet my daughter believes it.

"Why?"

"Dunno."

"Oh come on, Ellen, you can do better than that. I need to know everything before I go in there and kick off."

"I don't want you to kick anything!" She covers her face with her hands. "I want you to drop me off and go home! There's nothing you can do. They won't take George back, and we'll have to put up with more horrible phone calls."

It takes me a few seconds to work out what she means. "The horrible calls I'm getting are because you stuck up for George?"

She seems to be thinking about it. "I don't know," she mutters after a while. "I don't know . . . everything."

"Then tell me everything you *do* know, even if it's not much. Please, Ellen. What are you keeping back?"

A long silence. Then she says, "You're getting the calls because you're picking up the phone. It'd be too obvious if they asked for me, but it must be about me. You haven't got any enemies in Devon, have you? You haven't been making a nuisance of yourself, calling the head teacher a crazy tyrant. I have!"

Then why haven't I been summoned to the school for an earnest talking-to? None of this adds up.

"Whoever it is, she's telling you to go back to London knowing you'll take me with you," says Ellen. "I'm the one they want gone. I'm the one sticking up for George—the only one!"

I can't bear the idea of anyone thinking of Ellen as an enemy, especially when her only crime is loyalty to her friend.

We'll leave Kingswear. Tomorrow. Stuff the new house and the new life . . .

No. That's insane. What Ellen is saying is insane. There has to be another explanation. I love my daughter, but she might be wrong.

I can't tell her what I'm thinking; it would only make her believe I'm against her too.

"Why would the school have it in for George and Fleur?" I ask. "Are they particularly difficult pupils?"

"No. But it's not only the children the school gets landed with, is it? See exhibit A." Ellen points at me, attempting a smile. "Angry parent on the rampage."

"Right, so it's not about George and Fleur, then? Them as individuals, I mean."

"It's about the Donbavands," says Ellen. "They're a particularly difficult family."

Chapter 2

The Perrine Compromise,
and Taking Turns

Perrine, the third daughter of Bascom and Sorrel Ingrey, was brought up in a way that could be called the very definition of compromise. Her parents—both of them equally, in full cooperation—made sure she did her homework so that she never got into trouble at school. They also encouraged her to play a musical instrument, and made sure she did the amount of flute practice that her flute teacher said would be ideal, but when after a year Perrine said she hated these lessons and didn't want to play the stupid flute anymore, her parents let her give up.

When she got home from school, she was allowed to do what she wanted until dinnertime, unless what she wanted to do happened to be so ridiculous that it wouldn't be a sensible choice. So, unlike her sister Allisande, who had once spent an entire afternoon squirting pink conditioner all over an expensive Persian rug without either of her parents making a move to stop her, Perrine was allowed to do whatever she wanted *within reason*.

Her diet consisted mainly of lean meat, healthy oily fish, leafy green vegetables, juicy fruits and fibrous wholegrain cereals, but once a week she was allowed a delicious chocolatey treat, and sometimes she got to eat chips or crisps, though not too often. She was allowed sweets at Christmas, and Easter eggs at Easter. (Lisette wasn't. To this day, she thinks chocolate is evil and will not countenance its presence in her home. And Allisande wouldn't know the difference between broccoli and spinach if her life depended on it.)

Perrine was made to tidy her room once a week, but didn't get into trouble if it got a bit messy in between these times. (This was very different from the case of Lisette, who had been taught from day one that she must keep her room meticulously tidy at all times, and that anything found not to be in its proper place would be instantly thrown in the outside bin with no hope of it ever being retrieved.)

Up to a point, Perrine was allowed to choose what to wear. She wasn't prevented from dressing up as a princess as Lisette was (because her Socialist father disapproved of any collaboration with the monarchy), but neither was she allowed to walk to the nearest shops in the rain wearing nothing but a black bikini, a pink string vest and flip-flops, as Allisande was when she was only nine.

Friends, acquaintances and members of the extended family were relieved when Perrine came along. "Finally!" they said to themselves and to each other. "Finally Bascom and Sorrel Ingrey are bringing up a child in a normal, well-balanced way." All those people ought to have been more cautious in their celebratory banter. They ought to have kept in mind that, in spite of their extreme upbringings at either end of the strict-to-lenient spectrum, Lisette and Allisande were both very nice girls.

Perrine Ingrey, on the other hand, would not have been described by anybody as a pleasant child. She was sulky, selfish, prone to enormous tantrums, spiteful and dishonest. She never laughed or made anyone else laugh, and she didn't have a grain of charm in her. She looked lumpy and had a lumpy, difficult personality to go with her looks. It was impossible to find any good in her at all, however hard you tried. Bascom, Sorrel, Lisette and Allisande all tried very, very hard, and, until Perrine was murdered, they never gave up, but it seemed that nothing could be done to improve Perrine's character.

"How can this have happened?" everybody in the nearby villages and towns asked, when Perrine Ingrey and not one of her sisters was said to have murdered Malachy Dodd. "Isn't she the third child?" they asked. "The one who was brought up normally?"

This proves that ninety-nine people out of a hundred refuse to use their brains most of the time. True, Perrine was brought up in a well-balanced way that was a model of compromise, but both of her parents were constantly frustrated because they were unable to do things entirely their own way. Neither Bascom nor Sorrel could think, "Ah yes, I am rearing this child precisely as I believe a child should be reared." And neither of them could think, "I'm rearing this child in a way that's the exact reverse of the method I think is best"—which is a far more calming notion than you might think, because you simply submit and follow someone else's ideas, instead of feeling as if your way is making progress one minute, then being thwarted the next.

Unfortunately—and Bascom and Sorrel did not foresee this when they made their grand plan for three children—the Perrine compromise led only to constant foiling for both of them. Each parent was enough in charge of policy to feel frustrated at not being able to be more in charge. Surely you can understand this? "My thing ruined" is a far more upsetting prospect than "Not my thing."

It is therefore no surprise at all that Perrine Ingrey was the problem child. Her character was fatally damaged by two disgruntled parents who felt constantly impeded. Anyone in that situation might grow up to be a monster. (I'm not sure if Perrine was a monster, or whether she was sick in the head. Is there a difference between the two? No one is sure to this day.)

Malachy Dodd's regular visits were another compromise between Bascom and Sorrel Ingrey. They were for Perrine's sake, to cheer her up. That was the only reason they happened every Tuesday and Friday afternoon, regular as clockwork. Bascom and Sorrel didn't even like Mr. and Mrs. Dodd. They found them trivially suburban and unimaginative—the kind of people who buy each other cards with "Darling Wife" and "Darling Husband" printed on them by the card manufacturer, and who would rather buy an ugly house with storage space and a double garage than a beautiful dilapidated palace with a ballroom and secret passageways hidden behind bookcases but no off-road parking.

Still, if it would make Perrine less sullen, Bascom and Sorrel decided that they could put up with the company of the Dodds twice a week. They thought that perhaps Lisette and Allisande, being so close in age and such a devoted pair of sisters, made Perrine feel excluded. Malachy Dodd and Perrine were also very close in age. At the time of Malachy's murder, they were both thirteen years old. Malachy's family lived nearby, and so the plan involving these twice-weekly visits was hatched.

Perrine hated Malachy Dodd more and more with each visit. "How can you hate him?" Bascom (who believed passionately in rational discussion) asked his youngest daughter. "He seems good-natured and harmless to me. What's wrong with him?"

"He always makes me cry!" Perrine complained. "Me and only me!" It was true that Lisette and Allisande both adored Malachy, which wasn't fair because they didn't need to be made any happier. Also, Malachy seemed to like them far more than he liked Perrine. This made Perrine jealous. Her envy was the beginning of her downfall. If she hadn't been jealous, she wouldn't have ended up becoming a murderer, and if she hadn't been a murderer, she wouldn't have gotten murdered.

Perrine wanted Malachy to love her even though she hated him—this is an illustration of how warped a child she was. The fateful visit, the one that included the sadistic untimely death of Malachy, was to be the last, Bascom and Sorrel Ingrey had decided, unless some remarkable improvement occurred.

I think we can all agree that splattering all over a terrace and dying in agony is not an improvement. The friendship between the Dodds and the Ingreys, such as it was, ended on that day.

How, you might be wondering, was Perrine's jealousy to blame for all the misfortune that befell her? Well, she would never have risked murdering Malachy if the two of them had not been alone in her bedroom together, and they were alone up there for one reason and one reason only: Bascom Ingrey agreed with Perrine that Malachy preferred Lisette and Allisande to her, and decreed that he should not be given yet another chance to ignore Perrine in favor of her more appealing sisters. Sorrel disagreed with her husband and didn't like the idea of trying to force a bond between Perrine and Malachy if it wasn't happening naturally. "Wouldn't it be a better idea to cancel the Dodds' next visit and never invite them again?" she suggested. Bascom said, "Yes. That will be an excellent idea, once we know for sure that there's no way of making it work. Let's try it my way first, and then, if that fails, we'll put your plan into action."

"Why is it always your way first?" Sorrel asked.

"I've noticed that in any situation where we take turns, your turn always comes before mine."

"You're right," said Bascom, who was a little nonplussed. "I hadn't noticed."

"It must be because you're a man," said Sorrel. "It's the unavoidable sexism of everyday life."

"No, dear, it is not," said Bascom. "It's that I'm a person who prefers to take action, and you are a person who prefers to let things happen. It stands to reason that someone with my personality type would be keen to act, and would therefore go first, while someone with your personality type would never be in a hurry about anything."

"True," Sorrel agreed. "Though in this case, I'm keen to prevent yet another tooth-grindingly awful afternoon with the Dodds from taking place."

"Yes," said her husband. "But I'm afraid that here once again, we have to let me have my turn first. The other way around would be scientifically impossible. We can't cancel the Dodds, never invite them again, and then, next time they come, arrange for Perrine and Malachy to spend some time alone together—because there wouldn't be a next time, would there?"

Sorrel admitted that he was right. "There will, however, be a next time that we disagree about what to do and how to do it," she said. "And whenever that is, whatever the subject of disagreement, it's my turn first."

"Absolutely," Bascom agreed.

And that's how it was decided that on the fateful

day of the Dodds' final visit to the Ingreys' house, Perrine and Malachy should be sent up to Perrine's bedroom together, so that they could properly get to know each other.

But as we know, no bonding took place that day, only the crunch of bone and the seeping of blood on the terrace beside the fountain.

3

I knew Beaconwood was the right school for Ellen before I'd set foot inside it. The building is a former manor house, longer and deeper than it is tall. It's painted pink on the outside, with elaborate pargeting all over the front wall. There are beautiful formal gardens of the sort that wouldn't look out of place outside a stately home, as well as a wildflower meadow and acres of rolling green lawns for the children to make use of. The first time we came here, while we were waiting to meet the head, Alex whispered to me, "Keep an open mind, okay? We're not going to send Ellen here just because the grounds and the building are stunning."

"Not *just* because of that, no," I said. "And not *just* because I went to a secondary school that looked and felt like a high-security prison, but maybe a bit because of those things."

My mind was open enough; if we'd walked into Beaconwood and found sadists in billowing black capes cackling as they whipped the children, I'd have thought twice. Instead, Alex and I found Lesley Griffiths, the head, wearing blue plastic carrier bags over her shoes to protect them from mud while she watered plants in the flowerbeds outside her office. I knew at once that I was in the right place.

I lean against the car and draft a text to Alex, telling him I need to talk to him as soon as possible. Then I button up the coat I still own because I haven't donated it to a friend in need, and walk up the long path to the school's front door. Ellen leapt out of the car, mumbled, "See you later," and ran away before I'd turned the engine off. She wants no part of what I'm about to do, even though I'm doing it to help her best friend in the whole world.

"Justine!" a woman's voice calls out.

I turn around. It's Kendra Squires, the young Canadian teaching assistant who inflicts extra one-to-one maths sessions on those children like Ellen who hate the subject most. Despite this regular torture, Kendra is one of the sweetest people I've ever met. If she were an actress, she would be endlessly cast as the good-hearted innocent who dies tragically young.

"Is Ellen with you?" she asks me. "I mean—sorry, of course I can see she's not *with* you, but is she in school now?"

"Sorry, we had a late start this morning. Yeah, she's there now. Did she miss a session with you?"

"No, no, it's nothing like that. I wanted to talk to her, though. Unless . . ." Kendra tucks a stray strand of her wispy blond hair behind her ear. "Well, maybe I could . . . we could . . . ?"

"You want to talk to me instead?"

"I feel . . . I mean, I don't want to put any extra pressure on her, but there are times when it would really help me if I could set her some work sheets for homework? You know, covering what we've done together that day? Like I used to?"

"That's fine. I didn't realize you'd stopped."

"I know I'm supposed to wait until she's finished this story she's writing for English, but—"

"What?"

"She's writing a story? A murder mystery, I was told." Something about the way Kendra says it suggests that the person who told her wasn't Ellen.

"You were told?"

"Yes, by Mrs. Griffiths. She said you don't want Ellen getting other homework until she's finished her story. Is that not right?" Kendra's forehead creases in concern.

It's certainly not right—I said no such thing—but I'm keen to avoid the torrent of apologies that would follow if I set her straight. I smile and say, "It's no problem. I'll talk to Lesley about it. But yeah, from my point of view, I'm happy for you to set Ellen some maths to do at home."

"Fantastic!" Kendra beams. "I'd better scoot—can't keep the little darlings waiting!" She gives me a cheery wave and rushes on ahead of me.

My phone buzzes in my coat pocket. I pull it out to see if I want to answer, half-expecting to see the words "Anonymous Lunatic" on the screen. Thankfully, there's no evidence as yet that the loon knows my mobile number.

It's Alex. "Oh," I say, caught off guard. "I wasn't expecting you to call so soon."

"Your text made it sound important. Everything okay?"

"Um . . . I think so, but . . . Look, can I call you back later?"

"What's going on, Justine?"

"Nothing. How's Berlin? How's it all going?"

"Great. All's well my end. What about you? Has something happened?"

"No, nothing. Look, you must be busy, and I'm . . . out and about. Let's talk tonight."

"I'm not busy. I'll be busy later, and you sound shifty. What aren't you telling me?"

The same thing I asked Ellen less than an hour ago. I know how infuriating it is to be fobbed off.

"Don't make it sound like some kind of conspiracy," I say, feeling guilty.

"Don't try to put off telling me, hoping you can sort it out on your own and pretend there was never a problem."

I sigh. "All right, just . . . I hope you're in a patient mood." I sit down on the wide stone steps in front of the school, and start listing all the things I'm worried about: unjustly punished George Donbavand, Ellen's best friend in the whole world that I hadn't heard of before today; the peculiar family tree and story fragment; George's strange-sounding parents; Ellen's suspicion that his sister Fleur is also about to be unfairly expelled; the weird misunderstanding about Ellen's homework; 8 Panama Row—or Germander, as I suppose I ought now to think of it—and my inability to push it out of my mind.

That's a long enough list for the time being. Plenty to be going on with.

"I'm at school now," I tell Alex. "Why don't I talk to Lesley, then call you back?" I can hear another country's traffic in my ear, and plenty of it. It's distracting.

"The homework thing's pitifully obvious, isn't it?" Alex says. "No mystery there. El's keen on this story assignment. She doesn't want to waste her time on anything else, so she fibbed to ward off boring maths homework." He chuckles. "Ingenious. I suppose we'll have to come down hard on her about it."

Did we make a mistake? Choose the wrong school? Most would require a note from a parent in a matter of this sort. Only at an eccentric private school like Beaconwood would they take a child's word for it if she told them she wasn't to be given any homework. In my first conversation with Lesley Griffiths, I asked her if Beaconwood was a school that made exceptions—that could be flexible. "I can't do *anything*," I warned her, "so Ellen needs to go to a school that asks nothing of me—literally, nothing. I can't make Viking costumes, or send tins of soup for the harvest festival, or bake cakes for a fundraiser, or manage a stall at the Christmas fair—nothing. And Ellen might turn up without her gym bag one day or her school bag or homework—that all has to be okay. Whatever I *say* is okay, with regard to my daughter, has to be fine with you. Any other regime's going to be too stressful for me."

Like Ellen's current school, I thought but didn't say, *where I'm made to feel like a reprobate by the head and the other parents, because I'm too busy and keep messing up all the things mothers are expected to get right, and I can't take it anymore.*

"You don't need to worry at all," Lesley Griffiths chuckled. "We're about as eccentric and family accommodating as it's possible to be. Examples: we have one family that goes to Denmark for a long weekend every single week. There's a lonely and infirm grandparent situation, and so the children don't come to school on Fridays or Mondays. We accept that." She shrugged. "There's also—between you, me and the gatepost—a mother who drops her child off every morning, then comes back just before lunchtime to inspect the food we're about to dish out and check that it's nutritious enough and appetizing enough. I've offered to let her see our menus in advance, but that won't do—she wants to see each day's lunch with her own eyes and monitor how much her child eats. Really, you're likely to be one of the least unusual families at Beaconwood if you do come here."

I found this reassuring. Alex didn't. "Everyone there sounds like an oddball," he muttered as we left. "Everyone everywhere is an oddball," I reminded him. "Think of Ellen's current school—the parents, I mean." He rolled his eyes. I didn't need to say any more.

"Why does this story matter so much to Ellen?" I ask him

now. "I've seen her write stories before. This one's different. She's password-protected it on her computer. And why didn't she tell us about this George ages ago? If he's her best friend—"

"Her *male* best friend," Alex cuts in. "We all know what that means. Hopefully young George will soon be given his marching orders, and Ellen's next love interest will be someone able to provide his own clothing."

"I'm glad you think it's all so funny," I say as if I don't mean it, though in fact it's true: I am glad. Alex's levity makes me feel better. "I read a bit of her story, not only the family tree. It was creepy, and I don't mean it's a scary story. It's . . . you'd have to read it to understand. I can't believe she made it up."

"You think she copied it from somewhere?"

"No. That's the strange thing. I don't think she'd do that, but I also don't think the three pages that I read are the product of her imagination. And those are the only two possibilities, aren't they?"

"I wouldn't have thought so, no," says Alex cheerfully. "There are always other possibilities, ones you haven't thought of."

"Even the names . . . *Especially* the names." I shake my head, convincing myself once again that something's wrong. Can I convince Alex? "There are three generations of the same family: a married couple, Bascom and Sorrel Ingrey, with three daughters called Lisette, Allisande and Perrine. Then Lisette's got two children called Garnet and Urban. Do those sound like names Ellen would have chosen to put in a story?"

"Yes. They're over the top and weird. Sounds exactly like a fourteen-year-old's invention to me."

"I'd agree if the names were, I don't know, Florentina and Star, but Bascom Ingrey? Urban Ingrey? They're so austere and Victorian.

I keep telling myself I'm making a fuss about nothing, and then I think of those names and I *know* it's not right. They live in our house."

"Who does?"

"The Ingreys. Except they don't and never have, only in Ellen's story. I've Googled. There's definitely never been a family called Ingrey at Speedwell House. Our home is officially an architectural treasure, so there are online records going back to the year dot."

The next words I hear are quiet and German. They fade quickly. Someone walking past, no doubt.

"Please tell me your paranoia isn't veering toward the supernatural," says Alex. "Is that what you're hinting at? Speedwell House is haunted by a ghostly family called the Ingreys, and their spirits have infiltrated our daughter and made her ghost-write—ha, get it?—their family history?"

"Don't be daft." At least now I get a turn to sound like the sensible one.

"Then I don't see what you're worried about. Is this going to be another weird obsession that drags on, like 8 Panama Row?"

"Who can tell?" I say breezily.

"Darling, don't jump down my throat, but how sure are you that all this obsessing over trivia isn't some kind of stress hangover from the Ben Lourenco business?"

I feel either sadness or a sort of amused disbelief when I hear Ben's name these days, not boiling anger. I'm over it. I hope he is too.

"Very sure. All Ben Lourenco stress was blissfully canceled out when I decided never to work again," I say.

"Good." Alex sounds doubtful. "I suppose there's a common theme: Ben, like this George Donbavand, was unfairly maligned and accused. Look, either Ellen's written this story herself, and thought of the names herself—Googled 'unusual Victorian names' or whatever—or she's copied it from somewhere. Ask her."

"I tried. She was cagey as anything. Oh, she's put her own name on the family tree too, so there's an Ellen in the story. Urban Ingrey's wife is Ellen."

"I wouldn't worry about that," says Alex emphatically. Of all the not-worrying things I have told him, he has identified this one as the least worrying. "Writing's a kind of fantasizing, isn't it? Ellen's probably cast herself in the heroine's role. Look, I'd better go. Dieter and—"

"Wait." I wasn't planning to tell him the rest, but it seems crazy not to. I don't want to alarm him; on the other hand, he is as anxiety-proof as it's possible for a human being to be. "I've had two threatening calls. One this morning and one yesterday."

"What? Threatening how?"

I take him through the two conversations word for word.

"Jesus, Justine! You've wasted ten minutes on Victorian character names when you're being pursued by a fucking psycho? Why didn't you tell me straightaway?"

"Alex, calm down. I'm hardly being pursued—"

"Twice in two days, threatening to hurt you if you don't go back to your old life in London? I call that being pursued. Please tell me you've told the police."

"No, I—"

"Right. I'll get off the phone and let you do that straightaway while I book a flight home. Tell them—"

"Book a flight home?" I cut him off. "You can't come back. You've got concerts."

"Justine, we need to take this seriously. Promise me you'll call the police, and look after yourself and Ellen *properly* until I get back. Okay?"

"All right, but . . . please don't cut short your tour just for this. I agree, it's worrying, but I don't think we need to panic."

"I don't intend to panic, but I'm also not going to swan around Germany singing *Die schöne Müllerin* while a psychopath eyes up my home and family with a view to attacking them," says Alex impatiently. "I hope you'll agree that's reasonable?" In a kinder voice, he says, "I can't help being a heroic man of action. I've got my own coat and everything. Bought it myself. Didn't have it given to me by a girl."

I smile. "Well, if I can't talk you out of it . . ."

"Text me when you've spoken to the police. I'll go and get this flight booked. See you soon."

I smile as I put my phone back in my pocket. I'm pleased Alex is coming home. If there's any danger at all, I decide, it will now sense that my husband is on his way and beat a shamefaced retreat.

All of which means the police can wait half an hour or so. First, it's time for school.

Lesley Griffiths, a chunkily built woman in her late fifties with waist-length silver hair, welcomes me into her office with chalk all over her clothes and a cake tin stuffed under one arm. She neither explains nor apologizes for her appearance—which I'm used to by now—and radiates the sort of confidence and authority I would expect from the CEO of a multibillion-dollar company. Each time I see Lesley, she resembles a scarecrow that's had random objects stuck to it; last time she was holding a potted cactus in one hand for no discernible reason.

"Justine! This is a nice surprise. We never see you! That's the school bus for you—never see the bus parents! Sit, sit." Lesley points me toward the chair opposite her desk, and I hurry to seat myself as quickly as I know she wants me to. She's a clever and efficient woman who can often anticipate where things are heading, and her tendency is to try to speed them toward their final destination. I've been physically pushed down into this same chair before when I dawdled for too long. The challenge today will be to remain in Lesley's office long enough to get answers to my questions. I've let her hustle me out into the corridor prematurely on previous occasions, then had to knock on her door twenty seconds later and say, "Sorry, me again. I did have one other thing to ask . . ."

Above Lesley's desk there's a framed collage of holiday photos, mainly taken at her house in the south of France. Most are of her husband and three children messing around in their pool, but two are of Lesley in a green kaftan, reading in a deckchair. The kaftan looks much worse in one picture than in another—torn and faded. I suspect about ten years passed between photograph one and photograph two.

Apart from the collage, Lesley has nothing on her office walls apart from framed hunting and shooting pictures, which look like illustrations from old books. It's odd to see so many images of guns in a head teacher's office. Beaconwood is an eccentric school. I used to think this was a good thing.

I'm wondering where and how to start when Lesley says, "How's your girl getting on with that creative writing project of hers? I'm going to have trouble keeping her teachers at bay if she doesn't get some speed up. Has she hung a sign on her bedroom door: 'Do Not Disturb, Genius At Work'?"

"I wanted to ask you about that. I bumped into Kendra Squires on my way in. She seems to think I asked for Ellen not to be given any other homework until she's finished her story."

"That's right. Parents' orders." Lesley sits down at her desk and looks at it as if something's missing that ought to be there.

"In that case, there's been a misunderstanding," I say. "I'm Ellen's parent and I haven't ordered anything of the sort. It's fine for her to be given other homework. Especially maths, where she needs all the practice she can get."

Lesley squints at me. It's as if, by saying what I've said, I have made myself less visible somehow. "You didn't say no other homework while she writes this story?"

"No."

"Hm. That's interesting. Ellen told me you did. She was quite unambiguous about it. It didn't occur to me to doubt her." Finally, Lesley removes the cake tin from under her arm and drops it on the desk between us. It sounds like a small cymbal as it lands.

"Well, I'll sort out the misunderstanding." Lesley chuckles. "Ellen won't thank you for all the extra homework. Pretty single-minded about that story, she is. She's spending every spare second on it. On the bus, break times, lunchtime. Budding Jane Austen you've got there, I reckon."

"Break times *and* lunchtime?"

"Lately, yes. You can't drag her out of the library. We've all said to her, 'You'll give yourself RSI at this rate,' but she's hooked. It's no bad thing. They say children ought to go out three times a day and get fresh air, but look where we are." Lesley raises and spreads her arms—to indicate Devon, I think, though it's not absolutely clear. "Can't avoid clean air round here, inside or outside. It's not as if we're in Hammersmith or . . ." She shrugs, apparently unable to name another polluted part of London. "But, yes, absolutely. Normal homework for Ellen as of now."

"There's something else I wanted to talk to you about," I say quickly, recognizing Lesley's I'm-about-to-throw-you-out voice.

"Oh?" She taps her fingernails on the lid of the cake tin.

"Sorry. It won't take long." I try to persuade myself that this will be easy. Perhaps Lesley will be grateful to me for setting her straight.

"It's about George Donbavand, and Ellen's coat. Ellen's quite upset about it. She thinks you don't believe her, and I can totally understand why it might seem as if she's protecting George—"

"Justine, I think we'd better—"

"The thing is, George honestly didn't steal the coat." It's so unusual for Lesley to interrupt me that I decide to pretend she hasn't. "Ellen gave it to him as a present, which I know is a bizarre thing to do, but—"

"Justine."

"What?"

"Dear oh dear." Lesley sighs. The fingernail rapping on the cake-tin lid grows louder and more insistent, then stops altogether. "Times like this, I wish I were a different sort of person. I know I can be blunt and undiplomatic, and it's not always what people want."

"What do you mean? Be as blunt as you like. I have been. George didn't steal Ellen's coat. He doesn't deserve to be expelled. It's very wrong that he has been. There, you can't get much blunter than that." I smile in an attempt to soften the blow.

"Justine, there is no George."

"No . . ." It's the last thing I expected her to say. "Pardon?"

"There is no boy called George at this school."

We stare at one another. At a loss, I say, "I don't mean this to sound sarcastic, but . . . isn't that because you've just expelled him?"

"No. There never was a boy called George Donbavand at Beaconwood. No one has been expelled for stealing a coat they didn't steal. What you're worried about . . ." She looks doubtful for a second.

"Yes?"

"It didn't happen. Now, I have too much to do, as ever . . ." She stands up.

"Wait. I'm sorry, no. You're asking me to believe that Ellen dreamed up a boy called George Donbavand out of nowhere? She told me he was her best friend in the whole world."

Lesley is wearing a determinedly patient smile. "Justine, again, let me reassure you. There is no George, there never was, and nobody has been falsely accused or wrongfully expelled." She moves toward the door of her office and clearly intends for me to do the same.

I sit in silence for a few seconds, trying to process what I've heard.

Finally I say, "Then . . . if there's no George Donbavand and there never was, you should know I'm not going to be reassured at all. Much as I don't want to see innocent boys punished, I'm going to be a hell of a lot more worried if I think my daughter's insane or a complete fantasist."

Halfway through my speech, Lesley ditched her fake smile. She's not even looking at me anymore. She doesn't answer.

"What's going on, Lesley? When you said 'Dear oh dear' before—you weren't surprised that I'd brought up this nonexistent boy, were you? You knew exactly who and what I was talking about. How come, if there's no George Donbavand at Beaconwood and never was?"

"Justine, I'm so sorry—really—but I'm going to have to draw a line under this now. Ellen's a lovely girl. We love having her here. You can rest assured that there's no problem at Beaconwood. I've never expelled a child from this school, and I hope I never will."

I cannot fucking believe this.

"Is that a threat?" My palms are hot and itchy. I could so easily leap out of my chair and . . .

"A threat? No, of course not."

"So you weren't insinuating that if I don't drop this and agree to pretend George Donbavand never existed, you'll expel Ellen?"

"No." Lesley looks shocked. "Not in any shape or form."

"Oh. Okay, well . . . that's something at least. Can you come and sit down? I can't think straight with you hovering by the door."

Lesley hesitates. I'm surprised when she returns to her chair.

Good. This is progress.

"Listen," I say. "Ellen's not been herself lately. Not at all. I've begged her to tell me what's wrong but she won't. She's kept whatever it is entirely to herself until today, when she told me about George Donbavand, the coat, him getting expelled—the story that I *know* you know as well as I do."

Lesley nods—or at least, I think she does. The visual evidence is inconclusive. She's not committing herself to anything.

"Lesley, if my daughter has invented a whole narrative involving the persecution of a boy who isn't real, you have to tell me. If the reason you know the George story is that Ellen's been in here, sitting where I am now and pleading with you not to expel her friend *who doesn't exist*, that's something I need to know. I needed to know it five seconds after it happened."

"Do you trust me, Justine?"

"Not recently," I mutter—an immature response, but I can't help it.

"Yes, you do," Lesley corrects me with a smile that looks more genuine than its predecessor. "You entrusted Ellen to me and to this school, and I fully intend to honor that trust. I'm a mother too, remember."

"I do. As one mother to another: tell me what the hell's going on."

"Take it from me, there's absolutely nothing wrong with Ellen."

My body sags with relief. Then I'm annoyed with myself for taking her word for anything.

"I don't mean she isn't unhappy," Lesley qualifies. "I agree, she's seemed rather down in the dumps lately. But there's nothing wrong with her psychologically. She's not living in a fantasy world if that's what you're worried about."

"All right." I try to breathe evenly. "In that case, her best friend George Donbavand has just been expelled for stealing her coat. Hasn't he?"

Lesley says nothing.

"At least you've stopped denying it. I suppose that's something. Lesley, Ellen gave George the coat as a gift. Apparently he lost his, and his mum would have given him a hard time, so Ellen—who has a sap for a mother, willing to buy endless coats—gave him hers as a present. Please unexpel him."

"I can't." Something passes across Lesley's face. For a second, she looks crushed. Defeated. Moments later, I wonder if I imagined it.

"Why not?" I ask.

"I've told you why. We haven't expelled a George Donbavand. There's no wrong to put right here. If there were, I would rectify it immediately, I promise you."

"You haven't expelled him," I repeat in a stunned monotone. Can this really be happening?

"That's right. We haven't," says Lesley. "There is no George Donbavand. He was never here at the school for us to expel."

Chapter 3

Standards of Evidence and the Almost Hanging of Perrine

Perrine Ingrey did not go to jail for the murder of Malachy Dodd. There were no witnesses who could say for certain that she had killed him, and she denied it with more and more outrage and incredulity every time she was asked.

One night when Perrine was asleep, the rest of the Ingrey family discussed the upsetting subject. "I know she did it and so does Lisette," said Allisande. "We heard her say 'Ha!' at the precise moment that Malachy's body hit the ground." (The Dodds, oddly, did not seem to have heard this clearly audible "Ha!," and neither did Bascom and Sorrel. Perhaps they all mistook it for carried sound from the other side of the river, or a drunken reveler on the deck of a passing yacht. If so, they were indeed mistaken. It was Perrine's voice without a doubt, and instantly recognized by her two sisters.)

Lisette, the eldest, disagreed with Allisande that Perrine must be guilty. She strongly suspected that her youngest sister was a murderer, but she was not willing to use the words "must be" without proper evidence. "The 'Ha!' doesn't prove she killed him,"

Lisette told the other three. "All it proves is that she was pleased to see him fall to his death."

"He couldn't have fallen by accident," said Sorrel. "The window in Perrine's bedroom is set too high in the wall for that to be possible."

"We can't know what happened for sure since we weren't there," said Bascom, who, like Lisette, had strict views about standards of evidence. "For example, maybe Perrine was trying to perform some kind of strange trick, and it went wrong."

"What trick?" Sorrel's voice brimmed with disbelief.

"I don't know! Or . . . maybe she wasn't planning to let go of him, but he slipped out of her grasp."

"You're saying she was dangling him out of the window for fun?" said Sorrel sharply. "Or to scare him? Oh, well, that's all right then! Look, instead of wasting time speculating, why don't we concentrate on deciding what to do?"

Bascom, Lisette and Allisande were shocked. Sorrel did not usually say organized-sounding things like that.

"Do?" said Bascom (which was a more typically Sorrel-ish thing to say).

"Yes," said his wife. "Everybody for miles around believes Perrine murdered Malachy, including all of us. Something is going to happen. Somebody—not the Dodds, who are too dull-witted, but somebody else—will try to avenge Malachy's death. Can't you feel the darkness in the atmosphere? I can. I can feel hatred for Perrine brewing, everywhere I go. Something will befall her. She hasn't noticed, but I have. There is danger

all around, and not only for Perrine—for us as well.
What if someone throws boiling water in my face one
day for bringing an evil child into the world?"

"Mum!" Lisette and Allisande protested in unison.
"Don't scare us!"

"I'm afraid I might need to scare you in order to
protect us all," Sorrel murmured.

Bascom asked for evidence that the danger to their
family was real, but Sorrel didn't have any.

Perrine carried on as usual—devious, charmless and
prone to tantrums. She stopped being willing to answer
questions about her role in Malachy Dodd's death. She
started to say, "I've put all that behind me," whenever
the subject came up. This only set the village folk
even more passionately against her. It was whispered
on street corners and in local hostelries that Perrine
Ingrey now referred to Malachy's tragic death as if it
were her ordeal and not his—she was the main victim,
and she had survived and moved on.

One day, during an away rounders match at a local
school, Perrine was standing on the grass of the sports
field under a tree and suddenly felt something fall
around her neck. It was a noose made of rope that had
been dropped from above her head. She looked up. There
was someone sitting on one of the higher branches of
the tree. Their denim jeans and black running shoes
were visible but not their face, so Perrine never saw
who her attacker was.

(You're starting to think that Perrine is about to
get murdered, aren't you? Wait and see.)

She felt the noose tighten around her neck as her

mysterious enemy pulled the rope from above. Luckily for Perrine, her next impulsive action saved her life. She grabbed at the rope with her hands, so that as it tightened and tightened, and as she was hoisted slowly into the air by whoever was sitting on the branch of the tree, her fingers were just about able to pull the noose away from her neck so that she could still breathe, though only barely. Her fingers were badly hurt, but her windpipe was not crushed.

"Hanged by the neck until dead"—isn't that the saying? What a chilling phrase.

Perrine Ingrey didn't die. Not on that occasion. Do not think you can work out what is going to happen before I tell you, because you can't. It's impossible. There are some stories so unimaginably horrifying that no normal imagination could produce them. Even people who had known the Ingrey family for years would not have been able to predict what happened. Afterward— after Perrine was eventually murdered—still nobody guessed who had done it, why or how. To this day, if you visit the vicinity of Speedwell House, you will hear the local legends and rumors about Perrine. From the crab-and-lobster-strewn tables of the Anchorstone Café in Dittisham to the steeply sloping streets of Dartmouth with their rows of little art galleries all selling identical paintings of pastel-colored beach huts, and all up and down the River Dart on every kind of boat you care to mention, you will hear the name Perrine carried to you by the wind and whispered by the trees on the river bank. Sometimes it's as if the water itself is gushing the name, as if hundreds of wooden

oars are pushing it through the foam toward you: "Perrine, Perrine, Perrine!" (But of course many people
are quite fanciful and melodramatic, so I wouldn't
necessarily advise that you trust anyone who asks you
to believe that water and trees can speak.)

One thing is for certain: most of the human beings
who live in or around Kingswear still tell the terrible tale of Perrine Ingrey. And the irritating thing
is that when they reach the end, they all say the same
thing. They all say: "The mystery was never solved. No
one knows who murdered Perrine Ingrey."

That is, quite simply, not true. I know who murdered
Perrine. And those who don't know could easily work it
out if only they used their brains. All the information they need is in their possession by the time they
reach the end of the story. It's really as plain as day,
but they are not capable of guessing the truth, even
though there is only one logical possibility.

(To be fair, I'm not sure I would have been able to
work it out either if I hadn't been told.)

Let's get back to Perrine, who is hanging by her
neck from a tree. How thoughtless of me to leave her
dangling there while I digress and rant about people's
lack of imagination.

Perrine might have died eventually if her would-be
murderer had persisted. Even with her fingers between her neck and the rope, there wasn't much room
for breathing. Fortunately for Perrine, her killer saw
that she had grabbed the noose with one hand, and this
disheartened him or her. "Oh dear," he or she must have
thought. "A noose is supposed to have a neck in it

and nothing else. My plan has gone dreadfully wrong." The miscreant decided to give up and take off. Perrine later told her family that she heard footsteps a few seconds after she dropped to the ground. As she lay there choking and rubbing her wounded neck with her swollen, bruised fingers, she heard her attacker running away.

If you asked Perrine (which you can't anymore, but apparently someone did while she was still alive), she would have said that the worst part of her ordeal was not hanging by her neck from a tree and fearing that darkness without end was about to swallow her up. No, the worst part was seeing the looks on the faces of her teacher and fellow pupils as she hung there, suspended in the air. Each and every one of them believed that Perrine was doomed, and not a single one made any move to save her life. Twenty-nine pupils and one teacher stood perfectly still and watched with smiles of admiration for the murderer on their faces, happy that soon Perrine would be no more.

It was only when it became obvious that she would survive that her teacher sighed and said, "I suppose we'd better call an ambulance."

4

'm in the wrong place: sitting next to a tree in a terracotta pot in the lilac-walled reception area of the police station, when I should still be at Ellen's school. I can't believe I allowed myself to be steered out of Lesley Griffiths's office and whooshed out of the building with a stream of encouraging but meaningless pleasantries: Ellen is a lovely girl, she'll go far, she's so creative . . . Yes, all true, all good to hear, but not the point.

George Donbavand is the point.

Why was I so utterly useless in the face of Lesley's manipulation? Why did I leave without a satisfactory explanation? I know people do strange things when they're in shock, but it isn't as if I was tortured or assaulted—only mightily confused. It's hard to stand up for yourself when you're too bewildered to think straight.

Deliberately bewildered—that's how it felt.

If there was never a boy at Beaconwood by the name of George Donbavand, why wasn't Lesley more alarmed to hear about my daughter's invention of him? Why would Ellen make up a sister for him, also in danger of imminent framing and expulsion?

I wish I'd asked Lesley about Fleur Donbavand. As soon as I'm finished here, I'm going to go back to school and interrogate some other people: Kendra Squires, Mr. Fisher, any children I can get my hands on. *Hurry up, Police Constable Phoebe Hilton.* That's who I've been told I'm waiting for.

Dozens of pupils would have known George if he was at Beaconwood, and all the teachers. You can't force that many people into a conspiracy to lie, not with someone like me pestering them, determined to find out the truth.

I keep coming back to this: Lesley Griffiths isn't crazy. So what is she? Something much worse? If she's lying to me—telling me there's no George when there is one—that's so unacceptable, I can barely believe any head teacher would do it.

No one would do it. Yes, the world is full of grotesque characters who behave appallingly, but . . . this is too outlandish, too out-and-out bonkers. I can see the headlines in the *Sun* and the *Mail* now: "Head teacher who denied existence of pupil is revealed to be . . ." What?

"Justine Merrison?" I look up to find a young woman smiling at me. "I'm PC Hilton. Call me Phoebe, though." She doesn't look much older than Ellen. Blond hair sprouts from the top of her head in a high ponytail.

Is it illegal for a head teacher to lie to a parent? I might ask. The mystery of George Donbavand is all I'm interested in discussing at the moment. I'm less worried about the nuisance phone calls; they're a problem I might be able to solve without police help. If living in Devon means putting up with threats from strangers and sending my daughter to a school where pupils get "disappeared" in the manner of a fascist regime, then I have no desire to stay in the county. I don't want to go back to London, either. Maybe the deranged lisper would accept a compromise: Somerset, or Cornwall.

I love Speedwell House, but I don't love it that much. We could sell it in less than a week, probably—to one of the four families that lost out in the auction we won. Alex would insist that quitting is for cowards, but I've heard that nugget of alleged wisdom before and I've never agreed with it. If there's an aspect of your life that's making you unhappy and you can escape from it, why wait? Too many people stick around and try to improve things, which often means slogging your guts out to compensate for the deficiencies of others. Personally, I'm a fan of the discard: leave it; move on.

Or, as Ben Lourenco so memorably said the last time I spoke to him, "Chuck it in the fuck-it bucket."

"Shall we go somewhere where we can talk in private?" Phoebe Hilton asks.

"I don't mind. Here's fine."

"I think we'll be better off in a less public place. Reception's not usually this quiet. You never know who'll turn up."

"Fine." Then why ask me? I don't care. I want to get this over with so that I can go back to Beaconwood.

PC Hilton starts a conversation about the weather as we walk down a series of corridors. I do my best to participate without yawning. After we've established that it might or might not get colder over the next few days, she asks me about my accent. When I tell her I'm originally from Manchester, she says, "Whereabouts?"

"Northenden."

"I knew it! Near me. I was born in Wythenshawe."

"Really? You sound very Devon for a Mancunian."

"We moved here when I was fifteen. I gave myself a quick change of voice, so as not to get the bejesus kicked out of me every day at school. Still go back to Manc, though—my nan's been there all her life. Northenden's posh, if you ask her. S'pose anywhere's posh compared to Wythenshawe."

"Apart from Miles Platting." I smile.

Phoebe Hilton laughs. "Miles Platting! That's a name I haven't heard for a long time."

"I had a boyfriend who lived there. My dad and stepmum disapproved." *And my mum called them snobs and told them to get over themselves, because Northenden was hardly Mayfair.*

What would PC Hilton say if I told her my mother was killed by a family tree? She'd probably say it can't be true.

It isn't. I know it isn't. It only feels true.

Family trees are nothing more than pictures on paper. Do your worst, Bascom and Sorrel Ingrey. You can't harm me, whoever you are.

We end up in a long rectangular room with horrible pleated orange curtains, and lots of chairs and tables pushed back against the walls as if to make space for an imminent barn dance. "Grab a chair," PC Hilton says, doing so herself. She sits down and pulls a small notebook and pen out of her pocket. "Right. Tell me about these funny phone calls, then. Funny peculiar, I mean—not funny ha-ha."

I start by describing my anonymous caller's sort-of lisp, then do my best to reconstruct both conversations in their entirety. Next I explain the oddest part: that this woman talks as if we know each other well and have a history together when we don't. "I wouldn't be here, except when I called my husband and told him about it, he insisted I tell the police."

"He's right. If you've been threatened, it's always best to report it. Even if it's all hot air, as it seems in this case."

"You mean—"

"It's unlikely this person will do you any physical harm." Phoebe Hilton looks up from her note taking and smiles.

"What makes you say that?"

"Well, most antagonistic anonymous callers get all the aggro out of their systems by making the calls. That's enough for them."

I wait for her to produce something more persuasive. When she doesn't, I say, "Most?"

"Yes. Admittedly, a small minority do take it further, but there are usually very specific warning signs—things we look out for. I'm comfortable that none of those red flags are cropping up here."

I pull a chair over from the side of the room and sit down opposite her. "You don't think this woman's going to attack me and my family if we don't leave Devon immediately, then?"

"No, I wouldn't say so."

Damn. It would have been nice to be able to tell Alex, "The police advise us to run for our lives. If we stay, it'll be at our own risk." I'm confident that I could turn abandoning Devon into as much fun as abandoning work.

Is it weird to glean so much pleasure from booting troublesome things out of your life?

I say, "What about the red flag of this woman knowing where we used to live and what my job used to be? What about 'I don't want to have to hurt you'?"

PC Hilton's face twists in sympathy. "That's a horrible thing to hear, but it doesn't mean she's going to do anything. Honestly, for most of them, the calls are enough to give them the buzz they're after."

"Are there lots of unhinged anonymous callers in this part of Devon?" I ask. "You talk as if you meet hundreds of these people every day."

She laughs. "No, not at all. It's very rare, this kind of behavior."

"Then how—"

"I'd expect the calls to stop fairly soon. That tends to be the pattern with people who do this. If it continues, obviously come and see us again."

"It already has continued. From one phone call to two—that's a continuation." I didn't want to come here, but I did, to please Alex; now I'm getting angry on his behalf, knowing that Phoebe Hilton isn't saying any of the things he'd want her to. "Couldn't you try to trace the calls? I might not be quivering with fear and in imminent danger, but it's still harassment. People get prosecuted for this kind of thing, don't they?"

PC Hilton nods. "If the calls continue, we'll certainly look into tracing them," she says. "To be honest, it might be easier if you were to have a think about who it could be, and maybe try and talk to them? Confront them. Not alone, obviously, and as diplomatically as possible. Perhaps your husband'd go with you?"

Inside my head, all movement stops for a few seconds. Did I not explain myself clearly enough?

"If I thought I could work out on my own who's doing it, I wouldn't be bothering you," I tell her. "I'm here because I'm certain this is *nobody I know*. It's a voice I've never heard before."

"People can distort their voices," says PC Hilton.

"I told you: this *wasn't* a distorted voice. A distorted voice sounds muffled or altered, or . . . This woman was speaking in a perfectly ordinary, clear voice, with a slight lisp, though not the usual kind—not *th* for *s*."

"You said it sounded as if she might have had something in her mouth?"

"I don't think she actually did—I was trying to describe the lisp. It's more likely her tongue was catching on her teeth as she spoke. The point is, I'd have recognized her if she were someone I knew. She isn't. This is no one whose voice I've heard before."

"But you said she knew you used to work in the world of TV and live in Muswell Hill."

"Yes."

"So she must know you."

"No. She knows *of* me, evidently—she knows facts about me—but she doesn't know me because I don't know her. I can't believe I need to say it again, but it seems I do, so please listen carefully this time: the person making these calls is a stranger to me."

PC Hilton blushes and writes something down in her notebook. I hope it's the words "Note to self: stop being a dick immediately."

"All right," she says, looking up. "So you can't think of anyone you might have offended? Any incident that might have sparked this off? Obviously, if you do think of anything or remember anything, let me know."

"Are you serious?"

"Without meaning to," she adds quickly. "I'm not saying you've deliberately intimidated anybody, but people can take offense at the strangest things, can't they?"

"They can, yes." It's important to sound conciliatory. Three words of mollification: that'll do. "But you're missing the point. These phone calls aren't about me or anything I've done or not done. Yes, of course I've upset people from time to time—plenty of them."

"Exactly." PC Hilton sounds relieved that at last we are in agreement. "We all have."

"Yes, and if I thought there was any chance this caller was one of the people I've annoyed over the years, I'd tell you. But she isn't. She's a complete stranger. Look, she might have gotten a few details about my life right, but there's a lot she got wrong. She thought I should know who she was and what she was talking about, and I didn't. She's confused. She thinks I'm a different person, someone who's involved in . . . some kind of ongoing situation with her that I know nothing about! You're not going to find her by looking at my life. Trace the calls if you want to know who she is."

"If it continues, we'll look into doing that," says Phoebe Hilton. "Justine, you have to understand that in my job, so often I'm hampered by people withholding the details that would enable me to help them most effectively. While it's understandable that people are embarrassed or ashamed to share certain pieces of personal information—"

"I'm neither embarrassed nor ashamed. I'm irrelevant."

"How do you mean?"

"Whatever's going on, it has nothing to do with me. It's about her, whoever she is. I can't help you beyond what I've already told you. You're the one who can help me. You can get the calls traced. Taking action to protect civilians from threats is your job, not mine. I don't have a job." I can't help smiling as I say this. "I've done my bit. I've reported the threatening phone calls. Over to you."

"Leave it with me," she says.

And you'll do what? I want to ask. *Don't I have a right to know? When can I expect to hear from you?*

Instead, I do what a nonpushy person would do: I thank her, exactly as I would if I were grateful for something, and leave.

This time I head straight for the school: no dawdling to admire the beauty of the grounds. I park the Range Rover and march up the path, fixing my eyes on Beaconwood's pink decorated façade, as if by keeping it in sight I can prevent the building from vanishing into thin air.

If it can happen to a schoolboy, why not to a school?

I know what I believe and I am eager to be proved right or wrong. I believe that, until very recently, a boy called George Donbavand was a pupil here. He must have walked up this path every weekday morning, heading for the big wooden door as I am now.

I believe it because Ellen says it's true and she isn't a liar. Not usually, anyway. Only about homework.

One person who's willing to tell me the truth—that's all I need.

The school's door has an arched top and a large iron knocker that parents have been asked not to use because it's too loud. I press the less disruptive buzzer, remembering Alex's and my first visit to Beaconwood. We heard the scrape of the key in the lock, followed by the creak of ancient-sounding hinges, and Alex whispered, "A rotund, red-cheeked monk will emerge any second now."

I giggled.

"Brown robe, shaved circle on top of his head, pint of foaming mead in his chubby hand," said Alex.

Instead, the door was opened by the same woman who opens it now: Helen Minchin, the school secretary. Today she's wearing gray wool trousers with a mustard-colored cowl-neck sweater. Pearl earrings and necklace, black shoes with ornaments on the toes featuring more pearls. She looks out of place in a ramshackle country-house school like Beaconwood, where there's usually a pair of muddy boots or two, or sometimes as many as ten, lined up along the front and side walls. The idea of Helen and muddy boots inhabiting the same universe is jarring. She ought to work in a sleek glass and metal building with lifts that speak several languages.

Her two teenage daughters are sixth formers at Beaconwood and regularly babysit for other school families. Disconcertingly, their names are Leonie and Leanne. Alex and I had an argument about this shortly after Ellen started at the school. I said, "There's something sinister about effectively giving your two daughters the same name," and Alex said, "Why do you care? That's more sinister."

Helen breathes in sharply when she sees me on the doorstep. "Oh. Justine." Her shaky smile arrives several seconds too late. It's not convincing and leaves me in no doubt that my status has changed from Esteemed and Valued Parent to Unwelcome Pariah. *In the space of one school day. Unbelievable.*

I smile as innocently as I can manage. "I've just popped in with something for Ellen—hope that's okay!" I try to walk in as I have so many times before.

Helen stands in front of me, blocking the way. She holds out her hand. "I'll make sure she gets it, whatever it is."

I widen my smile by an inch or so. *Time to have some fun.* "Whatever it is?" I repeat Helen's words back to her. "You know what it is? It's a watermelon."

"A watermelon?"

"Yes. You know . . ." I use my hands to convey the approximate size. "Green on the outside, pink on the inside. A big healthy fruit—at least thirty-seven of your five a day. That's the official watermelon slogan, I believe. Anyway, it's Ellen's lucky fruit. I bet you didn't know she had one, did you? Well, she does." I ditch the smile and say, "I'm not going to give it to you. I'm going to come in and give it to Ellen myself. Remember those other times I've walked right in and everyone thought it was fine? So . . . I'm going to do that—the same thing I've done before—again."

Helen stares at me, stunned, as I stroll past her into the building. Lesley Griffiths prepared her for questions about George Donbavand, no doubt; she didn't tell her what to do in the event of a fictional watermelon attack.

Blatant lies are horrible. They're also fascinating: the way I can go nowhere near a watermelon for more than a decade, physically or mentally, and then suddenly plant one in Helen's mind that's impossible to dislodge. She knows I'm lying—I spoke in a way that deliberately drew attention to the ludicrousness of my lie. If everyone else around here can tell lies that aren't at all convincing, why shouldn't I?

"Justine," Helen calls after me. "They're not there."

I turn around.

"They're at swimming, the whole of Year 9. The buses won't be back for another half hour."

"Right." I forgot today was swimming day. "Don't worry—I've brought the watermelon in a plastic bag. I'll hang it on her peg."

Helen returns to her desk, temporarily defeated. She's waiting for me to leave her alone so that she can pick up the phone on her desk and alert Lesley to the emergency. Which means I might not have long.

I move fast through hallways full of children's paintings and sculptures. The two Year 9 classrooms—9G and 9F—are empty. Mr. Goodrick and Mr. Fisher won't be around if the children aren't. I move on to Year 8's part of the building, where lessons are in full swing. I'm not sure I want to barge in and interrogate any teacher in front of a class, though I will if I have to. One of them taught George Donbavand last year, presumably.

Kendra Squires would be a good person to corner, if I can track her down. She's one of those drifter-teachers, not attached to a particular class. She's also deferential and eager to please. I can't believe I wouldn't be able to drag the truth out of her, whatever strictures Lesley Griffiths has put in place. Even if all I get is lots of tears and an admission that there's a truth she's not allowed to tell me—that would be a start.

"Mrs. Morrison!" booms a voice behind me.

It's Mr. Goodrick, in paint-splashed jeans and a Jayhawks T-shirt.

"Not really," I say. "My name's still Justine Merrison, and I'm still Ms., not Mrs. Keep trying!"

"I'm not trying, that's the problem." Mr. Goodrick chuckles. "You're too easy to wind up."

I laugh as if I appreciate his banter. "True. I am exceptionally easy to wind up. You know who's done it most recently? Lesley Griffiths. Why haven't you gone swimming with the rest of them, by the way?"

"It's Art Week. They can't run Art Week without their very own Renaissance man"—Goodrick points at his face with both index fingers—"so AAG's filled in for me at the pool."

He means Ayesha Al-Ghannam, Beaconwood's Head of Seniors and sex education pioneer. She's probably interrupting the scheduled front crawl at this very moment—pulling spotty fourteen-year-old boys out of the water to make sure they haven't forgotten about polycystic ovaries.

"I'd better dash," Goodrick says. "Good to see you, Justin."

"Wait. I need to ask you something."

"Be quick, then. Seriously, I'm out of time."

"George Donbavand."

"Who? Sorry, never heard of him. George . . . Dunnerband, did you say?"

He might be God's gift to art, but he's no actor.

"Donbavand," I repeat. "He was a pupil here. He's recently been expelled."

"No. Uh-uh. I've never heard that name."

"You've never heard of George Donbavand?"

"Nope. No one's been expelled, far as I know." Goodrick lets out a little whistle—because, as we all know, those who whistle innocently must be innocent.

I want to jump on top of him and beat him to a puree.

"You have no idea how obvious it is to me that you're lying," I say. "Just as, this morning, it was clear to me that Lesley was lying. It couldn't be more obvious if you all wore T-shirts emblazoned with the words 'We're all lying!' Exclamation mark."

"I have to go, Justine Merrison. See?" He grins. "I'm not that bad with names—I'd remember a George Donbavand. There isn't one at Beaconwood. There never has been."

What can I do to stop him walking away? Nothing. My imaginary watermelon, so effective against Helen, is useless now. I can't throw it at Mr. Goodrick's head and knock him out.

Marilyn Monroe.

Why did that name come into my mind? That's right: the pictures on the wall behind me. Did I see . . .

I turn and look. Marilyn's one of the better efforts. Beneath her face—half photograph, half oil painting—is the handwritten name of the artist: "Fleur D."

"What about Fleur?" I call after Craig Goodrick.

He stops, but doesn't turn around.

He doesn't know what to say. Lesley told him to lie about George, but she didn't mention Fleur. He has to decide for himself, without knowing what she'd want him to do.

"Fleur Donbavand, sister of the nonexistent George," I say. "A pupil at this school. Look, this is her portrait of Marilyn Monroe. The one that says 'Fleur D' at the bottom."

Goodrick stuffs his hands into his pockets. "Yeah, Fleur," he says with not a trace of guilt. "She's a talented artist."

"So that I'm clear: you're talking about Fleur Donbavand?"

"Yeah. She's in Year 12."

"Yet not two minutes ago you pretended not to recognize the surname Donbavand. Dunnerband, you said."

"I didn't hear you properly." He stares at me defiantly.

"Still. When I repeated the name, you didn't jump in with, 'No, I don't know a George but I do know a Fleur Donbavand.'"

"I was in a hurry. You asked about George. I don't know any George Donbavand. I answered the question you asked. You didn't ask about Fleur so I didn't bring her up." Goodrick starts to walk away again.

"What do you think Fleur will say if I ask her about her brother?" I shout after him.

He's gone: vanished around a corner. It would be undignified to chase him. Pointless, too.

Should I burst into the Year 8 class on my right and demand the truth? Surely someone in the room would raise their hand and say "Me!" if I blurted out, "Who knows George Donbavand?"

Of course he's real. There's no doubt. If Fleur exists, then George must.

Years ago, while working on a TV thriller, I spent some time with a psychotherapist who profiled for the police. She told me the most dangerous and frightening liars are those who attempt to deceive even when there's no chance of convincing anyone, who savor the inability of the honest world to believe they would maintain their pretense in the face of proof to the contrary.

It chills me to think that this category now includes the head of Ellen's school and her form tutor.

I hear glass smashing. Not loud, like a window breaking, but small and contained. The blare of an alarm fills the corridor. I flatten myself against the wall as children start to pour out of classrooms, guided by teachers pointing and mouthing inaudible words.

Lesley Griffiths hurries past me, then turns back. She frowns and gestures at me. "Why are you standing still? You need to leave the building. Fire alarm," she mouths.

"It was you," I say to her departing back. "You smashed the glass, to get me out."

She can't hear me. I can't hear myself.

Chapter 4

Pas Devant les Enfants

After the unknown miscreant tried to kill Perrine by hanging her from a tree, everything changed for the Ingrey family. Later that same night, once Perrine had been checked by a doctor and the rope burns on her neck had been attended to, Bascom and Sorrel said something to their three daughters that they had never said before: "We need to talk in private, girls. It is likely to take a long time. You'll have to forage in the fridge and pantry for your own supper."

Lisette, Allisande and Perrine were shocked. Their home, Speedwell House, was one that had never contained an apartheid system with the grown-ups on one side and the children on the other. It always struck them as peculiar, when they visited the homes of friends, that other families behaved in this way. Lisette's friend Mimsie Careless, for example, had parents who ended conversations midsentence the instant she walked into a room, plastered bright smiles on their faces and said in falsely hearty voices, "Hello, darling! How lovely to see you!" For years, Lisette had been convinced that Mr. and Mrs. Careless were spies for a foreign power, until Sorrel had explained to her that a lot of adults suffer from weird neuroses that they keep at bay by depriving their children of important information about life.

Allisande had a friend called Henrietta Sennitt-Sasse whose mother wouldn't answer any questions in front of her daughter, not even the most innocent ones. If Bascom or Sorrel drove Allisande to Henrietta's house to drop her off and happened to ask Mrs. Sennitt-Sasse a question like, "Oh, is that a new lavender plant I see in your front garden?" or "What do you think of Marathon bars changing their name to Snickers?," Mrs. Sennitt-Sasse would tighten up her face and mutter through shrunken lips, "*Pas devant les enfants*," which means "Not in front of the children" in French. Only after Allisande and Henrietta had gone up to Henrietta's room would Mrs. Sennitt-Sasse answer, once she'd checked that the girls were nowhere in earshot.

The Ingreys had great fun mercilessly mocking the Sennitt-Sasse approach. Sorrel would rock with laughter as she told her family the punchline each time: "And after all that, and with me waiting on tenterhooks to hear this alluring secret that couldn't be spoken of in front of little pitchers with big ears, all the stupid woman said was, 'Yes, it's a new lavender. I bought it half price from the garden center on the weekend. There was a sale.' "

Until the day that someone tried to hang Perrine from a tree, Bascom and Sorrel Ingrey had been willing to discuss anything and everything in front of their three daughters. They did not hide strong opinions, or critical ones. In truth, they didn't have very many opinions that were not strong and critical, and it would have been ridiculous never to allow the girls to hear them speak! In the Ingrey household, the children were not protected from contentious or controversial subjects, because almost anything you cared to name was contentious and controversial for the Ingreys, from when to set off for an important event (with at least an hour to spare in case something goes wrong, insisted Bascom; no, at the very last possible moment to avoid wasting time, countered Sorrel) to how best to handle the family finances (employ an expensive accountant to save yourself a lot of trouble, said Sorrel; keep per-nickety, encyclopedic records and fill in every form yourself in order to save money, said Bascom).

I hope you will understand, then, that for the three girls to be told to make themselves scarce while their parents had a private discussion—in their bedroom with the door shut and locked—was so unusual, it was fright-ening. For Lisette, Allisande and Perrine, being excluded in this way and being able to make out only whisper-ing and hissing was nearly as traumatic as the whole hanging-from-a-tree-attempted-murder incident. Yes, even for Perrine.

The girls didn't go down to the kitchen and forage for their supper. Instead, they pressed their ears against their parents' bedroom door to see if they could hear what was going on. At first they couldn't, but then, as Bascom and Sorrel grew more irate, their voices became more audible.

"But we agreed!" Sorrel yelled. "You promised: next time it would be my turn first!"

"Will you listen to what you're saying?" Bascom

snapped. "How *can* it be your turn first? How would that work, exactly?"

Lisette, Allisande and Perrine started to cry. They had never heard their parents verbally attack each other in this way before. You see, although Bascom and Sorrel Ingrey argued and disagreed about everything, they never fought. It was always perfectly friendly and no one ever got upset. Disagreement, traditionally, was something they enjoyed. It was their hobby.

Until now.

"It is scientifically impossible for you to go first!" Bascom bellowed. "It's exactly like the business with Malachy Dodd—you wanting him never to come around again and me saying he should come around one last time. I didn't *want* him in the house again, or indeed at all—in an ideal world, I wouldn't have let him cross my threshold! But we'd agreed he might be good for Perrine. And we had to do it my way first, because the alternative was conceptually and practically impossible. The same is true in this instance!"

"But you promised that next time, *no matter what,* I would have my turn first," Sorrel sobbed.

"All right then, dear wife, tell me this: If you have your turn first, how on earth will we arrange for me to have mine?"

"We won't be able to. On this occasion, you will have to accept that you won't get a turn."

"No!" Bascom roared. "In any other circumstance I might agree, but this is the most important decision we've ever had to make. The stakes have never been higher!"

On hearing the word "stakes," Lisette, Allisande and Perrine remembered how hungry they were and that they hadn't had any dinner. They didn't care, though. They were all three quite happy to starve to death if their family life was going to be this miserable from now on.

"It's because the stakes are so high that I'm going to insist upon this point of procedure," Sorrel said to Bascom. "You vowed that, no matter what, it would be my turn first next time. I intend to hold you to that."

"You can't," Bascom told her. "Without my cooperation, your plan won't work. I simply won't go along with it! You need me, and you'd realize that if you weren't so stubborn. Do you want to ruin all of our lives?"

"You know what I want." Sorrel's voice was weary now.

"Darling," said Bascom, still sounding strict but not quite so angry. "Listen to me and try to keep an open mind. Let's try my way first. If it works, you won't want to have your turn afterward. If you still want to, that will mean that my method hasn't worked. Then, I promise you, you will have my full cooperation and we can do it your way without destroying our family. You know it makes sense."

"I hate sense!" Sorrel protested. "I'm not sure I can bear to wait!"

"Deep down, you know it's the right and fair thing to do," said Bascom.

"Oh, stop being so . . . *wise!*" Sorrel snapped at him.

Lisette, Allisande and Perrine knew that their mother had given in. Soon the only thing that could be heard through the locked door was kissing and affectionate murmurs. There was some more crying, but it was "Wasn't that horrible?" crying rather than "I hate you" crying.

About twenty minutes later, the bedroom door started to creak open. The three girls sprinted across the landing and leapt down the stairs so as not to be caught eavesdropping. They pulled open the fridge door, grabbed random soft cheese triangles and slices of ham and stuffed them into their mouths to make it look as if they were getting supper on their own.

Their parents appeared in the kitchen in the fullness of time. They were smiling and holding hands. "Girls," they said, "we have an announcement to make."

5

Nobody is dressed. Dressing, moving, would require deciding what to do, and we don't know how. Our drinks—one coffee, one hot water with lemon and honey and one orange juice—sit untouched in front of us.

By now, if all were well and this were a normal weekday morning, Ellen would be in her forest-green school uniform and on the bus, almost at Beaconwood. Alex, in torn jeans and a sweatshirt, would be asleep on a train from Berlin to Hamburg, en route to his next German concert.

I should be the only one in pajamas, sitting at the kitchen table. Instead it's all three of us, which feels horribly wrong. We can't all drop out of life and do nothing. The idea terrifies me. I need to sort out this mess so that Alex can go back to singing and Ellen to school. Not Beaconwood. Somewhere else. Somewhere sane.

Which school will George Donbavand go to next? I'll send Ellen there. I need the phone number of his new school, now, and I'm furious that I don't have it.

It's selfish of me, but I'm panicking—on the verge of tears because I haven't got the house to myself and don't know when I next will. I want to be able to do nothing alone, in this enormous house that I bought for that specific purpose—or lack of purpose—without anybody in my way. I can't have Alex and Ellen milling around here too. I'll have to . . .

What? What will you do? It's their house as much as yours.

I need to be with nobody as much as I need to do Nothing—for several hours a day at least. I didn't know this about myself until this morning.

Maybe I'll pretend to get a job—go out and spend all day Monday to Friday sitting on a bench somewhere far from home. I can do my relaxing obscenity-meditation anywhere; it doesn't have to be at Speedwell House.

Now that my former career is not my only source of anger, I can add a new verse to the mantra: *fuck Beaconwood, fuck Lesley Griffiths, fuck Craig Goodrick, fuck George Donbavand's mother who caused the trouble in the first place by being the kind of person who can't be told about a lost coat. Oh, and fuck my anonymous caller.*

Ellen still insists it's someone from school. I asked her about it again last night while we waited up together for Alex to come home. "Mrs. Griffiths has a grudge against the Donbavands," she said. "It has to be her."

I lost count of the number of times I pleaded, "*What* has to be her? But *why*?" like an irritating toddler.

Because they're a difficult family.

I don't believe that's the explanation. Every school is used to dealing with nightmare families by the dozen, surely.

"Ellen, talk me through the chronology of all this," says Alex. Within seconds of arriving home, he was asking why I hadn't sorted out a clear "timeline" for the George Donbavand business. The word made me shudder. It's only ever used by busy people who need to be efficient.

I'd better face facts: I'm going to have to become that brisk, capable person again, at least for the foreseeable future, if I want to get my old life back. My old new life, that is: the one in which my daughter was happy and her best friend in the whole world had not been expelled.

I feel sick when I try to imagine what might be required of me. I was efficient for too long—most of my life—and it nearly broke me. How can I go back to that? I can't bear the thought of having Things To Do—things that matter. I spent most of last night lying awake fantasizing about starting a new new life. Not in Devon; nowhere near here. Remotest northern Scotland, perhaps, or Florida.

And abandon poor George Donbavand to his fate?

You've never even met the boy. Forty-eight hours ago, you hadn't heard of him.

Look what happened when you stuck up for Ben Lourenco: nothing. It made no difference.

"Ellen?" Alex prompts. "Can you tell me what happened when, starting from the beginning?"

"Do you want exact dates and times?" she snaps. Her eyes are red, with semicircles of purple-gray shadow beneath them. She came downstairs looking like a ghost, carrying her laptop under her arm.

She's been awake all night, crying and writing her story.

"Don't jump down my throat, El," Alex says. "I'm on your side. I just—"

"Then why are you asking about chronology, like a policeman who doesn't believe my alibi? You don't believe me, do you?"

"Yes, I do."

"We both do," I tell her.

"We also believe there's something very strange—strange and wrong on every level—going on at your school," says Alex. "That's why it's important that you tell us everything that's happened from your point of view, and when it happened. I want to get to the bottom of this mess."

"It didn't happen 'from my point of view.'" Ellen's voice vibrates with anger. "It happened from everybody's point of view. It objectively happened."

"We know that, El." I reach over to squeeze her hand. She pushes me away.

"George is real," she says, blinking away tears. "He's as real as the three of us. Two days ago he was expelled. Mr. Goodrick's lying. Mrs. Griffiths is making him lie. She's probably threatened to sack him if he tells the truth about George. She's evil."

No, she isn't. That can't be the answer.

"She's the head. The other teachers would do what she told them."

"So George was in on Tuesday?" asks Alex. "Was Tuesday his last day at school or his first day not at school?"

"His last day," says Ellen. "He told me he'd been expelled and wouldn't be in again. And he was right. Yesterday, the day Mum drove me in, he wasn't there. There was no sign he'd ever been there. The bits of the wall displays that he'd done, with his name on them—his impressionist painting and his photo of a kingfisher—they'd gone. And all the others had been moved around."

Alex shakes his head. "Unbelievable," he says. "No, I don't mean I don't believe it, I mean what the fuck. Sorry. Five quid in the swear box from me."

"Yeah, the swear box we haven't got and have never had," Ellen mutters.

"Thought that counts," says Alex. "It's unbelievable. A school expels a pupil for stealing a coat he didn't steal—and they've been told he didn't steal it by its original owner—and then they remove him from the classroom wall as if he never existed?"

"What did you mean about all the others being moved around?" I ask Ellen.

"I meant they didn't only take George's stuff down from the wall—that would have left some gaps, and there weren't any. Someone took down the whole lot and put them up again so that there were no obvious spaces where George's work used to be."

"Ellen can't go back there," I say to Alex.

"Mum, I have to."

"You two are arguing about the future. I'm still struggling to understand what's happened so far," says Alex. "Ellen, when did you speak to the teachers about George and the coat? On Tuesday? Before? Who did you speak to?"

"Miss Squires first and then Mrs. Griffiths, when Miss Squires told me to. I explained—"

"On Tuesday?" Alex cuts in. He's not giving up on this timeline thing.

"No, Monday. George knew he was in trouble on Monday morning. He was crying in assembly."

"This story makes me want to kill people," I say through gritted teeth.

"George told me what he'd been accused of, and I told him not to worry. I made it worse by making him get his hopes up. I thought there was no way they wouldn't listen to me—it was my coat! How could they still expel him once I'd told them I gave it to him as a present? Mrs. Griffiths was really nice when I told her, or pretended to be. She smiled and nodded as if she believed me, and praised me for being such a kind and loyal friend. And then she went and expelled George anyway! I thought back over everything she'd said to me, and I realized what was missing. All that smiley praise was to shut me up and get me out of her office. She never once said, 'All right, George can stay. We won't expel him now that we know the truth.'"

"But you assumed she wouldn't," says Alex.

"Totally. She seemed to believe me."

"She did," I say.

Alex and Ellen look at me.

"I mean, yes, she hoodwinked you, clearly—she wanted to expel George, and she let you think you'd changed her mind when you hadn't. But I'm certain she believed you."

"Presumably George protested his innocence too," says Alex.

"Of course he did! He told Mrs. Griffiths exactly what I told her, but she didn't believe him either. Why would she expel him if she knew he'd done nothing wrong?"

"The coat thing's an excuse," I say. "A smokescreen story."

"Where are Mr. and Mrs. Donbavand in all this?" Alex asks. "Why are you the one going in to inquire and complain? Why not them? George is their son."

"Dr. and Professor Donbavand," Ellen corrects him. "They don't care about their children. George hates them."

"I'm sure they do care," says Alex. "What does he look like, this George?" It's a question I haven't thought to ask.

Ellen wrinkles her nose. "What's that got to do with anything?"

"I'm just interested. Is he tall, dark and handsome? Short, dark and weedy?"

Ellen sighs. "He's a Caucasian male, about three inches taller than me, with light brown hair and blue eyes. Satisfied?"

George hates his parents. They don't care about their children.

There's a half-formed idea in my mind. I like it so far and can't be bothered to wait. "I think Lesley Griffiths was trying to communicate something to me without being too explicit," I say. "She was using a kind of code. Telling me everything's all right, even if I think it isn't. If I ignore her actual words, which were implausible at best, everything about her manner was saying, 'Trust me, Justine. I've done the right thing. You'd agree with me if you knew what I know. Everything's fine, really.' Ellen, does that sound similar to how she was with you?"

Is it possible that Lesley expelled George to protect him from his parents in some way? I can't think how that would work, though— that's the only problem with my theory.

Ellen shrugs. "Have I got a clean uniform?"

"No." In the chaos and drama of yesterday, I forgot about the laundry I'd been meaning to put in. "But you don't need it."

"Yes, I do. I'm going in. Can you drive me to school, Dad?"

"Absolutely not!" I'm on my feet, prepared to stop them forcibly if I have to.

"Will you both sit down?" says Alex. "No one's going anywhere until I've had more coffee. This one's cold."

"That'll happen if you don't drink it," Ellen tells him.

"We also need to discuss the homework-dodging issue."

Shut up, Alex. Of all the stupid things to say.

"What?" Ellen spits the word out like a hard stone.

"You told your teachers Mum and I had said something we hadn't said, El. That's not ideal, is it?"

"Nor is bringing this up now, when she's upset," I say. "Can't we tackle one thing at a time?"

"Dad thinks the two are connected," Ellen says in a shaky voice. "Don't you? You think me lying is the connection."

"I've already said I believe you about George."

"Only because you can't prove it's not true. Not because you trust me. What time is it?" Ellen asks me. "Is it half past nine yet?"

I look at the digital display on the microwave. "Just gone quarter past. Why?"

Triumph flares in Ellen's eyes. Before I know its cause, I'm pleased for her. I want her to win everything. Yes, even arguments with her parents, paradoxically.

"I'll prove to you that George exists. You can see him for yourselves! I know where he's going to be at half past nine. Come on." Ellen darts past me. I lunge to try and stop her, but she's out of the door before I can grab hold of her pajama sleeve. Seconds later, the front door slams.

"We're letting her go out without clothes?" Alex complains. The flat of his hand rests on the coffee plunger, as if he's considering pressing an emergency alarm.

"She won't go farther than the garden dressed like that," I say, hoping it's true.

"None of this makes any sense!" Alex is angry suddenly. "Is George Donbavand going to be in our garden at nine thirty? Why would he be? Is he even real? I mean, why would Lesley Griffiths deny the existence of a boy who, until the previous day, was a pupil at her school?"

"I don't know, Alex. If we want answers, we need to follow Ellen."

"We're not dressed."

"So what? The world won't end if we go outside in pajamas. Ellen wants us to go with her. We need to move." *The river.* Is that where she's headed, to where the land belonging to Speedwell House ends and the water starts?

"Justine!"

I'm in the hall, about to open the front door when Alex calls my name.

"What? Aren't you coming?"

"Do we believe in this George Donbavand?"

"Yes," I say without hesitation. "I do."

Ten minutes later, the three of us—Ellen, Alex and I—are standing at the lowest point of our garden, looking out over the wall. Sunlight spreads itself into the dimples on the water. It's restful, just watching, forgetting I'm part of a story I don't understand. I wonder if Ellen and Alex feel the same.

Waiting in silence. Not knowing what for, not in charge, unable to anticipate. This moment, out of time and context, is how I would like my whole life to be. *This is it: what I want.* Here and now is the first time I've found it—my own peculiar holy grail—since we moved to Devon. Then the questions rush in and ruin it: Is George Donbavand about to appear? From where? If he was only threatened with expulsion on Monday, why has Ellen been withdrawn and distant for so long? Was she so wrapped up in her new friendship with George that she lost interest in us, her family?

"So. Here we are," Alex says: a not especially helpful public service announcement.

"It must be half past nine by now. Is it, Mum?"

"I don't know." I haven't worn a watch for years. "Maybe not quite. Another few minutes." When I worked, my BlackBerry was never not in front of my eyes. I was never not staring at its screen, trying to calculate whether I could spare the time to notice what time it was.

"I know neither of you is expecting to see him," says Ellen. "You don't believe he's real."

"If he's real, it can easily be proven," says Alex. "Which makes me wonder why school would pretend never to have heard of him."

Shut up, for God's sake.

"If they're lying, it's going to become obvious pretty bloody quickly. Why doesn't that worry them enough to stop them?"

"So they must be telling the truth?" Ellen says bitterly.

"I believe you, El," I say.

"Look!" She's staring hard at the river. Something's happened. What? What has she seen? Is George Donbavand about to come out of the water in a wetsuit and climb over our garden wall?

Please don't let Ellen be crazy. Please let George be real.

I stare at the river. Alex does too. Counting down without numbers, without words. It's like waiting for a magic show to start. Where is the magic element going to come from?

I see and hear nothing that surprises me, only boats and birds: an orange sail tied to a mast; a seagull sick of having to repeat itself.

No George Donbavand.

"There it is!" Ellen points out over the water. Standing beside her, I can feel her excitement. "Lionel's boat!"

Lionel—never referred to with a surname attached—is a well-known local painter with a booming voice who has a tendency to finish his sentences with the words "Are you with me?" He exhibits his wares in pubs and cafés, hoping to sell them for between £40 and £90, depending on their size. Lionel has considerable skill as an artist, but his pictures are stomach-churningly awful. He paints attractive Devon scenes and landmarks—Budleigh Salterton beach, Exmoor, the Royal Naval College at Dartmouth, Torre Abbey—then spoils the beauty he's created by painting a caricature of himself, complete with broken-veined nose, tufty white hair and tobacco-stained teeth, over the landscape in a completely different cartoon-like style that clashes horribly.

All his paintings have titles that begin "Lionel Woz Ere": *Lionel Woz Ere At Wortham Manor*, *Lionel Woz Ere On Burgh Island*—those

were two I particularly enjoyed leaving behind at the Anchorstone
Café in Dittisham to put people off their food until the end of time.
Lionel's pictures don't sell, and so end up being exhibited relentlessly, forever, by owners of establishments who tolerate and even
encourage him because he's "a character." His paid work is to pilot
his boat *The Kingswear Treasure*, a large wooden dinghy with an out-
board motor, from Kingswear to Dartmouth and back again dozens
of times a day, seven days a week. God knows when he finds time
to paint.

"What's Lionel's boat got to do with George?" I ask Ellen as *The
Kingswear Treasure* chugs over to our side of the river.

"George'll be on it when it goes back across to Dartmouth. The
Donbavands live on the other side. His dad always took him and
Fleur to school on the boat. Now he's been expelled, only Fleur
needs to be taken, but George's dad would never leave him in the
house alone and his mum always leaves for work at about five thirty
in the morning to avoid rush-hour traffic. George will have gone
across on the boat with his dad and Fleur. He must have!"

I see what she means. "Lionel's boat leaves for Dartmouth on the
hour and the half hour, so given that they'd miss the nine o'clock
because school only starts at nine—"

"They'll be on the nine thirty," Ellen completes my sentence.

I can't help smiling. It's funny to talk about "the nine o'clock"
and "the nine thirty" when we're talking about the same battered
wooden vessel, steered by the same white-haired windbag.

"Isn't Fleur in sixth form, didn't you say?" Alex frowns. "Surely
she's old enough to go to school on her own by now."

"George's mum doesn't think so." Ellen cranes her neck, nearly
toppling over the wall. "I wish I could see the jetty from here. Why
are there so many trees in the way? George and his dad will be on
the jetty, waiting for the boat."

"Here we go," I say as *The Kingswear Treasure* slides back into view on a burst of foam.

"There he is!" Ellen shrieks next to my ear. "There—see that man with blond hair and glasses in the brown coat and red scarf? That's his dad. The boy next to him, that's George. George! *George!*"

I step back to avoid being deafened by her screams.

Turn around, George. Please turn around.

"He's never going to hear you over the noise of all the people on the boat," says Alex. "Plus the water, the wind . . ."

"That's him, Dad," Ellen says mournfully. "I knew he'd be on Lionel's boat and there he is—too far away to hear me!" She bursts into tears and starts to run back toward the house. Alex follows her.

I stay where I am, staring at *The Kingswear Treasure*.

You're disappointed that he didn't turn around. Admit it. You think it might mean something.

I stare at the boy who might be George as he drifts farther away. He could easily be the person Ellen described. Light brown hair. I'd call it dark blond, but it amounts to the same thing. He's sitting with his back to me, so I can't see if his eyes are blue.

A boy in a boat. No proof that his name is George Donbavand.

Once I'm sure that both Ellen and Alex are inside the house, I shout, "George!" as loud as I can. He doesn't respond. Of course he doesn't. He's halfway to Dartmouth. As Alex said, it's a windy day.

It doesn't mean anything.

I'm sitting in the gazebo when I hear Alex's car pull up on the gravel on the other side of the house. I've left a note in the kitchen telling him where I am.

Ten minutes later, I see him coming across the lawn with two mugs in his hand, steam rising from both. He'll have made me tea—too strong, as always, with not enough milk. It's a running joke. Alex calls my kind of tea "beige water."

"What happened?" I ask as he hands me my drink.

"Nothing interesting. I dropped El at school, then drove home."

"Did you go in?"

"No."

"Speak to any teachers?"

"No. Let me try this again." Alex clears his throat. "I dropped Ellen at school, and then I came home. Nothing else happened. If it had, I'd tell you."

"Sorry." I swear under my breath. "We should have kept her at home."

Alex sighs. "We didn't, though, so why have the argument now?"

"She's knackered. I don't think she got any sleep at all last night. She stayed up writing her story."

"It won't kill her to be tired."

"We need to see that story. There's something not right about it. It's not what it seems."

"Not this again. How is it not what it seems?"

"I don't know!" The smell of Alex's coffee is ruining the sea-salt smell that I love. I move away from him, wrinkling my nose at his mug. "If I could be more specific, I would. There's something wrong, Alex. I thought so yesterday and I think so today, hence the repetition. Why do you think Ellen was so determined to go to school today?"

"She explained why: she can't ruin her education just because she's upset about George. Sensible, if you ask me."

"That was a lie, to placate us. She's frightened. Can't you tell? I think she believes the threat—to her, George, us, whoever—will be greater if she acknowledges it. By staying away from school, she'd be signaling that she knows how serious the problem is. She's trying to . . . appease the danger by pretending to be unaware of it. She's gone in today intent on acting normal."

Alex sips his drink. "That sounds vague and woolly to me. I mean, you could be right, but . . ." He shrugs. "By the way, how old do you reckon Lesley Griffiths is?"

"Why?"

"Ellen asked me. I didn't know the answer."

"When?"

"Just now, on the way to school."

"I've always assumed late fifties. What else did Ellen ask you?"

"Nothing. Oh, wait, no, she did. She asked about some family photos in Lesley's office. I didn't know what she meant. I've only been in her office twice, and I didn't notice any photographs."

"There's a framed collage—Lesley and her husband and kids at their house in France, messing around by the swimming pool."

"Apparently so. Ellen saw it when she was in the office sticking up for George."

"Why? Why would she care how old Lesley is?" I'm asking myself more than Alex. I don't believe Ellen suddenly, randomly, wondered about her head teacher's age.

My phone starts to ring in my pocket. I grab it quickly, in case something terrible has happened to Ellen at school since Alex left her there.

If you think that's likely, she shouldn't be there.

But if she's terrified of what might happen if she stays away . . .

"Hello?"

"You're still there, in the house. You're not going to make this easy for either of us, are you?"

"Hello, crazy stranger. Alex, it's that crazy stranger I was telling you about. She's got my mobile number now too—isn't that fantastic?"

"Three empty graves," says the unidentified voice. "One smaller than the other two."

"I beg your pardon?" My heart thuds like a bullet hitting bone.

"Two for a mummy and a daddy, one for a child."

I cover my mouth with my hand. Swallow hard.

"Three graves to fill, and all because you're too stubborn to see sense and go back to London. Is it worth it? Does winning mean that much to you?"

"Fuck you."

"That's very mature, isn't it?" says the lisper. "That's going to solve everything."

"You just threatened me with murder if I'm not mistaken. How mature is that?"

Alex is gesturing to me that I should pass the phone to him. No. This enemy is mine.

"Who are you?" I ask her.

No answer.

I don't know why I say what I say next. I know there's a reason, but it's not one I can put into words. "Is your name Olwen?"

Alex mouths, "Who?"

"Olwen? Is that you?"

I hear a click. She's gone.

Chapter 5

Homeschooling

As soon as they heard the details of the changes that were about to rock their lives, the three Ingrey sisters burst into tears all over again.

"From now on, no more school," said their mother brightly. "You will be home-educated. I will teach you everything creative and interesting—fun, arty things like dressing up and putting on improvised plays—and your father will take care of all the boring stuffy-shirt subjects like maths, physics, history, big yawns all around."

"No, I will teach you the *important* things," Bascom contradicted her. "Important things, which are also interesting. I'm afraid your mother's knowledge of history consists of little more than remembering that she used to find Mick Jagger of Rolling Stones fame more attractive than either John or Paul from the Beatles."

"Only a stuffy-shirt would use the expression 'of Rolling Stones fame,'" said Sorrel.

"The expression is *stuffed* shirt," Bascom corrected her stuffily. She laughed at him.

Lisette, Allisande and Perrine were unable to feel pleased that their parents were once again disagreeing in a loving and jovial manner. They did not want

to be homeschooled. They were aghast at the prospect
of losing this important dimension of their lives. It
wasn't about the education, it was about seeing their
friends, and the gossip that they couldn't live without. (No human being should be expected to live without gossip—that is an indisputable fact.) For example,
Mr. Coote had recently told off Henrietta Sennitt-Sasse
for spraying her floral deodorant spray all over the
school bus, but he had not done this during school
hours, or even on school grounds—oh, no. Shockingly,
Mr. Coote had bumped into Henrietta in the park one
weekend and started reprimanding her most severely
when he wasn't even in loco parentis. Every idiot
knows that a teacher can't harangue a pupil for a
school-related offense once the school day is over.
Henrietta had told Allisande that the "*Pas devant les
enfants*" her mother had spluttered to her father on
this occasion had been positively vicious, and she was
sure her parents were going to do all they could to
have Mr. Coote fired. Henrietta was determined that he
should be sacked, and if her parents didn't make this
happen, she planned to catch him out in another way.
Mr. Coote had a habit of ruffling children's hair and
slapping them on the back, and Henrietta thought this
behavior could easily be presented as violent pupil
battering.

It was because of ongoing sagas like this that Allisande and Lisette Ingrey did not want to give up
going to school, and they said so to their parents.
They begged and pleaded, to no avail. Perrine, surprisingly, felt the same way as her sisters. Everyone

was rather shocked to hear this. "But Perrine, last time you went to school, someone tried to hang you from a tree," Allisande pointed out.

"Yes, but that could have happened anywhere," said Perrine. "There's no way of knowing that the person who tried to kill me was someone from school. Anyway, I'm not scared. I was off my guard, but not anymore. If anyone else tries to kill me, I guarantee I'll choke the life out of them first." Perrine giggled, then let her eyes roll back in her head. She poked her tongue out of the side of her mouth and mimed pulling up a rope behind her head. She made a noise that sounded like gargling and the snapping of a neck all at the same time. Then she giggled some more.

Lisette and Allisande exchanged a look. Some of the time they were able to pretend to themselves that Perrine was normal-ish, but then something like this would happen and it became obvious that she really wasn't.

"Wait a minute," said Lisette. "Mum, Dad . . . no one has tried to kill me or Allisande, have they? Why can't we go to school as normal, and just Perrine can stay home?"

Sorrel shook her head sadly. "I wish I could say yes to that, I really do. But I'm afraid Perrine needs company."

"No, I don't," said Perrine. "I'm fine on my own."

"No, you're not," said Bascom. "Listen to your parents who know what's best for you. Families must always stick together, no matter what. Very close together."

"It's not only about keeping Perrine company," Sorrel

explained. "It's also a safety measure. Your father and I are determined to keep Perrine confined to this house so that no one can get to her. We will succeed, because when we join forces, we always triumph."

"Indeed," Bascom agreed. "That's the secret of our happy marriage."

"So, everyone who hates Perrine and wants her dead will be frustrated," Sorrel went on. "How long before they think to themselves, 'Okay, then, if we can't kill her, we'll make do with one of her sisters'?"

"I don't think anyone would think that," said Allisande. "Everyone likes me and Lisette. They wouldn't punish us because Perrine murdered Malachy Dodd."

"Oh, not that again!" said Perrine irritably. "I didn't murder him."

"Allisande's right," said Lisette. "I've lost count of the number of people who have said how sorry they are for me, having Perrine as a sister. I've had offers from teachers and pupils for me to go and live at their houses, join their families."

"Girls, I'm so sorry," said Sorrel. "It has to be this way. You two will be a good influence on Perrine, and I don't want to have to worry about you at school all day. Yes, most people have been reasonable and sympathetic to you both, but remember, it only takes one person to drop a rope noose down from the branch of a tree."

"But . . . we can still see our friends, can't we?" said Lisette. "Mimsie can still come round for tea after school sometimes, and at weekends?"

"And Henrietta?" said Allisande.

"I'm afraid not," said Sorrel, who looked genuinely upset. "Anyone who comes to the house might try to harm Perrine. Even if they have no desire to do so themselves, they might unwittingly be used as a pawn by someone who wants to hurt or kill her. We can't take the risk. From now on, for the foreseeable future, it'll just be the five of us. And . . . perhaps we will eventually move out of Speedwell House, away from Kingswear, to somewhere where no one knows the names Perrine Ingrey and Malachy Dodd."

"No!" protested Lisette and Allisande in unison. They had both started to sob. "We don't want to leave our friends!"

Sorrel looked at Bascom. "You see?" she said softly. "My way wouldn't have involved cutting Lisette and Allisande off from their—"

"Darling," Bascom said with a warning tone to his voice. "Come on. We agreed."

"Yes," Sorrel sighed. "We agreed."

"So . . ." Bascom rubbed his hands together enthusiastically. "It's going to be just the five of us for a while, and it's going to be lots of fun! We'll do all kinds of exciting things! We're going to introduce some new, extra-special security measures here at home, so that no one will be able to break in and threaten us. It'll be like playing hide and seek, but . . . for a long time, and with no one being able to find us."

"But you and Mum both have jobs," said Lisette.

This was true. Bascom worked as a supervisor in a timber frame factory, and Sorrel worked part-time as a receptionist for a vet in Kingswear. She would have hated to work full-time, or be a boss, whereas Bascom was ideally suited to a managerial role. He enjoyed delegating work, nurturing employees and being responsible for bringing everything together. Even when one of his workers fell into one of the machines at the timber factory and lost an arm, Bascom was pleased that he was the one sorting it all out (though there was nothing he could do about the lost arm, sadly).

"We will give up our jobs," Bascom told his three daughters. "We'll manage. We have some money saved up. This is why it's so sensible to save for a rainy day."

At that moment, the twilight sky lost all its color and turned jet black, and rain started to pour forth from above, drumming and hammering on the roof of Speedwell House. The Ingreys huddled together for comfort, but it was hard to feel safe when it seemed as if even the weather had turned against you.

6

'm sitting in my car on Cravestock Road, a narrow one-way street of redbrick interwar semis. Less than ten meters away are Panama Row and Germander; less than twenty, my old friend the North Circular Road. I'm trying to convince myself that coming here isn't the most senseless thing I've ever done.

There's no reason to believe that my anonymous caller is Olwen Brawn, a woman I've never met. I know this. I also know I'm going to suspect her until I prove that she's not the culprit.

If we speak—if her tongue doesn't catch on her teeth and she has nothing resembling a lisp—then I'll have made progress. I'll have ruled her out. I should get on with it. Get out of the car and do this.

Just once more: Why, exactly?

Silently, I present my justification to the imaginary judge in my head, who is a physically implausible composite of all the judges I've seen in *The Good Wife*.

Strange things have been happening lately: the anonymous calls; the overpowering feeling I had when I first saw 8 Panama Row; the fragment of Ellen's story I found, containing bizarre names I don't believe my daughter would invent; George Donbavand, who either isn't real or else was expelled for something he didn't do and then erased from the school's collective memory; Ellen telling me she Googled the house I'd been unable to forget, and discovered that its name was Germander.

She's keeping something from me for sure, and she was interested enough in 8 Panama Row to try to find out more about it. Maybe those two things are linked. Maybe my reaction to Germander was triggered by something I sensed in Ellen—a powerful emotional response? It must happen occasionally that a mother picks up on her child's unspoken feelings.

That's why I'm here. If I want to find my threatening caller, it seems sensible to start searching in the compartment of my life labeled "Freakish Things I Can't Explain," rather than in "Absolutely Ordinary." Most of the people in "Freakish Things" have voices I've heard more than once—the women at Beaconwood, for example. Lesley Griffiths, Kendra Squires, Ayesha Al-Ghannam, Helen Minchin and the rest. I've been through every female member of staff, and I'm certain it's none of them.

Olwen Brawn, owner and resident of 8 Panama Row, is the only woman in "Freakish Things" whose name I know and whose voice I've never heard. That's why I'm about to knock on her door.

Alex thinks I'm being irrational.

"Speedwell House," I said to him over breakfast this morning. "Germander. Germander Speedwell. You really think it's a coincidence?"

"Yes," he said emphatically, as if he'd been waiting to say the word all his life. "Why would Olwen Brawn, resident of a random ugly house beside the North Circular, be the person making these calls?"

I don't know. I've driven all this way to find out and I'm too scared to get out of the car.

I force myself, finally, by imagining the Range Rover is about to burst into flames. Then, as I walk toward 8 Panama Row, I imagine myself walking in the opposite direction—later, once this is all over, as it soon will be.

I ring Germander's doorbell and trigger a chorus of barking. At least two dogs in the house, if not more. I hear a woman's voice telling the dogs to calm down, not to be silly. Olwen Brawn?

If so, she's not my telephone stalker. There's no lisp, and her voice has a higher pitch. *Too late to run away.*

The door opens and I find myself face to face with a woman who looks a few years older than me—late forties. Her dark brown hair is short and spiky at the front. She's wearing a waistless black knitted dress with black tights and bright pink sandals. Dark red lipstick. Around her legs and behind her, there's a collection of what look like small bluish gray sheep, except sheep don't bark or have long, pointy faces. Therefore: strange dogs, each with a ridge of curly fur protruding between its eyes. One is more neatly groomed than the others. Its long ears end in perfectly round fur pompoms, like earrings: dog-cum-topiary.

Before I have a chance to say "Sorry, wrong house," the woman smiles and says, "He . . . eey!," as if she's been waiting to welcome me for hours. "You're here for Yonder!"

"I . . . Pardon?" I must have misheard.

"He's in the back garden with his remaining brother." She extends her hand. "I'm Olwen Brawn. And you must be Deborah Fuller."

Instead of thinking "No, I'm not, and I'd better say so," I find myself wondering if that's what's wrong: it's only because I think I'm Justine Merrison that nothing in my life makes sense. The moment I admit I'm Deborah Fuller, everything will fall into place.

"Come in, come in." Olwen Brawn disappears into her house,

clearly expecting me to follow. I should make a run for it, before the real Deborah Fuller arrives, but I want to see inside—see if there's anything in Olwen's home that explains the feeling I had when I first saw it.

The narrow hall has a wood-laminate floor and pale blue walls covered with framed photographs of dogs—different colors and sizes, but all with the same topiary look, and some wearing rosettes. Unsurprisingly, the house has a strong animal smell.

"Come through," Olwen calls out. Then she yells, "Yonder Star!" She's in the living room at the end of the hall, rearranging dogs on a sofa.

Yonder Star? As in "Star of wonder, star of night" from the Christmas carol?

A tiny gray furball of a puppy trots over to me and tries to climb up my leg. "Down, Figgy!" shouts Olwen. To me, she says, "That's Figgy Pudding pestering you there—Yonder's little brother. Oh, damn, he's got mud all over you. He's just come in from the garden."

"It doesn't matter."

I think back to what Olwen said before: *his remaining brother.* Okay, I've got it: Yonder Star is the name of a puppy. No one would talk about dead brothers in such a cheerful way, so "remaining" must mean the puppies that haven't yet gone to new homes. Figgy Pudding, presumably, is one of these.

He's still attached to my leg, looking up at me hopefully. "Hello," I say. What else can one say to a dog? Not much point asking if he's read any good books lately.

He jumps up, trying to bite the bottom of my coat, but he can't reach it.

"You're all named after bits of Christmas carols, are you?" I whisper to him. "That's . . . unusual."

He barks and darts off up the stairs, leaving me free to follow Olwen to the living room.

As well as a sofa, two chairs and a television, there's a large metal cage, like a room within a room, running nearly the full length of one wall. It's full of squashed beanbags and stained mats. And more dogs—mainly larger, older-looking ones. On one of the armchairs a chunky puppy—bigger than Figgy Pudding—is vigorously chewing a cushion.

I'm picking up nothing significant inside Germander—no feeling of belonging, no atmosphere. I ought to be relieved, but I'm disappointed. I'm not going to be solving any mysteries today. There will be no reward for hours and hours on the motorway.

Olwen's living room leads to a narrow galley kitchen with French doors that are standing open. Beyond these, there's a long, thin garden, all scruffy grass and dog-chewed tennis balls.

I want to ask why the house is called Germander, but Olwen only wants to talk about dogs. "This is him." She beams and points to the puppy attacking the cushion. "Yonder, don't *chew*! You have to be firm with him about chewing."

"I'm not Deborah Fuller."

She stares at me. Laughs. "What?"

"I'm not Deborah. I haven't come to pick up a puppy."

"Oh." Olwen giggles. "I'm sorry, I just assumed—"

"Please don't apologize. I'm the one who should apologize."

"If you're not Deborah, here to collect Yonder, who are you and what do you want? Oh—do sit down! Here, let me shift Beth out of your way. Don't worry, there's no hair—they don't shed. Come on, Bethlehem, off you pop. I sometimes think they forget they're dogs, the way I spoil them. Go on, go and run around in the garden! Cup of tea? Coffee?"

"No thanks." I'm finding her lack of suspicion a little unnatural. "It's very trusting of you to offer me a drink. You don't know who I am."

"Oh, you're a good enough egg." Olwen smiles. "I can always tell. And . . . well, I'll be blunt: I've still got one puppy to place—Figgy, the one you met in the hall—and I'm *desperate* to find a good home for him. He's so bright and sweet-natured, but he was also the littlest of this particular litter—I *hate* the word runt, I refuse to use it—and so people don't want him because of all the bilge that gets spouted about how the smallest is likely to have health problems. It's nonsense."

Olwen sits in the chair opposite me, scooping Yonder up into her lap. He has to make more of an effort to chew the seat cushion now, but he seems to think it's worth it.

"Figgy's a perfectly healthy lovely boy. I mean, you saw him. Did he look like a weak and feeble runt to you?"

"No. He looked . . . fine." Until today, I wouldn't have believed myself capable of having this long a conversation about anything to do with dogs.

"He *is* fine. But all the buyers rejected him in favor of his bigger siblings, and even after Yonder goes, when Figgy's the only one, people will say, 'Why's he the one left over? Why did no one want him? Was he the runt?' I'm not going to lie to them, but it's disheartening the way they're all so *stupid*."

"Yes." Here I can agree wholeheartedly. "I know nothing about dogs—I'm not an animal person, I'm afraid—but the bottomless stupidity of almost everyone you're likely to meet is deeply depressing." *I gave up work forever because of it.*

Olwen laughs. "Well, since you're evidently not stupid yourself, I won't try to hoodwink you. If you're wondering why I offer refreshments to any old stranger who turns up, this is why: Figgy needs a good home. You look like you might have one. And . . ." She shakes her head. "Okay, this is going to sound weird, but when you told me you're not Deborah, I had this really funny feeling—like a shiver all up and down my spine. I thought, 'This is Figgy's new owner.' Actually, I didn't even *think* it—the words were just there, in my mind."

No. Oh no. That's not fair. I smile and try to stay calm. The words "I am not Figgy's new owner" are powerfully present in my mind, and mine counts for as much as Olwen's. So what if she had a feeling? Feelings are nothing. *Do not attach significance to this.*

"I don't want a dog," I say. "That's not why I came."

I've nearly finished telling Olwen about my peculiar North Circular experience when my phone rings in my pocket. "Sorry," I say. "I'd better . . ."

"No problem." She hauls herself out of her chair. "I'm going to nip upstairs and retrieve Figgy. He's probably weeing and pooing everywhere, bless him."

Yes, bless him—as long as he lives in this house, not in mine.

It's Alex on the phone. "I'll have to be quick," I tell him. "I'm midconversation."

"Did you find her? Is she the one making the calls?"

"Yes, and no, she isn't. She's a very nice breeder of . . . odd-looking dogs. Can we talk later?"

"Sure. I just wanted to let you know I've been on to the police. They're coming to talk to us tomorrow and they've promised not to send PC Hilton."

"Great. I'll see you this evening. Before midnight, with any luck."

"Here he is!" Olwen bounces back into the room with Figgy under one arm. "Oops, sorry! Didn't realize you were still talking."

I make a "no problem" face at her.

"Is that her?" Alex asks. "Who's 'he'?"

"Figgy Pudding. I'll explain later." I press the "end call" button.

Olwen drops Figgy into my lap without asking if I want him there. "So carry on," she says. "You'd got to the part about your daughter telling you the name."

"Right." Is it acceptable to foist a dog onto someone who has expressed no wish to hold said dog? Figgy settles in and starts to lick the fingers of my right hand. "Yes, Ellen told me she'd Googled your address and found the house name: Germander, not German."

"Both equally awful, if you ask me," says Olwen. "The name was here when I moved in, and not my doing. I meant to take the sign down, but I was always too busy with the Beds, so I opted to let the letters fall off one by one instead. Three down, six to go."

"The . . . beds?"

"Bedlingtons. Ha! Of course, you're not Deborah. She's a Beds nut like me, or so she said on the phone." Olwen glances at her watch. "She's not turning up, by the look of it—probably another fantasist who never had any intention of buying Yonder. I get them all the time. But, yes, Bedlington terriers. All my dogs are Beds. They're the loveliest breed."

Figgy stops licking and looks up at me, as if to make sure that I'm taking this pep talk seriously.

Don't stare at me like that, please.

"Shall I tell you what's so great about them?" says Olwen. "I don't want to bombard you—"

"I'm really not in the market for a dog," I interrupt. "Sorry. Figgy's lovely, but my life's difficult enough at the moment."

"Ah, that's the classic mistake everyone makes. You think a dog will make your life harder, but that's so not true. It's quite the opposite. Figgy will solve all your problems."

I laugh. "Really? How will he do that?"

"You think I'm exaggerating. You'll see!"

I shake my head. "So . . . are *all* the dogs in the house named after bits of Christmas carols, or just the new puppies?"

"Oh yes, all of them," Olwen says proudly. "It's my signature theme. You'd be amazed how many carols there are, and you can get a decent name out of almost every verse if you think creatively. I've got a five-year-old Wenceslas—Good King Wenceslas—and a three-year-old Stephen—Feast of Stephen. Same carol!"

I do my best to look impressed. "I'm afraid I really can't take Figgy. You won't persuade me."

"That's fine," Olwen says. "I won't need to. You'll persuade yourself. Or Figgy will persuade you, won't you, Figs? Do you believe that some things are meant to be?"

"I might have, a little, until today. Coming here's persuaded me I was wrong."

"Oh dear." Olwen chuckles.

"I thought this house had some special significance for me, but it was just the name. I must have seen the outline of the missing letters, registered the name Germander subconsciously—"

"And?" says Olwen. "How does that explain it?"

"My house—the one I moved into that same day—is called Speedwell House. Germander Speedwell is the name of a plant."

"Ah. So you think that's all it was? The sum total of why you felt the way you did?"

"That and the stress of a house move, yes. I feel guilty for taking up so much of your time with my daft superstitions." Gently, I move Figgy from my lap to the sofa and stand up. He makes a squeaky noise without opening his mouth.

Quit it, Figgy. You're not helping.

"You know why I think you had that feeling when you first saw my house?"

I can guess.

"Because of Figgy. You knew you were looking at the house where your future dog would soon be born." Seeing my face, she laughs and adds, "It's no crazier than what you said you believed until today: that one day you'd live here, and be desperately grateful to live here."

No, it isn't. I want to jettison the crazy, not replace it with something equally nuts.

"Figgy's gorgeous." I move toward the door. "I'm sure you'll have no trouble selling him."

"I'm not going to sell him. I'll keep him if you really don't want him. But—look, this is the last thing I'll say about it, I promise— if you change your mind, give me a call. Any time. Or email me via the website: GermanderBedlingtons.co.uk. Yes, I'm afraid I called my business after the house—thought I might as well, since the name was there and kennel names are, as a genre, usually ridiculous-sounding."

"Thanks. It was lovely to meet you. And the dogs."

"Justine?"

"What?"

"I don't want any money for Figgy. You can have him, gratis."

"That's silly. Why would you want to miss out on . . . however much someone would pay for a puppy."

"About four hundred and fifty quid. Because I trust my instincts." Olwen's voice is authoritative and mischievous at the same time. "You and Figgy—it's meant to be."

No, it isn't. No, it isn't. Why do people keep telling me things are true when I know they can't be?

The doorbell rings, prompting a surge of dogs into the hall. Great. Maybe I can hide in the crowd, sneak myself out the door. "This is probably Deborah Fuller," I say. *Come on, Deborah—buy Yonder Star, like you promised you would. Be the silver lining.*

"Ooh! I hope so!" Olwen rushes to the door. I hear her say, "Are you Deborah?" and then, "Oh, wonderful!"

Right. Good. That's me off the hook. Yonder will go to his new home as planned, and Figgy will stay here at Germander.

Why do you care, for God's sake?

"Yonder!" Olwen yells.

"Come on, Yonder," I say with as much authority as I can muster. "We're off. Both of us." He ignores me, so I confiscate the cushion he's chewing. That does the trick. He hears Olwen call him a second time and runs to the front door, barking. She yells at him to be quiet. It's a who-can-make-the-most-noise competition. I regret leaving the living room.

Yonder leaps up and starts pawing at Deborah, who looks as if she's trying to say hello to me, though I can't actually hear her.

Figgy pads out into the hall to see what all the fuss is about.

"Oh *look* at this little one," Deborah coos.

"I know," says Olwen proudly.

Figgy sniffs at Deborah's shoes, then turns around and comes back to me. He starts to climb my leg like he did before, but changes his mind and drapes himself across my foot instead. His eyes close.

"Aw, he's *gorgeous*," Deborah gushes. "He's having a nap on your shoe, bless him!"

"His name's Figgy Pudding," Olwen tells her. "I know you said you didn't want the smallest one, but Figgy's really special."

"I can see that. Hmm, this is tricky . . ."

What? She's going to change her mind and leave Yonder stranded, having promised to take him?

Not that I care. Not that any of these people or dogs are any of my business.

"Poor old Yonder," I say pointedly, thrown by this new development. Deborah has to take him. She owes Figgy nothing. Figgy will be fine staying here with Olwen. Whereas Yonder's got his hopes up—you can see by looking at him.

"Hm?" says Deborah. "Oh, no, I'll take Yonder, of course. But maybe I'll talk to my husband about also—"

"No."

I said that. Me. Oh God, this is stupider than stupid. I am about to do an insane thing.

"I'm afraid you're too late," Olwen tells Deborah. "Justine's taking Figgy."

Chapter 6

Who Was It, Sitting on That Tree Branch?

Later that night, after their parents were asleep, Lisette and Allisande met in the library to discuss the startling new developments that the day had brought. Perrine was not invited to their secret meeting. Since the death of Malachy, the bond between Lisette and Allisande had grown stronger, and they left their younger sister out of as much as they could.

They talked in whispers so as not to wake anyone, though they needn't have worried. The library's book-lined walls did not let any sound escape. Every word spoken in that room was muffled and swallowed up by the decades-old, yellowing pages of such volumes as *Brideshead Revisited* and *A Passage to India*.

"I wish Mum could have had her turn first," said Allisande miserably. "Her way wouldn't have involved us never seeing our friends again. She said so."

"I'm confused," said Lisette. "Mum said we might eventually move away, to somewhere where no one knows Perrine's name—which made me think *that* would be her turn. But then she also said that if her turn were first, we wouldn't have to be cut off from our friends. So . . . if we put those two things together, what could her favored plan of action possibly be?"

Allisande shrugged. Lisette was the sort of person who was always determined to get to the bottom of everything. Allisande was too miserable to dream up theories. She didn't care what Sorrel's plan would have been, only about what was going to happen to them all now, with Bascom having it his way.

"I loathe and detest him," Allisande thought to herself, knowing that she didn't really mean it. She thought her father's approach to almost everything was idiotic and counterproductive, but she loved him because he was her dad, and it's sensible to love your family unless one of your relatives is a truly evil murderer like Perrine.

"Maybe Mum's plan was to move us all away but take our favorite friends with us?" suggested Lisette.

"I doubt it," said Allisande. "I know Mum's impractical at the best of times, but even she knows you can't take your children's best friends and move to the other end of the country with them. I don't think the Sennitt-Sasses and the Carelesses would be very pleased if Mum packed Henrietta and Mimsie into her suitcase and took them miles away from Kingswear."

The absurdity of this idea made both girls laugh. "Thank God I've got you," Lisette said to Allisande. "I couldn't cope with any of this if I didn't have the best sister in the world."

"Right back at you," said Allisande (or whatever fifteen-year-old girls said in days of yore that meant the same thing). Then she said, "I think, when Mum has her turn, we'll go back to school. That's what I'm going to believe, anyway."

"I don't think so." Lisette frowned. "I might be eighteen by then, or nineteen." (She was seventeen at the time of this secret conversation in the library.) "I'd be too old to go to school. I'd have missed all my A-levels. In any case, the minute we went back to school, anyone who wanted to kill Perrine would be able to do so, wouldn't they? I doubt a year or two would be long enough for everyone to forget how much they hate her. Even if they did, they'd remember as soon as she walked into the classroom again, wouldn't they? They'd think, 'Oh, there's that murderer,' and rush off to fashion a noose out of a sturdy rope."

"Yes, Mum and Dad must know this," said Allisande. "Which means no more school for us, and no social life. I can't bear it!"

"Who do you think did it?" Lisette asked her sister. "The noose thing. Who was it, sitting on that tree branch?"

"Mr. or Mrs. Dodd, I expect."

"I don't think so. I can't see either of them climbing a tree. If they wanted to murder Perrine, that's not how they'd do it."

"Then who do you think it was?"

"Well, obviously someone who knew Perrine would be playing rounders in the field that day. Someone who knew her school timetable—and the Dodds certainly didn't. It wasn't you, was it, Allisande?"

"No. It wasn't me."

"Nor me either," said Lisette.

"You don't think we ought to . . . ?" began Allisande.

"No," said Lisette, shocked. "Look at the lengths

Mum and Dad are willing to go to to protect Perrine—taking us out of school, even. They'd be devastated if we killed her."

"You're right," Allisande agreed. "I could do it to her, but never to them. Forget I mentioned it."

Lisette tried but she couldn't. As those with personal experience of such a thing will know, it's hard to forget one of your sisters suggesting the murder of the other.

7

"Ellen, I swear: that's not why I brought him home. I didn't think about you, or George, *at all*. I'm not trying to replace George with a dog. The thought didn't cross my mind."

The three of us are in her bedroom. Four if you count Figgy, who is gnawing on the corner of Ellen's school satchel. I wish he'd chew up the whole damn thing and all the exercise books inside it. Then, when he's finished, he could make a start on the green cardigan Ellen's about to put on, and her black uniform shoes.

I realize it's pathetic, relying on an eight-week-old Bedlington terrier puppy to prevent my daughter from going to school when I've failed to do so.

Ellen could not be more determined. I see it in her granite stare as she stands in front of the full-length mirror in her bedroom, knotting her Beaconwood tie. No fourteen-year-old should look like this: braced, alert, resolute. Anyone would think she was about to stand trial for murder. It makes me want to weep. I long to help her, but how can I if she won't tell me the whole truth?

She pulls off her tie and starts from scratch for the third time. Suddenly, today, it matters to her to make a perfect knot—the same child who, as recently as last week, would happily set off to catch the school bus with her tie draped around her neck like a scarf. She couldn't have cared less about neatness before George was expelled.

If he was expelled. If he's real.

"Answer Mum, El," says Alex. "She's trying to talk to you."

"And I'm trying to get ready for school."

"You've already missed the bus," I tell her.

"Because you didn't wake me up. You *knew* I wanted to go in, and you let me oversleep. You hoped I'd say, 'Oh, has the bus gone? All right, I'll just stay here and play with my new puppy, my friend-substitute, since I'm obviously so lonely without any human friends.' Well, I'm not going to say that. I'm going to get Dad to drive me in."

"I'll drive you in once you've apologized to Mum. You're assuming the worst about her and not letting her defend herself."

"I'm not stopping her. She can say whatever she wants."

"While you ignore her and snark at her?"

I walk over to the window and look out, so that Ellen can't see how angry I am. If only I could sail away from all this on one of those boats I can see in the distance . . .

"If the presence of a dog in the house is going to turn you nasty, I'll take him back to Olwen," I say, enraging myself further with the idea that I might have to do this, and for no sensible reason. "She'd have him back in a heartbeat. Just say the word."

"Figgy's not going anywhere," says Alex. "Look at him—he's just a bundle of fur. We shouldn't be using him to score points."

"You've changed your tune since last night," I mutter. "Then, it was all, 'How could you take such a radical step without consulting me?' and 'Are you out of your mind?'"

"I'm adaptable and I have a sense of proportion, unlike everyone else around here," Alex says. "For God's sake, El, be unfairly angry with Mum if you have to, but don't take it out on Figgy."

Ellen whirls around to face him. "Have I done anything to the dog? Like, whatsoever?" she snaps.

"You've refused to look at him. You haven't once called him by his name. His admittedly absurd name, but still . . ."

"Lots of kennels do that, Olwen said. They give their dogs themed names: Christmas carols, ABBA songs, whatever."

"I suppose Figgy Pudding is marginally better than The Winner Takes It All," says Alex.

"Mum, I *know* you got him to make up for George being expelled. As if I'm going to forget about my best friend and love an *animal* instead! I'm so sad and friendless, I need a pet who can't get away from me—that's the only way I'll ever not be lonely!"

"Not true, El," says my husband and valiant protector. "That's not the reason we have a dog. We have a dog because this Olwen character is an excellent saleswoman—"

"She gave him to me. I paid nothing."

"—who correctly identified your mother as a gullible fool and served up some vague pronouncements about destiny and fate accordingly."

I smile.

"What?" Ellen asks. "What is even remotely funny?"

"I think you're right," I tell her. "About my motivation—but it's nothing to do with you. *I'm* the one who wants to forget about human beings and hang around with a puppy instead. Look at him." I nod in Figgy's direction. He's moved over to the small mint-green door beside Ellen's bed and seems to be trying to insert his front paw into the thin groove between it and the wall.

"That's uncanny," says Alex, watching him. "We buy a house with a tiny green door embedded in the wall, and then, lo and behold, we acquire a new family member for whom that door is exactly the right size. You see, El? Destiny."

I haven't finished expounding the advantages of dogs over people. "Would Figgy ever ask anyone to rewrite three hundred and sixty minutes of TV drama—an entire series—removing the very thing he'd forced you to spend six months weaving in there in the first place, that you'd always thought was preposterous, while denying he'd ever insisted on its inclusion?" I ask of nobody in particular. "Would he expel someone for not stealing a coat, then deny that person ever existed? It's going to be so relaxing having him around, knowing he'll never do anything that shitty and irrational. The worst he'll do is wee on the floor and chew stuff."

"He'd better not wee on my carpet," says Ellen. Her voice sounds strange to me until I realize what's changed: her anger's gone.

"He should be okay for now," I say. "He had an accident in the kitchen five minutes ago. Let's hope he got it all out of his system."

"You honestly didn't buy him as a friend consolation prize for me?"

"I swear. He's my new best friend, not yours."

Ellen turns back to the mirror. Our reflected eyes meet, and she says, "I love George, Mum. I don't only like him. He's not just a friend. I love him."

"I know, El." Kind of a lie. I didn't know. I do now.

"It's not romantic love. I don't *fancy* him." She pulls a face. "You can love a friend as passionately as you love a romantic partner. That's how much I love George. Even if I never see him again, I won't stop loving him."

"Passionately?" Alex queries.

"Ellen, I get it. I'm not sure Dad does, but I do." Her intensity frightens me.

"I'm getting chucked on the pyre as Crap Oafish Dad, am I? After all I've done for this family."

"I'm sorry for being horrible to you about Figgy, Mum. He's cute. He looks like a gray fluffy sock."

"So, next contentious issue," says Alex. "Is Ellen going to school today or not?"

"Yes. I am."

I decide to try a new tactic. "The police are coming this morning, El. It'd be good to have you here to tell them about George, school, everything that's happened."

"Why?" She looks alarmed. "I thought they were coming because of the phone calls."

"They are. And you believe the calls and George's expulsion are linked, don't you?"

"I don't know anything. I don't want to talk to any police. If you make me, I'll tell them it's illegal to keep a child out of school who wants to go."

"Ellen, calm—"

"No, Mum! I'm going to school today. I'll go to my lessons and just . . . blend in."

"Why? What are you afraid will happen if you don't?"

"Justine, you've asked her that at least ten times. You're browbeating her."

"I don't *know* what I'm scared of!" Ellen covers her ears with her hands, as if she can't bear to hear what I might say next.

I feel sick.

"All I know is: If I behave normally, normal things might start to happen again. If I stay away, it'll be obvious why. Whoever hates us at Beaconwood will hate us more because they'll know we haven't forgotten about the George business." Ellen's voice sounds shaky and constricted, as if there's a hand inside her throat, choking her.

I can't cry. It would only upset her more.

"They'll know we haven't forgotten, whatever we do," says Alex. "No one forgets the kind of exchange Mum had with Mrs. Griffiths."

"I need to go in and act like nothing's happened," says Ellen. "That'll reassure school that we're not planning to cause any trouble."

"I'm planning to cause stacks," I say. "Soon as I work out the specifics."

"Mum, no!"

"You can't just wail 'No!,' El. I don't understand, and you won't explain. If you think something's wrong at Beaconwood, if you think someone there might be making these threatening calls, why isn't the obvious answer never to go back there? There are other schools!"

"Justine, you've asked and asked. If she wanted to answer—"

"Because of George! What if he escapes and comes looking for me? On a weekday, he'd go to Beaconwood, wouldn't he? That's where he thinks I'll be, so I have to be there. I know what you're both thinking."

Alex and I exchange a look. I am thinking about the word "escapes," as uttered a few seconds ago by our daughter; I wonder if Alex is too.

"You're going to say George wouldn't turn up at school, having been kicked out," says Ellen. "I thought that too at first, but then I thought of the bus. He could meet me at the bus stop one morning, just outside school grounds. I think that's what he's going to do, as soon as he can. I know him better than I know you, Mum—better than you and Dad know each other."

Alex frowns. "That's a big claim, El."

"It's true. You should have woken me up in time for the bus, Mum."

"Why did you say 'if George escapes,' as if his home's some kind of prison?" I ask her.

"Because it is. He's not allowed to go anywhere, do anything, have friends. It's prison without the official label."

"Don't his parents know you're his friend?"

Ellen laughs. "No way. They'd go mad."

I try to catch Alex's eye, but he's busy trying to pull one of Ellen's balled-up socks out of Figgy's mouth.

They would go mad, or they have gone mad?

What if George's mother, Professor Anne Donbavand, is the person making the deranged phone calls?

"That's why I didn't tell you about George for so long," says Ellen. "He made me promise. He said if his mum found out about our friendship, she'd lock him in a cupboard to stop him seeing me. She's a freakoid. George is always saying he wishes he had a mum like you."

I hear her, but I can't take in what she's saying. Something about her bedroom window has distracted me and provoked a flicker of recognition. As she was speaking, my attention snagged elsewhere, but on what?

It felt important.

Was it something I saw outside? I walk over and stare out. Everything looks normal: the grass sloping down to the river, the trees in our garden, the boats on the water, the wooded hillside studded with cottages.

Nothing is leaping out at me.

I inspect the window itself and find nothing remarkable or significant, only an ordinary sash window that needs repainting at some point.

"Justine? What's up?"

"I . . . Nothing." There's no way I'm telling Alex and Ellen about another strong, illogical feeling that probably means nothing. I've used up my allowance for the year, I think.

Could it be connected to the story Ellen's writing about the Ingrey family? This is, after all, the same window out of which Malachy Dodd fell to his death, pushed by the evil Perrine.

But you weren't even looking at the window, not at first. You were facing the other way, watching Figgy running around in a circle with Ellen's sock in his mouth. Then you turned to face the window, expecting to see . . . what?

"Justine, are you with us, darling?"

My mobile phone starts to ring. The sound clears my head, like a plunge into cold water. "Police or psychopath?" I say brightly as I pull it out of my pocket.

"Or school bus driver, wondering why Ellen never turns up these days," says Alex.

"Hello?"

"So you're still there. Bold as brass. You're not going to go, are you? Well, neither am I. I'm staying put too. You won't drive me away."

"You're mad," I say quietly. "Where are you staying put? Do you live nearby?"

"Why are you doing this to me, Sandie? I've kept quiet all these years. I've kept a vile secret that I wish I didn't know *because you wanted me to*. Not only because I was scared of what you'd do—though I was, terrified—but also to please you. So why are you punishing me now?"

"My name isn't Sandie."

"Tell me what you're planning to do to my family!"

Ellen starts to sob. Alex moves to comfort her, but she runs from the room.

"You're mixing me up with another person," I say, detached from my words as if it's someone else speaking. "I'm not Sandie. My name's Justine Merrison."

"Don't lie. I know your name and you know mine."

"No. Neither of those things is true."

"Shut up! This is your last chance." The words come out like a controlled scream. She's hysterical, but trying to keep her voice down. Trying not to be overheard, perhaps? "Your last chance, and your family's too," she says. "I'll bury you all. Go home, Sandie, if you want to live."

"First things first," says Detective Constable Euan Luce. "Your two phone numbers, landline and mobile—who has them? Let's make a comprehensive list."

He's in his late forties and comprehensive about everything. When he arrived—an hour earlier than expected, with no apology—he spent so long wiping his feet on the mat that I thought we'd have to have our conversation standing in the hall.

Alex and Ellen were getting ready to leave, with Figgy rolling over their feet. Luce had to wait while I Googled local vets and brands of worming tablets, and made a list for Alex of everything he needs to buy at Pet World after dropping Ellen at school.

Now he's asking me questions in the living room, in what he plainly regards as less-than-ideal circumstances. I had to bring Figgy in here with us so that he didn't try to follow Alex and Ellen out of the house. Luce has tutted several times at Figgy's harmless pottering around the room. I'm guessing he has zero experience of dogs, and a wife who jumps to smooth down curtain pleats every time she hears his key in the door.

He must be this uptight for a reason. Maybe he has a mountain of a workload that follows him around in his mind like a big bully. I was the same when I had a career. My days often started with a strong desire to kill my poor postman, and tear up letters without opening or reading them, because the mail had fallen messily all over the hall floor. When you work too hard for too long, you start to suspect innocent objects and people of conspiring against you.

I don't know why Luce is saying "First things first" when it's not "first" at all. He's spent the last half hour asking me for pointless details: my full name, Alex's, Ellen's; how long we've lived at Speedwell House, where we lived before, what Alex and I do.

"I do Nothing," I told him gleefully and enjoyed watching him recoil. *I stare at the strange, protruding chins of visiting policemen.* Luce's is separated from the rest of his face by a deep crease and has a foldaway look about it—as if it ought to be pushed back in or extended more fully.

His was the best reaction I've had so far to my "I do Nothing" announcement. I wish I'd given him a longer, fuller answer: *I can't remember the last time I was in a hurry. If every clock and electronic device in the house died on the spot and I had no way of knowing what time it was, it wouldn't matter in the slightest. Guess how many people will seek me out today, in person, by email or by phone? None!*

Well, none apart from my psycho caller. Come to think of it, she doesn't count, since I'm not the person she's after. I hope this is as clear to Euan Luce as it is to me. I've told him everything she's said to me since her campaign of intimidation started, word for word. I did more than tell him; I reenacted each phone call for him, imitating the crazy woman's voice, mimicking her tone as best I could.

"Let's start with the landline," says DC Luce. "Who knows that number?"

"My father and stepmother, Alex's parents. A few old friends."

"How many?"

I total them up in my head. "Seven."

"And you can give me names and contact details?"

"Well, I can, but I promise you none of them—"

"You can't promise me anything," he dismisses me briskly. "You don't know what anyone's capable of, however many years you've known them. So only eleven people know the phone number for this house?"

"A few more than eleven. Ellen's school obviously has all our details."

"Doctor, dentist?"

"Yes. Utility companies, our bank, credit card people. I can't think of anyone else."

"All right. And your mobile number? Who knows that?"

"Hardly anyone. My father and stepmother, and Ellen's school."

"Not your husband's parents?"

"No. They have his mobile number."

"What about your mother?"

"Dead."

"And the seven old friends?"

"They're all people I . . . Figgy, *down*. Come here. Sorry."

Tut tut.

Figgy is oblivious to the disapproval being beamed his way. He sticks his head under the sofa and wags his tail as if he's seen something under there that he's excited about.

"I see those friends once a year at most," I tell Luce. "They wouldn't need to call me on my mobile, so I didn't give them the number."

"So if you're meeting somewhere, you don't swap mobile numbers? That's unusual."

I might as well tell him; there's no reason not to. "This mobile's very new. When we moved from London to here, I ditched my old phone and number—deliberately. I didn't want anyone from my London life to be able to contact me."

"How come?" DC Luce looks up from his note making.

"I was sick of them all. I wanted to shake them off."

"Without exception?"

Except Ben Lourenco.

"Yes. All my friends—my entire social circle—were TV industry people. They all kind of merged into one after a while—in my mind, I mean."

"Did something bad happen to you in London?" asks Luce. "Is that why you moved?"

"I don't mean to be uncooperative, but this London angle's a waste of time. Honestly. No one I knew there has my new mobile number. This is nothing to do with London."

"You're not in a position to know that for certain," Luce says. He's allowed to be sure of things; I'm not. "Your husband and daughter know your mobile phone number, yes?"

I nod.

"All right." He writes in his notebook. "And anyone who knows it could have passed it on to someone else—there's no way we can know who, or how many, so if we're looking for pointers we'd better concentrate on you."

"That's a waste of time. These calls have nothing to do with me. Can't you trace them?" Above my head, the ceiling creaks. I hear raised voices, and the words "brush" and "minutes." Alex and Ellen. I thought they'd gone but obviously not. They're arguing about what constitutes adequate cleaning of teeth. Figgy looks at me and barks. Do we need a toothbrush for him, and special dog toothpaste? I'll have to call Olwen and ask.

"There's someone else who's got my mobile number," I tell Luce. "Olwen Brawn, Figgy's breeder. But she's not our woman. She didn't know me or my number until yesterday, and she has a completely different voice."

"I'll make a note of her anyway. As for tracing the calls—yes, we will, in the light of the death threats."

"Thank you."

"It's interesting that you say the calls have nothing to do with you."

"Not interesting," I contradict him. "Just stating a fact."

"You're the one receiving the calls."

"Yes, but they're not intended for me. They're intended for someone called Sandie."

"Which isn't your name and bears no resemblance to it."

"Correct."

"Anyone ever called you Sandie?"

"Yes." I wait for him to look up in surprise. "The woman making these calls. She called me Sandie this morning, twice. No one else has ever called me Sandie because it's not my name."

"All right, I'll rephrase the question. Does the name Sandie have a particular significance for you? Was it a childhood nickname, maybe? Does it strike a chord, bring anything to mind?"

"Um . . . the movie *Grease*? Olivia Newton-John, John Travolta."

"How is that film significant to you?"

"It isn't. I like it in the way that I like lots of films. Look, if I'd had a *Grease*-themed fling with a man who called me Sandie, I would mention it, wouldn't I? I can think of no reason at all why anyone would address me as Sandie apart from the *actual* reason, which I've already told you: this woman has me confused with someone else."

"Though she knows you lived in Muswell Hill and worked in television. And from what she said about graves, she knows that your family consists of two adults and one child."

"Yes." I want to scream with frustration. "Can we not waste time telling each other what we already know? I'm sure you're busy. Yes, this woman knows some things about me. I'm not denying that. And either because of those things, or in spite of them, she thinks I'm Sandie, which I'm not—scary Sandie who's determined to destroy her. She's clever, you see. She's the one intent on scaring and intimi-dating me. She's justifying her desire to attack with the lie that I've done it to her first, or Sandie has."

DC Luce grimaces. "Odd way to scare someone," he says.

"I disagree. I think it's a bloody excellent way to scare someone. You've got your basic, always-effective death threat—'I'll kill you and your family'—with an added layer of fucking with the person's head. You accuse them of doing to you precisely what you're trying to do to them so that they'll feel needlessly guilty, paranoid and confused as fuck, as well as mortally afraid. They'll grow more and more convinced that they must be to blame for what's happening to them, even though no evidence is provided. It's quite brilliant if you think about it."

Luce shakes his head. "Sorry. I don't see it."

Please crap down his trouser leg, Figgy.

I smile and say, "You might not see it, DC Luce, but I'm living it."

"Following your logic, though, she's not aiming this at you, she's aiming it at Sandie. Sandie may have tried to terrorize her."

"True, but . . . when I tell her over and over that I'm not Sandie, she flat-out contradicts me and tells me I am. So maybe I'm the in-tended target after all." I'm trying to work it out as I speak. "How can she have such a strong, intimate-sounding grudge against Sandie and fail to realize I'm a different person? I don't buy that. It's more likely to be someone who hates me and wants to mess with my head as much as possible before . . ." I don't want to say before what. I'd rather not think about it.

"But at the risk of blowing my own trumpet," I continue, "*nobody* hates me that much—not enough to do what this woman's doing. Maybe she's someone who was mildly pissed off with me, and also angry with someone called Sandie, and she had a psychotic breakdown and fused us into the same person. Schizophrenemy: when you merge two enemies in your mind to make only one."

DC Luce looks unimpressed.

"Or maybe we're crazy trying to find any logic in it at all," I say. "She might be out-and-out mad for all we know. Foaming-at-the-mouth insane—in which case, tomorrow she could well ring up and call me Gertrude or Montgomery."

Figgy springs up, in alert mode. He tries to bark and sounds hoarse. A few seconds later I hear the front door close quietly. "It's just Alex and Ellen setting off for school, Figgs. Relax." I keep my voice unemotional, embarrassed to be talking to a dog in front of a policeman.

"Your husband's name is Alex," says DC Luce.

"Yes. I know."

"Short for Alexander?"

"Yeah."

"Sandie's a common short form of Alexander."

I laugh. "Try calling Alex 'Sandie' and see what happens."

"Has anybody ever—"

"No. Whoever Sandie is, it's not Alex. Let's fast-forward what's coming next, shall we? Yes, Alex travels a lot for work—he's a very-much-in-demand opera singer who sings all over the world and is away as often as he's at home. No, he doesn't have another woman who knows him as Sandie and who's hatching a plan to kill him, his wife and his daughter."

"I'd like to ask your husband if anyone has ever addressed him as Sandie," says Luce.

"They haven't."

"He's just gone out, has he? Do you know how long he'll be?"

I groan. "The caller addressed *me* as Sandie. Not Alex. How

often do you call a friend and then, when the friend's spouse answers the phone, think, 'Oh well, even though Susan's answered, I'll
just say, "Hello, Geoff" anyway because she's Geoff's wife and that's
close enough.'"

"How long is your husband likely to be out?" Luce asks again.

Allisande Ingrey. Sandie could be short for Allisande.

"Ms. Merrison?"

Shut up for a minute. Let me try and work out what this means.

How can it mean anything? Allisande Ingrey is a fictional character. It's another irrelevant coincidence, like Sandie being a diminu-
tive of Alexander.

"Justine? How long is your husband—"

"Instead of scouring our lives for a cause or connection that isn't
there, how about just tracing the calls? How long will it take? I mean,
could you do it this morning—could you be doing it now, instead
of waiting for Alex to come back so that you can ask him pointless
questions? He'll be gone a good while, I'd imagine. He's dropping
Ellen at school, then doing dog-related errands and . . ."

I stop as the person whose morning activities I'm describing appears in the doorway. "Alex? I thought you'd taken Ellen to school.
What's wrong?" His face is tight and pale.

"Where is she?" he says. "I can't find her."

"You can't find your daughter?" asks DC Luce.

"I took a call from my agent. When I'd finished, Ellen had vanished. She's nowhere in the house, I can't see her in the garden. Have
you seen her?"

No, but I heard her close the front door behind her. So did Figgy.

"I'm sure there's no need to panic, Mr. Colley," DC Luce stands
up, ready for action.

"It's okay," I say. "I know where she is."

———

I find Ellen down by the wall at the bottom of the hill, as close to the river as she can get without leaving our land. She'd have made sure to be here in time to see Lionel's boat make its return trip.

She's crying. Copiously but silently, as if she hasn't noticed the tears streaming down her face. Or the cold. She's got no coat, but she's not shivering, though the sight of her in her thin white blouse and almost-as-thin green cardigan makes me shiver.

Where is her coat now? If George Donbavand was expelled for stealing it, wouldn't he also be made to return it? In which case, why hasn't Ellen brought it home?

I take off my coat and wrap it around her. She doesn't seem to notice.

"Is she there?" Alex is behind me, with Figgy on the leash. I don't answer. If I can hear him, he will soon be able to see Ellen for himself. I need to stay focused on what's in front of me: the scene of a terrible tragedy, judging by my daughter's face.

"Ellen? What's wrong? Has something happened?"

"Leave me alone."

"No. You're going to need to tell me what's wrong."

She looks at me coldly. "Who even are you?" she says.

"Who am I?" I'm not sure what I was expecting her to say, but it wasn't that.

"I know you're my mother because we have the same face, but maybe that's all I know."

"Ellen, what are you talking about? How have I turned into the bad guy?"

"The freak who keeps calling you, who you say you don't know— she called you Sandie."

"Yes, she did."

"Why?" ·

"I've no idea."

"I don't believe you. People don't just ring up and call you by a different name for no reason."

Great. First DC Luce and now Ellen. "Not usually, no," I say, "but apparently now and again they do."

"What's going on?" Alex asks.

"I'm not and have never been Sandie, Ellen. You've been to Granddad and Julia's house. You've seen my old school reports with my name on them."

"El, what's going on here?" Alex sounds angry. "You're surely not questioning Mum's identity?"

"It's okay," I say. "It's understandable. Anyone'd take the word of an anonymous stalker who makes death threats over that of the mother they've known all their life."

Figgy looks up from the grass he's been chewing and makes a mewling noise. I know how he feels.

"I'm sorry, Mum."

Not good enough. Mothers are supposed to be all-forgiving. I'll have to admit defeat and relinquish my anger eventually, but not yet.

"Mum?"

"Call me Sandie," I say in a monotone. "Everyone else does."

"Why do we never go to Granddad and Julia's house?"

"We don't never go. We go sometimes."

"Hardly ever. When we do go, they always say they'd like to see more of us. You pretend to agree, but then you never arrange it. You still haven't invited them here, and we've lived here for five months. And that time Granddad asked if they could come and stay for my birthday and you said someone else had dibs on the guest room— that was a lie. You just didn't want him to come."

I exhale slowly. "El, if you want to have this discussion, we can have it. Soon."

"But not now," she says bitterly, as if this sort of disappointment is what she's come to expect from me.

"No, not now. For now, this will have to do: my reasons for keeping Granddad and Julia at a distance have nothing to do with me being called Sandie, because I'm not and never have been. My name has always been Justine Merrison."

"All right, you've made your point," Ellen snaps. "Forget I said it."

Oh, easy. No problem at all. In ten minutes' time, I will have no memory whatsoever of being accused by my daughter of faking my identity.

"This is madness, El," says Alex. "You're out here crying because you've suddenly got a yen to see more of Granddad? No offense to Granddad but—"

Ellen lunges at him and snatches Figgy's leash from his hand. "And I can't believe we've got a puppy! Just when some psychopath starts harassing and threatening us! What if she kills Figgy?"

I flinch at the suggestion. It's a paranoid fantasy, but I know where Ellen's coming from. Psychopaths are supposed to escalate from animals to people, aren't they? If we assume our anonymous caller has never killed a human being . . .

I shudder and tell myself not to be neurotic.

"It's not safe for him to be with us, Mum."

It breaks my heart to hear her express worry for Figgy while not saying anything about herself. She must be scared. I wish I hadn't told her about the phone calls. I should have gone to any lengths to prevent her from finding out about them.

"El, Figgy's going to be fine," I say with a confidence I don't feel. Should I call Olwen and ask her to come and take him back? Would that be the right thing to do? "We're all going to be fine. DC Luce has said he'll trace the calls. I trust him to sort this out." I'd better get back to him, having left him in the living room. Is he taking advantage of our absence to ransack the kitchen cabinets, hoping to find an old photograph of me with the name "Sandie" scrawled across the back? That's what would happen in a film.

"Aren't some calls untraceable?" Ellen asks.

"If you're a tech-savvy criminal mastermind, perhaps," says Alex. "Not if you're a crank with a lisp."

"We should go back to the house and finish up with DC Luce," I say. "What do you want to do, El?"

"The same thing I wanted to do before: go to school." She glances at the river.

"Were you crying because you saw George?"

Her face hardens. "No."

Gently, I take Figgy's leash from her hand, pass it to Alex and send him a silent signal with my eyes.

"Come on, Figgs," he says. "You and I have got an appointment with Five-O in the drawing room, yo."

When they've gone, I say to Ellen, "You must miss George a lot. You're used to seeing him every day. Well, every weekday."

She nods. "He wasn't on Lionel's boat today."

"Are you sure?"

She gives me a withering look.

"So that's why you were so upset."

"'Were'? I *am* upset! I've lost him. I thought I could at least see him from a distance, but now I can't even do that anymore." She starts to cry again. "If George doesn't come looking for me, I'll never see him again—and how can he come with his parents watching him every second of every day?"

"Hold on, El. Today's only one day. Just because George wasn't on—"

"You don't understand!" she shouts over me. "Today's a school day, and he wasn't on the boat. Neither was his dad. They would have been if Fleur had gone to school this morning, so she obviously hasn't. I knew they'd do it eventually but I didn't think it would be so soon."

"You think Fleur's been expelled?"

"They've gotten rid of her, just like they got rid of George!" Ellen turns and runs toward the house. Too slowly, I reach out a hand to stop her and find myself holding nothing but air.

Chapter 7

A Bumcracker Dies

Lisette, Allisande and Perrine never went back to school. It took nearly six months for Bascom and Sorrel Ingrey to make Speedwell House completely safe for the protection of Perrine and all of them. They got rid of the rickety old wooden gate at the end of the long driveway, which hadn't closed properly for years, and replaced it with a pair of enormous tall gates with a strong lock. These gates looked like wood but had metal inside them. A high wall was built all around the grounds, enclosing the land owned by the Ingreys. As if all this wasn't enough, there was also electrified barbed wire and the best alarm system that modern technology could provide.

Bars and grilles were fitted over all the windows so that light could get in but nothing else would stand a chance. The front and back doors already had locks on them, but several more were added, as well as chains, bolts and alarms.

Bascom and Sorrel didn't want to risk using local tradesmen, so they arranged for all the laborers and experts they needed to be brought in on a bus from Nottingham, which was far enough away for Sorrel to be certain that no one there would have heard of Perrine or what she had done. As well as sorting out the house, these workmen also doubled as guards. Until Speedwell House and its grounds were impossible to breach, there was a risk, and all those men knew that their job was to keep their eyes peeled for dangerous intruders, or even harmless-looking ones, because often they are the most dangerous of all.

For six months, the Ingrey family lived with locksmiths, wall-builders and barbed-wire specialists all around them. Sorrel had to teach her three daughters art, drama, literature, film studies and creative writing with drilling and hammering going on all around her. She adapted by making the girls do sketches of carpenters and welders at work, and encouraging them to write stories in which families have to shut themselves away behind inscrutable gates for a variety of reasons. For film studies, she made them watch a movie called *The Money Pit* on video (this was the popular way of watching films in that era). *The Money Pit* is about a couple who are forced to cohabit with loads of workmen while they have their wreck of a house done up.

The tradesmen who were sorting out Speedwell House did not sleep in the house with the Ingrey family. They slept under blankets and in sleeping bags on the two buses that had brought them to Devon from Nottingham. This wasn't because there was no room in the house, nor was it because there were no local hostelries that would take them. The workmen slept on the buses because Bascom and Sorrel Ingrey had made another of their famous compromises! Sorrel didn't want the men to stay in the pubs and hotels nearby, in case they heard tell of the murderous Perrine and decided to use their saws and soldering irons to attack her instead of to attend to the fabric of the building. Bascom didn't want the workforce sleeping in his home in case some of them sneaked into his daughters' rooms and molested them. True, all the laborers from Nottingham seemed absolutely lovely, but one could never tell, said Bascom.

So, in order to keep both him and his wife happy, the men had to sleep on the buses.

All the lessons, it had been decided, would take place in Speedwell House's library, but even the insulation provided by books as fat as *War and Peace* and *Dombey and Son* wasn't enough to absorb all the clanging and banging from the workmen, so Lisette, Allisande and Perrine had to try to concentrate on their studies with a dreadful racket going on all around them. Perrine was her usual sullen self, so there was no change there. Lisette and Allisande were the ones who changed. They had always been sunny-natured before, but now their abject misery was etched upon their faces quite unmistakably. They hated the noise, they missed their best friends from school, and they were distracted from their studies by the sweaty bottoms of the workmen, who didn't seem to know how to make their trousers go up as far as their waists. Lisette and Allisande didn't understand this at all. Surely someone who can cover a sash window with an elaborate metal structure should not find it too hard to conceal the whole of his bum crack?

(I apologize for the vulgarity, but it is necessary for what I'm about to tell you: within days of the buses from Nottingham arriving, Lisette and Allisande Ingrey had given the workmen a collective nickname: the bumcrackers.)

Lisette, a conscientious girl who was still hoping, somehow, to be able to do her A-levels and go to university, applied herself to her studies in spite of everything, and became even cleverer and more knowledgeable than she'd been before. Allisande, who was naturally more of a skiver and a coaster-along, did as little as possible. She was thrilled to find that, during Sorrel's lessons, it was generally possible to do nothing at all. The trend of watching videos, which had started quite legitimately with *The Money Pit* as part of film studies, soon spread to all of Sorrel's lessons. Lisette complained bitterly when a double art lesson involved nothing more than watching the movie *Vertigo*, which features a painting and includes a scene in an art gallery. She complained again when drama lessons were taken up with watching *An Officer and a Gentleman* and *American Gigolo* (Sorrel loved the actor Richard Gere).

Fortunately for Lisette, her father's lessons contained no such indulgences. Bascom Ingrey taught the girls maths, English language, history, geography, French, Spanish and science. Or at least he tried to. Bascom found it much harder than Sorrel did to concentrate with the bumcrackers making a din all around him. Unlike his wife, he was not a go-with-the-flow sort of person who secretly wanted to watch videos all day. He was determined that the girls should learn more at home than they ever did at school. He wanted them to improve their minds and characters.

One Tuesday, he lost his cool during a history lesson. He was trying to explain to the girls about Bismarck and the Dreikaiserbund, when one of the bumcrackers suddenly appeared in the library: a young man with fair hair and flaky patches of skin under his eyes, as if a load of croissant crumbs had fallen off his eyelashes and landed just underneath.

Entering the library was strictly not allowed; all of the bumcrackers had been instructed never to interrupt lessons. Without apologizing for bursting in, this young man said to Bascom, "Need yah to hold a piece of wood in place for me, mate. Won't take long."

Bascom turned purple with rage. Apart from anything else, he didn't think being a manual laborer was any excuse for using incomplete sentences. He stormed out of the library, marched upstairs and locked himself in his bedroom until he'd calmed down. On his way up the stairs, the girls had heard him shout, "Sorrel! Can you take over? I'm too angry to teach!"

"I'll hold your piece of wood for you," Perrine volunteered, and she was soon following the flaky-eyed bumcracker out of the room. "Nice one, darling!" Lisette and Allisande heard him say, and they realized that they had never before—not since Malachy Dodd's death and not before it either—heard anyone say anything so nice and appreciative to Perrine. Then again, they had never heard her selflessly offer to do anyone a favor either.

Strangely, it did not occur to them that Perrine

might not have volunteered to help the bumcracker for kind or noble reasons. They were too shocked to think about it. Their father had not only abandoned a history lesson, but also suggested that their mother take over, when he knew perfectly well that Sorrel dismissed history as "a big bowl of yawns." Lisette and Allisande were afraid that Bascom might be having a nervous breakdown.

Perrine reappeared in the library after about five minutes. "Mum's on her way," she said. A few seconds later, Sorrel swept into the room with a video in her hand. "Okay, girls," she said. "Since your father's having a tantrum, let's watch *Gone With the Wind*. Lots of history in that. Men! They can't cope with anything. They're big babies, the lot of them!"

"Perrine just helped a bumcracker to do something to the house that he couldn't do on his own," said Allisande.

Sorrel put on *Gone With the Wind*, but stopped it almost immediately afterward and said, "Can you hear that? I think that's your father shouting for help. I'm going to ignore him. Oh, I can't concentrate on a movie! What shall we do instead?"

Before any of the girls could suggest anything, Sorrel's eyes narrowed deviously and she said, "I know. Let's talk about a different kind of history—the more interesting kind. Not your father's interminable three-field systems and Kellogg-Brioche pacts—"

"Briand," said Lisette defensively.

"Let's talk about the day someone tried to hang Perrine from a tree," said Sorrel.

"I'd rather not," said Perrine. "I've put that behind me and moved on."

"Rubbish," said Sorrel. "You're thirteen, and I'm your mother. You don't get to move on until I say you can."

Perrine sighed, as if she had just been set an incredibly tedious essay topic for homework.

"Here's what I'd like us to discuss," said Sorrel. "We know that a rope was hanging from a tree, and that it dropped to the ground eventually, which saved Perrine's life. We know that Perrine *said* she saw a figure in the tree, up in the high branches, holding the rope. She also said she heard footsteps running away after this mysterious person had dropped the rope. But did anyone else see this attacker, either in the tree or running from the scene? Hmm?"

Perrine cocked her eyebrow mischievously. She seemed to understand what her mother was talking about. Lisette and Allisande were baffled. What could Sorrel mean? they asked themselves.

"I'm wondering, you see, if perhaps there was no aspiring murderer," Sorrel went on. "What if Perrine attached that rope to the tree, put her own head in the noose and made sure to grab on to it with her fingers so that she didn't choke to death?"

"I was dangling in midair!" said Perrine indignantly.

"All right, then," said Sorrel. "What if you climbed the tree, tied the rope to the branch, put the noose around your neck and jumped, clutching the noose with your fingers to avoid strangulation? Did anyone see you standing there when the noose fell around your neck as you claim it did? Did anyone witness you *not* climbing the tree and then tumbling out of it, attached to a rope?"

"I don't know who saw what," said Perrine. "You'll have to ask them."

"Hmmm," said Sorrel, her eyes narrowing again.

Lisette and Allisande were growing increasingly frightened. They would have preferred to hear all about Dreyfus's exile to Devil's Island and how it was really Esterhazy that committed the crime. They had taken for granted that someone had tried to kill Perrine, and now their mother was suggesting that perhaps it wasn't true.

"But Mum," said Lisette, "if no one is trying to kill Perrine . . ."

". . . then we don't need the bumcrackers! We can go back to school!" Allisande completed her sister's sentence.

"I'm sorry, but someone did try to kill me," Perrine insisted. "Ask yourself this, Mother: Why would I go to great lengths to fake an attempt on my life?"

"Sympathy?" Sorrel suggested. "Except you didn't get any, did you? All your classmates and your teacher were quite happy to see you choking to death. Still, you got to be seen as the victim instead of the murderer, which must have been a nice change."

"I'm sorry, is this lesson called 'history' or 'falsifying history'?" Perrine sniggered at her own joke.

Lisette felt sick. Did Sorrel really believe what

she was saying, or was she testing Perrine? Was she about to say, "I'm sorry, darling, of course I know you wouldn't fake an attack on your life."

Surely Perrine wouldn't. Staging the attempted murder of yourself was as bad as committing murder. Worse, perhaps, because it was more devious.

No one ever found out what Sorrel was about to say, because at that moment something dramatic happened. The three sisters and their mother heard the word "Help!" being wailed from somewhere high up. "Oh for goodness' sake," snapped Sorrel. "Just listen to him! This is how your father reacts when someone walks into a room unexpectedly."

"Mum, that's not Dad's voice," said Allisande.

"HELP!" wailed the male voice again.

"She's right," said Lisette. "It's not Dad."

Sorrel stood up. She was about to go and investigate when she saw, through the window, a man falling to his death, just as Malachy Dodd had done before. His arms flailed as he fell.

There was a loud crash. Sorrel and her three daughters ran to the window. The man's head had smashed open and there was blood spreading across the gravel where he'd fallen. "Oh my God!" said Allisande. "It's the bumcracker who came in here, who Perrine helped!"

Perrine emitted a throaty chuckle. Sorrel, Lisette and Allisande looked at one another. They were all thinking the same thing: What if Perrine had somehow pushed the bumcracker off the scaffolding that was still attached to one side of Speedwell House? What if he'd grabbed onto a metal pole, hung on for as long as his arms and fingers could bear, crying for help and being ignored, and then fallen to his doom?

"Don't look at me," said Perrine, even though no one was because no one could bear to. "I didn't kill him. He's only a bumcracker, anyway. It's not as if his life matters to anyone."

8

Finally I'm alone in the house. DC Luce has taken his reams of notes and gone; Alex is dropping Ellen at school and then heading into town. I'm on my own with Figgy, who, thankfully, doesn't detract at all from my satisfying feeling of isolation. He's not going to stop me from doing what I'm about to do, or demand that I justify myself.

"I'll tell you, Figgs, because you're tactful enough not to ask." I sit down at the kitchen table with a mug of tea and my laptop. "I'm going to Google the fuck out of Professor Anne Donbavand. Why? Because . . ."

I stop to type her name into the search box, then press "return." First impression: no shortage of results, all relating to the right person. Most of this stuff looks deadly boring, possibly because I don't have a shred of interest in Assyriology.

I'm about to plunge into the first web link on the list when I realize I'd abandoned my explanation after "Because." That's a bit shoddy, even if one is only explaining to a dog.

"Several reasons, Figgy. All of them persuasive, in my opinion. Ellen's obsessed with George. She might have given him our phone number—my mobile too. She doesn't have a phone of her own, so anyone wanting to contact her would need to call me or the house."

Ellen has always been adamant that she'll never have a mobile. In London, mine ruined everything we tried to do as a family. Every trip, dinner and birthday treat was interrupted by between five and ten texts, emails or calls, most of which required immediate responses. Ellen once called my BlackBerry "the family destroyer."

"If George has the numbers, it's possible his mother also has them," I tell Figgy. "Am I saying that I think Professor Anne Donbavand is my mystery caller? No, not at all. But she could be. I've never heard her voice. She might have a weird lisp. She doesn't want George to have any friends, right? Ellen is George's friend. Doesn't that make Anne Donbavand the person most likely to want our family to leave Devon and go back to London?"

I try to make out the shape of a correct and wise answer in the silence, but Figgy offers no hint as to what he's thinking.

"I believe it does," I mutter, aware of how defensive I sound. "Whatever Ellen says, the idea that it's someone at Beaconwood calling and threatening me . . . sorry, but I don't buy it. And Alex will say I'm being ridiculous, but this Sandie business—"

I break off. Figgy looks at me expectantly.

"When I was talking to Lisp Woman this morning and Ellen started to cry—that wasn't general distress at having a stranger call us and threaten our safety. Ellen burst into tears and ran from the room immediately after hearing me say, "My name's not Sandie." It was the name that broke her, and someone applying it to me. Later, she accused me of hiding my true identity—of being Sandie. Somehow . . ."

I pick up my mug of tea and walk over to the window. Standing here looking out, I remember the feeling I had upstairs in Ellen's room. *Something not quite right about her window, or the view, or . . .*

No, it's not coming to me. It's silly to hope that it ever will.

Figgy appears to be asleep. I go over the rest of my theory in my head: somehow, there's a connection between Ellen getting so upset at the mention of Sandie, and Allisande from her story.

If she suspected me of being Allisande Ingrey, that means Allisande Ingrey is real.

Is it possible for three generations of a family, all with such unusual names, to have no online presence whatsoever? I Googled the Ingreys and found nothing. Maybe I should ask around about them—in pubs, in the post office at Kingswear. Not everyone is on Facebook or has a Twitter following, especially once you leave London. I'm the living proof. I haven't looked at my Twitter timeline or Facebook page since giving up my job—not once. If there are messages for me, I have no interest in receiving them.

I could have shut down all my social media accounts when I left London—could have and probably should have, but doing so would have meant going to each site at least once more, and I couldn't face that. I knew exactly what sort of messages would be waiting for me, and how many there would be, because I'd dared to disagree, publicly, with the dominant view of an issue that, in a sane world, would never have been an issue at all. I didn't want to see all the nonsense, and still don't. I chose instead to pretend that Twitter and Facebook had ceased to exist.

Devon must be full of people who feel the same way about the internet and shun electronic devices in favor of fresh air, horseback riding and mulch.

"But if Perrine Ingrey committed a murder, then surely I'd find something," I say to Figgy, who has opened his eyes.

He yawns.

I go back to the table, sit down and start to click on the search results for Professor Anne Donbavand. Here's her page from the University of Exeter's website. No photo, but a square in the top right-hand corner containing a head-and-shoulders silhouette template. *Damn.* I'd like to see her face. Would I take one look at it and think, "Oh yes—definitely an unhinged harrasser"? Or the opposite: "There's no way someone with that face would be capable of doing anything malicious"?

Professor Donbavand has three areas of expertise: the history of Mesopotamian medicine, the Babylonian language, and Akkadian grammar and textual criticism.

Wow. As someone with only two specialties—doing Nothing, and the internal politics of Lockhart Gardner, the law firm in *The Good Wife*—I can't help feeling comparatively inadequate.

"It's got to be her making the calls," I tell Figgy. "If I had to spend my days researching 'Cuneiform Tablets on Eye Diseases,' I'd soon be issuing hysterical death threats too."

I've looked through three pages of results and haven't found anything about Anne Donbavand that isn't connected to her work. If I have to read any more about the various papers she's presented at Assyriology conferences, I'll be tempted to bite chunks out of the kitchen table. Her email address is freely given on her university page. Should I email her?

In my head, I hear Ellen wail, "No, Mum!"

I start again with an empty search box and type in "Donbavand Exeter." Ellen said George's dad works there too. Yes, here we are: Dr. Stephen Donbavand, Economics Department. In format, his page is the same as his wife's, except he's been considerate enough to add a photo.

This could be the man I saw on Lionel's boat. I think it is. I didn't see his face, only the back of his head, but this looks like him. He has the absent-mustache look that some men have: not a trace of facial hair, but an oddly curved upper lip that makes you think about a mustache even though you can't see one.

Big smile. Big blue eyes. Glasses. He looks nice. Like a big, benign duck. Approachable.

I don't care that Ellen will scream at me later. Before I go to Beaconwood for round three of trying to get the truth out of somebody there, I'm going to send George Donbavand's parents an email. Both of them.

I go to my Gmail account and click on the "compose" button. An empty message box appears. "Dear Professor and Dr. Donbavand," I type. "My name is Justine Merrison. I'm the mother of Ellen Colley, who is a pupil at Beaconwood and an acquaintance of your son George." Better not put "friend," given what Ellen's told me. "Acquaintance" sounds formal and distant. No one could object to acquaintanceship.

Should I refer to George's expulsion directly? Probably better not.

"I believe there's been a kerfuffle recently about a coat that Ellen gave to George?" I write instead. "I'm having trouble getting any sense out of the school about what's happened, and I'd find it really useful to talk to one or both of you." I type out my home and mobile phone numbers and sign off, congratulating myself on my maturity in not adding, "Though of course you might know both these numbers already and be using them in a campaign of daily persecution."

I copy and paste the Donbavands' email addresses from Exeter University's website, press "send," then slam my laptop shut as if that will cancel out what I've done.

It was the right thing to do. Going to Beaconwood again is the right thing to do.

"The more determined everybody is to keep secrets from me, the more determined I am to find out, Figgy."

He's chasing his tail, going round and round in dizzy-making circles.

"Who are the Ingreys, though?" I sigh. "They can't be real. Can they? If they're real and they're nowhere to be found on the internet, where did Ellen get them from?"

The beauty of Beaconwood's grounds in the bright winter light is unwelcome today. These are gardens you should only be allowed to see, breathe in, walk through when you're happy. It's too jarring otherwise. I look at the lush, frost-speckled trees and berry-studded bushes and all I feel is anger and frustration because I can't enjoy them. Ellen's misery is weighing me down: the knowledge that it's there, inside her, and I can't take it out and demolish it. It's like carting a heavy rock around in a bag, with no choice about when to put it down.

I hear a child's voice behind me. "He's cute. Is he an Airedale?"

I turn and see a boy dressed in a Beaconwood Juniors uniform. He's about seven or eight, with auburn hair and missing front teeth. Like many children his age whose parents do their best but lead too-busy lives, he has a clean face and a dirty neck—a grime scarf, I used to call it when Ellen was little.

Imagine being too busy to make sure your child washes properly. Oh, wait: you don't need to imagine it, do you? You lived it.

A black BMW screeches out of the school parking lot onto the road as if it's auditioning for an Extra-Specially-Reckless Driving bumper episode of *Top Gear*. I catch a fleeting glimpse of a cuff-linked shirtsleeve and a man's hand, waving. The boy waves back. He's more sensible than his father. They're both late—for school and work respectively—but only the boy realizes there's no point hurrying when you've already missed half the morning. Might as well take your time.

"He's a Bedlington," I say. I'm such a dog novice, I don't know if that's a commonly used abbreviation, or if I should have said "Bedlington terrier." I'm guessing the short version's acceptable, since I'm pretty sure an Airedale is also a kind of terrier.

"How old?"

"Eight weeks."

"Called?"

"His full name's Figgy Pudding—that was the name his breeder gave him—but we call him Figgy."

I'm braced for mockery, but the boy nods. "We've got a bull terrier called Woody, but his real name's Cantorella Jumping Jack Flash. That's what it says on his pedigree certificate."

"From the Kennel Club, right?" Olwen told me about this.

"Yes. If your dog's a purebred you can get a certificate with all his ancestors on. Woody's ancestors have won loads of prizes. Have Figgy's?"

"I don't know." I ought to thank him for helping me avoid a chore. I was probably never going to send off for Figgy's pedigree certificate anyway, but now I definitely won't. I hate family trees too much. *Sorry, Figgs—even yours.*

"Can I ask you something else?"

"Sure." The boy tries to look modest. "I'm an expert on dogs. Before we had Woody, we had—"

"It's not about dogs. It's about a person: George Donbavand. He was at Beaconwood until recently. A bit older than you, I think. Did you know him? What's your name, by the way? I'm Justine." I smile and give him my hand to shake.

"Harry Shelley."

"Did you know George?"

"A bit. I'm not allowed to answer questions about him, though. They told us all not to. You'll have to ask one of the teachers."

So George is real. The heavy rock I'm carrying is suddenly lighter. My daughter might be unhappy, but she is not delusional.

"I will. Thanks. Nice to meet you, Harry."

He runs ahead up the path toward the school building. I try to follow, but Figgy has other ideas. He sticks his nose into the bottom of a hedge, where it stays for the next ten minutes, snuffling around.

I ring the bell and wait. When Helen Minchin appears, I don't bother with pleasantries. "I'm coming in, so please don't try to stop me."

"There's no need to be unpleasant."

"I agree. No need to be pleasant, either. I was going for neutral-informative. How did I do?"

When I try to move forward, she moves to stand directly in front of me. "I'm afraid we don't allow dogs in the building."

"I know that's not true, Helen. I've seen a large, white, curly-haired dog in here more than once."

"You mean Pippin. Yes." Helen's mouth tightens. "That shouldn't have happened. We've clamped down since then."

"Ha! I hate to think what clamping down means in a school that magics children out of existence whenever the fancy takes it. Guess what? I bumped into another Beaconwood parent last night and she knew George Donbavand. She confirmed that he used to be a pupil here." I don't feel guilty about lying. Anyone who would prefer the truth had better start using it themselves.

"You remember George, don't you, Helen?"

She looks at me as if I've said something offensive.

"He used to attend this school, didn't he?"

"I'm afraid you won't be able to go inside the building with a dog." Helen presents this as if it's an answer to my question.

"He isn't a dog," I say. Because you can lie even when it's ludicrous, even knowing no one will fall for it. You can present laughable nonsense as if it's the cleverest scam ever dreamed up by a human mind—that's what I've learned at Beaconwood. "Granted, he looks exactly like a dog, but in fact he's a bizarre-looking human. Figgy, say hello to Helen. He used to go to a different school, but he got expelled—can you believe this?—for looking too much like a dog. Now, please get the fuck out of my way."

Helen stands aside. I'd have sworn at her sooner if I'd known it would be so effective.

I head for Mr. Fisher's classroom, wishing I could remember his first name. Lincoln? No, that sounds too American. I'm sure it begins with L. Lachlan. Yes, that's it. Lachlan Fisher.

I peer through the thin glass panel in the door and see that he's in full flow, talking and gesticulating. I can see why Ellen calls him the Nerd King. It's easy to picture him hacking into GCHQ databases while dressed in cartoon-character pajamas.

His stupidly large glasses have slid down his nose, almost to the tip. The children laugh at something he says. They like him. I can tell from outside that there's a good atmosphere in the classroom.

I knock and steel myself for another difficult encounter.

Still talking and waving his arms to emphasize whatever point he's making, Mr. Fisher sidles slowly toward the door. He hasn't seen me yet. Any second now he'll look through the glass and his relaxed expression will give way to one of discomfort. I can't believe Helen Minchin has been warned about me and he hasn't. Lesley Griffiths would have left no member of staff unbriefed.

The door opens. "Hey, Justine." Mr. Fisher smiles at me. It looks genuine.

Wait. You haven't challenged him yet.

"Are you looking for Ellen?" He's doing that weird, obtrusive blinking that he always does: squeezing his eyes shut, then popping them open. It's offputting. Also difficult not to imitate. "She'll be in her classroom now, with Mr. Goodrick. Oh, who's this?"

"Figgy. He's very new."

"Hello, funny chap."

It occurs to me that some people might greet Mr. Fisher with those same words.

"He's a furry little character, isn't he?" He bends to stroke Figgy's head. "Or is he a girl?"

"No, she's a boy." I laugh. "Sorry—daft joke. *He's* a boy. I'm not here for Ellen. I need to talk to you."

"Me?" Mr. Fisher sounds surprised. "Oh. Huh. Okay, let me just . . . Class? 9F! Thank you. I'm going to step outside for a moment to talk to a parent. I don't want to hear the sound of chaos breaking out, okay?"

He closes the door on them and turns back to me. "This is good. I wanted to ask you something. I mean . . . funnily enough. Huh."

Someone at Beaconwood who isn't actively wishing me away: wow. I resist the urge to hug him. "You go first," I say.

"Oh. All right. I wanted to ask . . . This is kind of an out-of-the-blue question, but did you used to work in television? Did you make dramas and stuff?"

My stomach flips. How does he know? No one who isn't part of the industry notices the tiny names that appear in the end credits of a TV program.

I told Ellen at least ten times not to mention my former career to anyone at school. It's not a secret, but as soon as people know, they start asking questions, and I stop being able to pretend those years of my life never happened.

"Yes, I did. It was a form of slavery, albeit voluntary and well paid, and I'm delighted not to be doing it anymore. Ellen wasn't supposed to tell anyone. I don't like to talk about it—brings me out in hives."

"Oh, Ellen didn't . . . tell me," Mr. Fisher finishes the sentence uneasily. "So, there's something you want to discuss?"

Interesting that he doesn't want to reveal his source. Particularly as I can't think of a single other person associated with Beaconwood who would know what I did when I lived in London.

Hopefully this will work in my favor. He'll be feeling bad, hoping to compensate by being superhelpful from now on. "Mr. Fisher, I like you."

"I . . . I beg your pardon?"

"I approve of you. You teach my daughter about narrative perspective. I think you're a decent man. And recently I've been treated pretty indecently by some of your colleagues."

"Indecently?"

"Yes. Lesley Griffiths and Craig Goodrick have both lied to me about George Donbavand."

"Oh." Mr. Fisher hard-blinks at me.

"George was expelled for stealing a coat he didn't steal. I know he didn't, because the coat was Ellen's and she gave it to him as a present. When I tried to talk to Lesley Griffiths about it, she told me there was no such boy. She said George Donbavand didn't exist, had never been at Beaconwood, had never been expelled. Craig Goodrick said the same thing. They're both lying, aren't they?"

"Huh." Lachlan Fisher looks down at Figgy. "This is kind of awkward."

"It's okay. You won't be giving anything away if you tell me George Donbavand exists. I bumped into a kid on my way in today and he told me. I asked him directly."

"Justine, that's not true."

"What isn't true?"

"I'm not allowed to discuss it, but . . . you're wrong."

"Wrong how? George isn't a real boy? He wasn't expelled?"

"He wasn't expelled."

I turn away. I can't stand to look at another lying face. "What about his sister, Fleur? I suppose you'll say she wasn't expelled either."

"Most definitely not."

"So she'll be in her classroom now, will she, if I go and look for her?"

Mr. Fisher opens his mouth. No words come out.

"You know Fleur's not at school today, or else you'd have said, 'Yes, why don't you go and look for her?' Why isn't she at school?"

"Justine . . ." Lachlan Fisher clears his throat. "Sometimes, with the best will in the world . . ."

I wait.

"You see, it's complicated."

"That's okay. I can talk about complicated things. I'm forty-three. I've had lots of practice. Don't gawk at me like a shell-shocked goldfish. Will you at least admit that George Donbavand is a real boy, who until recently was a pupil at Beaconwood?"

Mr. Fisher stares down at his hands. His interlocked fingers clench and relax, clench and relax, as if trying to mimic a heart pumping blood.

"Lachlan, I have a distraught fourteen-year-old daughter who can't understand why her friend's been expelled for something he didn't do, even after she and he both explained to the head that he didn't do it. How do you think she feels when I tell her that same head teacher is now flat-out denying the existence of the boy she describes as 'my best friend in the whole world'? Is it the mission of this school to fuck with its pupils' heads until they can no longer distinguish between illusion and reality?"

"No. No, it isn't. Justine, I'm terribly sorry about all this. I really am."

"Then tell me the truth. What's going on?"

"I . . . Can you leave it with me?"

"No. Tell me now."

"That's impossible. I'm so sorry, but . . . if I could explain, you would understand. Truly."

"I think that might be the most irritating statement I've ever heard."

"Yes, I can imagine. Look, I promise—you have my solemn word—I'll do my best to sort this out. As soon as I'm able to, I'll be in touch. Hopefully later today. Do we have your current contact numbers in our records?"

"Yes." I want to scream at him and pummel him with my fists, but I've got to be practical. He's my best chance of finding out.

"I should get back to my class," he says. "Tell you what: I'll call you this evening either way."

"No," I say. "Only call me if you can tell me the truth. Come on, Figgy." *Let's get around this corner and then we can smash our fists against some walls. Well, I can.*

"Justine!"

I stop. "What?"

"George is real. He was a pupil at this school until a few days ago. He and Ellen were best friends."

I close my eyes for a second. "Thank you."

"Justine? The kind of friends they were . . . are, I should probably say . . ."

"Yes?"

"I've never seen anything like that between two secondary school students before. Between two *people* before," he amends. "It was . . . well, I suppose I can't say what it *was*, as an outside observer. But it *seemed* more intense than any relationship I've ever seen between adults."

Chapter 8

Remove All Sharp Items,
Chop Down All Trees

Bascom Ingrey blamed himself for the death of the flaky-eyed bumcracker, whose name turned out to be Jack Kirbyshire. Lisette and Allisande saw that there was no doubt in either of their parents' minds that Perrine had murdered him, and so they didn't doubt it either. It was now undeniable that those who found themselves in close proximity to Perrine were likely to fall to their deaths from high windows.

Bascom took this latest tragedy harder than hard. It half-destroyed him. He was unable to teach, and Sorrel took over all subjects. Every lesson, from maths to geography to science, consisted of watching videos and eating marshmallows. Sorrel had evidently stopped worrying about relevance. There had been three days of nothing but *Cagney and Lacey*, for example. To say that class discussions were no longer intellectually challenging was an understatement. Lisette was really worried. She knew she wouldn't get into Cambridge University on the strength of her ideas about why Harvey Lacey was always in his pajamas.

Officially, Jack Kirbyshire's death was recorded as an accident, but the local police knew the truth as well as all the Ingreys did. They just couldn't prove it.

The mood in Speedwell House was a dark one. The bumcrackers no longer sang, joked or listened to the radio. Bascom and Sorrel weren't sure if any of them suspected Perrine of murder. None of the family had said anything to them, of course, but Perrine was so obviously an alarming child that anyone intelligent would suspect her, they thought.

"We can't let her out of our sight," Sorrel told Bascom. "Any of the bumcrackers might try to kill her now. We must remove all sharp and heavy items from Speedwell House and chop down all trees from which nooses might be dropped."

"Would it be so terrible if a bumcracker tried to kill Perrine and succeeded?" said Bascom.

"You can't mean that!" Sorrel was shocked. "You don't want to give up on her, do you?"

"But what if she's evil? The sort of evil for which there's no hope."

"Well, then you ought to give up on her for sure."

"She can't be evil," said Bascom in anguish. "I refuse to believe it."

He stopped in his tracks. "Oh my sainted stars!" he whispered.

"What is it?" asked Sorrel. "Have you thought of a plan?"

"Music!" Bascom exclaimed. "We forgot music! The girls need to learn it. They did at school, though the lessons weren't up to much, were they? A few halfhearted choruses of 'The Windmills of Your Mind' while bashing some cymbals and a triangle."

Sorrel frowned. "I don't quite see what you're saying."

"Bach, Beethoven, Mozart—proper music lessons! That's what the girls need. That's what *Perrine* needs. That child has a soul, and I'm determined to find it. Music is the way. The pathway to the soul! Or it could be. I can't believe I forgot about music when I was devising their homeschooling curriculum. I know why I did: it's because I've got a tin ear. I'm musically illiterate, but I'm no philistine. I know how important music is. Obviously, it's not a subject I can teach . . ."

"Oh, I can do it," Sorrel offered cheerfully.

"Hmm. I'm not sure," said Bascom. "No offense, but—"

"Don't worry, I won't just play them old Rolling Stones albums."

"Oh good."

"I'll make them learn 'Sloop John B' by the Beach Boys, and then we can all sing it together, with the harmonies and everything." Sorrel was proud of her ambitious plan.

"No, no!" said Bascom, annoyed. "That's not what I mean at all. I mean *proper* music. Classical."

"Oh, don't be a snoot-nose!" Sorrel teased him.

"Sorrel, this is vitally important. We need to get someone in. A specialist."

"From Nottingham?" Sorrel asked.

"No, not necessarily. I'll make some inquiries."

"All right, darling, but please don't get your hopes up. I do worry that it might not work."

"It *has* to work," said Bascom. "It *will* work."

And so it was that, a few weeks later, David Butcher, a former organ scholar of King's College, Cambridge, arrived at Speedwell House with no idea at all of what was in store for him.

9

Thanks for coming in, Justine." Lesley Griffiths isn't smiling. She hasn't since I arrived. Oddly, this gives me hope. I've seen too many people slap a smile on a lie recently, to make it look better. If the truth is about to arrive on the scene, it's fitting that it should wear a serious face.

Lachlan Fisher didn't call me last night as I hoped he would. Instead, Lesley called to say she'd spoken to Mr. Fisher, and was I available to come in for a chat tomorrow afternoon? If so, they would both clear their diaries.

And now tomorrow is today and here I am in Lesley's office. She's sitting at her desk, with Lachlan Fisher behind her in the arm-chair in the corner of the room. I wish he'd pull it forward. He looks like a child who's been dragged along to an event against his will and told to sit quietly until the grown-ups have finished talking.

I want him in this conversation. Without his intervention, I'm convinced it wouldn't be happening.

"No puppy today?" he says.

"I left him with my husband. And Ellen. She's at home today."

"Is she okay?"

"No. When I woke her up this morning, she told me she didn't want to go to school. I said, 'Wonderful. Hooray.' I've been encouraging her to stay away from Beaconwood since pupils started vanishing into thin air and having their existences erased, so . . . today's a good result for me."

"I understand your anger," says Lesley. "No doubt I deserve it. This is an unusual situation, and I suspect I've made a mess of it. The handling of it, I mean. Only I'm not sure how else I could have dealt with it without—" She breaks off and sighs. "Would you like a cup of tea before I launch in? I could certainly do with one. Lachlan?"

"Glass of water for me, please."

They're both looking at me, waiting for my order.

"Before we get on to drinks . . . Lesley, was there a boy at this school until a few days ago called George Donbavand?" I am actually holding my breath.

There's a gap that no one's putting any words into. I stare at the clock on the desk, reminded of its presence by the ticking that's suddenly audible.

"Yes," Lesley says eventually. "There was."

I knew that already. I knew it. I didn't need you to tell me.

"He was in my form," says Mr. Fisher.

"So you lied to me?" I say to Lesley.

"Yes, I did."

Presented with a longed-for, long-suspected fact, my first impulse is to doubt more strenuously. Suddenly, I'm being told there *is* a George Donbavand—but what if the truth after the lie is just another lie?

"Did you expel him?" I ask Lesley.

"No."

"Did you expel his sister, Fleur?"

"Again, no."

"Is she still a pupil here?"

"No. Much to my regret. Justine, I know why you think I expelled George. I pretended to."

"You . . ." I sit forward in my chair. "You *pretended* to expel him?"

"I did, yes. George believes he was expelled."

"Right. The only problem with that is: It doesn't happen, does it? Ever. Why would a child who hasn't been expelled believe that he had been?"

"This is what I'm going to try and explain to you," says Lesley. "Are you sure you don't want tea or coffee before we start?"

"I'll have a coffee." Damn. The words slipped out before I could stop them. I haven't drunk coffee since leaving London. Haven't felt the need for it. I do now, and that's a bad sign. If I'm craving an energy boost, that means I'm veering off my true path.

One cup. A solitary exception, not a relapse.

Lesley rings someone—probably Helen Minchin—and asks for a tea, a coffee and a water. Then she says, "All right, might as well start. No point us all milling around awkwardly while we wait for drinks. Justine, what you said before—'That doesn't happen, ever'— I must warn you that there's a lot of that in what you're about to hear. Unfortunately, many things one expects will never happen— because, frankly, one can't credit them—have been happening. As to how to deal with them . . . I've been in a bit of a quandary."

"Go on," I say.

Lesley glances over her shoulder at Lachlan Fisher, who nods his approval.

"George and Fleur Donbavand—both pupils at Beaconwood since preschool. Parents? My first impression was: nice, normal dad and unhappy, neurotic mum. Mum in charge, sadly. Dad totally under the thumb—a Prefect Parent if ever I saw one."

"Prefect Parent?"

"Yes: parent in name only. More like an older child with special privileges—ones bestowed by the Power Parent, who could remove them at any time. Anyway. Mum Donbavand wore all available trousers, so unhappy and neurotic carried the day as far as the family went. Always a shame when the better parent is the dormant one, don't you think?"

"I don't think you're any sort of good parent if you sit back and let your other half harm the kids," I say. Then I wonder if I've been unfair. I haven't met Anne Donbavand. Do I have the right to imply she's damaging her children based on a few second-hand comments?

"Oh, me too," Lesley agrees. "I didn't say 'good,' though. I said 'better.'"

"You're suggesting it's not difficult to be a better parent than Anne Donbavand?"

"What I'm *not* doing is denying that Stephen Donbavand could and should be stronger. But he isn't, and wasn't, so. After a while, over a period of some years, the parental anxiety levels became a problem. Emails asking for details of who was preparing the hot lunches, and did we make sure to get proper references for all those people. Demands to be informed whenever an exchange student or nonpermanent teacher came to school, the same questions about references there. In the end I invited Parents Donbavand in for a chat, hoping to get to the bottom of it all. I've met many an anxious parent in my time, but this was different. The security questions they asked . . . It was as if they thought someone was intent on attacking their children. So I got them in and asked them directly: 'Do you think someone's out to get Fleur and George? Someone who might stoop to applying for a job in our canteen so as to poison them?'"

"And? What was the answer?"

"Lots of incoherent screaming from Mum: Why was I asking? What did I know? That sort of thing. It was a short meeting. She stormed out almost immediately and Dad scuttled after her. A few days later there was an email from Dad: Could they come in again? They'd obviously decided—well, *she'd* decided—that she wanted to talk. I said yes, of course. She was perfectly calm for our next meeting. Apologized for her behavior on the previous occasion, then told me she and her family don't exist."

"*What?*"

"Her very words. I'll never forget it. No such people as Anne, Stephen, Fleur and George Donbavand. Those are false names, she said, because they're in hiding. In answer to my question from last time—was someone out to get her children?—she told me that, yes, she feared they were. Someone was out to get all of them, hence the assumed identities."

Is this some kind of joke? Apparently not.

"How long had Fleur and George been at the school when you had this conversation?" There's so much I want to ask, I don't know where to start.

"Hm." Lesley's mouth twists as she tries to work it out. "I could dig out my old diaries and check, but . . . Fleur and George were both still in Juniors."

"A long time ago, then?"

"Oh yes. We at Beaconwood have been living with this knowledge of the threat to the Donbavands for years. Each new member of staff we hire has to be informed. Lachlan'll tell you."

"It's true, Justine. I think we must be the most security-conscious school in the country because of it. Once you hear something like that, you can't help but worry. You're in charge of protecting two students whose parents have told you they're endangered. You start to see threats everywhere: visiting speakers, other children's parents . . ."

"We got used to it," says Lesley. "You get used to anything, don't you? We watched George and Fleur like hawks all day long, vetted everyone who entered the building as diligently as we could. Anne Donbavand asked to be informed in advance of anyone Fleur and George might come into contact with, so that she could vet them too."

"It was time-consuming," says Lachlan. "Long emails had to be sent every week: the names of anyone new who was due to be in school the following week, any new families starting at the school . . ."

"Wait. You're telling me that when Ellen came to Beaconwood, you had to email Anne Donbavand and give her our names, so that she could check us out?"

Lachlan hard-blinks at me a few times before turning to Lesley. He wants her to deliver the unwelcome news.

"I don't think she can have investigated every name we gave her, else she'd have gotten no work done—the woman's a workaholic from what I can gather—but yes," says Lesley. "When I knew that Ellen was coming to Beaconwood, I emailed Anne to tell her. I did it whenever we had a new family."

I'm annoyed to find myself believing what I'm hearing: believing, at least, that Lesley's no longer lying to me. I'd be happier if I still had doubts. This story is already too disturbing, and we haven't gotten to the expulsion part. Sorry: pretend expulsion.

"The first time Alex and I came to look round, without Ellen— did you warn Anne Donbavand in advance that we were coming?"

"Yes."

"This is unbelievable."

"Isn't it just? Thing is, we've never had a visitor to the school for whom secrecy is a priority. You and Alex weren't concerned that no one should find out you'd been here, were you?"

"No, but—"

"No one is," Lesley glides smoothly over my unfinished objection. "I figured it wouldn't do any harm to anyone else if I . . . kept Anne informed. Kept her off my back, more importantly."

"Didn't she also threaten to take Fleur and George out of Beaconwood?" asks Lachlan.

"Yes. Sorry, I missed out that part. It became clear at a certain point that if we weren't prepared to put these . . . reassurance measures in place, the ones Anne demanded, then she would remove both children." Lesley's mouth sets in a firm line. "I wasn't having that. At least with Fleur and George at Beaconwood I could guarantee they'd be exposed to six hours of sanity, five days a week."

"Hold on." I'm confused. "Are you saying Anne's insane, and there's no real threat to the family?"

"No, I believed her," Lesley says. "But think about living like that—in hiding, knowing that if anyone finds out who you are, it might be curtains for you. Imagine it! Anyone'd go loopy. I think that's what happened to Anne Donbavand. She wasn't as bad when I first knew her. She got worse. Told me she'd nearly not risked sending George and Fleur to school in their new life. Toss-up between us and homeschooling, it was. I thought about poor old Fleur and George in that house all day long, with Anne's dark, paranoid fears for company—frankly, I'd have done anything to keep them here, as long as it didn't harm anyone else. So, yes, I went along with most of Anne's strange requests."

"You believe her, yet she's also paranoid?" I say.

"She's a woman who makes heavy weather of things." Lesley's tone suggests this is a serious understatement. "For all I know, the danger she's forever referring to isn't something that would have induced a more . . . well-balanced person to start a new life with a new name."

"Wait. You're surely not saying you don't know what the threat is?"

"That's right."

"Well, who's making it?"

"I don't know that either."

Person or persons unknown. This would be funny if it weren't so appalling.

"So you've brought me in here to tell me a story you don't know yourself. Fantastic."

"I'm telling you what I know," says Lesley. "Should have done it sooner. I'm ashamed that it took Lachlan's involvement to make me see sense, but . . ."

Here comes the excuse.

"Paranoid neurosis—it's a funny thing. Ingest enough and it starts to infect you. Anne has impressed on me so many times that I must never breathe a word to anyone. I was afraid that if I told you the truth, something might happen to Fleur and George."

"Wow." Breathe, Justine, breathe. "You're not joking, are you? You're actually serious about all of this."

Two troubled faces stare back at me.

Not joking, then. Definitely not. Joking ruled out, despite being the only halfway plausible option.

"So you don't know who's after the Donbavands, or why, or what they used to be called before they were the Donbavands?"

Lesley nods. "Anne said—and on this I was with her all the way—it would be reckless of her to tell me. The less we at Beaconwood know, the more protected we are. I've no desire to be privy to details that might put my colleagues and pupils in danger."

"Is that what Anne said? That knowing would put you at risk?"

"Not explicitly. She said I was safer not knowing. I don't think she was necessarily implying that being in possession of the full story would be life-threatening for me. Could have been a case of 'Trust me, you'd rather not know.' She was dead right! Something so

dreadful that you'd flee your former life and change your name . . .
I'm happy to remain in the dark, thank you very much!"

Hearing this, I could almost start to suspect Lesley of lying all
over again. Is she an idiot? There's no greater danger than not knowing exactly what and who you're up against. However awful the
truth might be, how could Lesley have preferred to be ignorant?

"Have you—"

Loud knocking interrupts my question.

Our drinks are brought in not by Helen Minchin but by Kendra
Squires. She puts the tray down on the table with a nervous smile.
I manage not to push her out of the way to get to my coffee, which
smells divine. I'm going to pretend to myself that I have no intention
of drinking it until I take the first sip. Then I'll down the rest in a
few gulps, so that I can get it over with quickly and resolve never to
weaken again. That should trim away a bit of the feeling of failure
at each end.

"You were saying," Lesley picks up once Kendra's gone.
"Have I . . . ?"

For a moment, my mind is blank. Then I remember what I was
on the point of asking.

I'll sound crazy if the answer's no.

On the other hand, the lingering traces of my sanity are making
me stand out like a sore thumb around here.

"Has Anne Donbavand ever mentioned the name Ingrey?" I say.

Lesley fires questions at me for ten full minutes: "Whose name is
that?" "Are you saying the Donbavands used to be called Ingrey?"
"Why mention it in this context if it's nothing to do with the Donbavands?" "Is Ingrey a real name?" "Oh—you've only seen the first
three pages of the story? Why won't Ellen show you the rest?"

It seems she's suddenly acquired a wish to be privy to details.

"I've shared as much as I want to for the time being," I say. It's a line from *The Good Wife*. Lesley and Mr. Fisher are unlikely to be fans who know each episode by heart. *Too busy storyboarding for their own series,* The Dysfunctional School.

"You thought it was me, didn't you? I was showing an interest in George Donbavand—an interest for which there was a perfectly reasonable explanation—but you decided I was the person Anne Donbavand and her family went into hiding to avoid. That's why you lied to me."

Lesley's shoulders slump. "Lachlan convinced me it couldn't be true. Told me he'd always had a good feeling about you, which reminded me that I had too. I decided to trust my instincts."

"I knew you'd never hurt George or his family." Lachlan Fisher fixes his solemn eyes on me, pushing his glasses back up his nose. "Ellen would be distraught if any harm came to George. If she were distraught, you'd be distraught, therefore . . ." He finished with a shrug.

"Did Anne Donbavand ever say that I was the danger?" I ask Lesley.

"Never."

"Then why assume the worst about me?"

"You have to remember, Justine: for years, I'd been hearing from Anne about nameless enemies hell-bent on wreaking their revenge on her via her children. I'd seen no evidence that what she was saying was true. No one seemed unduly interested in Fleur or George. Then suddenly Ellen comes along, and she and George are spending all their time together."

"And you thought, 'Aha, this fourteen-year-old girl must be the secret agent of destruction'?"

"Put yourself in my shoes. I was in an impossible situation. Long before Ellen turned up at Beaconwood, Anne had asked me to tell her if anyone got close to either of her children. For years, no one did. The teachers mostly liked George but the children didn't know what to make of him, and, though they were friendly enough, they mostly kept their distance as far as politeness would allow. He's an odd boy, George. Charming as anything, witty, incredibly erudite, but he could be blunt-verging-on-rude, too. And embarrassingly direct. Some people found his charm a shade too much and wondered if it was an act. He never really had a proper friend until Ellen turned up. She's also very mature for her age, intellectually. The two of them were inseparable from the start."

"You told Anne about Ellen, then?"

"No. I didn't, and felt remiss about it. I couldn't bear the prospect of her taking George out of Beaconwood and opting to home-school him instead."

"Did she threaten to do that if he ever made a friend?"

"No, but I know Anne," says Lesley. "I could imagine the frenzied whisking away of children that would take place if I referred to George's new best friend."

"Friends weren't allowed," says Lachlan Fisher. "Neither were pets—Fleur would have loved a cat—she came to school crying one day because she'd been told in no uncertain terms that she could never have one. No phone calls, internet access, sweets, crisps or chocolates. No residential school trips, nothing that involved leaving the grounds of Beaconwood, even supervised by teachers—even when Anne was invited to come too, as a parent-helper, to check that everything was in order."

"Well, she wasn't interested in that, was she?" Lesley snorts. "Always too wrapped up in her work."

"Tell me about the fake expulsion," I say.

Lesley nods. "I didn't tell Anne about George's friendship with Ellen, but he must have given something away himself, or else

Anne had other spies in school. She came in one day a couple of months ago, buzzing with rage and fear. Worst I've ever seen her. 'Does George have some kind of special friend?' she wanted to know. The way she said 'special friend,' as if it's a terrible thing to have, a curse . . . Brrr. It gave me a chill."

"What did you say?"

"At that point, asked a direct question, I couldn't lie."

"You told her about Ellen?"

"I had to."

"What, exactly?"

"She wanted to know about the family. I told her Ellen's father is a famous-ish opera singer, that you used to live in Muswell Hill in London. I'm sorry, Justine. I can see how upsetting this must be for you."

"How did Anne react?"

"She went very quiet. It was peculiar. I was expecting a hysterical meltdown and got the opposite. Almost as if, now this was serious, she couldn't afford the histrionics. She needed to keep a cool head, go away and plan . . . Or maybe that's hindsight, in the light of what happened next."

I wait.

"More than a month passed. Then Anne came in—again, very calm, uncharacteristically composed—and told me she was taking George out of the school. I'd dreaded and half-expected it, but I nearly dropped dead of shock when she ordered me to pretend to expel him. She told me about the coat Ellen had given him. She knew it was a gift, but explained to me how I could insist it was theft and use it as grounds for expulsion."

"But . . . why?" I ask. If I had a large piece of paper and a pen to hand, I would write down that one word, so that I could keep holding it up. *Why?*

"Poor George," Lachlan Fisher mutters.

Never mind sympathizing with him. How about doing something to help him?

"So that he wouldn't hate his mother," Lesley explains. "The way Anne tells it, Fleur has always been good as gold, but George never stops kicking against all the restrictions. He understands they're to keep him safe, but he resents it. Anne begged me."

And you should have told her to fuck off.

"Said she finds George nigh on impossible to control as it is, and he'd only get worse if he blamed her for taking him away from Beaconwood and Ellen. She asked me to play the villain of the piece. I know what you're thinking, Justine, but it wasn't only a desire to shift blame onto someone else. George is extremely bright, and he's . . . spirited. Stubborn, some might say. If he thought we'd be happy to have him here, he would never have stopped trying to return. He'd have badgered his parents relentlessly and they're at breaking point as it is. Horrible though it was, I could see Anne's point of view. If it wasn't safe for George to stay with us—and for that I had to take her word, since I didn't know the facts myself—then it was probably easier all around if he believed that option wasn't open to him."

"No," I blurt out, unable to keep a lid on my frustration any longer. "You're telling me it's better for a boy who's done nothing wrong to think he's been unfairly expelled? Better than for him to be told that, despite his wishes, his parents don't think it's safe for him to go to that school? What a load of bull! You don't really believe that, Lesley. You made your decision based on your fear of George's mother, not out of concern for George and what would be good for him."

"You're wrong." Lesley sighs. "Did I make the right call? Who knows. Maybe not. But I was thinking of no one but George when

I made it. Try to understand: I didn't, in all honesty, have a clue if I believed Anne Donbavand or not. I tied myself up in knots trying to work it out, but . . . I had nothing solid on which to base my opinion. And in the meantime, while I wondered and debated— with myself and others—I had to choose how to interact with Anne. That couldn't wait until the truth arrived, unfortunately. I needed a way of . . . *being*, in her company. In the end, I decided to behave as if I believed her, since . . . well, proceeding as if I didn't wasn't an option, really. I suppose I wanted to give her the benefit of the doubt . . ." Lesley sounds uncertain. "It was inconceivable to me that she might have invented it all, really. It still is."

"Benefit of the doubt? And that extends to pretending to expel her son, knowing he's done nothing wrong?" I'm not sure I've ever felt as disgusted by anything in my life.

"Justine, I know Anne Donbavand. You don't. I know how hard it must be for poor George to live with her, and I judged that it would only get harder for him if another powerful grudge were to be added to the mix. George loved this school, and he was going to have it taken away from him. I didn't want him to endure that pain. So . . . yes, it's unorthodox, but Anne's logic made sense to me: cancel out the pain by extinguishing his love for Beaconwood. Would you want to attend a school that booted you out on a bogus charge? Or would you hate that school, and consider yourself fortunate to be rid of it? I was led to believe lives were at stake, Justine. What would you have done?"

"Not what you did," I say angrily. How dare she play tag with her moral dilemma and try to make me It? I'm not head of Beaconwood and this isn't about me. Though, since she's brought it up . . .

I know exactly what I'd have done. It's something I can still do. My not being head of a school will present no obstacle at all.

Pleased with my decision, I feel slightly less hostile toward Lesley.

In a milder tone, I say, "So, what, you called a special school meeting, told everyone not to mention George at all, pretend he'd never been here?"

"On Anne's instructions, yes. She warned me that people would come and ask about George once he'd gone—seemingly with his best interests at heart. She as good as ordered me to deny he'd ever been here."

"And then I came in asking the very questions you'd been warned about."

"Well . . . yes." Lesley sounds apologetic.

"I have no grudge against the Donbavand family, Lesley. I've never met any of them, and hadn't heard of them before this week. Whoever this threat is, it's not me."

"Of course it isn't," says Lachlan Fisher vehemently.

"You broke the glass and set off the fire alarm, didn't you?" I ask Lesley. "You, personally. To get me out of the building."

"Yes. I couldn't think of a better plan at that moment." She looks embarrassed.

"The police?" I suggest, though I have less faith in them than I did this time last week. "If the Donbavands' lives are at risk . . ."

"I mentioned the possibility of seeking police help more than once. All I got was screaming from Anne. She told me I didn't understand, that involving the police would be the most dangerous thing of all."

"And you believed her." I can't keep the scorn out of my voice. "And so an entire school acts out the private lunacy of one disturbed woman."

"I didn't and don't think it's as simple as that," says Lesley. "Yes, Anne was irrational much of the time. Frankly, she was a woman delirious with fear. Did she magnify the threat out of all proportion? I don't think that's for us to say, do you?"

Am I being unreasonable? I'm not sure I care at the moment. I'm not the one who pretended to expel George Donbavand, then pretended he didn't exist.

"But none of this adds up, Lesley. Anne's behavior makes no sense. If sending your children to a school puts their lives at risk, you don't send them. If the threat's that serious, and it's all so top secret, why are you okay with the headmistress and all the teachers knowing about it? Aren't you worried there'll be some nosy teacher who'll try to find out more?"

"I can't answer for Anne." Lesley looks away.

"No, but you can think critically about what she's told you. You said before that her enemies were hell-bent on wreaking their revenge on her via her children. That suggests that Anne herself is the focus of the anger or grudge, whatever it is—not Fleur and George. Right?"

Lesley chews the inside of her lower lip as she considers this. "That hadn't occurred to me, but . . . yes, everything Anne's let slip suggests she's the target."

"Then how come Fleur and George are on twenty-four-hour lockdown while Anne goes about freely all over the world giving papers at academic conferences? Yes, I've Googled her—why wouldn't I? My daughter is obsessed with George Donbavand, therefore so am I. She told me he's got weird parents, so I thought I'd have a look online. Anne Donbavand is a university professor. Universities typically have thousands of new people joining them all the time—staff, students. Each new academic year, Anne starts from scratch with a sea of unknown faces, presumably. How come she's not terrified one of *them* will be this enemy from the past that she's so terrified of, moving in for the kill?"

"It's natural to worry more about your children than about yourself," says Lesley.

"Also, Anne might know which face to look out for," Lachlan Fisher contributes. "George and Fleur may not."

"I don't buy it," I tell him. "Is it normal to take on new identities, go into hiding, then announce, 'This is our secret new identity! We're not really the people we're pretending to be!'?"

"I think it's fairly common for key school personnel to be taken into a family's confidence, yes," says Lesley.

No. Not like this. Something smells very wrong here.

"What about Fleur?" I ask. "Was she fake-expelled too?"

"No. There was no need to lie to her. Unlike George, Fleur was never happy at Beaconwood. She was timid as a mouse, always anxious. She'll be happier at home—even the Donbavands' home."

"Fleur was as worried for her parents as they were for her," Lachlan tells me. "She hated being at school because it took her away from them. If she wasn't with them, she didn't know they were safe."

"Her concentration was appalling," Lesley says. "As anyone's would be if their mind was on whether or not they'd find their parents still alive at the end of the school day, I suppose."

There's a hot ball of fury in my chest. "So Professor Anne manages to write conference papers and books—travel around the world to present her words of wisdom, advancing her stellar career—and meanwhile her daughter can't concentrate on school work for fear of violent attacks on her family? Does that sound right to you? Why are the children the ones doing all the obvious suffering here?"

"Oh, Anne suffers," says Lesley. "You only need to speak to her to see it. Besides, George wasn't anxious. He was remarkably sanguine about it all. I once raised the subject with him, tactfully—mainly to see how he was bearing up. He tried to make light of it, as if having someone out there aiming to kill you and your family were no more than a minor annoyance."

I need to get out of here. My head's spinning. "I'll have to tell Ellen what you've told me," I say, standing up.

"I'm sure she already knows that George Donbavand is not George's real name," says Lesley.

My heart thumps faster. In my head it sounds like footsteps, running to catch up. "Why . . . why would Ellen know? She hasn't said anything to me about that."

"She wouldn't. She'd think telling anyone, even you, would put George at risk."

"You have no idea what Ellen knows or doesn't know," I snap. "Soon she'll know that George wasn't expelled—that's the main thing."

Is it?

I came here hoping for answers. Instead, I feel as if I've been given a bigger, more impossible puzzle than the one I came in with.

What if whoever wants to kill the Donbavands has added Ellen to their list because of her friendship with George?

No. Don't even think it. You don't believe in this mysterious threat to the Donbavands. Do you?

I mumble something—it's meant to be "Thank you"—on my way out of the room.

Halfway down the corridor, I hear footsteps slapping the lino behind me. I turn and see Lachlan Fisher. He's holding something: a typed document. "For you," he says.

"What is it?"

"All the Year 9s were asked to write stories. George gave me his before he left. He wanted me to have it: his last piece of work for Beaconwood. It . . . it meant a lot to him."

"Thank you." I take it from him. "I'll give it to Ellen."

"No. I mean, you can if you want, but read it first."

"What's it about? His family?" Wouldn't it be great if the solution to the Donbavand mystery were contained in a fourteen-year-old's creative writing homework?

"No, it's not at all autobiographical."

Then don't waste my time.

"It's about injustice," Lachlan Fisher says, with a hard-blink for a heavy word. "And madness."

I've had enough of both for one day, but I take the story and put it in my bag because he persuaded Lesley to talk to me and I owe him a good deed.

"Ellen's story is about murder," I tell him. "A weirdly real-sounding murder."

He doesn't like the sound of that at all. I watch him try to blink my words away.

"Mr. Fisher? Are you okay?"

He mumbles something inaudible, then turns and hurries back to Lesley's office.

Chapter 9

No Lock on the Little Green Door

David Butcher, the Ingrey girls' new music teacher,
introduced himself to Lisette, Allisande and Perrine
with the help of a Hungarian folk song. "My name is
Mr. Butcher," he said. "And so that you never forget
it, here's a song called 'The Handsome Butcher.'" Then
he cleared his throat and began to sing:

> *Seven locks upon the red gate,*
> *Seven gates about the red town.*
> *In the town there lives a butcher and his name is*
>   *Handsome John Brown.*
> *In the town there lives a butcher and his name is*
>   *Handsome John Brown.*
>
> *John Brown's boots are polished so fine,*
> *John Brown's spurs they jingle and shine.*
> *On his coat a crimson flower, in his hand a glass*
>   *of red wine.*
> *On his coat a crimson flower, in his hand a glass*
>   *of red wine.*
>
> *In the night, the golden spurs ring.*
> *In the dark, the leather boots shine.*

*Don't come tapping at my window now your heart no
longer is mine.*

*Don't come tapping at my window now your heart no
longer is mine.*

The Ingrey girls never did forget David Butcher's name,
but it wasn't because of the butcher in the song. It
was because Perrine murdered him.

(I know he has barely been introduced, but there's
no point allowing you to get to know him. He's nothing
more than a victim in this story, however brilliant
and life-changing a music teacher he would have been
if he'd lived.)

David Butcher did not fall to his death from one of
Speedwell House's upstairs windows. Instead, he was
found lying cold and still on the library floor. It
was one day when he arrived early for the lesson, and
Perrine did too. When Lisette and Allisande entered
the library at the correct hour, they found Perrine
sitting curled up in a chair with a smirk on her face,
and Mr. Butcher's dead body at her feet.

There was not a mark on him.

"What did you do to him, Perrine?" Bascom wept.

"Nothing, Father," came the nonchalant reply.

"Don't 'Nothing, Father' me! Did you poison him? You
must have poisoned him, since he has no visible wounds."

"I don't think she did," said Sorrel Ingrey quietly.
"I think she simply removed her mask—the one she
always wears in our presence—and let him see who she
truly is. I think that scared him so much, it stopped
his heart."

"Or perhaps she did nothing more than wish him dead," Allisande suggested. "That might have been enough."

"You're talking about me as if I'm a witch," said Perrine indignantly.

"Come on, Perrine." Sorrel clapped her hands together. "I'm taking you upstairs to your room and locking you in there."

"For how long?" asked Perrine.

"For as long as I feel like!" Sorrel snapped.

"Don't forget the little green door," Bascom told Sorrel. "You'll have to push the chest of drawers up against it on the other side, or else she'll be able to get out there. There's no lock on that door."

Lisette immediately rewrote "The Handsome Butcher" song in her head:

> No lock on the little green door.
> Put a chest of drawers in the way.
> In this house there lives a killer and her name is
>   Perrine Ingrey.
> In this house there lives a killer and her name is
>   Perrine Ingrey.

"What choice do Mum and Dad have, Perrine?" asked Lisette, who still desperately hoped a rational approach might prevail. "When you're free to do so, you kill. If you would only admit it and promise to stop . . ." Lisette broke off when she realized none of her family were listening to her.

"Shouldn't she have a worse punishment than being

locked in her room for a while?" said Allisande. "This is her third murder!"

"I'd appreciate it if you would leave this to your father and me," Sorrel said sternly.

Perrine was taken upstairs. Everyone heard the key turning ominously in the lock. Bascom Ingrey sat quietly weeping in an armchair in the corner of the library until his wife reappeared. She took one look at him and pursed her lips. "Pull yourself together, Bascom," she said briskly. "This is no time for sentiment. We have important business to discuss."

Sorrel sat down. "Girls," she said. "We have difficult times ahead of us, but Dad and I have made a plan, and if we all follow it to the letter, everything will be all right. Okay?"

Lisette and Allisande nodded eagerly. Lisette wondered when this plan could have been made. Sorrel made it sound very new, but they had all only just now discovered David Butcher's dead body.

"No matter how much we all wish it were otherwise, we must face facts," Sorrel began solemnly. "Perrine is a killer. She has killed three times, and we can't let it happen again. That would be socially irresponsible. We must call the police and tell them what we know. The only problem is that we have no proof. Perrine is extremely skilled at leaving no solid evidence of her crimes."

Now Bascom joined in. "There's a strong chance that the police wouldn't be able to do anything, because we have nothing concrete to offer them, and they can't just lock people up willy-nilly. So . . ." Hesitantly, he looked at his wife.

"So we're going to have to fake the evidence," said Sorrel. She produced a small knife—the one she used mainly to chop garlic—and held it up in the air.

Lisette and Allisande gasped.

"I'm going to plunge this knife into David Butcher's heart," said Sorrel. "And maybe slice his neck with it too. We need to make him look more murdered. It's okay—he won't feel a thing, so it's not harming him in any way. I don't want to do it—I hate the thought of vandalizing a corpse—but I need to, to make it look as if that's how he died. A stabbing—something that can be *witnessed*."

"You mean . . . ?" Lisette began tentatively.

"Yes. We four must pretend to the police that we all saw Perrine stab David Butcher with this knife. Then there will be proof, and hopefully they will lock her up for a long time. Of course, it will still be her word against ours, and I'll have to make sure I wipe all my fingerprints off the knife, but I'm confident the police will believe us."

"As would any jury," said Bascom.

"But we'd have to lie in court, under oath," Lisette protested.

"Yes," said Sorrel. "I'm afraid you would, darling. It's a terrible thing that we're asking you to do, I know. But if we don't do this, Perrine will kill again. I think we all know that. Don't we?"

Bascom and Allisande nodded.

"But . . . can't we just tell the police the truth?" Lisette asked. "That we know Perrine is a murderer, but can't prove it? It's their job to prove it, not ours."

"And if they fail, as they surely will?" asked Sorrel.

"But . . . but . . ." Lisette spluttered.

Sorrel walked over to sit beside her. She put an arm around her eldest daughter's shoulder. "Dearest Lisette," she said. "I know you're a person of high morals and principles. I very much admire that about you. But sometimes, one runs up against something that's more important than principles. Look at poor dead David Butcher . . ." (David was still lying life-less on the floor in front of them all.) ". . . a bril-liantly talented musician, cut off in his prime by an act of evil. Can there be any higher, more vital prin-ciple than making sure nothing like this ever happens again?"

"Mum's right, Lisette," said Allisande. "We all have to stick together on this."

"I suppose so," said Lisette reluctantly.

"Good," said Bascom. He stood up. "I'll go and call the police."

"Not yet, silly," said Sorrel. "First I have to . . . you know. Stab the body."

"Oh. Oh yes, quite."

"Why don't you and the girls go and start getting lunch together while I sort it out. There's no need for any of you to be involved. I know what needs doing."

(It might strike you as odd that Sorrel, the lazy

parent who always preferred to do as little as possible, took the lead here. The sorry truth is that, whatever one's natural inclination and personality type, when it comes to an abysmally unpleasant chore, it is the woman and not the man who ends up taking care of it in 99 percent of cases.)

Lunch was all laid out on the table by the time Sorrel reappeared: ham, chutney, French bread, hummus, taramasalata, salad and stuffed vine leaves, with apple juice to drink. "That looks lovely," said Sorrel. "Good job, everyone."

"What about your . . . side of things?" asked Bascom.

"All taken care of! Girls, please don't go into the library again until further notice. I don't want you to see the carnage. Bascom, you needn't look either."

"I certainly don't want to," her husband replied with a shudder. "Have you phoned the police?"

"Not yet. I intend to do so first thing tomorrow morning." Sorrel started to pile food onto the plates that were laid out on the table.

"Tomorrow morning?" Bascom exclaimed. "Have you taken leave of your senses? We can't just let a body lie around—"

"I'm not planning to leave him there indefinitely," Sorrel cut him off. "I have a very good reason for waiting until tomorrow. I want other people to be present when the police arrive. I'm going to invite the Dodds, for a start. And the families of Jack Kirbyshire and David Butcher. I think they deserve to see justice come for Perrine, don't you? I think we owe them that, especially since we've protected her all

this time, hiding her away in our specially strength-
ened fortress of a house! I want to make it clear that
we are not on her side against the families of her
victims, and that we are the ones who, in the end,
enabled justice to be done."

"Yes. Of course," Bascom agreed, as if all this
should have been obvious to him.

"Mum, if people are coming, please could Henrietta
Sennitt-Sasse come?" asked Allisande.

"Oh, and Mimsie Careless?" said Lisette. "Please!"

"Very well," said Sorrel. "I shall invite the
Sennitt-Sasses and the Carelesses as well." She handed
them each a plate with their lunch on it, then loaded
one up for herself and laid it down on the table in
front of her chair. She sat down and was about to
start eating. Suddenly she leapt to her feet with an
"Oh!" She went to get another plate, and piled it high
with food. "I forgot Perrine," she said. "We mustn't
starve her, whatever she's done."

"No, we mustn't," said Bascom with a sob of paternal
anguish.

"I'll take this plate up to her," said Sorrel, shov-
ing a stuffed vine leaf into her mouth because she was
quite hungry and didn't really want to wait for lunch.
"Won't be a second."

"Are you going to tell her?" asked Lisette. "About
the police?"

"No." There were tears in Sorrel's eyes. "Given what's
going to happen tomorrow, I'd like her to have one last
nice day."

It occurred to neither Lisette nor Allisande that it

might be difficult to have any sort of nice day while locked in one's bedroom. The whole Ingrey family had been hibernating in seclusion for so long, they all took it for granted that life now involved a certain amount of being shut away, unable to get out.

10

Alex is in the garden with Figgy when I get home. "Everything okay?" he asks as I get out of the car. I see he's got a new leather leash for Figgy, who is using it to drag him toward a shrub called—I think—butcher's broom. I still don't know the names of half the things growing in our garden. Whatever it is, Figgy is determined to poke his nose into it.

Just like his owner.

"George Donbavand is real," I tell Alex.

"Real, and in our house," he replies with a grin.

A sharp pain in my head. Above my right eyebrow, from nowhere.

"What? Our . . . He's in our . . ." I'm stumbling over my words. "Which house?"

"Do we have more than one?" Alex points. "That one over there. Speedwell House, Kingswear. Remember it?"

"This isn't funny, Alex. George Donbavand is in there? With Ellen?"

"With a completely transformed Ellen, yes. Barely recognizable: radiant, witty, bubbling over with joy. It's a bit of an eye-opener. I hadn't realized how miserable she was."

I told you a hundred times.

I start to march in the direction of the house. Alex catches my arm, pulls me back. Or maybe we're both being pulled by Figgy, who is now thoroughly embedded in greenery. The only sign he's still there is his taut leash protruding from the leaves.

"Justine, relax. Abandon all plans to embarrass the living daylights out of your daughter. No harm's going to come to them. They're fourteen, not three. They're playing Monopoly."

"*Monopoly?* Who plays that these days? We don't have Monopoly."

"George brought it. He seems remarkably civilized for a teenage boy, I have to say."

"I wish he hadn't come. Not today. I need to talk to you, without visitors around—especially not him. Can you ask him to leave?"

"Why? That's absurd. What happened at Beaconwood? You've come back all wound up."

"He's not allowed to be here. For as long as he's in our house, we're not safe." I'm not sure I believe this. So why am I saying it?

"Darling, with the greatest respect, you're sounding a bit"—Alex makes a winding gesture with his index finger, next to his head—"out to lunch."

"Why's the blind down?" I ask.

"What?"

"The kitchen blind's down. And Ellen's bedroom curtains are pulled shut. How could you not notice? How long have you been out here?"

"Hour, hour and a half? Figgy seems happy pottering around the garden, I thought I might as well—"

"Was the kitchen blind down when you came out? It wasn't," I answer my own question. "I don't think it was down when I got out of the car. I'd have noticed. They've done it just now. Why?" I set off toward the house again: great big strides.

"Justine, wait! Can you put the brakes on and not overreact? Think about it: it's getting dark. People draw blinds and curtains when it gets dark, don't they? Come on, Figg—looks like we're going in."

"Have you ever known Ellen to notice that the curtains need drawing?"

"I don't know."

"I do." I hurry ahead. Whatever is about to happen, I'd rather Alex and Figgy stayed in the garden, but I can hardly stop my husband from entering his own house. "Ellen never touches a blind or a curtain—not in her bedroom, not anywhere. I do it. As you can see, I'm not inside the house at the moment. Which means George Donbavand must have—"

"Justine, you're going off at the deep end for no—"

"On his first visit to my house, he's seen fit to close the blinds and curtains in two rooms. Why?"

"I don't know. Let's stretch the boy on a rack until he tells us, shall we?"

I run into the house through the open front door. "Ellen? Ellen!"

"Hi, Mum," she calls out.

This house is too big. I can't get to the kitchen quickly enough. When I do, she isn't in it. "Ellen? Where are you?"

"Upstairs, with George. In my bedroom!"

In her bedroom with a remarkably-civilized-for-fourteen boy from a severely dysfunctional family, with the curtains closed. Closed by him.

Remarkably civilized means unusually mature—intellectually, and perhaps sexually too.

"I'm coming up!" I yell. I try not to look at Alex but still manage to see him shaking his head at the spectacle I'm making of myself.

Ellen's door is wide open. She and George are sitting on the floor with glasses of orange juice beside them and a Monopoly board between them.

Curtains closed, door open. What does that mean? Did they only open it when I called Ellen's name? They look as if they've been sitting like this for a while; there's no sign from either of them of recent exertion, they're both fully clothed . . .

Alex was right. They're playing Monopoly.

George springs to his feet and walks toward me, holding out his hand. I shake it. "Ellen's mum," he says, with a wide smile. "It's a great pleasure and an honor to meet you. You have a supremely brilliant daughter who's about to beat me at Monopoly."

Ellen giggles. Her eyes are bright, her cheeks pink.

"It hardly seems fair, when I'm the one who brought the game. I won't be making that mistake again. What a wonderful house you have, incidentally."

"Thank you." I have to say something. "George, did you . . ." What am I doing? I can't ask him, but I have to know.

Alex appears at the top of the stairs. This must be how escaped lions feel when their tamers hove into view.

"Do please ask, whatever it is," says George eagerly. "Ask away!" He's got a wide, square face, fine golden-brown hair, thin lips, big eyes that I'm trying not to stare at. It's the irises. Instead of circles of color, they look more like hollow cylinders—curved blue surfaces and gray interiors. It's as if they go back a long way into his head, like tunnels down which the black pupils of his eyes are falling.

I clear my throat and say, "It's nothing, really." George's willingness to be grilled makes me feel guilty.

"Oh, do ask, or I'll wonder for*ever*," he says theatrically. "I'm insatiably curious."

"In that case you have something in common with my wife," Alex tells him.

"I was going to ask you if you closed the curtains. Ellen's window."

You see, George, I had a peculiar feeling in this room recently. I thought, "There's something wrong here—something to do with the window." And I couldn't work out what it meant. Still can't. And Ellen never closes her curtains, but here they are: closed.

Malachy Dodd was alive on one side of that window and dead on the other. But he's not real, is he?

"Oh. Yes, I did indeed," says George. "It was getting dark." His smile has vanished and he looks stricken. "Oh—should I not have done that? I know some households like to leave curtains open day and night. I come from a family that closes them as soon as the light starts to fade, but maybe you're different?"

"It's fine, George," says Ellen contentedly. Everything is ideal in her world at this moment. She looks . . . joyful is the only word I can think of that comes close to describing it. "Mum always closes the curtains when it gets dark. Don't you, Mum?"

She's not angry with me for asking an embarrassing question. She's too elated; resentment would be impossible.

"Yes, but I'm in someone else's house," says George, his brow still furrowed. "Your mother's right. I shouldn't have touched the curtains without asking." He turns back to me. "I should confess that I also lowered the blind in the kitchen, when Ellen sent me down to get orange juice. Unilaterally, without permission. I'm so sorry. What must you think of me?"

I'm thinking more questions: Why lower a blind in a room that you're only going to be in for a minute? Where do his parents think he is?

He speaks like a fussy old retired colonel with a monocle.

And that surprises you? After all you've heard about his family life, you expected him to be a normal kid, playing Grand Theft Auto *on his Xbox?*

"Don't give it another thought, George," says Alex firmly. "It's fine. Helpful, in fact. Isn't it, Justine?"

"Yes. Very. Thank you, George." I smile, feeling a stab of pity for this child who obviously wants so much to be liked and approved of.

Instantly, he produces a broad grin of his own to mirror mine and says, "It's cozier if you keep the darkness out, I think."

"I agree," says Alex. His deliberately jolly tone annoys me. He's trying to compensate George for what he sees as my unreasonableness.

"My house should be cozy, as it's a little cottage, but it isn't at all. I hate it."

"You . . . you hate your house?" I say.

"Oh, I don't mind the building itself. It's the people in it that are the problem. They're positively unnerving. Every day they unnerve me." He pronounces every word loudly and deliberately, like an entrant in a diction competition performing before the judges. "That's another reason I closed the blind and the curtains. But we don't need to go there. In fact, we shouldn't."

I look at Ellen, hoping for a clue. She's deliberately avoiding my eye. Alex has fallen silent.

Wonderful. The conversation's taken a turn for the awkwardly unfathomable, and suddenly I'm its sole custodian.

"Who unnerves you?" I ask. "Are you talking about your family?"

"Justine, I don't think he wants to talk about—"

"Hell, yes, my family!" George laughs and rolls his eyes, giving the lie to Alex's tactful warning. "They're a sorry bunch. I'm the only normal one of the four of us. Ellen is so lucky to have you two—loving, reasonable parents."

I have no idea what to say. I've known this boy less than five minutes.

"And you're lucky to have her, and so am I," George goes on. "Even if she does beat me at Monopoly."

"I haven't yet," says Ellen. "Let's carry on playing. You two can go downstairs."

"George . . . you said something about another reason you closed the blind and curtains?"

"Mum, you're obsessed," says Ellen.

"It's all right," says George. "Yes, I didn't want to be seen."

"By . . . ?" I ask.

"The secret police, otherwise known as my dad. Our house is halfway up the hill on the other side of the river, directly opposite you. I don't think he'd be able to see me in here from there, but I didn't want to take the risk. He doesn't know I'm here, you see. I'm not allowed to go anywhere. You can imagine how oppressive I find it!"

I glance at Alex, whose face is caught halfway between a smile and a grimace. He can't decide if George is joking.

I'm sure he isn't.

"Where does your dad think you are now?" I ask.

"He has no idea. I'm hoping to keep it that way."

"But if you're not allowed to go anywhere, how did you . . . ?"

"A very good question!" George follows this compliment with a small bow. "I snuck out. Is it sneaked or snuck? I think it's snuck. I left a note saying I'd gone out for a long walk. My mother's away at a conference, which makes life easier—in too many ways to list. I waited until I knew she wouldn't be able to call for several hours, then I wrote a note for Dad and slipped out."

Seeing my look of concern, George adds in his strange, booming voice, "It's perfectly all right, really. You're safe. Dad's more likely to saw off his own head than tell Mum, even if he finds out where I've been. She'd make him suffer horribly."

You're safe. He takes for granted that the whole world is as afraid of his mother as his father is. And as he is, despite his bold manner. This isn't confidence I'm looking at; it's a very frightened boy, putting on an act.

I ought to tell him that if he isn't allowed by his parents to be here, then he can't stay.

And send him back to the madhouse halfway up the hill? Ellen would never forgive you.

"You're welcome to stay as long as you like, George," I say. "Make yourself at home."

"Thank you, Justine. You're too kind. As long as I like would be forever, which is impractical. Still." He sighs. "I wish I had a nice, normal mother like you. Oh!" He turns from me to Alex. "Would the two of you like to join Ellen and me in our Monopoly tournament? It would be a convenient excuse to scrap the game we're in the middle of—the one I'm losing—and start a new one. You'd be helping me out greatly."

He's real, I find myself thinking, but is he really fourteen? While knowing that he is, I am simultaneously wondering if there's any way at all that he might not be. Could he be a seventy-five-year-old trapped in a child's body? He's so polite, yet he calls me "Justine" without waiting to be asked. Scrupulously polite and overly familiar—it's an odd combination.

"But if you abandon a game—any game—then whoever's winning at the moment of abandonment has won," Ellen teases him. That's my daughter, who, until today, thought board games were the dullest thing in the world.

"The moment of abandonment," George repeats, amplifying each word. "What a marvelous phrase. Doesn't it sound like a romantic novel?"

"You've got a better chance of not losing if you keep playing," says Ellen. "It's your only hope, however remote."

George turns to me and rolls his eyes conspiratorially. "Your offspring is an evil genius. I am completely in thrall to her. Next time I come, I'll make sure to bring a jigsaw puzzle instead. Collaboration, not competition! That's the way forward."

No doubt New Ellen will declare herself to be a devotee of jigsaws any moment now.

"Righto," says Alex decisively. "Justine and I'll leave you to it. We'd better go and track down the dog, who at this moment is probably crossing 'Destroy the entire downstairs' off his to-do list."

Ellen laughs. "You're funny, Dad."

"Oh." George looks disappointed. "Well, if you change your minds, you'd be most welcome to join us at any time. The dog too! Monopoly's fun with two players but four or five is ideal. It's a game for all the family!"

Two hours later, with my mobile phone hot in my pocket from a long call, I'm returning to my house again, this time in a dripping raincoat and drenched running shoes and socks. Figgy is soaked too. Without the padding of dry, fluffy fur, his legs look perilously thin. Luckily he doesn't seem to mind. He and I have walked three times around the perimeter of Speedwell House's grounds, on the inside. I'd have ventured beyond the big iron gates, but Alex, shocked to hear that I took Figgy to Beaconwood, was adamant that he can't leave our land again until he's had his second lot of vaccinations. I think he's being neurotic, but arguing would have kept me in the house longer.

I had to get out. Being told by George that I would be "most welcome" to join an activity taking place in my own house made me feel the opposite. I escaped so that I wouldn't have to speak to him again before he left.

I don't dislike him. How I could I fail to like a boy who's so lovely and complimentary to Ellen, and so charming to me? I fled because I was upset for him—too upset to stay and endure any more of his weird conversation, to watch him set off for what passes for home and his god-awful parents, knowing there's nothing I can do to help him. If I can't solve a problem, I don't want to be around it.

You're a coward.

I unlock the front door and open it. Figgy rushes into the house ahead of me, only to be jerked back by his leash. I unclip him and he goes racing toward the kitchen to find his food bowl.

"Is that you?" Alex calls out from the family room. "I was about to send a search party."

"Sorry. I had an important call to make." It's not the sort of thing someone who does Nothing should be saying, but I'm too tired to worry about my life plan having drifted off course. "Where's Ellen?"

"In her room iPod-ing. Or Instagram-ing, or Video Star-ing. George left about an hour ago. Come and tell me about the call, which I assume was George-related. Bring alcohol if so inclined."

I pull off my raincoat, hang it up in the hall, and swap my soaked socks and running shoes for my indoor flip-flops.

Alcohol. Excellent idea. On my way to the fridge for tonic water to add to my gin, I stop in front of the kitchen window, raise the blind that George lowered, and stare out. All I can see in the blackness is moonlight bouncing on the water and small, square patches of gold from across the river: the windows of the cottages opposite.

One of those houses belongs to the Donbavands. Which one? I'm not close enough to see what's going on in any of the rooms, though I can see flickers of movement. Perhaps with binoculars . . .

I don't have any, and I doubt there's anywhere nearby where I could get some. When I lived in London, if I didn't have something I wanted, I went out and bought it. Since we've moved here, I've adopted a different attitude: anything I haven't already got, I accept that I can't have. When the view from your every window is leaves and water, it seems a sensible and hassle-free approach to take. If I ever wake up and find a department store on my lawn, I'll rethink my policy.

Alex has made a fire in the family room, the only one with a working fireplace at the moment. All the others need attention before they can safely be used. Personally I'd rather manage with just the one than have to call a chimney sweep, but Alex might disagree strongly enough to sort it out himself.

I pass him his whisky and tell him I've hired a private detective.

"*What?* You've done what? Tell me you haven't!"

"I have. Don't worry, it's a reputable firm. They've got coverage all over the UK, a website, thousands of Twitter followers."

"Justine, are you demented or something?"

"Not when I last checked. Why? Do I seem it?" I sit down on the floor in front of the fire with my drink. Figgy dashes in from the hall and plonks himself down in my lap. Great. Another soaking from his wet fur.

"Is there such a thing as a reputable private detective?" Alex asks. "Aren't they all crooks?"

"I've no idea. Neither have you. We have no experience of that world."

"True, but—"

"Let's not waste time arguing. It's done. I've paid upfront. He'll either prove useful or he won't. I thought it was worth a try."

"So you asked him to find out who's making these phone calls? I think there was another one while you were out, by the way. The landline rang. When I picked it up, there was breathing, then they hung up."

"I mentioned the calls, yes, but we mainly talked about George."

"Why? There's no mystery about George anymore, is there? He's real. I assume Lesley Griffiths explained to you why she expelled him?"

"She didn't expel him. She only pretended to."

In between sips of gin and tonic, I tell Alex everything that happened at Beaconwood this afternoon. He listens without interrupting. When I'm finished, he says, "So you've asked this investigator to find out . . . what? The Donbavands' original name, before they changed it?"

"Not only that—also where they used to live, what happened to make them want to run away, who's after them with a view to harming them . . ."

Alex is wrinkling his nose dismissively. "Can he find out any of that stuff? How?"

"I don't know. He didn't sound fazed by it at all. He said, 'Yeah, should be able to get something for you,' as if I'd asked him for a cup of tea and a chocolate biscuit."

"I can't think how he'll do it," Alex says.

"That's because you're an opera singer and not a detective," I say impatiently. "I assume he has methods that he uses regularly, if his firm's been in business for thirty years."

"Maybe." Alex sounds unconvinced. "I hope he's not planning to break any laws, making you an accessory."

"I don't care if he breaks every law known to man if he gets me the information I want," I say. "I've given him Anne and Stephen Donbavand's email addresses and suggested he hack their accounts."

Alex throws his head back in despair. "That's idiotic! That could land you in jail. What did he say?"

"He said hacking emails was against the law. He didn't say he wouldn't do it."

"Good on him. Justine, I'm worried about this." Alex slides off the sofa, landing on the floor next to me. It's hard to deliver a stern lecture while reclining with your feet up. "It's not only the possibly dodgy detective and the legality issues, it's the chance that you might find out. Lesley Griffiths's approach is the one I'd favor: something fucked up and dangerous is going on, therefore keep as far out of it as you can."

"For as long as George and Ellen are intent on doing their Heathcliff and Cathy bit, we're involved whether we like it or not, Alex."

"Don't be daft. George popping around once in a blue moon when he can escape from his parents isn't going to put us at risk, but—"

"Isn't it? Are you sure? George was pulled out of school by his parents *because of Ellen*—because, after years of loneliness, he made a friend. His mother doesn't want anyone getting close to him. Lesley said so. All right, maybe someone's out to get the whole family. *Maybe.* If so, it's made Anne Donbavand paranoid and she's decided to take it out on George. And on us."

Shall I go further and risk being wrong? I can't keep it in. "I think she's the one making the threatening calls."

Alex makes a weary face. "You've no proof of that."

"Which is why I said 'I think.' I've never heard her voice. She didn't answer the email I sent her—neither did her husband. But now we know Ellen's friendship with George bothers her. To her disturbed mind, it must look as if our arrival here meant she had to take her kids out of Beaconwood. So, yes, when I think about who might want to call me and say, 'Go home or I'll kill you and your family,' she's at the top of the list. She *is* the list."

"Did you tell your detective you suspect her?"

"Yes. I told him everything."

"Darling, you don't know this man from a bar of soap."

"Oh, so what? He's doing some work for me, that's all. We don't need to be blood brothers."

We sit in silence for a while. I stroke Figgy's chin with my knuckles and he makes a sound I'd call purring if he were a cat. Do dogs purr, or is there a different word for it?

"I'm going to make another phone call you'll disapprove of," I tell Alex. "To Olwen Brawn. I thought about asking her when I was at her house but I chickened out."

"Asking her . . . ?"

"If she's heard of the Ingrey family."

"The . . ." Alex's baffled expression gives way to wide-eyed disbelief. "Seriously? You're proposing to ask a random dog breeder if she knows some fictional characters invented by your daughter, and you're calling Anne Donbavand disturbed?"

"Ellen's imagination didn't produce what was on the pages I read. It was her handwriting, but not her creation. You have to trust me on that."

"Well, I don't *have* to," Alex mutters apologetically to his whisky glass. "I could disagree with you instead. I could say, 'Does anyone know what another person's imagination is capable of?'"

George Donbavand's imagination, for example . . .

I swallow the last of my drink. "The anonymous caller called me 'Sandie.' On the family tree attached to Ellen's story, there's someone called Allisande Ingrey. Sandie could be short for Allisande."

"Justine, stop."

"On the same family tree, there's somebody called Ellen—sound familiar?—who appears to be married to one Urban Ingrey. He's Allisande's nephew, son of her older sister Lisette. Lisette and Allisande had a younger sister called Perrine—"

"Darling, these people don't exist!"

"Perrine murdered a boy called Malachy Dodd and was then murdered herself. *If* the Ingreys are a real family, that means Lisette and Allisande suffered two fairly severe traumas—severe enough to explain Anne Donbavand's neurosis."

"All right," Alex says slowly, thinking. "So your theory is what? Ellen's story isn't made up, it's the true story of Anne Donbavand's childhood? Told to Ellen by George, I suppose."

"Maybe. I think it's possible."

"Lisette Ingrey is Anne Donbavand? Urban Ingrey must be George if he's married to Ellen on the family tree."

"It's exactly the sort of thing Ellen would do," I say. "It's obvious she worships George. She's making a family tree of his family, and she writes herself in as his future wife."

"Let's assume that's true," says Alex. "Lisette Ingrey has a— presumably equally traumatized by childhood events—sister called Allisande, but *that isn't you*."

"Of course it's not me. Though remember Ellen burst into tears when she heard me say, 'My name isn't Sandie' to the anonymous caller. And later she asked me if I'm really who I claim to be."

"Fuck." Alex shakes his head.

"That makes perfect sense, doesn't it, if George has told her all about his mother's past? Sandie—Allisande—is evidently a force for darkness in the story—a threat, a danger to Lisette and her family. Ellen hears that I've been addressed as Sandie and panics. Thinks, 'What if my own mother is the person out to get George and his family?' And before she thought that, she thought it was someone at school making the calls. That's why it seemed plausible to her that Lesley Griffiths might maliciously expel both George and Fleur. Maybe she thought Lesley was Anne Donbavand's dangerous sister? Remember she asked you how old Lesley was?"

"But if Anne Donbavand is or was Lisette Ingrey, she must know you aren't her evil sister Allisande. And . . . all of this sounds made up," Alex rounds off dismissively.

I hold my breath for as long as I can, then exhale slowly. "If she were sane, then, yes, she would know I'm not Allisande. Now think about what might happen if she isn't. She's had a terrible childhood—a murderer sister who's then murdered. Somehow, she and her surviving sister end up as enemies. Lisette flees to get away from Allisande, whom she's come to fear. She changes her name to Anne Donbavand, starts a new life, but grows increasingly neurotic, fearing that Allisande will track her down. Allisande never does, but the threat grows and grows in Anne's mind. She keeps her kids under lock and key, scared her sister might harm them when she's not there to protect them. Then she hears George has a friend—she does the maths and works out that this friend might have a mother roughly the age of scary sister Sandie, and a delusion is born. In her mind, I'm Sandie. She's probably got some whole crazy narrative about how Sandie disguised herself as a TV development producer and changed her name to Justine Merrison to make it easier to get close to Anne and her family without arousing suspicion. Which is why it'll be great if this detective can find the real Sandie. Maybe then Anne will snap out of this fantasy of hers and realize it's not me."

"You Googled all those Ingrey people and found nothing," Alex tells me, as if I might have forgotten. "If one of them had murdered someone called Malachy and been murdered herself, they'd *all* show up in an internet search. Guaranteed. And didn't you say they lived in our house in the story?"

"Yes, and I know no one called Ingrey has ever lived here. But what if Ellen changed the names as a security measure? I can see George asking her to do that, can't you? Names changed to protect the guilty and the innocent—loads of writers do it. I've wondered if the characters' names might all be anagrams. They're so . . .

unnatural sounding, somehow. I tried to rejig the letters of Ingrey in my head, but got nowhere."

"Anagrams? That sounds unlikely. I mean . . . more unlikely than everything else. Why don't you ask Ellen? It's her story."

No, it isn't.

"She wouldn't tell me. I've tried. Now do you see why I called a private investigator? He'll be able to provide me with concrete facts: where Anne Donbavand grew up, what her name was, where her sister is now."

Alex nods. "Admittedly, facts would be useful. Though I still don't see what Olwen Brawn has to do with any of this."

"Probably nothing. I just . . . I looked at her house the day we moved and had such a powerful feeling, as if someone were trying to tell me something. And then more weird things happened—lots more. What if . . ."

What if Olwen Brawn is Allisande Ingrey, Anne Donbavand's sister?

I laugh at myself. That's so stupid and irrational, I'm not going to say it out loud. Instead, I say, "You're right. Probably Olwen has nothing to do with any of it, but asking her if she knows the Ingreys or the Donbavands won't do any harm, will it?"

"I don't think there's much point," says Alex. "You'd be better off waiting for the police and this detective to do their jobs, and doing normal things in the meantime—like calling The Car Men and arranging for the Range Rover to be valeted. All right, joke—*joke!*—but there's no point keeping a dog and barking yourself. Is there, Figgs? You're a dog—you should know. Let the investigators investigate."

Normal things. Alex might as well have suggested I fly to the moon. Normality is temporarily on hold. Hopefully not permanently.

"Though if you are calling Olwen, can you ask her advice about neutering? The vet said we absolutely should do it, but I don't want to ruin Figgy's future sex life for no good reason. It'd be useful to know Olwen's view."

"I'll call her now. Your question'll be a good pretext."

I'm in the hall when Alex calls out, "What about school? Do we send Ellen back to Beaconwood or not?"

"Neither name means anything to me," says Olwen. "I don't know any Ingreys or Donbarrands."

"Donbavands."

"Or them. Who are they? Doggy people?"

"It's nothing to do with dogs."

"I was going to say: if they were Bedlington breeders or Crufts people I'd know them, but I don't know all kennel owners."

"No, I wouldn't assume you did. Oh well, never mind. It's not important." I try to sound like someone making an ordinary chatty phone call.

"Do they want puppies?"

"Who?"

"These people—Donbavands and Ingreys."

"No. Really, it's . . . unrelated." Clearly Olwen finds it hard to conceive of pockets of the universe that don't center around dogs.

"Fair enough," she says. "It's just that I don't think I'll have another litter until this time next year. Are you all right? You sound tense."

"I'm fine, thanks."

"Figgy giving you the runaround? It takes a bit of getting used to, you know. Especially for novices like you and your husband. But stick with him and Figgy'll make a lovely family pet. Beds always do."

"He's already a lovely family pet," I say defensively, remembering the way George said "A game for all the family!" so enthusiastically, like someone in an advertisement. "We're managing really well, I'd say. He's been having fun going on long walks, nosing around in shrubbery and long grass."

"Walks?" Olwen sounds wary. "He shouldn't be out and about until ten days after he's had his second jabs."

"You said it was okay for him to be in the garden," I remind her, omitting to add that he's also been to school.

"Well, yes, but . . . you said long walks."

"We have a big garden."

"Big enough for a long walk?"

Fantastic. This is exactly the sort of conversation I want to be having with a woman who lives in a small end-of-terrace next to London's North Circular. No way for me to come out of it well. "Yes. Eighteen acres." *Plus, it's possible to walk around it more than once, and in different directions. Not that it's any of your business.*

Does she think I'm lying?

"Eighteen acres? So you live in a stately home?"

The conversation is plunging headlong into the unacceptable. Ellen has appeared in the kitchen, which might be the only thing that stops me from telling Olwen to stick her questions where the sun doesn't shine. "Remember the Germander/Speedwell thing I told you about?" I say instead. "Speedwell House is where I live. Google it. It's a registered historic building in Devon. If you think I'm lying about living there, let me have an email address and I'll scan and send you a copy of the deeds."

Ellen, from the sofa, twists her face into a cartoon-like expression that says, "Weird conversation much?"

"Justine—forgive me," Olwen says. "I'm being silly. And rude. Of course I don't doubt you. I panicked when I heard you say Figgy had been out on long walks, and you did sound slightly . . . well, *odd* at the start of the conversation. You asked so insistently about those two names, as if you thought I ought to know them, then you changed tack and said it didn't matter at all. The truth is, I'm *hopeless* at letting go of my dogs. I worry about them once they've gone, and always want to come and snatch them back for the first week or so."

"Please don't," I say. "I'd never have thought it possible, especially not so soon but . . ." I look down at Figgy. He's yawning. He's got some kind of seeds stuck in the fur around his mouth and nose. I'll have to fish them out later.

"That's all I need to hear," says Olwen. "Your panic at the prospect of me wanting him back is extremely reassuring. Tell you what, though—I'd love to come and visit him in his new home."

You've got to be kidding me.

"How are you fixed for tomorrow?"

"Tomorrow? That's . . . soon."

"I must admit, now that you've mentioned this grand house with eighteen acres, I'm itching to get a look at it. It'll be like visiting a National Trust mansion. Tomorrow's my only free day for the foreseeable future, but do say if it's inconvenient. It can wait a few weeks."

"No, tomorrow's fine."

Ellen does a pantomime "What now?" face.

Knowing that Olwen wants to come, I'm not inclined to delay it. There's something not right about all this. How many dog breeders are so intrusive? How many would be willing to travel from London to Devon to visit a puppy they last saw less than a week ago?

Is it a coincidence that I mentioned the names Donbavand and Ingrey, and almost immediately Olwen decided she wants to travel for hours to see Figgy?

Perhaps, in spite of her apology, she's still anxious about him and wants to give his new home the once-over. Or else she's the ruthless and deranged Allisande Ingrey who grew up in Speedwell House, and that's why she wants to come.

And you're letting her?

It seems I am.

Something's on its way. Something's going to happen, and I won't know what it is until it has. I have to advance toward it, or draw it toward me.

"What's your email?" I ask Olwen. "I'll send you my full address."

As soon as I'm off the phone, Ellen says, "Dad says George wasn't really expelled." I expected her to ask about the conversation she's just half heard. I should have realized George would trump everything.

"That's right."

"I'm going to tell him next time he comes," Ellen says defiantly. "That he was only pretend-expelled."

"You should," I say. "I think he deserves to know. Do you think there'll be a next time? Sounds like it's pretty difficult for him to get out of the house."

"He'll come whenever his mum's somewhere where she can't call and ask to speak to him."

"You knew he was going to come today, didn't you? That's why you asked to stay home from school."

Ellen nods.

"How did you know?"

"On Fleur's last day, he gave her a note to deliver to me at school."

"El . . . if you don't go back to Beaconwood, you'll have to go to another school pretty soon. You can't sit around the house every day on the off-chance that George might turn up."

"There are no off-chances involved, Mum. Me and George discussed it—yes, I know it's George and *I*, I don't care. Fleur's not at school anymore, so she won't be able to deliver messages. So we've agreed that whenever George is planning to come around the next day, he'll send a signal. Every evening at quarter to nine on the dot, I'll stand by the kitchen window. That's his house there, see—the one painted kind of tangerine color, with the black-painted wood? George's room is the one on the far left. His bedroom will be dark by quarter to nine—he has to turn his light off by eight thirty, can you believe that? He's fourteen! Anyway, if he turns his bedside lamp on and off three times, that means he's coming the next day. I'll reply by turning the kitchen light on and off three times to let him know it's okay to come."

I know what I ought to say: that if the next day is a school day, it won't be okay because Ellen can't miss school, ever, simply to see a friend.

Yes, she can. If it's a friend she loves, who loves her, whom she'd never see again otherwise.

I should say that if George isn't allowed by his parents to visit Ellen, then, however much I might sympathize with her predicament and however tyrannical his parents are, I won't have him in the house.

Fuck that. Fuck Professor Anne Donbavand and her vicious paranoia.

"All right," I say. "Then that's what you'll do."

"Really?" Ellen's eyes nearly pop out of her head. She was expecting resistance.

"Really. Let's hope you'll be able to squeeze the occasional day of school in between George's visits, eh?"

She throws her arms around me and squeezes me. "You're so the best mum ever. It might only be once every six months. His mum's out of the house quite often, but usually she calls every hour or so and she'd be suspicious if she couldn't speak to him. This time he knew she'd be on a plane for seven hours flying back from America, so there was no chance of her calling. Mum?"

"Mm?"

"What did you think of George?"

This is an answer I have to get right. When I lived in London and worked too hard, I was a less-than-ideal mother in many ways: often stressed and bad-tempered, never available to make Halloween costumes, or even to order them from Amazon. Sometimes Ellen used to creep up to me with a tentative "Mu-um . . . ?" and I'd snap, "No! Not now! Don't ask me to do anything, don't tell me you need something—I can't! If you can't sort it out yourself, the answer's no." I feared that to be assigned one more task might have broken me.

Terrible.

I compensated by being wildly enthusiastic about all the things I could see Ellen loved, by making sure never to steer away from her own wishes and needs in order to fulfill mine—something I saw so many of the always-armed-with-top-notch-Halloween-costumes mothers doing.

Top of Ellen's list of loves at the moment is George Donbavand.

"I think he seems amazing," I say. "You're very lucky to have him as a best friend."

"You know when you asked about the curtains being closed—did you think we were kissing and stuff like that? Sex-type things?"

"No." I give her a sharp look. "You're fourteen: too young for all that."

"Exactly," Ellen agrees. *Thank God.* If someone had said that to me when I was fourteen, I'd have laughed till I cried.

"No, that didn't even cross my mind," I lie. "It struck me as odd to close someone else's curtains, that's all. And I knew you wouldn't have done it."

"Mum, can you keep a secret? I mean even from Dad, because he wouldn't understand."

"Are you sure? Dad's quite enlightened."

"Not enough for this," says Ellen gravely. "You might not be either, but . . . I just really, really need you to be!"

All right, get ready, Merrison. Whatever she's about to tell you, you mustn't blow this. You support her, whatever she wants. If she wants to have George's name tattooed on her ankle . . .

Oh God, please let it not be that. Anything but that. She might not love him this time next year.

"When we're older—I mean *much* older, once we've been to university and everything—George and I are going to get married. He proposed to me and I said yes. We're engaged."

I give her a hug. "Congratulations," I say, and I mean it. University first: hooray. My child is sensible. Sensible enough, anyway. No tattoos, no fundamentalist religion, no body piercing, no blowing up laboratories that experiment on animals because George loves rabbits . . .

"Wait," says Ellen, extracting herself from my embrace. "It's not going to be a regular marriage."

"What do you mean?"

"George is gay. So you see, we'll *never* have sex. Oh, don't do your 'Say what?' face."

"Sorry, I didn't mean to . . . George is gay? But . . . then won't he want a husband rather than a wife?"

"No!" says Ellen triumphantly. "We want to be married to each other because we love each other more than anyone else, and that's who you should marry, isn't it? Your favorite person, the one you want to commit to and spend the rest of your life with?"

"Well, yes, but—"

"We might both have dalliances—just for fun—with people

we fancy, but that'll be fine. We can each have as many dalliances as we like and it won't threaten our relationship, because our marriage won't be about that. It'll be based on something much deeper. There'll be no romantic or sexual jealousy like there usually is in a marriage. George says everyone should do what we're going to do, and then fewer people would end up getting divorced when their desires change. He says romantic desires can only ever be fleeting, and it's important to marry the person who mirrors your spirit most exactly, whether or not you want to make out with them or go to bed with them. When you think about it, he's right, isn't he?"

"Honestly? I don't think there is a 'right' when it comes to relationships. I think everyone must do what works for them. If this plan works for you and George and will make you both happier than any other plan, then go for it."

Or make me happy and change your mind before you reach marriageable age.

Am I a conventional conservative at heart, despite my liberal pretensions?

It's unflattering to think that fourteen-year-old socially deprived George Donbavand might know more about life and love than I do.

I don't see why I should have to fret about this alone, so I say, "Dad would agree with me. You should tell him too."

"Really?" Ellen perks up at the prospect of having two understanding parents in on the secret.

"I think so." On impulse, I say, "Have you heard of Vita Sackville-West?"

"No. Who's she?"

"She was part of the Bloomsbury Group and had a long, happy marriage with a gay man. She was a lesbian, I think. I'm pretty sure she had the kind of marriage you and George are planning."

And the only reason you're planning it is because Professor

Anne—stupid twat that she is—doesn't realize that forcibly keeping people apart deprives them of the opportunity to get thoroughly sick of one another. If she followed a recipe entitled "Create a Doomed, Forbidden Love Out of Nothing," she couldn't possibly do a better job.

Ellen leaps up from the sofa. "I'm going to Google Vita Sackville-West," she says. "I hope you're right about her. George and I aren't telling *anyone* until we're eighteen, but it'll be easier to explain it if someone's done it before. George says people are more likely to hate and fear things that are new and different."

"Only bigoted people," I whisper to myself after she's left the room. I don't want to be one of those. Definitely not.

Engaged. My fourteen-year-old daughter is engaged. But it's fine, because there's no sexual strand to the relationship, and never will be.

Except that doesn't sound fine to me. A marriage should be about romance and physical love as well as friendship.

Where did I put George's story, after Lachlan Fisher gave it to me? I haven't seen it since I came home. Suddenly I'm desperate to read the creative work of my future son-in-law.

I go in search of my green bag, which isn't in the kitchen. God, I hope Ellen tells Alex quickly—in the next ten minutes, ideally. I need someone to talk to about all this. I could do with a steer from my own mother, but she's been dead more than ten years. I wish she'd lived and my stepmother had died instead. Julia. She's not a bad person by any means, but I've always been cool toward her. It would have been immoral to allow her to like me, knowing that every time I see her, the words "It should have been you!" ring out in my mind.

George's story is—thank goodness—in my green bag. It's folded in a way that borders on the I-don't-give-a-shit scrunched up. Without the announcement of Ellen's engagement, I probably wouldn't have looked at it.

I take it back to the kitchen, stretch out on the sofa and start to read.

Only a few words in, I recognize it. I know this story, start to finish. I'm in it. Reading it feels like being tricked into attending a dreaded reunion.

I skim quickly over the words, trying to take it in at a glance. Names of actors and directors jump out at me.

Christ on a fucking cracker.

I'm here, and so are my former colleagues, my reason for leaving London, for leaving my job. All of it.

George Donbavand has written my story.

"The Casting Ouch"
or
"The Ben Lourenco Affair"

by George Donbavand, 9F

No, it's not a typo! If I'd meant to call my story "The Casting Couch," I would have made sure to give it that title. Do you really think I am so slipshod as to send a story out into the world without thoroughly checking it first? If that's what you think, I'm surprised you've progressed this far. I wouldn't want to read a story by someone who wouldn't check for mistakes. How could you rely on anything they wrote?

You will see that there are two alternative titles above. That's because the first one, while perfect if readers interpret it correctly, will inevitably be taken as a typo by some, and this cannot help but mar its perfection. So it's no doubt safer to call it *The Ben Lourenco Affair*, after its tragic hero. Though in fact Ben Lourenco is not strictly speaking an embodiment of tragedy in the traditional dramatic sense, because he is not brought down by a fatal character flaw or moral weakness. There is plenty of moral weakness in the story, lashings of the stuff, but none of it is Ben Lourenco's.

Should I tell you that from the get-go? Too late!

I already have. I'll tell you something else as well: the yarn that I am about to relay to you is divided into what is known as "front-story" and "back-story," as many yarns have been since records began—or so I am told by the venerable Mr. Fisher, guru of Class 9F.

What follows is slightly different from that age-old format. Different and, I would venture to suggest, more interesting. Here, as you will soon discover, we have a known front-story wrapped around and rooted in an unknown back-story. Not unknown to everybody, natch. There are people who know what did or did not go down, but none of them are actors in the front-story. And, take it from me, there's nothing more taxing than being expected to play a lead role in a drama based entirely on another drama whose script you cannot read and must merely guess at.

That's no excuse for terrible acting, mind. And you are about to encounter, in these pages, human beings acting terribly, for which I apologize. On the plus side, you will hopefully enjoy being aghast, as I did when I first heard this sorry tale. It's completely true, which makes it so much worse. Though it also gets me off the hook for never revealing the truth surrounding the back-story. I can't, because I don't know it, so please take this warning of partial narrative disappointment and stash it away in your back pocket for later, as it were.

Luckily, I know the facts concerning the front-story, which is the only reason I haven't fired myself from my authorial position on the spot.

And now the moment has arrived when the introductory

pleasantries have been concluded and the dramatic
plunge must be taken, so here goes . . .

Who is Ben Lourenco? You might have heard of him, or
you might not. He's an actor: British, originally from
Billericay, which until recently I had assumed was in
Ireland. The name sounds so Irish, doesn't it? Frankly,
I think it should be moved there.

Let's get to know Ben Lourenco a shade better. I am
told he is six foot four, has big blue eyes with laughter lines around them, slightly scarecrow-esque dark
blond hair, and a dimple on his chin so deep that if
you were his loved one, you'd be tempted to try and
scoop dust or grime out of it on a regular basis with
the corner of your handkerchief. Yes, it is what you
might call a substantial dimple. It's a dimple that
you'd notice and think, "That dimple really ought to
be someone's responsibility."

Ben Lourenco has never been the star in anything,
but he's been a valuable not-quite-main character in
many TV dramas that see maladjusted and overlooked-
for-promotion police detectives frowning their way
around cloud-addled Yorkshire moors, litter-strewn
London government housing and antiseptic white mortu-
ary corridors. It's fair to say that, in his capacity
as non-lead-role player, Ben has shone—so much so that
he was shortlisted for Best Supporting Actor at the
2012 BAFTA awards. To nobody's eternal surprise, he
won. Hurrah for Ben!

The performance for which he won this accolade was
not his usual fare at all. Instead of a police drama,

it was a TV movie, a romantic comedy called *The Future Sex Diet*. It sounds intolerable, doesn't it, from the title alone? I wish I didn't have to describe its plot and themes but I'm afraid I do. I promise to be as compassionately brief as I can.

The Future Sex Diet: written and directed by Freddii Bausor, a well-known television and film director who has occasionally ventured as far as Hollywood. But in case her well-known-ness doesn't extend to you, gentle reader, fear not, for enlightenment is on the way. Freddii is a woman now, but hasn't always been. Or rather, her body hasn't always been, though her essential self has. Hence the need for masses of surgery, the net result of which is that Freddii is now a woman in all senses of the word.

The Future Sex Diet was a great success when screened on UK television. It's the story of a young, confident career woman who is quite happy being single, sleeping around in a fun and resolutely uncommitted way, and looking like an ordinary woman and not an overly made-up Barbie doll, until . . .

Have you guessed? Are you guessing? Shall I put you out of your misery?

. . . until she meets a man at a work drinks party one night, falls madly in love with him on the spot and decides, after he invites her out for dinner in a way that pointedly implies sex for dessert, that she simply can't take off her clothes in front of this man until she has lost half a stone in weight. For every other man she frolicked around in bed with, her body was perfectly all right and adequate in her opinion, but this man is so divine that she feels compelled to make herself perfect for him.

She erroneously supposes that the only thing wrong with her is the extra half stone, and not the fact that she becomes a blithering idiot the moment a gorgeous man hoves into view, but we must leave that aside for the time being since we were not invited to offer our editorial opinion, and in any case it is much too late. This film has aired, baby, as they're bound to say in Hollywood and BAFTA circles.

Our brain-bypass heroine accepts the dinner invitation from this hot geezer, and off they go to a restaurant. Sure enough, after the meal that the heroine has done her best to eat only the perimeter lettuce of, the hero, in a charming and winsome way, suggests that fornication should follow. Oh help! What a predicament! The extra half stone! He can't be allowed to see it, or he might run away screaming! What can our hapless lass do to avert disaster, yet still keep this good prospect hooked?

She has a brilliant* (*wholly moronic) idea. She remembers, from many a romantic legend she has imbibed since the year dot, that men are supposed to prefer women who don't joyously leap into bed with every halfway appealing chap that turns up. Men positively like women who make them wait and beg and suffer and petition, because they have all bought into the virgin/whore distinction (first coined by Sigmund Freud, points out the heroine's intellectual best friend with whom no one in the movie wants to have any sex at all because she's always lugging around a heavy book). Men think that women who are too easy are worthless, and only ever want to marry the ones who withhold sex for ages.

Our heroine sees the solution to her problem. It's staring her in the face! All she has to do is pretend to be one of those women for six months, while secretly dieting like mad. By the time the six months are up, she'll be at her ideal weight, and her romantic hero will like her all the more because of all the time and effort he had to put in.

This superb* (*utterly abysmal) plan works swimmingly for a while, until disaster strikes in the form of a chance encounter with a group of men in a bar, several of whom have done the deed of darkness with our mildly padded protagonist. These men all promptly say things that no one would ever say in reality, but that are needed to advance the plot in fiction: "Making you wait, is she, mate? She must have changed since we all had her! She couldn't wait to get our boxer shorts off, I tell you—wouldn't even let me finish my pint!" (The real dialogue is even worse, no doubt.)

Damnation: our heroine is revealed as a fraud! Our romantic hero is bepuzzled! What goeth on? thinks he. She admits to lying, finding herself with no choice, but does she take this excellent opportunity to tell her hapless chap the truth? Why, no. She invents a new and quite revolting lie. She pretends she recently escaped from an abusive relationship, and even bribes

one of her male friends (yes, this nincompoop has
friends, surprisingly) to play the role of the aggres-
sive ex-partner.

 This hoax, too, is eventually rumbled in the most
sidesplitting and cringeworthy of ways, and the romantic hero dumps the heroine for being an unparalleled
buffoon with appalling values. That's where the film
should end, in my opinion. Freddii Bausor evidently
disagreed, because the actual ending is: self-loathing
and excessive promiscuity on the part of the heroine, much weight loss resulting from misery, eventual
rescuing by forgiving hero who is willing to give her
another chance. (Clearly, for some men, every ethi-
cally bankrupt laughingstock is an opportunity for
improvement.) But the twist is—guffaw, guffaw—he says
she's too skinny and refuses to undress her lustily
until she's gained at least half a stone, and ideally
a whole stone. The final scene is the two of them
eating in a restaurant, and him shoveling profiteroles
into her mouth in a way that we're supposed to find
romantic, but that will make all right-thinking people
contemplate joining a terrorist organization if only
for the hunger strike opportunities that might become
available.

 The Future Sex Diet is the sort of film my parents
would never in a million years let me watch. I have to
say, I can see their point in this instance, which is
not something I am always able to do. They won't let
me watch most films, and squander their disapproval
on anything they think of as too adult, or violent,
or potentially upsetting in any way. And don't get me

started on their musical intolerance! They won't let me listen to any pop or rock music. I think they honestly believe that all flutes and violins will immediately cease to exist if one of their precious children catches even a note or two of *The X Factor*.

If I ever have children, I'll let them watch and listen to whatever they want—apart from *The Future Sex Diet*, which hopefully will have been roundly forgotten by then. Fairness obliges me to point out that the film did very well when it was aired, far better than most TV movies. It "won its slot," as they apparently say in the world of TV, and slot-winning is the holy grail. It means more people watched it than anything else on television during that same time period.

Back to Ben Lourenco, whom I hope nobody has forgotten. Ben played the heroine's friend who pretended to be her abusive ex-boyfriend. It was for this role that he won Best Supporting Actor. It drew him to the drama world's attention very forcibly, and so naturally he was grateful to Freddii Bausor, without whom he would be no more than a household dimple that everyone recognized but no one knew by name.

At the BAFTAs that night were two fairly eminent bods from a TV company called Factotum Productions, Donna Lodge and Justine Merrison. Donna was the managing director of the company and Justine was the head of development. This meant that, together, they were responsible for coming up with ideas for what programs and films to make, and deciding which actors they would like to be in those ideas.

Donna Lodge took one look at Ben Lourenco and

decided he would be perfect for a drama series they were trying to get off the ground. The development of this drama had hit the rocks somewhat because Donna and Justine couldn't agree about it. (My source was not allowed to tell me much about the project, as it has still not hit our screens and perhaps never will.)

It had started off very high concept, but then Donna had worried that the concept was too high, too big a risk. Would viewers buy into it? Would the BBC, ITV or Sky commission it? Donna was in favor of removing the high concept before "pitching" the drama, which means offering it to channels that might put it on. Justine disagreed. Without the high concept, the show would have no content, she argued. Imagine pitching James Bond as an idea, except, because it's pretty implausible that he's *such* an amazing, death-defying spy, you make him not a spy at all. Instead, he more convincingly wanders around his kitchen, sometimes making toast and sometimes just listening to a spot of news on the radio, but generally being a character full of depth rather than one hampered by a plot.

When Donna Lodge saw Ben Lourenco claim his award at the BAFTAs, she leaned over her champagne glass and said to Justine, "Ben Lourenco would be *perfect*." Silently, Justine thought, "Perfect for what? A lead role in a drama about a man who mooches around?" To make it worse, the setting of the drama and its title remained unchanged from the original idea that Justine had loved, so this show was set in a place that everyone associates with lots of amazing stuff happening, and this made it even worse that nothing amazing was going to happen. The title was suggestive of upheaval, mayhem and redemption, all three of which had been removed from the "treatment"* (*synopsis). Imagine a movie set in the world's most notorious prison, called *The Cells of Horror and Hope*, in which the inmates are quite content and civilized and the guards are suspiciously lenient and humane, and you might begin to perceive the scale of the problem.

Justine Merrison was pessimistic, to put it mildly. But Donna Lodge was her boss, and she couldn't think what to do. Most people who had fallen out with Donna had not subsequently fared well in the TV industry, and Justine suspected this was no coincidence. She didn't want to have to leave her job, and couldn't think of a way to discuss her unhappiness with Donna that wouldn't involve screaming at her to stop being such an imbecile.

Ben Lourenco was the first good idea Donna Lodge had produced for a long time, so Justine said yes, hoping this might be the beginning of Donna coming to her senses. The lead role in the drama-free drama was duly offered to Ben and he accepted it, though he humbly asked if he could have some creative involvement in the idea's evolution. "Of course!" Donna gushed.

Justine was astonished when Ben voiced her concerns, almost word for word. "We need a stronger hook, I think," he said. "I mean, we've got six hours of drama to fill. I think my character's potentially interesting, but something needs to be driving him. I mean, ideally we'd have a strong story of the week and an overarching narrative as well."

"What a fantastic idea, Ben," said Donna, to Justine's astonishment.

Justine cleared her throat and said, "You mean like . . . ," and then she described her and Donna's original idea, the high-concept drama, as if it were entirely new and had only just occurred to her.

"Yesss!" said Ben. "That's *wonderful*. Exactly that sort of thing."

"Well, let's go with that, then," said a radiant Donna. "Justine and I were thinking of something along those lines at first, but we worried it was too high risk. But actually, we should pitch what we're passionate about, not what we think they want, right?"

"Right," said Ben.

"Right," said Justine.

And in a flash, everything was back on track. Justine hated Donna more than ever, but in a way she knew she would enjoy and make a fun hobby out of, not in a seriously problematic, miserable way. The main thing was that the show was back on—the proper show, in its ideal form. Or, rather, the pitch was back on. Who can tell what the channel controllers will say yes to?

As it turned out, the pitch never made it to the inbox of the head honcho of any channel. Why? Because of Freddii Bausor. Or, it might be more accurate to say, because of Freddii Bausor's enemy, the woman who used to be the wife of Fred Bausor, as Freddii was known before her operation. This former spouse, an American historian called Carine Hartwell who had dumped Freddii after her surgery, went to the police and claimed that Fred had frequently battered her and done all kinds of other unsavory things to her during their six-year marriage. Several of her close friends said they had known about the abuse. But just as many other people who had also known the married couple said that it was absolutely untrue. One friend said that Freddii had once tearfully confessed to being violent and unable to help it. Another said Carine Hartwell had announced many times that she was going to break Freddii if it was the last thing she did. Yet another claimed to have heard her verbally draft a plan that involved pretending Freddii was a wife-beater and rapist. In the end, it boiled down to everybody's word against everyone else's.

With all these contradictory accounts buzzing around, the press and the public, who all wanted to be able to bray in a particular direction and had no idea which one to pick, were obliged to look further than what everyone was saying, so they looked at the work of Freddii Bausor and Carine Hartwell. Here is what they found:

Freddii: detective shows featuring grotesque murders and psychopaths who pretend not to have committed them. One TV movie about a woman who believes seven pounds of extra weight renders her unloveable, and who lies about having once had an abusive partner.

Carine: one scholarly tome about Christian missionaries in Malaysia.

Most interested parties decided* (*completely kidded themselves) that the above comparison of works was pretty conclusive. In the television industry, many prominent producers, actors and directors let it be known that they completely believed Carine and would never work with Freddii or partake of her cultural artifacts again. This seemed to be the dominant opinion. Famous stars of screens big and small started to tweet infographics to one another: endless rows of little gray men and then, huddling together for warmth, two small red men in the corner. The gray men were supposed to be all the men accused, and found guilty, of doing unspeakable things to women, and the two red men represented the tiny minority of men who'd been wrongly accused.

Endless heated exchanges took place on the internet about whether it was insulting and transphobic to apply a guilty-and-innocent-men infographic to Freddii, who had never been a man in anything but physique.

Carine Hartwell was informed that there was insufficient evidence for a prosecution of Freddii. This news was greeted with an outpouring of sympathy for her and an even bigger one of hatred for Freddii, who was seen as having gotten away with it, and loathed even more fiercely than she would have been if she'd been found guilty of something—though she would have been heartily loathed in either eventuality. There was so much venom sloshing around that Freddii, being only one person, couldn't soak it all up. It started to drench all those who made comments in chatrooms and on social media along the lines of "But we don't know for sure that Freddii did anything wrong," though the tide receded if the sinners repented with a follow-up like, "Though I personally suspect that she did and want her to die." The most enlightened folk of all expressed a wish to garrote Freddii with piano wire while making sure to chastise those calling her "him," because to do that was insensitive and reeking of cis privilege. ("Cis" is a relatively new word and it means "not trans." You, gentle reader, are probably cis.)

One day, Ben Lourenco could bear it no longer. He tweeted a tweet, which read as follows: "Please stop RT-ing *that* infographic, people. I get it. There are only two little red men. What if Freddii's one of them?"

The floodgates opened, and vitriol poured forth in the form of abusive tweets and savage blog posts. Ben Lourenco replaced Freddii Bausor as Chief Devil Incarnate. This was quite rational: Freddii had only maybe done terrible deeds, whereas Ben Lourenco had unequivocally done two horrendous things: 1) he had tacitly given succor to the violent patriarchy by failing to condemn a possible wife-beater, and 2) he had misgendered Freddii, and, in doing so, shown himself to be a hateful transphobe.

Ben explained that he hadn't meant to imply that Freddii was a man. He was merely using the metaphor of "little red man" to mean "rare and exceptional innocent person," and if his use of little-men symbolism was offensive, then surely all the people RT-ing the infographic were guilty of the very same offense.

The unmollifiable hordes remained unmollified.

A few days into this controversy, Donna Lodge told Justine Merrison that she no longer felt Ben Lourenco was right for the hero's role in their fledgling TV show. Justine was aghast. "He's clearly a misogynist," said Donna. "Why else would he choose to defend Freddii when Freddii might be . . . dubious?"

"But Freddii's a woman," Justine pointed out.

"Well, yes, but . . . not as much as Carine Hartwell is, let's face it," said Donna transmisogynistically. "Don't worry." She smiled. "I'm not going to change my mind again about the central concept. You were right about that."

"You were right to suggest Ben Lourenco," Justine countered. "And you'd be very wrong to boot him out when he's done nothing at all to deserve it."

"Hmm." Donna pretended to consider this. "I just . . . look, we want to get this show commissioned, don't we? Do you think having Ben Lourenco as our leading man is going to improve our chances or stymie them?"

"Do you think Ben has done anything wrong?" Justine asked.

"I know that an awful lot of other people do, and I'm worried about how it'd play with Joe Public," said Donna. "Jo *anne* Public." She tittered at her own joke. "We have to be pragmatic. We don't want to work with someone that half of our industry has taken against, Justine. Really, we don't."

"Actually, I do."

"Tough. Ben's gone. He's off the table."

"Then please may I be excused as well?"

"Pardon?" said Donna.

"From the table." Justine stood up. In her mind, she had already gone. She no longer worked with Donna. From now on, she worked with Ben Lourenco, though the two of them would probably never meet again. She did not work with Ben on any kind of TV project, but on something far more important: remaining rational in the face of frothing-at-the-mouth numbskullery. Be warned, all: this is frustrating work, and it pays badly.

After posting a sequence of tweets sticking up for Ben Lourenco and encouraging his detractors to do rude things to themselves, Justine Merrison walked out of her office and never went back.

Donna Lodge soon replaced her. She replaced Ben Lourenco with another leading man whose tweets were mostly accompanied by the hashtag #istandwithcarine, and she replaced the high concept of the putative drama series with nothing because you don't need a gimmicky concept if you've got multilayered characters you care about, according to Donna.

The show has been "greenlit," and will air sometime next year.

11

M um, this is the yummiest breakfast ever," says Ellen, shoveling another forkful of scrambled eggs into her mouth. Alex eyes her suspiciously, wondering about the identity of this charming visiting diplomat who resembles his daughter.

Light streams in through the window, creating a golden patch effect on the kitchen table.

I haven't told Alex about Ellen and George's agreement—I can't bring myself to call it an engagement. Fourteen-year-olds can't be meaningfully engaged.

"Seriously, Mum, you're the Queen of Egg Scrambling. Utterly delish!"

Is this how Ellen will be from now on? Mimicking superpolite George? My heart aches at the thought. I want her to be a typical teenager. Surely we'll get a few years of "You're so unfair / You're such an embarrassing idiot"? I don't think I can bear the prospect of a charming Ellen-and-George unit jollying me into playing Monopoly in the drawing room for the rest of my life.

Maybe I should provoke a row by demanding to read every word of Ellen's story about the Ingreys. Until I saw her this morning,

I intended to raise it with her first thing, but, coward that I am, I'm loath to do or say anything that might dim her radiant smile.

Having read George's frighteningly accurate account of why I gave up my career in television and escaped to Devon, I have a theory. I believe that he and Ellen agreed to swap. Each gave the other a true story to tell. George wrote the one that belonged to me, and Ellen wrote about his mother's childhood. It must have felt like a way of getting to know each other better—strengthening the bond.

Lisette Ingrey—mother of Urban, mother-in-law of Ellen—is Anne Donbavand. When the private detective gets in touch to tell me what he's found out, I'll be amazed if it isn't that. The names might be different—I still don't believe in three sisters called Lisette, Allisande and Perrine—but the substance is true. Anne Donbavand had a younger sister who murdered a boy and then was murdered herself.

But if only the names have been changed . . .

I remember my conversation with Ellen, after I read those first three pages. I asked her why she'd used our house as a setting, and she said, "Are you thinking Perrine Ingrey's going to get murdered in my bedroom? She isn't. Don't worry. She doesn't get killed in the house or the grounds."

Malachy Dodd does. He falls from a great height and smashes his head open on the terrace by the fountain.

What if that really happened—here, at Speedwell House? No family called Ingrey has ever lived here, but others have. One of them could have been Anne Donbavand's family. Must have been. Why else would Ellen make this house the setting for her macabre story?

If Malachy Dodd fell to his death from Ellen's window, might that explain the strange feeling I had in her room? Can tragic events leave an imprint on a place that's still perceptible years later? What does that say about the much stronger strange feeling I had when I first saw Olwen Brawn's house? Olwen who is coming to visit later today . . .

I don't want to live at Speedwell House anymore. I don't want Ellen sleeping in Perrine Ingrey's old bedroom, or whatever the murderous murdered child's real name was. It's all I can do to keep my mouth shut so that I don't blurt this out.

"You all right, darling?" Alex asks me.

I nod. Now would be too soon to say anything, even to ask more forcefully to see Ellen's story. I need to know, first, that I'm not wrong. The detective I hired should be able to find out if the family living at Speedwell House during the 1980s had three daughters, one of whom was murdered.

A well-known local secret. Don't tell the stupid Londoners—let them buy the doomed house so we can laugh at them behind their backs.

The doorbell rings. And carries on ringing. There's an index finger pressing hard. It stops after nearly five seconds of solid noise. Figgy, who was asleep under the kitchen table, starts to bark ferociously and scoots out of the room toward the front door.

"Early-morning harassment," grumbles Alex as I get up to go and see who it is.

I have to find Figgy's leash and attach it to his collar before I can open the door, or else he'll be off and we might never see him again. This takes several minutes, during which time there are two more short rings of the bell.

I find a policeman in uniform on the doorstep. He's middle-aged with a scrawny neck, stick-thin legs and a fat middle section in between. His face is red with dozens of small purple flecks from broken veins. It reminds me of a terrine.

"Well, it was a toss-up which was going to happen first," he says.

"Me calling on you or you calling on me. I'm glad I beat you to it—saves you the bother, too. I'm here now." His Devon accent is stronger than I would have believed possible. He bends down and pats Figgy on the head repeatedly. "Hello, little fella!"

Figgy lowers his head and slides out from under—a sensible reaction to being treated like a drum by an irritating stranger.

"I don't know what you're talking about," I say. "If DC Luce has delegated me to you, please tell him I don't find that acceptable."

"Euan Luce?"

"Yes. Has he sent you? About the phone calls I've been getting?"

"Ah, you know Euan then, do you?" He seems to think this is a pleasing coincidence. Fancy that: me, a person, knowing DC Luce, another person who probably lives less than a mile away—who'd have thought it?

"What phone calls are you talking about, Mrs. . . . ? Mrs. . . . ?" He turns his head and offers me his ear, as if I'm trying to tell him my name and he can't hear me.

"If you're not here about phone calls, why are you here?"

"About the signs." He nods as if he's said something profound and makes the shape of a square with his fingers.

"What signs?"

" 'What signs?' says she! You ought to know, since you've got one yourself. I expect you've not been out yet this morning, with it being so early. If you'd care to step outside, you'll see what I'm talking about."

"I've got nothing on my feet. Can you please explain what you mean?"

"You don't have to come far. It's right here." He points at the wall in front of him, next to the front door. He must mean the stone plaque with the house's name on it. Does he really want me to come outside and inspect it? I know very well what my own home is called.

"Wait a second," I say. None of my shoes are near the door. My flip-flops are nowhere in sight, even though I left them right here last night. Moving necessary footwear to untraceable locations is Figgy's favorite hobby. There's a pair of green boots—Alex's. I pull them on and step out into perfection that even the policeman's presence can't spoil: the dew-soaked grass sloping down to the ranks of leafy evergreen trees; the gorgeous winter sun; the sound of oars brushing water aside; the smell of the sea.

For a moment I forget what I'm doing out here with the policeman. Then I remember and turn and look at the house sign. Over the words "Speedwell House," someone has stuck a colored, shiny plastic . . . thing. I don't know what to call it. A sticker, I suppose: big and square. The background's purple and the writing on it is turquoise. It says "*Tide Glider*," and completely covers the house's name.

"You'll want to peel that off," says the policeman. "Yours is the only one this side of the river, far as we can work out, but you should see 'em over Dartmouth side. Houses on the boats, boats on the houses. Imagine if your doggy got lost and someone read his little silver medallion to see where to bring him back to—you don't want them delivering him to a dinghy over by the jetty, do you? I'd be peeling right now, if I were you."

This man might have many talents, but using words to convey meaning is not one of them. "Can you please tell me what you're talking about in a way that makes sense?" I say. "*Tide Glider* is . . . the name of a boat, I assume?"

"Oh yes. Last night, while you and I were getting our shut-eye, someone was awake playing silly beggars. They must have planned it, cuz I've seen nearly thirty of those big plastic sticker things so far, and that'd take time to do. Seen 'em on houses and seen 'em on boats, I have. Swapped! House names on all the boats attached to the jetty this morning, with the signs covering up the boats' proper names—including your one, *Tide Glider*."

"I don't have a boat called *Tide Glider*," I tell him through gritted teeth. "I've never owned one, sailed in one or heard of one. Never heard the name until I read it just now."

"I wasn't saying you did." He widens his eyes at me. "I'm saying there's boats all over the show with their names covered up with house name stickers: The Old Forge, Lilac Cottage, The Laburnums, what have you. Speedwell House is on one of them, which is why I come here. I wondered, see. Meanwhile, there's a fair few houses— the ones whose names I've mentioned, and others besides—with boat names stuck over their signs: *Oh, Buoy!*, *Watersprite*, *Wave Weaver*. Local paper's doing a piece about it. I think the photographer's over at the jetty now, snapping the boats. If you want to pose next to your new sign, give the paper a bell."

I claw at the "*Tide Glider*" sticker with my fingernails but can't prize loose a single corner. The policeman tries to help and ends up bashing his fingers into mine. I push his hands away and he shrugs as if to say, "No pleasing some people."

"Let me get this right," I say. "You're honestly telling me that during the night, someone has gone out with a load of these big industrial-adhesive stickers and put boat names on houses and house names on boats? And all these names belong to actual houses and boats—they're not made up?"

"Oh, no, they're all real. And yes, you've hit it on the nail. That's what's happened. As to why, I couldn't tell you. There's always a practical joker out to commit mischief, isn't there? I take it you heard nothing during the night—because someone was stood right here at some point, weren't they? Sticking it on."

Her name arrives in my head as the obvious answer: Anne Don-bavand. Outside my house at two in the morning, her nasty fingers smoothing down the sticker . . .

"It might be more than a joke," I tell the policeman.

"How so?"

"Someone wants to create confusion about which house is which and which boat is which."

"Now why would they want that?"

Because they're unbalanced.

Isn't there a Bible story about houses being marked for some kind of attack? I shiver.

"You want to build a higher wall and install some security cameras, I reckon," says the policeman, looking up at the top of the house. "As it stands, anyone could hop over into your garden and lurk here in the small hours, plotting mischief. I've never understood it myself: this yen rich folk have for living miles from other people, surrounded by all their acres, but no one to help them if they need it in a hurry. I wouldn't feel safe living out here—no offense. I wouldn't feel safe at all."

"This is an almost indecent helping of beauty!" says Olwen later the same day. "What you need up here's a hammock, or a big comfy armchair—right here, where I'm standing. Figgy, you are one extremely lucky pup. Oddly, I always knew that about you."

Her enthusiasm goes some way toward dissolving the knot of misgiving planted in my mind by the terrine-faced policeman, with whom I'm still angry. What kind of person says, "I wouldn't feel safe living where you live," before scuttling back to his own place of safety?

Olwen says, "If you were a social climber, you could aggravate people at parties by saying, 'Not only do I own a mansion—I can see the top of it from my own land. I can look at my own roof tiles anytime I fancy!'"

"Yes, well . . . anything rather than look at my own mortgage statements," I say, not wanting her to think I'm a spoilt rich person.

She's right, though: from the highest point in our garden, we can look down on our house from above. I knew this before today, but it's only now, as Olwen remarks on it, that I'm struck by how unusual it is.

"So you reckon this Ingrey family lived here, then?" she asks. I've told her the full story, or at least the fullest version currently available.

"Possibly. Though if they did, they weren't called Ingrey."

"It's odd that the surname doesn't change from one generation to the next. On the family tree, I mean. If Lisette Ingrey married this Grevel chap, why are she and her kids all called Ingrey?"

I stop walking. "Of course. How did I miss that? I wonder if the Donbavands did the same thing—chose Anne's maiden name as the family surname, not Stephen's. If they did, that's yet more circumstantial evidence the two families—Donbavands and Ingreys—are one and the same. I should call Ops and ask him to find out."

"Ops?" asks Olwen.

"Yeah, the detective I've hired. That's not his name, but his email address starts with 'Ops.' Short for 'Operations,' I guess."

"I see. Justine, I don't mean to be nitpicky, but I'm not sure 'yet more circumstantial evidence' is accurate. Is there *any*, really? I mean, absolutely, yes, Ellen's story *might* be about George's mother and her family, and the woman calling you Sandie on the phone *might* be Anne the professor whose sister *might* be Allisande Ingrey in the story, but isn't it equally likely that none of those things is true?"

This isn't what I want to hear.

"Humans are pattern-seeking animals," says Olwen. "Your theory neatly covers everything strange that's happening and ties it all together, but there are other less satisfying possibilities that are as likely to be true."

"Such as?"

"Your malicious caller is unconnected to George Donbavand. She has mental health problems that include confusion: hence, she knows you're Justine, but when she takes too many drugs, or too few, she gets your name mixed up with the name of her yellow Labrador, Sandie. Do you have any idea how many yellow Labs are given that name? Drives me crackers!"

"Yeah, why don't people call their dogs proper names, like Stood a Lonely Cattle Shed," I say, ducking out of the way when Olwen aims a pretend blow at me.

"George's mum's fear and paranoia might have nothing to do with the phone calls you're getting," she goes on. "It's also possible that George decided to write a story about you without giving his mother's story to Ellen to write."

"Yes, and it's possible that Ellen's *so obsessed* with this story, like she's never been about any homework ever before, for some other reason that's not linked to George, but now I think we're drifting into the realms of implausibility."

"Not implausibility. Patternlessness. The two are different."

"Anne Donbavand took George out of school because of his friendship with Ellen. At almost exactly the same time, these threatening calls started. If I'm seeing a pattern, it's because there is one. It's a fact, not an interpretation."

Olwen gives me an "I don't know how to break this to you" look. "Not to make excuses for the woman, but if George got overexcited and shared his future marriage plans with his family before Ellen shared them with you . . . well, it wouldn't justify hauling him out of school, but I can see how a parent might overreact in the face of something so unusual."

"That's a point." And something else I hadn't thought of.

"While I'm suggesting things, I've got more if you're interested," Olwen says.

"Suggest away," I say.

"You've signed over a stack of money to this Ops chap, and let's hope he can help, but in the meantime, you're not doing the thing that would be most useful."

"What's that?"

"Getting through to Ellen." Olwen holds up a hand. I half-expect her to order me to sit. "Let's say you're right and her story is George's family history—a traumatic history. It's no surprise she's resisting your attempts to invade what she sees as her and George's private world. And yet it seems you do need to read what she's written."

"She's writing it for school. If her teacher's going to read it, why can't I?"

"Justine, I'm not the one you need to convince. Children are oversensitive about their parents muscling in. Puppies are the same with their owners, at roughly the same point in their maturing. Between eight and twelve months—the teenage phase—they assert their independence in all kinds of inconvenient ways. Things they did before to please you, suddenly they won't do. It passes of course, but . . ."

"Ellen isn't a Bedlington terrier, Olwen."

"I realize that. Still, though . . . I'd approach her as an equal on this, not parent to child. Is there anything you've kept from her since all these funny goings-on started?"

I want to say no, but it wouldn't be the truth. There are things I could share with Ellen that I haven't wanted to: the reason I see as little as I can of Dad and Julia; why I hate family trees.

"Whatever's in your mind now, tell Ellen about it—all of it. Trust her with it. Once you've taken that leap, that's when you ask her to level with you about the story she's writing and to let you read it. Don't act as if it's your God-given parental right to know. Make her feel as if she has a choice."

"Okay, Wise Dog Woman," I say in a mock-resentful tone. "I'm going to put your advice to the test. If it works, the Crufts gold medal for family diplomacy is yours."

The word "medal" snags in my mind as I say it. There's something wrong about it. Where have I heard it recently? *Come on, brain, come on . . .*

"The policeman," I mutter.

"Which one?" Olwen asks. "Haven't you had three?"

"This morning. He mentioned Figgy's medallion. 'Little silver medallion,' he said. I didn't take it in at the time."

"This one? Keep still for a minute, Figgy. Here, on his collar." Olwen bends down to inspect it more closely. "Hmph. Wrong address. Did your husband get this made? Women don't generally forget where they live."

"No. Alex wouldn't have a tag made for Figgy and put it on his collar without showing me and Ellen. No way." I turn in a slow circle, fixing my eyes on one cluster of trees after another. Figgy's been in and out of every one since I brought him home. Many are dense enough to conceal a person.

"Well, some fool's put the wrong address on this tag," says Olwen. She moves out of the way so that I can take her place. I cover my mouth with my hand as I read the engraved words. On one side it says, "Little Dog." On the other: "Want to keep me safe? Then take me home: 19 Lassington Road, Muswell Hill, London, N10."

"It's our old address," I say.

"I suppose it's an easy mistake to make if you're on autopilot," Olwen says doubtfully.

"It's not a mistake." I pick Figgy up and wrap my arms around him. He's shaking, poor thing. Then I realize he only is because I am. "It's a threat," I tell Olwen. "From Lisette Ingrey, aka Anne Donbavand."

It's five A.M., I've failed to fall asleep, and what I must do now is obvious: email "prefect parent" Stephen Donbavand again, except more deviously this time.

When I wrote to him before, I was honest about who I was and what I wanted. Was he tempted? Did Anne forbid it? Is he in agreement with her, or is his compliance based purely on fear?

I need to find out more about him. Hopefully he'll agree to meet me—or rather, the person I'm going to pretend to be in my email.

"Dear Stephen Donbavand," I type, with the end of Figgy's leash clamped between my knees. Once she understood about the writing on the medallion and what it meant, Olwen pleaded with me to let her take Figgy back with her—only temporarily—for his own safety.

I should have agreed. It made sense, but I couldn't do it. The idea was unbearable. I promised Olwen that Alex and I would keep Figgy with us and on the leash whenever we were outside. I've taken it even further: here I am in the library with him on the leash in case . . .

Don't even think it.

When I went up to say goodnight to Ellen earlier, I pulled open the small mint-green door beside her bed, praying I wouldn't see feet walking quickly away. "What are you looking for?" she asked me.

"I thought I heard Dad there," I lied.

I was looking for Lisette Ingrey.

The silver tag with "Little Dog" on one side and Anne Donbavand's threat on the other is in my pocket, ready to be dropped onto the desk of DC Euan Luce tomorrow.

Concentrate, Justine.

I delete "Dear Stephen Donbavand" and type "Dear Dr. Donbavand" instead.

"I know you must be extremely busy, but I wonder if you might spare ten minutes or so, at your earliest convenience, to discuss with me the possibility of becoming my PhD supervisor. I'm thinking of applying to do my doctorate at Exeter, and my chief research interest is similar to research you have done that I've found interesting. I'm leaning toward working on microeconomic analysis of competition in online markets, but would love to discuss this further. Are you by any chance able to meet me in the next few days? As soon as possible would be great for me. I'm staying near Exeter at the moment, with relatives. I look forward to hearing from you. Very best wishes, Julia Vowles." I use my stepmother's first name and the surname of a detective from a TV drama I put a lot of effort into that never got commissioned.

I press "send." Then, still not ready to go to sleep, I Google all the names I've already Googled more than once. Unsurprisingly, all the same results come up. I swear under my breath. I'm not being imaginative enough, that's my problem. I should try something different.

I try "Ingrey anagrams," "Perrine Ingrey anagram," "Anne Donbavand formerly called." Nothing. "Little dog" yields plenty, but none of it's relevant.

On a whim, I type "*Tide Glider*" into the search box and press "return." I click on the first result that comes up because it contains the word "Totnes," though I'm not holding out much hope. When the page opens, I suck in a breath, not daring to let my thoughts flow until I've enlarged the picture.

Oh my God. The resemblance is unmistakable. I clutch the side of the desk as Figgy's leash slips from between my knees. He stays where he is, and looks up at me in a point-proving way: "See? I can be trusted to stay here of my own volition."

I'm looking at a 2011 article from the *Totnes Times* about a local artist, Sarah Parsons, whose painting *Anne, Tide Glider* won a local art prize. It's a portrait of a woman of about my age. The text beneath the photograph says that Sarah cares more about this painting than any of her others because of its sentimental value; she is delighted and moved that it has won this prestigious prize. The woman depicted is her estranged sister Anne. There's no explanation of the "*Tide Glider*" part.

Those features: the wide forehead, large blue-gray eyes with irises like hollow cylinders . . . The woman in the portrait has George Donbavand's face.

Get out of my house, bitch. I slam the computer's lid shut to banish her, and find myself staring at the library's wood-paneled wall. She could be behind one of the panels. Hiding.

I have to get out, get some fresh air.

I pick up Figgy's leash and give it a gentle tug toward the door. "Come on, Figgs. You must need the loo. Well, not the loo—the grass." He seems to agree and runs ahead to the front door.

I unlock and open it as quietly as I can and step out into the cold air that smells of deepest night. "Isn't this—" I start to say to Figgy, but straightaway I'm falling, leaving my words stranded up in the air as I hit hard blackness.

Chapter 10

You Know What? You Know What?
You Know What? I Don't Care

The following morning, the gates to the grounds of Speedwell House were opened and left standing open for the first time in absolutely ages. Guests were expected: the police, the Dodds, the Sennitt-Sasses, the Carelesses, Jack Kirbyshire's wife and children, and David Butcher's parents.

Bascom and Sorrel Ingrey had laid out a big breakfast spread: toast and jam, steamed prawn dumplings, fresh fruit, Parma ham and thin slices of Dutch cheese. To drink there was tea, coffee or freshly squeezed orange juice. Bascom was exhausted. He had been up all night squeezing oranges. (Sorrel had been asleep. One of her principles that she never broke was that she had to get nine hours' sleep every single night.)

The feast laid out in the kitchen seemed unnecessarily elaborate to Lisette and Allisande. "Why is this happening?" they kept saying. "Today isn't someone's birthday party. It's a horrible day. The food is too nice."

"We'll all need to eat," Sorrel explained. "You can't invite people to your house so early in the morning and not provide breakfast, and it might as well be a nice breakfast. Now go and sit in the drawing room, girls—you're getting in the way."

Lisette and Allisande went to the drawing room and Bascom brought them each a plate of breakfast while Sorrel clattered and swore in the kitchen. She hated the stress and the bother of entertaining.

Each of the guests grabbed a drink and a plate of food and congregated in the drawing room. (On the way to the drawing room, however, there was much to-ing and fro-ing in the wide Georgian hallway, much wandering into other rooms to have a peek at the famously locked-up house that was eagerly wondered about by all those who lived near it. For at least half an hour, people bumbled about and explored and roamed freely. I'm telling you this because it will become important later on.)

Eventually, everyone had quenched their nosiness for the time being, and they all ended up in the drawing room (apart from the police officers who had come to remove David Butcher's body from the library—they had gone). Only the police and the Ingreys knew what was about to happen. It was clear from the faces of the Dodds and the Kirbyshires that they were puzzled to be at Speedwell House, and wondered what they were doing there.

Once everyone had finished eating and boosted their energy levels for the ordeal ahead, Sorrel stood up and spoke to the crowd. "Thank you all so much for coming. These gentlemen here are policemen. In a moment, they will go upstairs and arrest my youngest daughter, Perrine, for three murders: the murders of Malachy Dodd, Jack Kirbyshire and David Butcher."

Gasps and exclamations exploded all over the room. "About time!" said Mrs. Dodd venomously.

Sorrel went on: "We, Perrine's family, have always suspected that she was a killer, though she vigorously denied it. But a mother knows when there's something askew in the mind or heart of her child, and I have always known this about Perrine, even before she murdered Malachy Dodd. When he died, and when Jack Kirbyshire died, I knew Perrine was guilty, but I couldn't prove it. It was only when I saw her stab David Butcher that I finally had proof."

"We all witnessed this stabbing," Bascom added. "Me, Lisette and Allisande too."

"We could have called the police straightaway," said Sorrel, "but we wanted you all to be here. We're aware that you see us as Perrine's protectors, and, yes, we have been. We've imprisoned ourselves in order to keep her safe. It's a natural impulse, to want to protect one's family."

"Bit late for some of us to do that, isn't it?" muttered Mrs. Dodd bitterly.

"Will you pipe down?" David Butcher's mother turned on her, surprising everybody. "I think we've heard just about enough from you. Do you *know* who my son was?"

"Leave it, dear," muttered her husband.

But Mrs. Butcher did not wish to leave it. "He was a former organ scholar of King's College, Cambridge!" she blurted out. "He had a glowing future ahead of him!"

"And so what?" said Mrs. Dodd, her voice trembling. "Are you saying that means my Malachy's life doesn't matter?"

"Let's not do this," said Jack Kirbyshire's widow. "Please. Let's not play hierarchical victim games."

When someone says a word like "hierarchical" in an everyday setting, it often has the result that everyone immediately assumes that person must be right about everything, because they know a long word. This was what happened here. The Dodds and the Butchers piped down.

"What's going to happen next?" asked Henrietta Sennitt-Sasse, rubbing her hands together in excitement. "Is Perrine going to be arrested while we watch? Will she go to prison forever?"

"*Pas devant les enfants!*" cried out Henrietta's mother, but to no avail.

You might think from Henrietta's remark that she was mean and relished the idea of long, endless prison sentences for others, but you'd be wrong. Henrietta had simply been starved of grown-up gossip all her life. This was the first interesting adult conversation she had ever been party to.

One of the policemen stood up and said, "It is overwhelmingly probable that Perrine will receive a custodial sentence, yes. But it's unlikely she'll go to prison forever. Remember, she's still only a child, and the law likes to try to rehabilitate such young criminals wherever possible."

"May I ask a question?" Jack Kirbyshire's widow rose to her feet. "Perrine seems to have committed three murders, but only one was witnessed. Does that mean she might be convicted of only one murder, the murder of David Butcher?"

Mrs. Dodd leapt to her feet again. "That can't happen! It would be an outrage! I want her to do time for Malachy, not just for some other murder!"

"There's a good chance she will, if the information I've been given by Mrs. Ingrey here is correct," said the policeman. "If there is no feasible way that Malachy could have fallen out of the window by accident—"

"There isn't," Sorrel Ingrey chipped in. "I've said this since the day he died. Malachy's center of gravity was too low for him to have fallen out of that window. It just wouldn't happen."

"And it didn't happen!" snapped Mrs. Dodd, red in the face.

Mrs. Butcher muttered something under her breath.

"What was that, you snide cow?" Mrs. Dodd demanded.

Mrs. Butcher shook her head. She had decided against saying what was on her mind, but then she couldn't resist. "Do you have any shame at all?" she asked Mrs. Dodd. "Are you even a *tiny* bit embarrassed about how much airtime you're taking up today?"

Mrs. Dodd replied with a sequence of obscenities so shocking that most people in the room turned red, and Mrs. Sennitt-Sasse screeched, *"PAS DEVANT LES EN-FANTS!"* louder than ever before.

"Ladies, please," said the policeman. "These arguments are not helping anything. To answer your question, Mrs. Kirbyshire"—he paused to smile in a noticeable

way, to reward Mrs. Kirbyshire for being better behaved than Mrs. Dodd and Mrs. Butcher—"I'm very sorry
to tell you this, but if we have difficulty making any
of these murder accusations stick, it's most likely to
be your Jack's murder that Perrine gets away with. He
was standing on some scaffolding when she pushed him
off, and so it really is possible that he could have
fallen—even though we all know he didn't."

"As long as that evil little monster serves some
years specifically for Malachy," said Mrs. Dodd determinedly. "Special Malachy years. Lots of them."

Lisette Ingrey at this point rose to her feet and
cleared her throat.

"Wait," she said. "This isn't right. We're all talking as if we know she's guilty."

"But you do!" said the policeman with a puzzled frown.
"You saw her stab David Butcher to death, didn't you?"

Lisette realized at that moment that she should not
have agreed to lie. Her parents and Allisande were all
glaring at her, scared that she was going to say, "Actually, no, I didn't see my sister stab David Butcher.
I just made that up."

She couldn't do that to them. "Yes," she said. "Yes,
I witnessed the stabbing of David Butcher by my sister
Perrine. I know, for certain, that she is guilty of
that one murder. About the deaths of Malachy Dodd
and Jack Kirbyshire, however, I can't be certain. All
I can say is that I strongly suspect Perrine killed
them both. That's all anyone can say." She turned to
the policeman. "You can't claim to know that Jack

Kirbyshire didn't fall," she said. "You're supposed to be an impartial officer of the law."

The policeman had turned bright red. "You're right," he said. "I suppose it's just so rare that someone's entire family tells me they're a killer—I assumed it must be true."

"It is true," said Sorrel.

"Even if it is, *he* shouldn't say so!" Lisette protested. "His standards of evidence should be higher. Perrine deserves a fair trial, however evil we might think she is. We might be wrong!"

"You are right, miss," said the policeman. "And if everyone has finished with the breakfast buffet, I will now go upstairs and arrest young Perrine, so that we can proceed as quickly as possible to that fair trial that we all agree she should have."

As he left the room with Bascom and Sorrel Ingrey following behind him, Mrs. Dodd called out, "I don't agree she deserves a fair trial! I think she should be hung, drawn and quartered in front of a large audience."

"It's 'hanged,' you illiterate fool!" said Mrs. Butcher, and Mrs. Dodd retaliated with an obscenity-strewn character assassination of Mrs. Butcher. Mrs. Butcher then did something that surprised everyone. She walked over to where Mrs. Dodd was sitting, put her face right in front of Mrs. Dodd's and chanted defiantly, "You know what? You know what? You know what? I don't care." (The rhythm was similar to when Eminem raps, "My name is . . . my name is . . . my name is . . . Slim Shady.")

All the aggression and swearing sent Mrs. Sennitt-Sasse over the edge. She started to chant frantically, "*Pas devant, pas devant, pas devant . . .*" as if she too were a white rapper. There was such a commotion going on that at first no one noticed when Sorrel, white-faced and shaking, reappeared in the drawing room. Bascom and the policeman followed close behind her.

"Mum?" said Allisande, rushing to her mother's side. "What's wrong?"

"It's Perrine," stammered Sorrel. "She's . . . she's not there! She isn't in her room. She's missing."

12

So, Mr. Colley, to be sure I've got this right: you were woken by the sound of your dog barking excessively, and you judged the barking to be coming from outside. You went to investigate, and found that a large hole had been dug in the lawn immediately in front of your house, and that your wife had fallen into it."

"That's right," says Alex.

Every morning has to start with a policeman. That's the new law. Today it's DC Euan Luce again, standing in the corner of the drawing room, holding his notebook at a forty-five-degree angle as if his ambition is to be a human lectern.

Alex and Ellen got dressed, knowing he was coming. I'm still in pajamas, robe and flip-flops, in accordance with my no-proper-clothes-before-lunchtime rule.

I take a few deep breaths to quell the accelerating tide of rage that's coursing through me. Luce has said "large hole" several times and not "grave," which is what I told him I'd fallen into.

"And you didn't see anyone?" he asks Alex. "You're sure?"

"No, but it was dark and I didn't look. My only concern was

pulling Justine out of that . . . pit, and calming Figgy down. He was going bananas."

"I slept through it," says Ellen.

"It isn't a pit or a hole," I say. "It's a grave. She promised me three, remember? This is the first."

"Not necessarily," says Luce. "The . . . recess you fell into isn't coffin-shaped."

It's like being hit in the face with a sock full of stupidity.

"Are you serious? Have you never attended a funeral?"

"Several."

"A burial?"

Luce's face stiffens.

"No? Then take it from me, because I have. There's only one coffin-shaped thing at a burial, and that's the fucking coffin."

"Justine," Alex murmurs.

"I'm sure DC Luce has heard worse, Alex. I'll swear if I want to—and everyone else can try not to make me want to. How about that? A game for all the family!"

"All right, point about shape of graves taken," says Luce.

"What's happening on the call-tracing front?" I ask him.

"It's proved more difficult than we'd anticipated. Whoever's behind the telephone harassment has taken steps to cover their tracks. Still, it's not all disappointing news. The last call, you think, was the one to the landline that your husband answered, correct? And the caller ended it without speaking?"

"Right," says Alex.

"That's good, then. That's a move in the right direction, from verbal antagonism and direct threats to silence, from longer calls to a shorter one. Let's hope hearing your voice will have put this woman off, Mr. Colley."

I can't believe what I'm hearing. Why the hell is Alex nodding along?

"Wait," I say. "The woman—and let's stop being coy and call her by her name: Anne Donbavand—has not been *put off.* That's why she came around in the middle of the night and *dug a grave* in my garden! Does that sound like the action of a deterred person to you?"

"I think DC Luce means that it's possible the digger was someone else," says Alex. "In which case, the caller might have been scared away by getting me instead of you, at least for the time being."

"For God's sake, do you honestly think two separate people are—"

"Ms. Merrison, did you say Anne Donbavand?" Luce interrupts.

"Yes. Don't tell me you know her."

"Wife of Steve Donbavand?"

I sigh. "Yes."

"I know Steve very well. We're part of a group that organizes charity fun runs every so often to raise money for good causes. I doubt very much indeed that his wife—who's a university professor—has ever vandalized anyone else's property or made threatening phone calls. Steve's one of the most likeable men I've ever met."

"Of course he is." I roll my eyes. "Every monster needs a weak, likeable sidekick to collude with them in their tyranny."

"Please put the idea of this caller being Anne Donbavand out of your mind," says DC Luce firmly. "Take it from me: it isn't her."

"Why? Because you're mates with her husband? Does she speak in the way I described to you last time? Almost a lisp, but not quite?"

"I've exchanged no more than a couple of brief hellos with her, so I couldn't tell you. It's more likely the caller is someone you know, holding a grudge—"

"Except I've told you she isn't—remember?"

Luce looks blankly at me.

"I understand why you find it hard to believe," I say. "You've watched the same movies I have, where a threatening figure from someone's past rings up and says, 'It's me.' The caller always knows a guilty secret about the heroine, don't they? It doesn't make for a good story to have the heroine say cheerfully, 'Sorry, I've no idea who you are. Bye!'"

I take a deep breath. "I don't know my anonymous caller, but I think I know her name: Professor Anne Donbavand. No, I'm not one hundred percent sure. You think I'm wrong, so how about a bet?" I suggest. "Five grand."

"Justine, for Christ's sake." Alex covers his face with his hands.

"Shut up, Dad," says Ellen. "Five grand's too much, though. A grand."

DC Luce glances at his watch. "We need to move this dialogue on," he says. "I have to be somewhere else ten minutes ago."

"Oh, sorry to keep you," I say. "Next time I'll try to fall into an unmarked grave when you've got more free time."

"Are you going to investigate what happened here last night?" Alex asks him. "I mean, grave or not, someone trespassed on our property last night and spent what must have been several hours digging up our lawn."

"I have to be honest with you, Mr. Colley. We'll look into it, of course, but at that time of night, dark, no one around—we'll be lucky if we find anything."

"Improve your odds by looking in the Donbavands' house. There's probably a muddy shovel on the kitchen table. Not that you'd be swayed by that. She's a professor, so even with a muddy shovel, she *must* be innocent!"

"Your attitude doesn't help," says DC Luce.

"It helps me."

"If you're worried, go and stay with a friend for a while, but in my opinion the risk to you isn't as great as you imagine it to be."

"And Figgy's silver tag? What about that?" I snap. "Someone had that made who wasn't us. That person attached it to his collar. Is that another example of the anonymous caller being put off?"

"As I've just said: Why not go away for a while?"

"And then what? When could we come back?"

If we leave, the harassment will stop, and the police will stop investigating it, assuming they ever started. However long we waited before coming back, the malicious campaign would start again as soon as we crossed the threshold of Speedwell House.

No. No way am I going to let anyone drive me out of my home.

"Are you going to question Anne and Stephen Donbavand?" I ask Luce. "Will you carry on trying to trace the calls?" I make sure not to look at him as I speak. I want him to know I've given up on him, that I'm asking only to highlight his inadequacy.

"Yes to the latter. If you really want me to talk to Steve and his wife, I will, but—"

"I do. Tell them I'm not prepared to put up with their antics indefinitely. I'm going to fight back, and they won't like any of the things I do."

"I'm going to pretend you didn't say that." Luce frowns. "Making threats is inadvisable, and that sounded like a threat."

"Did it? Good," I say. "Your job is to make sure the Donbavands believe I really mean it."

Ops, who has no idea that this is how I and my family refer to him, calls me on my mobile at noon. "Justine? That you? I can hardly hear you."

"Yes, it's me."

"Shall I call back when you're somewhere less noisy?"

"No, please . . ." I can't say *Please talk to me now.* It would sound too desperate. "Wait, I'll cross the road and get away from the beach noise."

I'm in Torquay with Figgy, on the promenade. I did some internet research and found a sensible-sounding website that said nothing bad would happen to a puppy taken for a walk before its second set of vaccinations as long as it didn't come into direct contact with other dogs.

I decided to believe it. I needed—need—to be in a crowded, busy place, not hidden from the rest of the world by a screen of trees so that no one would see if something happened to me. And Figgy's safer here than at home.

Alex and Ellen have gone to the cinema. They also didn't want to stay at Speedwell House, staring out of the window at the grave in the lawn.

We can't go on like this. Can't get into bed every night wondering if we'll wake up to find a second grave in our garden, then a third. Ops has no idea how much I need his help. *Please, please, let him give me something I can use.*

"Can you hear me better now?" I ask, once I'm across the street and tucked into a shop doorway.

"Yeah, a bit. I'm afraid I'm going to be awkward."

"How?"

"I'm not going to tell you what you're expecting to hear."

"I'm not sure what I'm expecting." I close my eyes and cover my free ear with my hand. I don't want to be distracted by the hundreds of faces and voices. Is Torquay always this busy? It's like central London, except here people look annoying in a completely different way.

If Ops has found something out that helps me—really helps—I'll ignore the reply I had from Stephen Donbavand this morning saying he'd be happy to meet my economics-expert alter ego. I won't go and meet him under false pretenses.

"All right, first off the bat," Ops launches in. "No Bascom and Sorrel Ingrey, or their kids or grandkids. All those names you gave me, the whole family—not a trace of them. So unless they've successfully erased all evidence of their existence—unlikely if they aren't in witness protection . . . and even when the police are involved in identity concealment—there are still trails you can follow, generally, if you know where to look. I've been in this business thirty years, and if you want my honest opinion? You're looking for a family that doesn't exist. Didn't you say you found these Ingreys in a story? I think they're fictional."

Or they're real but you didn't find them because Ellen changed their names to disguise a true story as invention.

"On to the Donbavands," says Ops. "They do exist, you'll be glad to hear. Stephen Donbavand, born 1968 in Edinburgh. Only child. Father a chemist, mother a dance teacher—"

"Wait. What was his name?"

"Whose name?"

"Stephen Donbavand. What was he called when he was born?"

"Unsurprisingly, he was called Stephen Donbavand."

"No, it is suprising." My heart pounds as I try to figure out what it means. Has Ops forgotten what I told him? "Remember, Lesley Griffiths, the head teacher of my daughter's school, said that the Donbavands had changed their names?"

"Because someone was after them, right? Based on what I've got in front of me, I'd dispute that. There's nothing to suggest either Stephen or his wife Anne did anything that would have generated that level of ill-will, or that they took on new IDs. Both their lives are well documented all the way, and there's no controversy in either. He had an ordinary upbringing in Edinburgh, went to Durham Uni, PhD at Leeds where he later got his first job."

Ops swallows the yawn that crept into his voice toward the end of his last sentence. Finding out the truth about people must get dull after three decades. "He left Leeds after four years for the Economics Department at Exeter, where he is now. His wife was born in Totnes. Maiden name Anne Offord—that's O-F-F-O-R-D. One sister: Sarah. Parents Martin and Denise. They're still in Totnes, got a kitchen design business they run together. He does the building and fitting, she does the design and accounting. Anne was a bright spark at school, went to St John's, Oxford, then to Pembroke, Cambridge, for her postgrad. First job in Leeds, where she met her husband. Then Exeter—they both moved at the same time. She was made professor three years ago. Two kids, Fleur and George—seventeen and fourteen respectively."

"Tell me about the sister," I say.

"She was married to a Gregory Parsons. They subsequently divorced."

Sarah Parsons the artist. With an "estranged" sister, Anne.

"She's a painter," says Ops. "Apparently Anne doesn't have much to do with her family, though. Christmas and birthday cards is about the extent of it."

"One sister living," I say. "What about dead ones?"

"Are you thinking the substance of your daughter's story might be true but the names altered? Sorry to disappoint again. Anne Donbavand—Offord as was—has only ever had one sister."

"But did you—"

"Give me a chance," he says wearily. "Yes, after I got your last message I looked into the history of Speedwell House near Kingswear. No murders or unexpected deaths associated with it, going back the last two hundred years. Nor with any of the families who've lived there. I double-checked to see if Anne was adopted by the Offords as a baby—I thought that might point me in the direction of this other family containing a murderer, but it was a blind alley. Anne wasn't adopted. So . . . how far do you trust this headmistress?"

"I don't know. Why?"

"Well, she's the one who's fed you this line about the Donbavand family changing their name and being in hiding, isn't she? That doesn't sit right with me, after looking into it. As I say, Anne and Stephen Donbavands' pasts look conventional and uncontroversial."

I think about the word "estranged." It implies a rift—something more dramatic than a gradual drifting out of touch.

"People that good at covering their tracks don't generally turn up in their safe haven of choice and immediately start blabbing to the local schoolteachers about their new identities and the terrible threat they've escaped from. It just doesn't tie in."

Fuck. Fuck, fuck, fuck. Where does this leave me?

I say, "I've got Anne Donbavand's work email address. Could you get into her account, do you think?" If what Lesley told me is true, some correspondence about taking George and Fleur out of Beaconwood would presumably be in there. Unless Anne has a different email account for nonwork correspondence.

"I could." Ops chuckles. "But it'd be illegal, and you and I could both go to prison." He said the same thing the last time I asked him about hacking; I hoped my increased desperation would net me a different answer. Apparently not.

This is ridiculous. Is he a private detective or a mouse? "I understand you might not want to take that risk, but I'm prepared to," I tell him. "Is it illegal for you to explain to me how to do it?"

"Listen, Justine—you don't want to go down the law-breaking

route. I've seen clients do it, against my advice, and it never ends well."

But does it end? I want to ask him. All I want is not to have to wonder anymore. I know that, somehow, the Ingreys are real. I just have to find out how.

You also want to be safe, remember? And keep your family safe?

"What about Malachy Dodd?" I ask.

"Right," says Ops sheepishly. "I must admit I haven't gotten around to that one yet. I'll try to fit it in tomorrow. Want me to have a look into this headmistress while I'm at it? No extra charge."

"Lesley Griffiths? You think she might be . . ."

"I think she might be telling you fibs, yes. She's done it before, hasn't she? Told you George Donbavand was never at her school, then admitted he was."

"Yes, but she had a fairly persuasive reason. I believed her."

"I don't doubt she was convincing, but it doesn't happen, does it?"

"What doesn't?"

"Heads of schools making out pupils they've taught for years are a product of someone else's imagination. Heads of schools pretending to expel kids, to make it easier for their parents to remove them."

But Lachlan Fisher endorsed every word she said.

"You want my best guess? She's changed her lie, but she's still lying."

"I don't think so," I say. I want to sit down on the pavement and close my eyes. Do I need to put Lesley back on my list of untrustworthy people? Lachlan Fisher too? When he gave me George's story and I told him Ellen's was about murder, he looked startled and fled. I wonder if he had the same idea I did once I'd read George's—that he and Ellen had swapped family stories.

Did Lachlan run away scared that the Donbavands' secret, the one they'd successfully kept from everyone at Beaconwood, involved murder?

"George told me things himself about his parents that tallied with what the headmistress said," I tell Ops.

"You said he gave the impression they were unreasonably strict. Did he mention them being on the run from a previous life?"

"No." I must sound naïve and clueless.

"Justine?"

"Mm?"

"Don't make the mistake of thinking that if something sounds far-fetched, it must be true. It's what we call No One Could Make That Up Syndrome. There's nothing so eccentric and bizarre that someone can't invent it."

"Can I ask you something? Something more psychological than factual?"

"Shoot."

"How far should one trust one's instincts about people? I mean, if I meet someone and get a strong feeling they're a good thing and inherently reliable, is that a hunch worth trusting?"

"If there's no opposing case to be made, absolutely," says Ops. "If it's all good, you trust the person. We all do. Life'd be impossible otherwise. None of us'd ever get married, for a start. Your dilemma comes when you start noticing details that don't fit with the overall picture, things that can't be reconciled. Personally, though I've never met this head teacher, I can't reconcile a trustworthy, sensible managing director—she's effectively managing director of the school, isn't she?—with someone who'd fake an expulsion to please demanding parents, then deny the existence of the boy in question."

"You're right," I sigh. "I should keep an open mind." Who asked Ellen and George to write their stories, after all? Craig Goodrick and Lachlan Fisher: Beaconwood people. What if they specifically asked for stories about family secrets? What if they did so at Lesley's request?

Which would mean . . . what? I've got so many suspicions spilling out in every direction, I'm losing track.

"I'll email you later with a list of names," I tell Ops. "Teachers at Beaconwood as well as the head. I'm happy to pay a bit more if it's a lot of extra work, but I'd like you to look into all of them."

There is generally no way to avoid going home eventually, however much one might dread it. I delayed my return for as long as I could, but Figgy got tired of walking up and down the hilly streets of Torquay in the rain. He plonked himself down on a pavement and refused to budge. I ended up carrying him back to the car and was dripping with sweat by the time I got there.

Now I'm lying in a lily-of-the-valley-scented bath with my eyes closed, wondering if DC Luce has spoken to Stephen Donbavand. *Hey, Steve, you don't know a lady called Justine Merrison, do you? Daughter at Beaconwood? I shouldn't tell you this but between you, me and the gatepost, she's only claiming you and Anne are trying to drive her out of Devon.*

"Mum?" Ellen appears in the doorway. "Wow. How much bubble bath did you put in? A whole bottle?"

"A lot," I say unashamedly. "Bubble baths should be like lemon meringue pies. The bubbles are the meringue layer, and it needs to be as thick as the—"

"Yeah, I'm not really interested," Ellen waves her hands to shut me up. "I just came in to tell you I Googled Vita Sackville-West."

"Oh. And?"

"She didn't exactly have the sort of marriage George and I want, though she kind of did."

"Oh." I desperately don't want to talk about this now. Or ever, in fact. I want it to go away.

"It's called a mixed-orientation marriage."

"Right. That makes sense. El, I don't suppose you've told Dad yet, have you?"

"Sorry. I didn't want to do it today. I just wanted to watch a movie and be a normal teenager."

I nod, hopefully not too hard. *Yes, yes, be normal.*

"Anyway, I was wondering," says Ellen. "Do you know any examples of famous dead people whose future mothers-in-law were so against them when they were only fourteen that they dug a grave for them? Like, on their property?"

I laugh. Ellen smiles.

"No, I can't say I do."

"Great. What a way to be unique."

"Ellen, I don't know for sure that the person who wrecked our lawn is George's mum. It might not be."

"That's not what you said to DC Luce this morning. You've got bubbles on your chin, by the way. It looks like a Santa beard."

"I know—about Luce, I mean, not the beard." I wipe my chin and pull myself up a bit. "It's strange. Sometimes I feel as if I have more proof than I could ever need that Anne Donbavand's out to get me and other times I worry I've got nothing. Nothing concrete. There's something you could do that would really help me, Ellen."

"Ask George?" she says. "I will when I next see him, but God knows when that'll be. He hasn't done the signal yet and he probably won't for ages. I know what he'd say, though. He'd say, 'I wouldn't put anything past my mother. She's a basket case.' He calls her that all the time."

More proof? Or still no proof?

"Will you let me read your story about the Ingreys?" I ask.

"No. Why do you want to?"

"I think you know why." Bearing Olwen's advice in mind, I say, "I'm sorry if I came on too strong the first time I asked to read it. It was the family tree. It rubbed me the wrong way. I've got a thing about family trees—almost a phobia."

"How come?"

I'm getting too hot in the tub. I haul myself out, grab the green bath sheet that's draped over the towel rail and wrap it around myself. "Remember you asked me the other day about Granddad and Julia—why we don't see more of them?"

"Yeah."

Ellen follows me across the landing to my bedroom. Figgy's sitting on the bed chewing a metal hair clip. "You should be on the leash, with Alex," I tell him. "Where's he gone, and why hasn't he taken you with him?" To Ellen I say, "Do you think I should call Dad 'Alex' when I talk to Figgy, or . . . something else?"

"Like what?" She narrows her eyes in suspicion. "Dad? Daddy?"

"No." I blush.

"Yes!" She points an accusing finger at me. "That's totally what you were thinking, and ugh, no. Gross! Dad isn't Figgy's father."

I might ask Olwen about this: get a second opinion from an expert.

"You changed the subject," says Ellen. "You were supposed to be telling me why you hate family trees, and why we never see Granddad and Julia."

"We don't *never* see them. Occasionally we see them."

"Mum! Stop . . . procrastinating."

"I think you mean prevaricating." Whatever you want to call it, she's right.

I sit down on the bed. Why is it so difficult?

Ellen says, "You know some people are phobic about their relatives? It's called syngenesophobia. George told me. He has it."

"Is there a name for a phobia specifically of *George's* relatives? Because I think I have that." I smile.

"Mum. Tell me about Granddad and Julia."

There's no putting it off any longer if I'm going to do it at all.

"When I was about your age, Julia made me a family tree as a present. I'm not talking about a quick sketch on a bit of paper. She was into genealogy and family history at the time, so she did stacks of research and, once she'd gone back several generations, she commissioned an artist to turn the information into a proper family tree for me. It was enormous, and quite beautiful, really. There was only one problem."

"What?"

It's easy to make it sound mundane because there was no big drama, no overt conflict. "Julia thought it would be inappropriate to start researching my mother's parents, grandparents, great-grandparents. Granddad had left my mother for Julia the year before, and Julia was sensible enough to work out that Mum, who was still heartbroken, wouldn't welcome her getting in touch and pestering her for details of her ancestors. So she didn't put anyone from Mum's family on the tree. Just Mum, as Dad's first wife, but as if she had no parents herself. Just on her own, in a little box sticking out next to Granddad."

"Did Julia put herself on the family tree as Dad's second wife?" Ellen asks.

"Yes. Which is fine, and what I'd expect her to do. But she also included several generations of her family above her."

"*What?*" Ellen's face contorts in disgust. "You're kidding! Julia put *Julia's* great-grandparents on the family tree she made for *you*?"

I nod.

"But . . . She did that when you're the daughter of the woman whose husband she nicked, and whose ancestry she left off the same family tree?"

"Yes." I ought to say that Julia didn't steal my father, that he went of his own volition. It felt like a theft, though.

"That's offensive," says Ellen.

"I hated the family tree from the second I laid eyes on it. There was barely any space for my mother in her isolated little box amid Julia's dozens of forebears. It didn't occur to Julia that Mum mattered to *me* if not to her—that I might be upset by a visual representation of her insignificance."

"She shouldn't have made or given you a family tree at all," says Ellen. "It's like, hello? You've broken up a family and now you want to make an *illustration* of that, and give it to the child of the home you broke?"

I'm impressed that Ellen can see the problem. I tried to talk about it with my father many years later, and he shook his head in disgust at what he saw as my ingratitude.

"When Mum died a few years later, I blamed Julia and the family tree. The official cause of death was cancer, but I saw that as a symptom, not the true cause. Mum saw the family tree. Julia and Dad—Granddad, I mean—gave it to me in front of her. At her house, in fact—one Christmas when we were all trying to spend a halfway decent day together. Mum tried not to show it, but I could tell she was devastated. That's when I think her cancer started. Though, like so many other things, I can't prove it. And I know it can't be true, really, I just . . ." I shrug. "Anyway, that's why I was funny about the family tree in your story."

"Right," says Ellen with venom in her voice. "I hate Julia now, and I'm glad we hardly ever see her."

"Me too, and me too," I say, knowing it's the opposite of the response I ought to give. "Granddad isn't blameless either. He should have stopped her and told her to buy me a book token instead. Stupid arse. But you can't hate him because he's your granddad."

"You can hate people who are related to you by blood," Ellen informs me. "George hates his mum. He says he'd be *so* happy if she died."

"Really?"

Ellen nods. "She never misses an opportunity to ruin his life, he says. I mean, he wouldn't kill her or anything, but he's definitely hoping she'll die young. Young for an old person, I mean. He wouldn't be sad."

"Ellen, listen, this is important. George's mum . . . I believe she might be a dangerous woman—"

"So does George."

"—and I think your story about the Ingreys might be about her in some way. If it is, I urgently need to read it. Any information, *anything* you know about Anne Donbavand, I need to know."

"Why?" Ellen looks away.

"So that I can keep us all safe," I explain.

"I don't see how it would help you to do that, though."

"So your story *is* about George's mum's childhood?"

Ellen chews her bottom lip.

"My guess is that you'd like to tell me but you can't because you've promised George. I understand that. If you're going to marry him, your first loyalty has to be to him." *Was that a step too far?*

"Maybe if I didn't *tell* you . . ." Ellen says tentatively.

"Yes," I say eagerly. "You could just let me read the story."

"No. I can't."

Damn. "Why not, El?"

"For the same reason you're so desperate to read it," she says tearfully. "If you use stuff in it . . ."

Use stuff in it to do what? This is what I've been after, isn't it? Proof? If it's not a true story, how would I be able to use it in a way that would harm anyone?

"Ask me a question I can answer without answering," Ellen mumbles, as if saying it inaudibly is the same as not having said it at all.

"All right. Unless you here and now tell me I'm wrong, I'm going to assume the story you're writing about the Ingreys is about Anne Donbavand. Perrine is her little sister. Anne is Lisette Ingrey. George told you about her childhood. If you don't contradict me, I'm going to take that as confirmation that I'm right."

"Hello?" Alex calls up the stairs. "Justine, is Figgy up there?"

"Yes, Dad, and he's *off the leash*," Ellen yells back.

"Fuck. Oops, I mean, damn! Fiver in the swear box. No, make that fifty quid, since I keep reoffending. His leash is still attached to his harness—he must have wriggled out of the damn thing. It's too big for him. We need a smaller size."

"I said that. You bought one for a medium dog."

"It was the only one Pet Guff had." That's what Alex thinks the pet accessories superstore ought to be called. He's leading by example.

He appears in the bedroom. "Hello, Figgs, you old Houdini, you. Where's El?"

I didn't notice that she'd left the room. "She was here a minute ago," I say.

"Bedroom!" she calls out, before slamming her door shut.

"Yes!" I say.

"Yes what?" asks Alex.

"I was right. Anne Donbavand is Lisette Ingrey."

I must hang on to this certainty. Mustn't let doubt creep in. What's just happened—Ellen leaving the room without a word— that's conclusive.

So why couldn't Ops find any hint of a murdered sister? Did he make a mistake? Is it not true that Anne grew up in an ordinary home, with her parents and one younger sister?

The Offords. And Sarah Parsons.

They're who I need to talk to next. If I want to be really sure.

Chapter 11

An Unlocked-House Mystery

All the people gathered in Speedwell House's drawing room listened and hardly dared to breathe as the policeman who had gone upstairs with Bascom and Sorrel told what had happened from his point of view. He had led the way upstairs, with Bascom and Sorrel following behind him. When they had reached Perrine's bedroom door, the policeman had held out his hand for the key, and Sorrel had passed it to him. "Be careful," she warned. "Perrine might go for you."

"Oh, I think I can fend off a teenage girl," said the policeman.

He unlocked the door and walked into the room. "Where is she?" he asked. "This had better not be some sort of prank."

On hearing this, Bascom and Sorrel rushed into their youngest daughter's bedroom. Perrine was not there. Even more peculiarly, her bed was not there either.

"She must be hiding," said Bascom.

"Where?" said Sorrel. "There's no wardrobe in here, only a chest of small drawers—all too small for her to fit in."

Bascom, Sorrel and the policeman searched the room.

Perrine was nowhere to be found. Her bed was nowhere to be found.

"What about that little green door in the wall?" said the policeman. "Might she have . . . ?"

"No," said Sorrel. "Absolutely not. You open it and see if you can get out. You can't. We pushed a very heavy mahogany wardrobe up against the wall on the landing on the other side.

"But . . . she must have escaped that way," said Bascom, his voice brimming with bewilderment. "The only other way out of the room is by the main door, which, as you saw, was locked."

"The window was locked too," said Sorrel, who kept turning around suddenly, as if she expected someone dangerous to sneak up on her. "She *must* still be in this room, but where? She can't be hiding under the bed because there is no bed!"

"Let's not get carried away until we've checked all available avenues," said the policeman. "I think your husband must be right, Mrs. Ingrey. The little green door seems to be the only possibility. I'll wager that if I were to open it now, I'd see the back of the wardrobe you mentioned, with a large hole cut in it—a hole big enough to allow Perrine to escape."

He pulled the tiny door open, and saw straightaway that he was wrong. There was unbroken solid wood pushed right up against the doorway. No hole. "Perhaps she pushed the wardrobe out of the way, climbed out, then replaced it."

"Try it," Sorrel suggested.

The policeman pushed and puffed and panted, but the

wardrobe did not budge one millimeter (or one inch, as people used to say in the old days).

"See?" said Sorrel. "You're a big burly man and you can't shift it. How could Perrine? She's a slender teenage girl."

"So then we searched the bedroom again, every nook and cranny," the policeman told everybody in the drawing room. "And we found neither Perrine nor her bed."

The Dodds and the Butchers looked furious, especially the women. "So, what, she's run off somewhere?" snapped Mrs. Dodd. "If you police let her get away with what she's done, I'll make your lives a misery, you mark my words!"

"There must be justice!" declared Mrs. Butcher.

Jack Kirbyshire's widow burst into tears. "I can't bear the thought of someone else being murdered like my poor Jack," she sobbed.

"Never mind your grief and your desire for justice," said Sorrel in a commanding tone. "Let us first focus on the practical side of things. It is not possible that Perrine escaped from her bedroom. It is utterly impossible, I tell you, unless one of you let her out!"

"One of *us*?" said Mr. Careless, Mimsie Careless's father. "Oh, I see! You mean me, don't you? You're accusing me of letting a murderer loose on the world!"

"No one's accused you, sir," said the policeman. "And I have to say that you're behaving rather suspiciously."

"No one's accused me *yet*," said Mr. Careless, "but they soon will, you'll see. Do you have any idea what it's like to go through life with the name Careless? The instant something goes wrong and there's no one

else obviously to blame, even your best friends start
to think, 'Well, what about that Careless chap? Careless by name, careless by nature, no smoke without
fire . . .' "

"I'm so sorry," Mrs. Careless said, blushing. "My
husband has the most enormous chip on his shoulder
about his surname. Whereas I rather like it. My maiden
name was a horrendous double-barreler. You'll never
guess, so I'll tell you: Common-Dowd. Can you *imagine*?"

"I don't give two hoots about your stupid husband
and his stupid name!" wailed Sorrel. "Where is my Perrine? I can't bear this! I have to know where she is!
I need to know she's safe! One of you has sneaked her
out of this house when I wasn't looking, and you're
planning to torture and kill her! Oh, *why* was I fool-
ish enough to let you all in?"

Bascom patted her and did his best to calm her down.
Once her hysterical fit had subsided, the policeman
took over the proceedings. "Now listen, everyone," he
said. "This is very simple. Well, actually, it is very
puzzling, and finding the solution will not be easy
at all, but what I mean to say is that the puzzle is
simple to explain. What we have here might seem to be
a locked-room mystery—how does a child disappear from
a room when to do so is impossible in every practical
and scientific sense?—but in fact it is *not* a locked-
room mystery!"

"It isn't?" said Lisette, who thought that it
clearly was.

"No," said the policeman. "Because that part is

simple: someone unlocked Perrine's bedroom door and took Perrine and her bed. Having removed them from the room, this person then locked the door again. We know that must have happened, because it's the only thing that *could* have happened. Now, let me show you what I found on Perrine's bedroom floor." He rummaged in his pocket and produced something so small that no one could see it. "A small metal screw," he said. "This strongly suggests that whoever removed Perrine's bed from the room took it apart first. Of course, it is much easier to remove a bed in the form of discrete pieces of wood than as a whole bed, so dismantling the bed would make sense."

The policeman went on, "I would argue that what we have here is not a locked-room mystery but an *unlocked-house mystery.* For the first time in months, this morning Bascom and Sorrel Ingrey unlocked their home and filled it with people, including my good self and your good selves. Before we all congregated in this drawing room, we were wandering about singly and in little groups, having a good old nosy and chatting to one another. *One of us*—not me, I hasten to add, being a policeman and therefore above suspicion—one of us stole the key to Perrine's bedroom, went upstairs, unlocked her door, dismantled her bed and took it and her out of the house. But why did they take the bed too? That's a real mystery! And did they take Perrine in order to punish her, or to let her escape justice?"

"We would have seen!" said Sorrel. "Someone would

have seen someone else with Perrine and a load of bed pieces under their arm, moving through the house!"

"No, dear," said Bascom. "*We* wouldn't have seen. You and I were in the kitchen serving breakfast right up until we moved through to this room. From where we were, we couldn't see the hall or the front door."

"Was anyone in the hall the whole time?" the policeman asked the assembled company. "Can anyone swear to me on the lives of their nearest and dearest that nobody went upstairs, and that nobody came down shortly or longly afterward with Perrine and the bits of bed in their grasp?"

Everyone started to talk at the same time, which made it hard to get the gist of what was being said, but it became clear in due course: nobody had been in the hall, or able to see the hall and the stairs, for the whole time.

"Aha!" said the policeman. "Then we have made some progress. We know now that my theory is perfectly possible."

"How did this person get the key to Perrine's bedroom?" asked Sorrel. "It was in my cardigan pocket. It was there just now, when I came upstairs with you, when you were going to arrest Perrine."

"Whoever took it must have replaced it," said the policeman. "Though I admit it's a bit odd that you didn't notice anyone reaching into your pocket, Mrs. Ingrey."

"Mum, you weren't wearing your cardy when you were sorting out the breakfast," said Allisande. "I remember, because there was a stain on your shirt, on the right shoulder. I thought to myself, 'Mum looks a total scruff, I wish she'd put her cardy back on.'"

"She's right!" blurted out Mrs. Sennitt-Sasse. "It looked like a coffee splash. I saw it too."

"Yes, I remember now," said Sorrel distantly, as if busy trying to coax the whole memory out of a dark and cobwebby corner of her mind. She pulled her cardigan down on the right-hand side, and everyone saw the stain that had been described. "Yes, I *did* take my cardy off. I remember now. I hung it on one of the coat hooks in the hall before I started in the kitchen."

"There you are, then!" said the policeman. "Anyone could have gotten to it, unseen in the hall."

"This all seems laughably unlikely." Mr. Careless proved his point by laughing. "No one would be able to do all this unnoticed: sneak upstairs, somehow dispose of a girl, not to mention a bed, which one would first have to dismantle. It's preposterous! There were people milling about all over the place—someone would have seen something."

"How would the person have known that the key to Perrine's room was in your cardigan pocket?" Bascom asked Sorrel. "Only the family knew that."

The policeman stared hard at Lisette and Allisande. "Girls?" he said. "Does either of you have anything you want to share with us?"

"No," said Allisande aggressively. "I didn't do it! I would never bother to dismantle a bed, for any reason whatsoever. It would be a major hassle."

"She's telling the truth," said Lisette. "I could

see her the whole time. She didn't go upstairs and set Perrine free. Or kill Perrine and hide her body in another part of the house."

The phone started to ring at that moment. Sorrel gave Bascom a weary look. "I'll get it," he said.

"'Set her free, or kill her and hide her body,'" mused the policeman, repeating Lisette's words. "That's the real question, isn't it? Which one was it? If the former, we might never find Perrine. If the latter, we will no doubt find her body either hidden somewhere here, in the grounds of Speedwell House, or locked in the boot of someone's car."

"We should check all the car boots quickly!" said Lisette. "What if Perrine's trapped in one of them still alive? Maybe whoever took her is planning to kill her later because they didn't have time this morning."

Everyone looked at Mrs. Dodd, who said, "I wish I did have her locked in my car boot so that I could make her suffer later as much as she's made me suffer . . . but I'm afraid I don't. Check if you don't believe me."

"On balance, I think I do believe you," said the policeman. "I have a question for you, miss."

Allisande nudged Lisette, who looked up and saw that the policeman was talking to her. "Yes?" she said. She hadn't noticed because she had an idea in her head that wouldn't go away.

"You mentioned that you could see your sister Allisande the whole time, so therefore she cannot be the culprit. Correct?"

"Yes," said Lisette.

"Very good. My question is this: Could *she* see *you* the whole time?"

But before Lisette, or indeed Allisande, could answer, Bascom Ingrey came back into the drawing room. In fact, it would be most accurate to say that he staggered in. His face looked like a slab of old gray meat. "That was the police station," he said. "Perrine has been found dead. Murdered!"

13

Anne's more than my sister," Sarah Parsons tells me. We're standing in her gallery, looking at the *Anne, Tide Glider* painting on the wall. "In a way, I've always regarded her as my creator. If it weren't for her, I wouldn't exist." She giggles. I was expecting it. Her laughter doesn't mean she finds something funny, I've discovered; it's a signal that she's finished speaking. It would be interesting to see if she did it after saying, "I'm bankrupt and about to lose my house." Maybe she has a different punctuation-behavior for sad conversations.

She's a short, round woman in her midthirties, with a mass of brown, curly hair, and—thank God—no reservations about inviting a stranger into her home. I emailed her via her website and said I loved her paintings, and could I come and look at them with a view to buying one? It worked.

Sarah lives on Fore Street in Totnes in a narrow three-story building that's squashed in between a shop that sells crystals and a real estate agent. The ground floor is where the paintings are: all hers, no one else's. Above is her home, spread over the top two floors. We've just had tea up there: delicious Earl Grey, complete with shiny silver contraptions to catch the twiggy bits. The teabag-tea I have at home doesn't taste as good but is less fiddly to make and pour.

"How did Anne create you?" I ask Sarah. She seems happy to talk about her family and strikes me as an exuberant innocent. Bare feet, no makeup. On the middle toe of her right foot, she's wearing a ring with a big red heart on it. As we chat, she swishes the skirt of her long blue silk dress from one side to the other, like Ellen used to when she was three and dressed as a Disney princess.

"My mum turned up at school to collect Anne one day, and another mother congratulated her—told her how fantastic she was looking, how excited she must be, and why was there no sign of a bump yet? Turned out Anne had told the whole school her mum was preggers with twins. Twins! Anne was quite lonely being the only child, and our parents weren't showing any signs of supplying a sibling, so she invented two of them. When Mum heard about Anne's lie, she felt guilty for depriving her of what she so obviously wanted, had a word with Dad, and . . ." Sarah stretches out her skirt on both sides, like low-down wings, and does a little curtsy. "Voilà! Here I am, thanks to my older sister."

And there's the punctuation laugh: my cue to speak. "Why *Tide Glider*?" I ask, looking at the picture.

"Oh, Anne and her family have a boat with that name, and it seemed appropriate as a name for Anne too. She's sort of glided away from us. Me, Mum and Dad, I mean. Still . . . maybe not forever." A sad smile instead of a laugh this time.

So Anne had a sticker made with the name of her own boat on it, and stuck it over my house sign. Why the other houses, though, and the other boats? Why involve them? To create extra confusion? So I wouldn't be able to convince the police that I and my house, specifically, were the targets?

"It's a beautiful painting," I say. This could be the biggest lie I've ever told. Sarah's a talented artist, but I find the picture of Anne offensive because of its subject. I might buy it and make one or two additions: a red arrow and the words "EVIL BITCH" in red capitals.

I was hoping to talk to Sarah and Anne's parents today too—Martin and Denise Offord—as they live nearby, but shortly after I arrived, Sarah mentioned that they're in the Algarve and spend most winters in their villa there.

I force my eyes to linger on the portrait in front of me. "I read something online about this painting, I think." I do my best to sound vague. "Anne was referred to as your estranged sister."

Sarah frowns. "Yes, I know exactly the article you're talking about. I never used the word estranged and was furious when they did. There's been no row, and we all get on perfectly well. Anne's busy with her own life and family, but we see her every Christmas and . . ." She shrugs. "To be fair to her, we're an in-each-other's-pockets family. It can be a bit stifling. I can understand why Anne needed to go her own way. I did too. Or I thought I did: fled to Scotland, got married. When we split up, my ex-husband gave my parents as the main reason he couldn't live with me." Big, loud laugh for this.

"He didn't like them?"

"No, it wasn't that. It was more that he said he felt as if he was married to all three of us. Mum and Dad called every night, we got together every other weekend . . . either they'd come to Scotland or we'd come here. Nathan got sick of only having one weekend in two to ourselves. To me it was just normal!" Small giggle.

"But Anne doesn't speak to you every night on the phone or visit every other weekend?" I say.

"No." Sarah sighs. "She comes with Stephen and the kids for two hours on Christmas Day. That's it. And it's clear she's not having a good time when she's there. She always seems kind of . . . removed from the festivities, as if she's present in body only. Stephen, her husband—he's really lovely!—he tries to overcompensate by being superfriendly, but it's a bit awful really. Ha!"

"Well, it's clear from this portrait—thanks to your skill as an artist—that Anne is a woman with many interesting facets to her character," I say.

"Seriously? That's so sweet of you!"

"What's she like? I hope you don't mind my asking. I mean, what was she like as a child? And—again, feel free to tell me to mind my own business—but was she always a bit distant and aloof from the rest of you, or . . . did something happen?"

"Nothing whatsoever. That's why it was so weird when she suddenly backed away from us soon after she left for university. I know everyone says, 'I did nothing wrong,' but, literally, there was *nothing* that happened. I think Anne must have had some kind of . . . psychological epiphany. Sometimes the people you grew up around remind you of the old you—the person you don't want to be anymore. Mum and Dad begged to know what they'd done wrong, but all they got in response was polite deflection. I told them: leave her be. If she's ever going to come back to us, it'll only happen if we back off."

"Sounds sensible," I say.

"I'm more optimistic than Mum and Dad," says Sarah. "Anne and I were close, despite the seven-year age gap between us. I was her adoring disciple. She used to tell me stories about film stars she'd met—Richard Gere and Harrison Ford—and pop groups that had asked her to join because they were in dire need of a female vocalist—Duran Duran, no less! I'd lap up the stories unquestioningly." Titter, titter.

"But . . . they weren't true?" I don't know why I'm asking when I know the answer. Teenage Anne Offord from Totnes did not meet

Richard Gere or Harrison Ford. She wasn't invited to sing with Duran Duran.

"Oh God, no, but Anne told them as if they were!"

It's called lying. Same goes for making up pregnancies.

"Anne had the most incredible imagination," says Sarah. "I was always the visual one and she was the storyteller. I was sure she'd be a writer. So were Mum and Dad. I actually wonder if she went into academia to spite us."

"It's odd that you think she'd want to do that, given that you say nothing happened, no conflict or rift, or . . ." I shrug. Mustn't seem too interested. Feigning a laugh, I say, "Are you sure there's no dark family secret? A third sister tucked away somewhere who might have driven Anne away?"

"Ha-ha. No, I'm afraid not."

Not a flicker of recognition or guilt.

"Literally, apart from being very close—closer than most, if you don't include Anne—there's nothing interesting about my family at all."

Apart from it containing a pathological liar. One who started early.

"I branched out into the semi-bohemian by being an artist, but other than that, my childhood was building-society-advert dull: 2.4 kids and a microwave kind of deal. The most dramatic thing to happen was when I seemed to develop a strange respiratory illness, but then even that turned out to be a massive anticlimax: I was just allergic to our dog!"

The mention of a dog makes me think of Figgy and how odd it is not having him with me. Alex has him today and I'm a bit jealous. I want to get back to him, bury my nose in the curly fur on the top of his head. If I could go back in time and tell the Muswell Hill, TV-producer Me that she would turn into someone who aspired to do Nothing and looked forward to cuddling a dog, she would be distraught.

And, what's more, it would serve her right—for what, I'm not sure.

"Is this painting of Anne for sale?" I ask Sarah.

"Ooh. Good question." She puts her thumb in her mouth and starts to chew it. "Can I think about it and let you know? I mean, I'm sure it will be for sale, but because of the sentimental value, I don't want to rush into selling it, if that makes sense."

"Of course." I smile. Inside, I'm cursing. I want the picture now. I want to deface it. Dig a grave for it on Professor Anne's lawn. Let her good friends Richard Gere and Harrison Ford try to stop me.

I write down my details for Sarah and ask her to email me once she's decided about the portrait. Hopefully she'll decide in my favor, and when I come back to collect it, I can ask her more questions. If she rumbles me, I can always tell her the truth: "Look, I'm sorry I came here under false pretenses, but here's the situation . . ." That's what normal people do—people who lie only occasionally, when they need to: they apologize and revert to the truth when found out. They have a sense of shame.

Pathological liars like Anne Donbavand produce new lies to explain away the old ones: "Oh, did what I said turn out not to be true? Here, then, have another nice but false story."

The teenage girl who pretended Duran Duran were headhunting her grew into an adult woman who pretended her family changed its name and started a new life because they were in danger from a nameless pursuer.

I believe Lesley Griffiths; I don't care what Ops thinks. I doubt he's ever worked in TV drama. I've probably read more documents than he has about the psychology of the compulsive liar.

Mythomania, it's called. I remember a document with that heading sitting on my desk for weeks, and me never having time to read it. Eventually I spilled coffee over it deliberately, hoping no one would provide me with another copy.

Someone did. I read it eventually. One line stuck in my mind: "The stories told tend to present the liar favorably, as the hero or the victim." I thought that was odd: Why would anyone want to be a victim? How did that qualify as favorable presentation?

If I ever meet Anne Donbavand, I might ask her.

Before I leave Sarah's gallery, I can't resist trying one more question. I throw it over my shoulder as I'm leaving, hand on the door, to make it sound trivial. If she reacts badly, I can always make a run for it. "I don't suppose you've heard of a Perrine Ingrey, have you?"

"No, I haven't. Though what an alluring name! Is she an artist?"

Again, not a flicker of recognition.

"I'm not sure she's anyone," I say, wanting to make my parting remark as honest as possible. "I think I've been given the wrong information."

I arrive out of breath and two minutes late for my four o'clock meeting with Stephen Donbavand. Getting from Totnes to Exeter was the easy part. Finding the right office once I arrived at Exeter University proved almost impossible.

I knock on the door. Two minutes only counts as late if you're a punctuality freak like me. It's another hangover from my London life, where it really mattered. Every meeting that needed two hours was squashed into one because you invariably had a stack of twelve to get through afterward, followed by an evening spent doing all your housework with one hand while arranging and rearranging the next day's meetings on your iPhone with the other.

I'm hoping Exeter University has a more leisurely ethos. I suppose it bodes well that no one I've encountered so far seems to know where any of the buildings or departments are. I found Stephen Donbavand's room by accident in the end.

Who am I supposed to be again? Too late: the door is opening. *Fuck.* This isn't a normal kind of forgetting; it's a panic-induced blanking out.

"Julia Vowles?"

Oh thank you, thank you.

"Yes. Dr. Donbavand?"

He extends a hand. I'm about to shake it when he turns abruptly and walks over to a table in the corner of the room that has a kettle, mugs and packets of Nescafé on it. "Pleasure to meet you," he says.

I put away my unwanted hand and try not to feel embarrassed. Is this a new thing: the air handshake, like the "mwah-mwah" no-contact kissing that TV people do?

I'm surprised by my racing heart and dry throat. One day I might tell someone I did this—Alex, for example—and I'll make it a funny story: how I snuck in and fooled Stephen Donbavand, pretending to be someone wanting to study micro-blah-blah economics. I won't mention that I was so scared, I could hardly breathe.

What if Stephen Donbavand sees through my act? What if he attacks me?

"Do come in and make yourself comfortable. Coffee? I can offer you caf or decaf, but no tea, I'm afraid."

"I'll have decaf. Thanks." It's not a breaking of my rule. Decaf instant Nescafé has more in common with juice than it does with real coffee.

"Good idea! I'll join you." He sounds delighted that we're going to have the same drink.

I know this man. Not him specifically, but his type. He's one of those people so steeped in niceness, he's unable to recognize its opposite. Of course Anne Donbavand would marry someone like him. He'd be the perfect enabler.

His office is tidy and impersonal. There are two shelves of economics books with titles like *A Note on the Existence of Nash Equilibrium in Games with Discontinuous Payoffs*, one small blue and white rug that looks pitiful at the center of such a large room. The mug in which my noncoffee arrives has a slogan on it: "150% of statistics are wrong!" No photos anywhere in the room, of his wife and children or of anything else.

It's as if Stephen Donbavand has dutifully put some things in his office to make it his own, but has no idea how to make it truly personal or homely. Either that's a typically male approach to occupying space or else I'm a sexist.

Already, I know more about George's father than I did when I knocked on his door. I know he didn't take one look at me and think, "That's not Julia Vowles, it's Justine Merrison." Or "That's my sister-in-law, Allisande Ingrey."

How much has Anne confided in him? People keep things from their spouses all the time. I set off to Totnes this morning without mentioning to Alex that I was going on to Exeter afterward to pretend to be Julia Vowles the economics student. It's possible that Anne Donbavand hasn't mentioned her harassment of me to her husband.

He must know the Ingrey story, though, if George does. But, no, that doesn't work. If Stephen and George—and Fleur too, presumably—think that Anne is Lisette Ingrey, daughter of Bascom and Sorrel, sister of Allisande and Perrine, who do they all think they're visiting each Christmas when they spend a tense afternoon with Martin and Denise Offord and Sarah Parsons?

When he sits down opposite me holding his own mug, which he's rather bizarrely wrapped in a blue tea towel, I look at Stephen

Donbavand's smiling face and think, *You could tell this man anything and get away with it.*

"So. Why Exeter University?" he asks me.

"Because you're here," I say. "As I said in my email, I've read some of your work and found it very interesting."

"Oh." He looks surprised. "Well . . . thank you!"

I wonder if there's a slogan on his mug, concealed by the tea towel: "150% of prospective PhD students are secretly here to ask questions about your mad wife!"

"And also I know your sister-in-law, Sarah Parsons," I add on a whim. I'm scared anyway; might as well escalate to very scared.

Stephen Donbavand looks surprised, but pleasantly so. "I see! How do you know Sarah?"

"From walking past her gallery so often—one day I plucked up the courage to go in. We got chatting—you know how friendly and chatty she is—and we've been good friends ever since. She's an amazing artist, isn't she?"

"Yes. Very talented indeed."

"You must have her paintings all over your walls, have you? Oh. I'm so sorry." I cover my mouth with my hand. "What a stupid thing to say. I know Anne doesn't like to have much involvement with her family—Sarah told me. So . . . there's no reason why you'd have lots of her work in your house."

"Think nothing of it." Stephen smiles. Still no suspicion on his face; still the benign duck expression. "In fact, what I know about art could be written on the back of a postage stamp, so rather than have a conversation that reveals my ignorance . . . shall we talk about your research plans instead?"

Interesting. I make a reprehensibly intrusive comment about his wife, and his response is to try to make me feel better.

"Yes. Though . . . I'm just thinking, does it matter that I'm a friend of Sarah's, from the point of view of you maybe being my supervisor?"

"No, I don't think it's any sort of conflict of interests," Stephen Donbavand says.

"Good. Neither do I."

We smile at one another.

"So tell me about your work, then."

Shit. What can I say? Sitting in a room with someone who believes I might be planning to do some work is making me sweaty and nauseous.

"Julia? Are you all right?"

"I will be. I feel a bit dizzy."

Think, woman. Economics. Help, quick. The budget. The Chancellor of the Exchequer holding up a red box. Until Alex set me straight, I thought the box was full of money and wondered why I never heard it jingle when George Osborne waved it in the air.

"Julia? Shall I get you some water? Coffee's not the best thing if you feel faint—even decaf."

"Water would be good. Thanks."

He puts down his drink on the shelf next to his chair. In his hurry to get the water he hopes will cure me, he lets the blue tea towel drop to the floor and I see that his mug does indeed have writing on it—the worst kind. It's one of those head-bashingly irritating "Keep Calm" slogans: in this instance "Keep Calm and Stop Caring."

"Here you go."

"Thank you."

I take two long sips of cold water. Stephen stands in front of me, too close. He's probably waiting to catch me if I faint.

"I'm fine now, really. Thanks."

As he turns to walk back to his chair, I catch sight of his palms and gasp.

He whirls round. "Are you all right?"

"Yes. It's just . . . the water's cold. In a good way." I smile, hoping he can't hear the terror-drumming of my heart.

His hands are livid red and swollen. Cracked at the bottom, with mud embedded in the cracks, brown lines across his palms. On the fleshy pad beneath one of his thumbs is a wound, like a burst blister, inadequately covered by a plaster.

That's why the tea towel. Without it, holding a mug of hot coffee would be too painful for him.

I've found the Speedwell House gravedigger. Not Anne Donbavand, but her husband: smiling Stephen. Or maybe both of them.

"Ouch, that looks sore," I say. "Your hands. Did you burn them?"

"What? Oh yes. No, actually, it was digging that did it."

How dare you, you fucker? How dare you look so jovial about it?

"Gardening? At this time of year?" My laugh comes out strangled. I'm nearly as bad an actress as I am an economist. Doesn't matter. Now that I know Stephen Donbavand dug a hole out of my garden to scare me and my family, I'm less worried about him suspecting my true identity. He's got something to hide, so he'll assume he's the only one in the room who has.

"Well . . ." He shrugs and laughs. "If it keeps my wife happy."

My breath turns solid in my mouth and throat. He has no idea who he's talking to, or what he's told me. Not that I didn't know it anyway. This isn't a man who would dig a grave in a stranger's garden off his own bat. Stephen Donbavand would never do that. What he would do, if he woke up one day and found himself married to a dangerous lunatic, is keep calm and stop caring. Or care, but do nothing about it.

He tries again. "Let's talk about your proposed PhD. And, if you could give me some background about your—"

"No."

He can't physically attack me without using his hands, and they're injured. If I have to fight him physically, I will. I think I could win.

"Let's talk about your wife for a bit longer. Before she married you, she was Anne Offord, with one sister, Sarah. Yet she pretends she grew up as Lisette Ingrey, with two sisters, Allisande and Perrine. Perrine murdered Malachy Dodd. Except none of these people are real, are they?"

I'm looking at a frozen man with a colorless face. He's not going to ask me what I mean. He knows.

"My name isn't Julia Vowles," I tell him. "I think you know who I am, don't you? Who would care enough to trick you into a meeting? Who's your wife tormenting at the moment? Who are you helping her to harrass? Any names spring to mind?"

"I . . . I think you ought to leave. I'm . . . I'm really sorry." The last word comes out as a sob. He's hunched in his chair, protecting himself with his arms. From words. Nothing but words.

"I'm Justine Merrison, Stephen. Your hands are sore because you spent most of the other night digging a grave in my garden—as you said, to keep your wife happy. You're scared of her, which I can understand. George is scared of her, and I can only assume Fleur is too. From my point of view, that's no excuse for going along with whatever she asks you to do."

"Justine, you have to leave." He isn't asking; he's pleading.

"I will, once I've had my say. Anne has been ringing me, calling me Sandie, telling me to go back to London or else she'll kill me, my husband and our daughter—that's Ellen, who's George's best friend. Except Anne took him out of Beaconwood, having first made the head pretend to expel him—apparently for his own good—so now he never sees his best friend anymore. What would Anne have to do before you'd think, 'Enough is enough'? Are you waiting for her to kill someone before you take action? If so, I'd like to suggest an alternative plan. As the person she's likely to kill first, I think it's my right to do so."

"Justine . . ." He raises his injured hands to try to stop me.

"What?"

"I can't talk to you. I wouldn't have agreed to meet you. You know that."

"Then I'll leave. But first I want to hear you say that you know your wife is a pathological liar and that she's harming your children. Tell me what you're going to do about that and I'll go. Tell me how you're going to stop her from causing me any more grief."

Stephen Donbavand gets up and walks over to the window. Eventually he says quietly, "I mean you no harm, Justine. There's nothing I can say that you'd want to hear."

"Expect a visit from the police," I tell him.

His face contorts at the word: a cartoon mask of horror. "No. Please, you don't know . . . Anne wouldn't hurt anyone. She's not violent."

"Are you serious?"

"You have no evidence!"

"I've seen your hands. And I haven't heard you deny what I'm accusing you of."

"Get out. Please."

I wonder if he's as desperate as he sounds. Desperate people will agree to anything. In my most reasonable voice, I say, "If you don't want me to tell the police, stop your wife from doing what she's doing. Can you do that?"

No answer.

"And tell me the truth. Where does the Perrine killing Malachy

Dodd story come from, and all that stuff about the Ingreys? Is it based on something true? Or did Anne make it up?"

"Please leave. You've no right to . . ." He comes storming toward me, then stops suddenly, as if he's realized that he can't. He is a person who always can't.

He walks over to his desk and picks up his phone. "I've never done this before, but I think I can have you forcibly removed from university grounds. This is your last chance to leave of your own accord."

"All right," I say, standing up. "I'll give you a last chance too: to stop Anne coming anywhere near me and my family. That includes phone calls, and it includes my dog—I don't know if she told you what she did to our puppy?"

Stephen squeezes his eyes shut. I hope he's imagining something worse than what happened, and all the bad things that are going to happen if he doesn't do as I ask.

"I know you hate this as much as I do, Stephen. So stop her. If you don't want to end up in jail and your children in care, you can't let Anne carry on the way she's going. It's not too late yet, but you haven't got long."

I slam the door on my way out.

"You're not asleep, so . . . I'm doing this." Alex turns on the bedroom light. It's not what's supposed to happen. He's supposed to watch the rest of the film I couldn't focus on, whose title I've already forgotten, and give me time to lie in the dark wondering what to do. Worrying, analyzing, trying to reconcile my disbelief—my strong urge to laugh at the absurdity of it all—with my fear, and the knowledge that, however impossible and ridiculous it might seem, it's real. It's happening.

I wish Alex had turned on a lamp instead of the overhead light.

"You're nowhere near asleep," he says. "I thought you were tired."

"I'm shattered." *But I can't sleep.* "Where's Figgy?"

"Snoring on Ellen's bedroom floor. I checked on him a minute ago. He's fine. They're both fine. Darling?"

"Mm?"

Alex sits down on the bed. "Where did you go today? Not Totnes—I mean afterward."

I haul myself into a sitting position and tell him about Stephen Donbavand. He listens without interrupting. When I've finished, he says, "I don't get it. He admitted to messing up our garden?"

"Digging a grave in our garden." It's important to me to keep stressing this. No one else seems to want to focus on it. Yes, it's a hole; yes, it's a mess, but mainly it's an empty grave, waiting to be filled with the dead body of Lisette Ingrey's hated sister, Allisande.

"He didn't exactly admit it," I tell Alex. "Didn't say, 'Yes, it was me, I did it,' but he didn't deny it either. And the way he looked and acted was as good as an admission."

"So why didn't you go straight to DC Luce?"

"What's the point? There's no proof. Stephen Donbavand would deny it, and Luce would believe him."

"We should still tell him. What can we do without police help?"

Excellent question. To which I don't know the answer. "That's what I was lying in the dark trying to figure out," I say. "It was easier when I believed I wasn't Allisande Ingrey. More straightforward."

"What do you mean?"

"Nothing. Forget it."

"Justine, explain. You're scaring me."

How? What's your worst fear? That I'm possessed?

"I thought it was a mistake," I say. "The anonymous caller was calling me Sandie, but I knew that wasn't me. I'm Justine. I can't be Justine *and* Sandie, so whoever it was must have mixed me up with someone else, I assumed—someone who'd been intimidating in the past, someone who was at war with the caller. Whether her name was Allisande Ingrey or an anagram of Allisande Ingrey, or something different altogether, I thought she was, at the very least, an actual person.

"Then I made progress, or so I thought: several clues pointed to her being Anne Donbavand's sister, and to both of them being characters in Ellen's story. When Ops told me Anne only had one sister—Sarah—and no connection with any murders, I wasn't completely convinced. I still thought the Perrine Ingrey stuff might be real, and very well hidden. And then when Ellen as good as told me that the story she was writing was true, and about George's mother, I knew I had to be right! That was until I met Sarah Parsons, and she told me about the lies Anne told as a child. That's when I realized that invention, if you're ruthless and deranged enough, makes anything possible."

"I'm not sure I know what you mean," says Alex.

"You can fabricate a past that includes someone who's out to get you—a fictional sister. You can use it as an excuse to exert unhealthy control over your husband and children: 'Everyone must do as I say—my children must never leave the house—because this person I've made up is trying to kill us all, and only I understand the danger.'"

"Hold on. If Allisande Ingrey is an invention, then you're not her. I mean, we know you're not anyway, but . . .'"

"Do we?" I say. He doesn't get it. Maybe no one ever will except me. "If Allisande can be proved to be somebody else, then I'm not her. But if she's nothing more than a figment of Anne Donbavand's imagination, then she can be anyone Anne wants her to be. See what I mean?"

"No. This makes zero sense to me."

"She can be me. She *is* me, because Anne says so, and the only sphere in which Sandie exists at all is one over which Anne has complete control. I have to face facts, Alex. I've been trying to find another candidate to be Anne's fake persona's fake sister. I even hired a detective! And I've found no one. Neither has Ops. There *is* no one."

"But . . . so the facts you want to face are Anne's lies?" Alex says. "Lies aren't facts."

"But they can create facts. So can fictions. That's what's happened here. There was no mix-up, no mistaken identity, no wrongly targeted anonymous calls. I'm the target—I have been from the start. Anne knew who she was calling. She was calling Lisette's sister."

"But you're not . . ."

"Yes, Alex, I am! I don't like it any more than you do, but I can't bury my head in the sand. In some fucked-up, invented world that I never agreed to be part of, I'm the middle sister: older than Perrine and younger than Lisette. I'm Allisande Ingrey."

Chapter 12

The Legend of Evil Perrine

Bascom Ingrey was able to say no more and collapsed in a shrieking heap on the Persian rug (the same one that the young Allisande had once squirted conditioner all over for fun. No fun was being had anywhere near that rug anymore, that was for certain).

The policeman ran to the telephone.

No one else moved. Everyone was watching Sorrel, expecting her to fall to the floor in a sobbing heap too. "What?" she said, noticing them all watching her for signs of distress. "I will wait for confirmation before I get upset. I hate suffering, and I won't do it any sooner than I have to."

A few minutes later, the policeman entered the drawing room again. "I'm afraid it's true," he said. "Perrine's dead body has been found."

Sorrel covered her face and moaned.

"Good!" said Mrs. Dodd.

"Where?" asked Mrs. Kirbyshire.

"This is the extraordinary thing," said the policeman. "She was found by Lionel the boatman—you know, the one who has *The Kingswear Treasure*—"

"He's got far too many tattoos," said Mrs. Sennitt-Sasse in a warning tone.

"Yes, well, be that as it may," said the policeman, who was annoyed to have been interrupted, "even those with tattoos can find dead bodies, and Lionel found one about ten minutes ago. He found Perrine. Said she looked like she'd been strangled—blue in the face, she was—but the really odd thing is this: she was in her bed, all neatly tucked in. And guess where the bed was? You never will, so I'll tell you: her bed was on the wooden jetty down by where *The Kingswear Treasure* leaves from to go over to Dartmouth. That's how come it was Lionel who found her." The policeman looked at his watch. "I must get down to the jetty right away," he said.

"Wait!" cried Sorrel Ingrey. "Please, before you go, take all these intruders out of my home, so that I can lock my family in safely again. Don't leave these strangers here. I believe they might kill us all. Their thirst for revenge knows no bounds."

"Intruders? But you invited me," said Mrs. Sennitt-Sasse.

"Don't be silly, Sorrel," said Bascom. "Nobody here could have gotten all the way to Lionel's jetty and back this morning without us noticing."

"Then they had someone waiting just outside the gates of Speedwell House, ready to take Perrine and the bed," said Sorrel.

"Don't worry, Mrs. Ingrey. We will get to the bottom of it, I assure you," said the policeman.

"I expect you to keep your word on that," said Sorrel, looking him sharply in the eye. "Remember this: I was ready and willing to hand Perrine over so that justice could be done. Now that Perrine is the one who has been murdered, I expect you to be dedicated and tireless in your search for justice for Perrine. Murdering a murderer is not acceptable. That is why civilized countries do not have the death penalty."

The policeman looked as if he disagreed, but he nodded anyway.

Fifteen minutes later, all the guest-intruders were gone, and Speedwell House was once again locked up so that the outside world couldn't get in.

Bascom and Sorrel Ingrey sat in the drawing room for hour upon hour. Bascom wept and Sorrel stared numbly into space. They didn't seem to notice that their two less troublesome daughters were still alive and in need of attention.

Ignored by their parents, Lisette and Allisande found it remarkably easy to sneak away. "Let's go to the library," Lisette whispered.

"But . . . it hasn't been cleaned yet," said Allisande. "David Butcher's body might not still be there, but there will be loads of blood. It'll be horrid."

"I know," said Lisette. "I need to look at it, though. Things are horrid at the moment. There's no way around that."

"I still don't see why I have to sit in a room full of blood," said Allisande sulkily.

Lisette felt it was important that she and Allisande should talk in the library. She had something momentous to say to her only living sister. She needed to confront her, and make her admit the truth. It stood to reason that the best place to do all this was in the library, where they would be forced to face the

horror that had taken over their lives—where the her-
ringbone parquet floor would be wet and red with the
blood of an innocent music teacher. It would be sym-
bolically right, thought Lisette, for them to have this
vital conversation in the library, in the presence of
this haunting visual spectacle, but she couldn't explain this to Allisande because you ruin a symbol if
you explain it.

In the end, she enticed her sister into the room by
saying, "I've got an exciting secret, and I won't tell
you it unless you come in here with me."

There was not quite as much blood in the library as
Lisette had expected. She had pictured almost enough
to swim in, as if the library were a pool but with no
deep end, just shallow all over the room. Like those
children's pools that you sometimes see next to the
main pool at hotels. Instead, there were drops and
smears and a couple of large-ish patches, but nothing
up to knee height as Lisette had imagined. Mostly the
library looked the same as it always had. "Why isn't
there more blood?" she asked.

Allisande (who had, remember, always been allowed
to watch whatever she wanted on TV, while Lisette was
busy doing only worthwhile, mind-improving activities
that Bascom chose for her) said, "It's because Perrine killed him ages before Mum slashed at him with a
knife. I saw a TV movie where that happened: someone
was stabbed to death, or looked as if they had been,
and the police worked out that they hadn't, and that
they must have been already dead for ages, because of
the lack of blood around the body. Apparently if you

stab someone who's already dead, nowhere near as much seeps out."

"Allisande," Lisette said gravely. "Who do you think murdered Perrine?"

Allisande snorted to show that she didn't think much of the question. "I've no idea!" she said. "I suppose the obvious answer is Mrs. Dodd, who is angry enough to turn into a raving homicidal maniac . . . but it can't be her."

"Why not?"

"Too obvious."

"This is real life, not a story!" Lisette exploded impatiently. "You're trying to be flippant, as if someone's made all this up for titillation, because *you know the truth*! You know it as well as I do, and you won't admit it!"

"I do not!" Allisande protested. Her face had turned red.

"Yes, you do. We know more than anyone else, don't we, you and I? One by one, the guests went to get their breakfast from Mum and Dad in the kitchen, but we didn't. Dad brought our plates in to us in the drawing room, remember, while Mum was busy in the kitchen?"

"Oh—yes, you're right," said Allisande grudgingly. "But I don't see why that means—"

"You *do* see," Lisette spoke over her. "Stop lying! I know it's difficult to face the truth, and nothing in your life experience has trained you to persevere when something is difficult—"

"I *hate* difficult!" Allisande flounced off to the other side of the room, making sure not to step in

David Butcher's blood as she went. "Let's not have this conversation, Lissy. Please? Let's go to the gazebo and make lists of names we're going to call our future children. I quite like Ptolemy for a boy and Arbella for a girl—what do you think? Not Arabella—that has 'arab' in it, which sounds like 'scarab,' and isn't that a beetle?—but Arbella. Do you like it?"

"We have to talk about this, Sandie," said Lisette. "You and I were sitting, the whole time, in chairs in the drawing room that faced the window. We were still there when everyone else came in and settled down for the big group meeting, and we know that Perrine can't have been murdered after that point because there was no one available to murder her—all the suspects were in the drawing room."

"Oh shut up, shut up!" moaned Allisande.

"Whoever took Perrine out of the house, with all the pieces of her bed in tow, they must have gone out through the front door and along the drive. There's no other way. The back door was never unlocked, and it's only reachable if you go down the other flight of stairs, the one on the side of the house where Perrine's bedroom isn't."

"That's not true," said Allisande. "Someone could have come down the stairs near the drawing room, straight from Perrine's bedroom, and then gone around to the back door instead of going to the front door. If they stole the key to the back door—"

"But they couldn't have done!" said Lisette in an impassioned voice. "The only key to the back door is kept in the drawing room in the glass-fronted cabinet, and we were in the drawing room the whole time! We'd have seen if any of the guests had gone to the cabinet and taken the key. No one went anywhere near it!"

"Intruders," muttered Allisande.

"What?"

"You called them guests. I call them intruders."

Lisette's heart sank.

"One of them murdered our sister," said Allisande.

"Sandie, you have to tell the truth—to me and to yourself! From where we were sitting, we would have seen if anyone went out of the front door. Who did we see? Who did *you* see?"

"Two policemen, taking David Butcher's body out on a sort of stretcher thing." Suddenly, Allisande's eyes lit up. "What if it wasn't only his body? What if Perrine was in there too? You know how the legend of evil Perrine has spread across the whole of the local area, and even as far as Paignton and Torquay—what if the police decided to take care of a murderer in a forbidden way, without any trial or anything?"

"I thought of that," said Lisette. "But it's impossible. David Butcher's body was in a bag, wasn't it? A zipped-up bag, exactly the shape of a person—*one* person, an adult male. Perrine wouldn't have fitted in the bag, no way—and even if she had, what about the big wooden headboard of her bed, and all the other bed pieces. None of the policemen were carrying any bits of bed at all."

"They might have hidden them under their coats," suggested Allisande, who was starting to seem nervous.

"You know that's impossible," said Lisette. "And you know something else too. Why won't you admit it?"

Allisande looked trapped. She put her fingers in her ears and started to sing: "Seven locks upon the red gate, seven gates about the red town. In the town there lives a butcher and his name is Handsome John Brown . . ."

"You know who else you saw going out of the front door," Lisette persisted. "I know that you know, Sandie, because I know you saw exactly what I saw. And I know."

"No one!" spluttered Allisande. "I saw *no one*. Nobody went out of the front door apart from those policemen with the body."

"Ah!" said Lisette. "I see what you're doing. You're telling the truth and lying at the same time."

Allisande began to sing again: "John Brown's boots are polished so fine, John Brown's spurs they jingle and shine. On his coat a crimson flower, in his hand a glass of red wine . . ."

"You know who killed Perrine," Lisette raised her voice to be heard over the song. "You know it not because of anything you saw, but because it's the only possibility."

"In the night, the golden spurs ring. In the dark, the leather boots shine. Don't come tapping at my window now your heart no longer is mine . . ."

"You know when it was done, and why."

"Don't come tapping at my window now your heart no longer IS MINE!"

"You know why Perrine's bed was dismantled, taken

and reassembled on the jetty. The police would never work that out, would they, Sandie? Not unless we tell them. And we have to. We have to explain to them why Perrine's killer or killers decided to make life difficult by taking apart furniture and putting it back together again."

"*No!*" Allisande roared. "We tell the police nothing!"

"We must, Sandie. It's the right thing to do. Telling the truth is right, and sticking together is even more right."

"No! Lionel the boatman did it! He's always hanging around that jetty!"

"Don't be silly—he didn't come to the house. How would he have gotten Perrine?"

"All I know is, he's *exactly* the sort for whom taking apart a bed and putting it back together again would be no problem at all. I bet he wouldn't even need the instruction leaflet!"

"You know Jetty Lionel had nothing to do with it," Lisette snapped tearfully. "All right, then, if you won't tell the truth, I will. I'll go to the police right now."

"No, you won't." Allisande smiled a menacing smile. "Because if you do, then as soon as you come home, I'll kill you, sister dear."

14

I t's up to you, El," says Alex. "If you want to go, you can go." He looks at me to check that I haven't changed my mind.

Ellen's standing by the front door in her school uniform, with her satchel over her shoulder. "I have to go to school somewhere," she says. "And even though it's sad being at Beaconwood now that George is gone, at least he was there once. If I started at a different school, there wouldn't be any memories of being there with George or of meeting him there. It would be worse."

"Then you should go," I say, shocked all over again by the strength of her feelings. I didn't love anyone as much as Ellen loves George until I was in my early twenties. "Alex, can you walk her down to the bus? Take Figgs?"

"We can do that, can't we, Figgs?"

Please let her tell him soon about her plan to marry George. I need him to reassure me it won't happen, that Ellen and George will both come to their senses by the time they reach marriageable age.

Whatever she says, Ellen's feelings for George are not platonic. Her eyes light up and her voice changes when she mentions his name. If they got married, it would be a disaster. George would fall in love with somebody eventually—the kind of love that would count for more than the friendship bond he has with Ellen—and that would break her heart. Meanwhile, if it took him too long to realize his mistake, Ellen might have missed out on her chance to have children.

"You sure you're okay with me going, Mum? Not long ago you were dead against."

"That was . . ." I clear my throat. "I've been a bit all over the place, El, but I was wrong to say that. I don't approve of the way Lesley Griffiths and her staff have behaved over the George business, but they were in a tricky situation. Now that the Donbavands have extricated themselves from Beaconwood, I'm hoping it'll revert to normal."

"No school is normal," says Ellen. "Any building with more than five people in it is going to contain weirdness. People just *are* weird."

I wonder if she's wiser than I am. It wouldn't be hard. Maybe she and George will marry and live happily ever after, always loving each other best in the world. What do I know?

It's a beautiful crisp morning. The kind of morning when even the grave that a malevolent stranger has dug in your garden without permission can't spoil the view. I stand in the doorway, watching as Ellen, Alex and Figgy disappear over the hill and out of sight. The fading voices I hear are talking not about mixed-orientation marriages but about when we'll be able to start watching *The Good Wife* again, or will Mum always say she's not in the mood, like she's started saying every night?

I can't help it. How can I immerse myself in fictional intrigue when I know Lisette Ingrey might be outside with a spade, moving earth around to create two more graves?

I realize the implication of "two more": that the one already there is going to remain as it is. *Unthinkable.* I've left it too long already.

I'm going to fill it in today. The contents of the hole are sitting beside and around it, in mounds on my lawn. I'll push them back in. Have we got a spade? Can I do it with my bare hands?

I think of Stephen Donbavand's red, mud-lined palms, and shudder.

I'm on my way out to the shed to see if there's a shovel there when the phone rings.

Her again. This time there's no hello, no "It's me."

"You'll never find me!" she says, her voice flailing and shaky, as if she's been screaming at me unheard for hours and has only just this second thought to call me so that I can hear her. "You don't know the name of my house, do you? If you did, it would be no use to you anyway. I've covered up the name, but I can find you. I know where you live, so I've got the advantage."

"So why did you cover up my house sign with the name of your boat, *Tide Glider*?" I say. "I mean, I can see the logic in covering *your* house sign if you think it'll help you to hide from me, but why mine when, as you say, you know where I live, and, obviously, so do I?" The more out-of-control she sounds, the calmer I feel. This isn't a woman with a clear head and a strategy. It's not the voice of someone who can't be outwitted. "Why swap around the names of so many houses and boats—was it because you wanted to disguise the fact that this was a thing just between you and me? Your family and mine? Would that have been too obvious, Anne? Created a link between us that even the dumbest policeman would be unable to deny?"

"How do you know what my boat's called?" Her voice rises and gathers speed. "How do you know I've got one? I haven't got a boat!"

"I know quite a lot about you. I know your husband has a mug in his office with '150% of statistics are wrong!' on it. I've seen the blisters on his hands from digging up my lawn at your request—ouch.

You should make him see a doctor, Anne. Those sores need treatment. He could get septicemia."

"I hope you get it!"

"Why would I get septicemia?"

"I'm going to laugh and laugh when you choke on mud and die!"

"Actually, I'm just about to replace the mud you . . ." I stop. Someone's pounding on the front door.

"Mum! Open!"

Ellen. I drop the phone and run faster than I knew I could. Why isn't she on the school bus?

She looks all right. Scared but unhurt. "What's happened? Where are Dad and Figgy?"

"Following me," she pants, out of breath. "George's mum was there."

"What?"

"She was at the bus stop, leaning against her car. Waiting for me. I knew it was her—she looks exactly like George. And then she smiled and beckoned me—like this!" Ellen does the gesture with her index finger. "I totally freaked out and ran."

"Ellen!" Alex is running toward the house. "Go inside, both of you."

At first I think Figgy's not there because he's not running alongside Alex. Then I see him in Alex's arms, a little gray bundle with surprised eyes. Figgy can run faster than any of us. If he's being carried, it means Alex thinks he needs protecting.

"What's going on?" I shout.

"She's coming—followed me up from the bus stop and didn't try to be subtle about it." As Alex crosses the threshold, he looks over his shoulder. "You should see her face. I think there's going to be trouble. Let's lock the door."

"Mum, seriously, she's in full beast mode," says Ellen. "I think she knows."

"About . . ." I nearly said "the engagement."

"About George's visit! She's going to go mad."

"This is . . . what does 'full beast mode' mean?" I ask. "Is she showing signs of violence?"

"Violence? I don't know," says Alex. "From her face, I wouldn't rule it out. No one's ever looked at me like that before."

"She's here," I say. Alex and Ellen turn to look. Fifty meters away, beyond the open grave in our garden, Anne Donbavand is standing where the lawn starts to slope down to the river.

"Dad, keep hold of Figgy," says Ellen. "Keep him well away from her."

"Can't we all keep well away?" Alex asks me. "We don't have to speak to her, and if necessary we can call the police and ask them to remove her from our land."

"Did either of you see her on a mobile phone?" I ask.

Alex nods. "She was speaking on one while she was following me. Looking angry. That wasn't . . . ?"

"Yup. My not-so-anonymous-anymore caller."

"Mum, why the fuck—sorry—is she just *standing* there?"

Very slowly, Anne Donbavand starts to walk toward our house.

I am very calm. I say to Alex, "Go to the kitchen. Take Ellen and Figgy. I'll deal with her." I sound like someone with a plan. That must be why Alex doesn't argue, when I am half-hoping he will.

I consider, then rule out, calling the police. A woman is walking toward my house, that's all. I have no evidence that I or my family are in danger. The police would be unhelpful, and I'll stand a better chance against whatever danger there is if I don't surround myself with unhelpful people.

What will I say when Anne gets close enough for us to speak? Will she start the conversation, or is that down to me? I'm the host, and she has arrived at my house. I can't imagine myself saying, "Hello, Anne." The only things I can picture myself doing are nonverbal. Violent. Perhaps I am the dangerous one.

Anne walks a curve around the open grave. Apart from the distinctive tunnel-effect eyes, she looks ordinary. Dark brown, shoulder-length straight hair in no particular shape or style. Royal blue wool coat buttoned to her knees, hands in her pockets. Black trousers, black boots with square heels, blue and brown checked shoulder bag.

Her face is not still. Her lips, eyebrows, nose, the skin around her cheekbones—all these parts are moving constantly, almost imperceptibly, as if someone's tugging them this way and that behind the scenes. Either she has a neurological condition that causes twitching or else she's rehearsing the exchange we're about to have. Isn't that most likely? Inside her head, a dramatic scene is playing out. She's arguing, winning, enjoying it. Trying not to mouth the words. By and large, she's succeeding, but I can see the effort.

As she comes closer, the facial tremors become less frequent. By the time she's standing in front of me, they've stopped; she's abandoned her imaginary conversation in preparation for our real one.

"I took the *Tide Glider* sticker off my sign," I tell her. "I've still got it if you want it back. Did it ever end up in the papers, do you know, the feature about the day the houses and the boats swapped names?"

"I don't know what you're talking about. I'm too busy to read newspapers."

Newsspaperss.

It's her. That voice: the not-quite lisp. My last doubt smoothes itself away, flattens into absolute certainty.

"It must have taken you ages to have those stickers made," I say. "Did you delegate it to your husband? Like the digging?"

"I didn't come here to talk about stickers or house signs."

"Or digging?"

"Are you Justine Merrison?" What she says matters more to her than what I say, clearly. Her hard stare warns me that this will remain the case, however long we spend talking.

"Pardon? Oh right—you're pretending not to know who I am. Yes, I'm Justine. Though you prefer to call me Sandie, remember?"

"I've never called you anything before. This is the first time we've met."

"Met, yes. Spoken, no. I'm surprised you don't recognize my voice. I recognize yours from all your threatening phone calls, including the one about ten minutes ago."

"I really don't know what you're talking about. You're Ellen's mother?"

"Yes. Justine Merrison, Ellen's mother, and therefore not your sister Allisande Ingrey."

"Who?"

"Well . . . yes! Good point. Because we both know Allisande doesn't exist."

Anne stares at me coldly. "I have no idea what you mean. May I come in? I need to discuss something with you." She looks over my shoulder into the hall.

"We can talk here. I'm not letting you in."

"What? No, not here. I'd like to come inside."

"But you can't."

"Why not, for heaven's sake?"

"Because you're disturbed and dangerous. You think you're someone called Lisette Ingrey, but you're not. Or maybe you don't really think it. Maybe you're pretending because it suits you to do so."

Not a flicker of guilt or discomfort in her eyes. "No, you're the one pretending. Wait—let's call it what it is: lying. You're making up lies about me—which is no surprise, I have to say. The thing is . . ."

She glances at her watch. "I need to get to work, and I have a problem I need to discuss with you, so I'd appreciate it if you would stop talking rubbish and let me in."

"No." Could she push past me? Will she try? "You don't have a right to come in if I want to keep you out, and I do. This is my house, not yours. It's never been your house."

She flinches at that. Which, if she doesn't believe she's Lisette Ingrey who grew up in Speedwell House, makes no sense.

"I don't know what's real in your mind and what's an act," I tell her, "but you've told your children that you're Lisette Ingrey. That your sister Perrine murdered Malachy Dodd and was then murdered. Somehow this led to Allisande, your other sister, wanting to kill you, and so you and your family all had to change your names, and George and Fleur aren't ever allowed to do anything or go anywhere in case that gives the dreaded Allisande an opportunity to get to them. That's what George and Fleur believe, isn't it? They believe it because it's what you've told them."

Anne stares at me as if I'm a big, ugly obstacle in her way. "I don't know any Ingreys or Dodds," she says.

"You made your husband come here at night and dig a grave in my lawn—that one there, see?—after making a threat on the phone about three graves. You sometimes hide in the trees on my property—you saw I had a new dog, and you had a silver nametag made for him, which was also a threat. Really, the reason you want me and my family to go back to London is to separate Ellen and George—the same reason you took him out of Beaconwood, after you persuaded Lesley Griffiths to pretend to expel him. Will you admit that you did that?"

"*Pretend* to expel him?" Anne laughs. "I don't know what line you've been fed, but—"

"Lesley Griffiths said you asked her to pretend to expel George so that he would turn against the school for being unfair to him, and not want to go back there."

"If that's what Lesley's told you, she's lying. Now, are you going to let me in?"

Unbelievable. "Will you at least admit that you've been phoning and threatening me? I recognize your voice."

"No. I've had no contact with you of any kind until you opened that door."

Is there any point in saying "Yes, you have"?

If a person won't admit they've been caught out and doesn't care what you think of them, what can you do? They're as free as they've always been to make up ridiculous stories—ones that don't need to convince anybody. If someone doesn't obey the basic rules of logic and doesn't fight fair, how can anything be proven against them?

Yet Anne Donbavand is capable of rational thought. She's had dozens of articles published, and three books; presumably she can construct arguments that make enough sense to satisfy her editors. Everything she's said to me since she turned up on my doorstep has sounded ultrareasonable, and everything I've said to her has sounded unhinged. An objective observer, witnessing this dialogue without knowing the background, would probably take her side.

What can I do? I can't make an arrest, can't place her under oath for further questioning—not that she'd care about committing perjury, I'm sure. I have no power to punish or restrain her.

"What did you mean before, when you said me making up lies about you is no surprise?" I ask.

"I meant that, given your daughter's character, yours is unlikely to be up to much. I've been asking myself what kind of mother might have a child like Ellen, and—"

"And that's the end of this conversation," says Alex, who has appeared behind me. "Now that you've insulted my wife and daughter,

I'm not interested in anything else you might have to say. I'm going to close this door now—excuse me, Justine—and I expect to see you walking away. If you're still on my property in five minutes' time, I'll call the police."

He slams the door in Anne's face.

"Alex, I don't want to stay here." I'm shaking. I can't believe what she said about Ellen. It's worse than the death threats. *Given your daughter's character . . .* The idea that someone could say that about my lovely child . . .

"I think she'll go," Alex says. He doesn't sound sure.

"I don't care. Let's get out of Devon. I don't want to be anywhere near that woman, even if she's not on our land—even with a river between us. She's obsessed with this house." It's more than I can bear: the thought of Anne Donbavand, every night while we're asleep, silently and resentfully roaming around our garden, imagining herself to be the wronged Lisette Ingrey whose home it once was.

"But if we go, she's won," I argue with myself.

"It'd be temporary," says Alex. "We can have a higher wall built, a lockable gate." He runs his hands through his hair. "Do you think we're overreacting?"

"No."

"I've never had such a bad feeling about anyone as I have about her."

A loud scream snatches my breath.

Ellen.

Alex is running. I freeze for a second, then run after him.

Kitchen.

All the rooms in this house are so fucking far apart. Too much time to think between here and there. To fear the worst. *No, no, no.* This is not happening. Nothing bad will happen.

Anne Donbavand is in my house. In the kitchen, sitting on the sofa. The window's open. Ellen's crying, curled up against one leg of the kitchen table, hugging Figgy close. His leash—navy blue with a pattern of pale blue paw prints—is lying on the floor, pointing from Ellen to George's mother.

"Dad, make her go," Ellen sobs. "She climbed in. I opened the window to hear what she was saying to you at the door. I couldn't stop her and grab Figgy at the same time. I thought she'd gone! I was nearly in the hall, coming to find you, and I heard this noise. She was pushing the window open more from the outside, so that she could get in. She picked up Figgy's leash and yanked him toward her. I think she was going to take him."

"That's all lies," Anne says.

"All?" I say. "So you didn't climb in through my kitchen window?"

She smiles at me. Now that she's inside, she's happier.

"Wow." The disgust I feel almost overpowers me. "You really don't give a shit what you say, do you? You'd literally say or do anything."

"Anne," says Alex.

"Yes?"

"What are you doing in our kitchen when Justine expressly said you couldn't come in? Do you remember her saying that?"

"Yes. But I need to talk to you both. It'll be simpler if you allow the conversation to happen. It's necessary, or I wouldn't be here."

"If you want to talk, Justine and I will meet you somewhere—as soon as you like—but we don't want you in our house. So please leave."

"No." Anne smiles. There's a laugh behind it that she's holding in.

"All right, this is completely unacceptable," I say. "I'm going to call the police and report an intruder." I move toward the phone on the wall.

"Go ahead," says Anne. "When they arrive, I'll tell them you harbored my fourteen-year-old son in your home against my wishes. You knew George wasn't allowed to be here, but you did nothing about it. You let him stay. You didn't phone his worried parents to let them know he was safe. That's unforgivable."

I laugh. "I'll be happy to confirm to the police that it's true. If I'd known what George was going back to, I'd never have let him leave."

"His family—that's what he was going back to." Anne sounds annoyed. "We're a very close, happy family."

"It's not true," says Ellen, who has composed herself. She's still holding Figgy tight. "George was never here. He's never been to this house. Mum's just angry. Ignore her. George would never come here without permission. He knows he's not allowed to."

Shit. Have I landed George in it by admitting he was here? Anne evidently knew already; I assumed he'd told her.

She throws back her head and laughs. "You're a shameless little liar, aren't you?" she says to Ellen. "Have you told your parents you've talked George into agreeing to marry you?"

"It was his idea," says Ellen. She looks at me, her eyes full of panic. No words, but I'm in no doubt about what she means: I'm not to think that because Anne knows about the marriage, she knows everything. She doesn't know George is gay.

I nod: *got it.*

"That was what I came here to talk about: this marriage rubbish," Anne says. "Then, lo and behold, I overhear Ellen talking about 'something something George's visit'—the visit she's now denying ever took place!"

"Wait." Anne has made a mistake, and I pounce on it. "Ellen, when you first came into the kitchen just now, did you touch the phone?"

"Yes." Ellen looks surprised. "I hung it back up. It was off the hook, dangling against the wall."

I turn to Anne. "Exactly. When Ellen mentioned George's visit, you were nowhere near this house. You appeared a few seconds later, right at the bottom of the garden. You can't possibly have overheard, unless . . ." I laugh. "Anne, you've just totally given yourself away! I was on the phone to my deeply unpleasant anonymous caller when Ellen banged on the door. I dropped the phone and ran, without hanging up—as Ellen's just told us. She came in here and found it off the hook. So, there's only one way you could have caught what Ellen blurted out about 'George's visit,' and that's if the anonymous caller was you. Ellen's voice couldn't possibly have reached where you were in the garden. The kitchen, on the other hand . . . I'd dropped the phone in the kitchen, but you were still listening. Weren't you?" I raise my voice. "And Ellen's scared, raised voice in the hall was just loud enough for you to hear. Admit it!"

"No. I heard Ellen from the garden," says Anne calmly, but her skin has changed. *Like a snake.* Her face is dark and mottled. I've riled her.

"George wasn't here, I swear," Ellen tries again. "What you heard—yes, I said 'George's Visit,' but I wasn't talking about George coming here. He's never been to this house, honestly."

"Do you think I'm an idiot?" Anne asks her.

"No, listen. Dad's a singer. I've grown up listening to a lot of opera, and my favorite's *Carmen*, by Georges Bizet. When I was a child, before I'd learned any French, I saw his name on a CD case and pronounced it wrong. Mum and Dad thought I'd said 'George's Visit,' and it stuck. We've all called Bizet 'George's Visit' ever since. Haven't we, Mum? It's become like . . . a family joke."

A game for all the family!

Ellen's not looking at me, but a little to my left. I turn to see what might have caught her eye.

The noticeboard. Alex's list. "CAR MEN!!" at the top. Bizet's *Carmen*. So that's what gave her the idea.

"It's true," I lie. "That must be what you heard, Anne." Is this what Stephen Donbavand does—colludes because he can't bear to expose lies told by someone he loves?

"Justine, why are we justifying ourselves to this woman?" Alex asks me. "Why are we talking to her at all?"

Anne walks over to where Ellen is sitting and stares down at her. "George's Visit instead of Georges Bizet?" she says, with ice in her voice. "You honestly expect me to believe that?"

"Yes," says Ellen defiantly.

Figgy barks.

Anne opens her bag. I open my mouth to shout, expecting her to pull something out—a knife or small spade—but she doesn't. She lowers the open bag, holds it in front of Ellen's face and says, "Stay away from my son in future."

"Dad, she's got a dead thing in there!" Ellen cries out.

Alex moves to grab Anne's bag, but she slides out of his way, snapping her bag shut.

"What have you got in there?" I ask her. "Show me!" *Please don't let it be some poor person's puppy or kitten.*

"It was covered in blood. Its head was half torn off," Ellen sobs.

"She's lying again," says Anne.

"Fuck you, you rank bitch, it had a fucking tail!"

Oh God. A squirrel? Our garden's full of them.

"What appalling language from a child."

"If you don't want to hear more of it from two adults, I suggest you get the fuck out of our house," says Alex.

"Don't worry, I'm going. I've made my point." Anne sweeps out of the kitchen. I hear her heels clack along the hall, and then the front door bangs shut.

I run to the drawer beneath the sink, pull it open and grab the biggest knife I can see. I lift it above my head and bring it down with force, stabbing the wooden work surface as hard as I can, again and again.

I wish I'd killed her, wish I'd killed her, wish I'd killed her.

"Justine, stop. Give me that." There's a gap in the red mist in my head. Through it, I see Alex taking the knife from me. "Don't take it out on the house."

I have to do something. I'm not going to stand here and talk about this anymore—not to anyone. It's time to stop talking and start acting.

"I'm going out," I say.

"Where?"

"Don't be stupid, Mum!"

"I'm forty-three. I can go where I like."

"Yes, and you can kill Anne Donbavand and end up in jail," says Alex.

"I'm not going to kill anybody."

"Tell me where you want to go," says Alex.

I haven't got the energy to lie. I shouldn't have to. "Her house."

"She said she was going to work. Even if she isn't, she won't let you in."

"I didn't let her in, but she got in, didn't she?" I say bitterly. "I can do the same to her. You think she's on her way to Exeter University? That might have been her original plan, but it changed when she heard the words 'George's visit.' She'll be driving back home, fast as she can, to make her son's life more of a misery than it already is. Or maybe she won't scream at him—maybe screaming's what she does when she's only mild-to-medium angry. For a serious mutiny like this, she might dig a grave for him in the back garden."

"So if you're right, Anne's on her way back home now," says Alex. "You want to turn up and get in the middle of a huge family row?"

"I'll get there before the row starts."

"And do what?"

"Bring George back with you, Mum. *Please.* He can live with us."

"No, El, he can't," Alex says. "That would be kidnapping."

"George would *love* to be kidnapped, Dad. Wouldn't you, if that . . . *thing* was your mother?"

"Yes, but . . ." Alex groans and turns to me. "Justine, stop and think a minute. If you're right and Anne's heading home, she'll get there before you."

"No. I'll get there first."

"How can you? She's had a head start, and you're not even dressed. What do you want to go to Anne's house *for?*"

I ignore the question and sit down on the floor beside Ellen. "Don't cry, El—it's going to be okay." I stroke Figgy, who growls. I've never heard him do that before. Could he be upset by all this? His eyes widen and he licks my hand, as if to apologize for growling.

"Ellen, listen—you said Anne was leaning against her car at the bus stop. Right?"

Ellen nods.

"If she's going home, she'll drive there," I say to Alex. "The only other way is Lionel's boat. Why would she take the boat and leave her car on this side of the river? She'd only have to retrieve it later." I glance at the time on the microwave. "Lionel's boat leaves in eight minutes. I can make it if I take the Range Rover—then it's five minutes across to the Dartmouth side, and it looks like no more than five up to George's house. If Anne's driving, she'll have to go all the way around, which is forty-five minutes at least—probably more like an hour, this time of day."

"But what will you do when you get there?" Alex asks. "What's the point of this trip?"

"No time to tell you."

Or to work it out myself.

I grab my bag, phone, and car keys and pull on a coat over my pajamas. In the hall, I slide my feet into what's left of my puppy-chewed flip-flops and I'm on my way, with Alex's question ringing in my ears.

What will I do when I get there? I'm about to find out. If I can just get there before Anne does . . .

In the car, I'm disciplined. Can't look at the clock on the dashboard or I'll worry about time, make frantic calculations, measure each second as it knocks itself out of the race. That'll take my concentration away from driving as fast as I can. I keep my foot pressed down on the gas.

If I meet another car coming in the opposite direction up this narrow lane, I'm finished. I'll miss Lionel's boat.

Don't think about that either. Don't think, don't feel, don't breathe, don't be human. You're used to this, remember? It's how work used to be.

I get to the boat with seconds to spare and sweat pouring down my face. The other passengers take care not to look at me. There are nine of them, all doing a convincing impression of Happy Tourist Under No Time Pressure At All. I hope they all drown—not literally, but in my head, to make me feel better.

Lionel, not known for his subtlety, leans his face in front of mine and says, "Somebody's in a tizzy this morning!" I tell him to get me across the water as fast as he can, then blank out his reply—something about journeys taking as long as they take; currents, headwinds, am I with him? If I allowed myself to hear the detail, I'd push him into the river, which would be counterproductive.

It seems to take years, but at last we're moving across the Dart. A white-haired woman in a green raincoat points at my house as it comes into view at the top of the hill and says, "Look, Morris, up there—is that the Agatha Christie house?"

"Don't be silly," Morris replies.

Is he suggesting Speedwell House isn't good enough for Agatha Christie? He can drown too.

I love my house. There's only one thing about it that I hate: its proximity to Anne Donbavand.

Using another trick from my London taxi-grabbing, meeting-hopping days, I get out my purse and prepare the exact change for the fare, so that I can press it into Lionel's hand on the other side and make a quick getaway while the other passengers are fumbling in their pockets for pound coins.

Finally we arrive at the jetty on the Dartmouth side. While we were sailing, I identified the best footpath to take up the hill. I've never sprinted uphill before, and would have said it was something I couldn't do, but there's no such thing. Everything's something you can't do until you have to do it.

Now the foothpath has run out, or else I've lost it. That's more likely. I scramble up the wooded hillside, nearly slipping a few times. Flip-flops aren't the ideal footwear for this sort of thing. If I fell now, I might land in Lionel's boat as it fills up to set off back to the Kingswear side.

Against the odds, I arrive in one piece. The Donbavands' tangerine-colored cottage has a wooden sign attached to its wall to the left of the front door. It must have a name, but I can't see it. The sign has a large sticker covering its surface—the same size and shape as the one that was stuck over my house sign. This one says "*Wavebreaker.*"

To hide the cottage's true identity, so that vengeful Allisande Ingrey can't find her sister Lisette and kill her.

It's too crazy, but now isn't the moment to wonder how any of this is possible.

I knock hard on the door. Nothing happens. I hear no movements from within.

Bending down, I shout through the letterbox, "Hello! Anyone home? George? Stephen?" I look in through the narrow, rectangular slit. All is still: an unoccupied house.

"Justine? Is that you?"

I cry out and jump back. The voice is so clear and close. He must be sitting in the hall beneath the letterbox. "George?"

"Yes. Hello! This is a nice surprise."

"Are you sitting against the door?"

"Yes. It's what I like to call 'going out.' The closest I get these days, I'm afraid."

Unimaginable. Yet, on this side of the river, in this house: normal.

"Let me in, George."

"I can't. The door's locked and I haven't got a key."

Shit.

"My mother took it. She's no fool, my mother. She knows that if I had access to a key, the chances of her finding me here when she got home would be slim to say the least."

"Are you alone in there?"

"Yes. Mum and Dad are at work, and Fleur's having a trial day at a new school."

"But not you?" My fingers are starting to ache from holding the letterbox open.

George laughs. "Don't be silly. I can't be trusted to be out in the world. Fleur can. She's our mother's creation. No mind of her own whatsoever. She'd never be so audacious as to make a friend, or—God forbid—*trust* someone outside the nuclear family. No danger there."

Where did he learn to talk this way? From his mother? I wonder how many times she's told him the story of Lisette, Allisande and Perrine Ingrey.

"George, I need to get in."

"And I need to get out," he says. "I can't work out if we share a dilemma or not. I think we probably do."

"Your windows look single glazed. I'm going to smash one."

"Really?" He sounds thrilled. "Justine, you are exceptionally cool."

"I'm not, George. I'm just . . . I have to get into the house."

"Where's Ellen? School or home?"

"What? No, you should stay here. I think your mum might be on her way back. She's angry. She knows you came to our house."

"She's always angry. Or crying, or worrying. Trust me, she'll be at work all day. She's never back before seven. Dad gets back around five."

"And they think it's okay to leave you here alone all day?"

"Well, Mum knows I can't get out. Until recently they wouldn't have left me unattended, but a state of emergency has been declared. I told my parents that Ellen and I are engaged."

"Yes, I . . . Right." Is he waiting for me to congratulate him?

They can't leave him locked in the house all day long. For how many days? What's the plan?

Instead of breaking and entering, I should call Social Services. If I'm lucky, they'll send someone to speak to me who doesn't organize charity fun runs with Stephen Donbavand.

"Can you smash the living room window?" George asks. "At the back, the farthest one on what will be your right. That will upset Mum most."

I release the letterbox and run around to the back garden. I nearly laugh when I see what's lying on the grass: a large, mud-encrusted shovel. Stephen must have been exhausted after staying up all night digging a grave in my lawn. He came home, dropped his spade and hasn't been able to bring himself to pick it up since.

It's too heavy for me to lift above my head, so I swing it upward toward the glass. The window smashes instantly. George is standing on the other side, wide-eyed with what looks like joy. "Use the spade to go around the frame and push out all the jagged bits," he advises. "That's it." There's no question of me getting in before he's out. He's already got one foot up on the sill.

"Careful," I say. "There might be fragments. Don't cut yourself."

"I'm fine. Where's Ellen? School?" He propels himself out and lands on the grass next to me. He's wearing dark blue jeans, red shoes and a khaki T-shirt, frayed at the neck. It looks as if it might once have had letters on it.

I think of Germander—the three letters that fell off the sign.

"I don't know where Ellen is now," I say. "She was at home when I left—your mother paid us a visit, so she didn't go to school on the bus."

"Ugh. I'm so sorry Mater inflicted herself on you."

"I think Alex will probably have taken Ellen to school by now, but I'm not sure. She might want to wait at home for me to come back. She knew I was coming here."

"Right. I'll try school first, then Speedwell House," says George. "I'd better hurry or I'll miss Lionel's boat. Help yourself to tea and coffee." He laughs. "That's funny, isn't it? I mean, in the circumstances."

"It is. George, wait. Would you be able to hide something and get away with it? I mean . . . does your mum search your stuff?"

"No. She wouldn't bother. She knows I don't have anything apart from 'permitted items.'" He makes air quotes with his fingers.

I pull my mobile phone out of my bag and check to see if it's getting a signal here. It is. I hand it to George. "Take this. There's an envelope icon—that's my email. Click on it and you'll go to my inbox. You'll find some emails Ellen sent me—click on reply and you can email her. Hide it in your room, somewhere your mum never goes, and you can email Ellen whenever you want. Do you know how to send emails?"

George nods. "Ellen showed me, on her iPod." He turns the phone over, inspecting it from all angles. "But what about you? How will you manage without it?"

"I'll buy another one."

"But until you do, how will you call people?"

"I don't want to call anyone. I don't want anyone to be able to call me. The less time I spend communicating with other people, the better—Ellen and Alex not included."

"You're the opposite of me. I just love people!" George beams. "I want to talk to anyone and everyone, apart from my mother. Dad and Fleur don't count. They're just replicas of her. When I told them all about me and Ellen being engaged, they all said the exact same thing."

He wants me to ask, but I can't face it. I nod and try to look supportive—as if I'd have said something better.

"So . . . Justine, are you sure about this?" George asks. He's weighing my phone in the palm of his hand as if it's a bar of gold. "It's so generous of you. Do I deserve it?" He frowns. "What if I read all your personal emails? I promise I won't!"

"You're welcome to. There's nothing secret in there." I invented a different email address for my correspondence with Ops, and those messages don't automatically upload to my phone. Even if George searched the internet history, he wouldn't be able to get into the account. It's password-protected. "If you dig deep enough and get to last year, you'll find me ranting and swearing like a madwoman about injustices in the world of TV drama, but then you know all about that already: the Ben Lourenco business."

He looks worried. "How do you know I know about it? Did Ellen tell you?"

Wait. My turn first. "George, who's Lisette Ingrey?"

His eyes widen. His Adam's apple jerks up and down in his throat.

"Did your mother tell you that was her name, before she changed it? Did she tell you your name was once Urban Ingrey?"

"What do you mean did she tell me? Are you saying it's not true?"

I shouldn't have brought it up. Terrible timing. Whatever George believes about her never getting home before seven, Anne might be on her way back. I may not have long.

"It's true, Justine—everything Ellen's told you." George looks upset. "I hope you don't believe in . . . bad blood or anything like that. I think that's a silly superstition, with no scientific basis," he blurts out defensively. "Just because my aunt was who she was, that doesn't tell you anything about me. I could no sooner murder anybody than rollerskate to Mars!"

"George, I . . . really, I don't think anything bad about you. Please don't worry about that."

He hates his mother. He's clever enough to see exactly how destructive she is. But he believes what she's told him about her past history—believes it unquestioningly.

It can't be my job to tell him his mother's as much of a liar as she is a tyrant. In an ideal world, that task would fall to Stephen Donbavand—useless waste of space that he is.

"Thank you, Justine—for your faith in me. I promise you, I won't let you down."

"We can't have this conversation now, George," I say. *I need to search your house.* "Take the phone. Hide it."

"You are truly the loveliest of people."

My eyes fill with tears. It's pathetic, no doubt, but I can't help it.

"Justine? When you've finished in the house, before you leave, make sure you don't block up the window or anything. Leave it open or I won't be able to get back in. I'm going to pretend I was upstairs all day and didn't hear it smash."

I nod. George stuffs the phone into his jeans pocket, bows to me as if I'm the Queen and he's my humble servant, and tears off down the hill to Lionel's boat.

I climb into his house through the window. The first thing I spot in the predominantly brown and beige living room is a sideboard with open doors. There are board games and jigsaw puzzles inside it, and more piled high on top. In a corner, there's a TV but no DVD player. Nondescript landscape paintings on the walls, two sofas that have an aged, crushed look about them. Two fat bookcases full of all kinds of books: novels, dictionaries, Assyriology tomes, books about economics. Why so many dictionaries? I wonder. There are more than ten, and none for foreign languages. Did Anne keep buying new editions in the hope that the meaning of "truth" might change—that suddenly, in 2010 or 2011, the word might be redefined in her favor?

Truth: whatever shit you feel like inventing, to make everyone who knows you wonder if they're going mad. Former meaning: that which is in accordance with fact or reality.

There's a dreary gray and black galley kitchen at the back of the house, and a downstairs loo that ought to have been left as an understairs cupboard. Apart from that, the whole ground floor is the living room. I go upstairs and find what I expected: three bedrooms—a double and two singles—and a bathroom.

This isn't right. If I didn't know better, I would assume a normal family lived in this house. Fleur's bedroom is spotlessly tidy. All over the walls, there are posters of what must be some kind of girl band: The Saturdays. George's room is mainly tidy, but not immaculate like his sister's. There are a few heaps of clothes on the floor. He has a bookcase in his room that's stuffed full of novels: Dickens, Jane Austen, Charlotte Brontë, Robert Graves, Tolstoy.

Interesting. It looks as if Anne has no objection to her son reading novels, as long as he doesn't have access to the internet. It's other real people that she fears. She's not worried about the influence of *Jane Eyre* or *Oliver Twist*.

Clever people can be the stupidest of all.

Anne and Stephen's bedroom is the messiest room in the house. The bed is unmade. There's a large pile of clean, ironed laundry balanced on one corner and spilling over onto the floor, where there are nearly as many crumpled, dirty clothes and discarded bath towels. An ironing board is pushed against the wall under the window. There's a dressing table in a corner with two laptops on it, as well as makeup, deodorant, perfume, balled-up socks.

The Donbavands need a bigger house. Incarceration doesn't have to be this cramped.

The phone begins to ring, startling me. I stare at the old-fashioned handset on the bedside table nearest to the window. It's covered in dust. I don't want to touch it. It might stink of liar breath. My stomach heaves at the thought.

It could be Anne, calling to speak to George. When he doesn't answer, won't she panic and drive straight home? I need to get out of here as soon as I can. There's nothing to stop me leaving now. I've done what I wanted to do: invaded Anne's home the way she invaded mine.

Randomly, I pull open the dressing table drawers and find nothing interesting. One contains between ten and twenty plug adaptors. Furious, I slam it shut, thinking about Anne jetting around the world, sharing her ideas with other academics while her son's not allowed to make one friend without getting removed from school.

In the next drawer down there's a heap of hair accessories on top of a brown envelope file, which I pull out and open. My breath catches in my throat.

At the top of the first typed page, in a large font, are the letters "A.I.," underlined. *Allisande Ingrey.* Beneath the heading, there's a numbered list of what look like gravestone inscriptions. It goes on for pages and pages, starting with the short and basic—"In Loving Memory of," "In Remembrance of"—and moving on to longer, more elaborate suggestions: "A tiny flower, lent not given / to bud on earth and bloom in heaven." There's a blue-ink checkmark next to number forty-six on the list: "Our family chain is broken. / Nothing seems the same. / But as God calls us one by one / The links shall join again."

That's a reference to Perrine Ingrey having been murdered, no doubt.

The phone has stopped ringing. In the ensuing silence, I tell myself what I know is true, though I wish I could pretend otherwise: Anne Donbavand has chosen the inscription for my gravestone.

In the same file, there are three coffin catalogs, showing pictures of every conceivable kind of model: dark, shiny and expensive; plain, light and cheap. There's a blue checkmark next to one of the priciest.

An odd choice if you're planning to murder a person, some might say, but I understand. Allisande might be hated and feared by Lisette, but she matters to her. When someone is that important to you, you don't choose cheap.

There's a black eyeliner pencil on the dressing table. I remove its lid and draw an "X" next to Anne's checkmark. I start to write, "Good quality, but too baroque. I'd prefer a plainer style—okay, sis?" Halfway through writing "quality," I give up. I don't want to make a joke, even one that will make Anne angry. I don't want to call her "sis" because she's not, has never been and will never be my sister.

This isn't funny. I can't quip my way out of it. A delusional, dangerous woman is fantasizing about killing and burying me and I have the brochures to prove it. She's been thorough: as well as coffins, there are hundreds of pictures of urns in the file: another two catalogs' worth. Anne mustn't have been able to decide at first between burial and cremation.

I take several deep breaths. She might not go any further than she has already. Maybe the contents of this file and the hole in my lawn will be enough for her.

And Figgy's nametag, and climbing into your house when you told her she wasn't welcome, and the anonymous calls, and the dead creature in her handbag . . .

I pull out all the drawers, one by one. There's nothing else in the dressing table, nothing in the wardrobes.

I find two more files—one red and one green—in the drawer of Anne's bedside table. I flip open the first and see something that belongs to me. I catch my breath. *When did Anne have the chance to . . . ?*

No. She didn't. She didn't steal it. This is her own copy of the real estate agent's brochure. She must have seen that Speedwell House was for sale, as we did; sent off for the details, as we did.

Here's the beautiful picture of the staircase, Ellen's bedroom with the little mint-green door in the wall . . .

Why am I wasting time staring at something I know by heart? I close the brochure and pull out the other papers in the file: information about Speedwell House, printed off a website . . . I gasp when I see what's at the bottom of the pile: another set of real estate agent's details, but this time much older—fifteen or twenty years older, perhaps. The colors in the photographs are faded. Again, there's the little door from Ellen's room . . . *Perrine's room* . . . I vow to myself here and now that I'll paint that door a different color as soon as I can, whether Ellen agrees or not. I am coming to loathe that mint green. Why has nobody ever changed it?

Over the years, Anne has been collecting all the information she can about Speedwell House, the Ingreys' family home. Except the Ingreys never lived there, and Anne Donbavand is not Lisette Ingrey.

I stuff everything back into the green file, shuddering.

The red file is worse. In it, there's a list of names, email addresses, Twitter handles, workplace details and phone numbers. Bile fills my throat. I swallow it, wincing at the foul taste, then sit down on the edge of the bed so as not to lose my balance. Once the dizziness recedes, I look again.

Everyone I know or used to know is on this list. Ben Lourenco, Donna Lodge, Freddii Bausor, Dad and Julia, childhood friends, neighbors, casting directors, makeup artists, agents. Everybody who was part of my life, even a tiny part; people I followed on Twitter and who followed me, and the same for LinkedIn and Facebook.

Everyone.

Why didn't I set my Facebook privacy settings to maximum? Why, all those years ago, didn't I make my Twitter account private? Anne's presence in my digital life has more than made up for my absence from it.

I could so easily have avoided this invasion. Alex gave me a little speech about digital privacy a few years ago, and I laughed at him, told him he sounded like a mad conspiracy theorist. "I'm not hiding from anyone," I said. "I hate this obsession with privacy. It's so much effort apart from anything else."

Anne must have spent hours researching all my contacts. There's a thick wad of paper here. A quick flick-through tells me that she's thoroughly investigated each and every name on the list. Somehow, she's found the addresses and phone numbers of more than twenty people, details I didn't know myself, in some cases. Matthew Read from the BBC, Peter Fincham from ITV, Will Peterson from Independent Talent, my friend Cassie from primary school who tracked me down and made contact a few years ago, much to my annoyance . . . Anne has found and listed their addresses, along with assorted other details.

Obsessed with me, obsessed with my house. Which came first? It had to be the house, surely. Or perhaps a combination of that and Ellen's friendship with George. I dared to move into Speedwell House, and then my daughter stole Anne's son's loyalty . . .

Here's my dad's mobile phone number, and here, directly beneath it, she's written mine. *Thanks, Dad. Cheers for giving my number to a maniac. I didn't think you'd ever go one better than the family tree business, but it seems you have.*

What do I do? Do I take these files straight to DC Luce? What do they prove? My name isn't anywhere in these pages. It looks like a harmless list of names and addresses. And the other file, the coffin and urn catalogs and the inscriptions . . . there, too, my name is absent. Anne knows, and I know, that A.I. stands for Allisande Ingrey and that, in Anne's twisted mind, Allisande Ingrey is me, but there's nothing here that proves any of that to someone who doubts it. The abbreviation "A.I." has other common meanings: artificial intelligence, advance information. In London, publishers constantly used to send me Advance Information sheets for books they were about to publish, in case I wanted to snap up the TV rights. Anne could plausibly tell DC Luce that she'd headed the inscriptions list "A.I." because it contained useful information to have in advance of dying. She could—and I've no doubt she would—pretend that the blue checkmarks were things she'd chosen for her own funeral, not mine.

I press my eyes shut. For a few moments, I am filled with such intense fury that I can't speak, think or move. Then I breathe it all out, all the heat and anger. With it goes my last hope of getting any help from the police. I no longer resent Euan Luce's inability or unwillingness to help me, whichever it is. That's just how things are.

I open my eyes and stare out of the window. There's no sign of any cars heading toward the house. From here I'd see anything driving up from the main road, which is useful. The view from the Donbavands' cottage isn't as beautiful as the view from Speedwell House. It's partly because both the ceilings and the windows are so much smaller and lower . . .

My heart jolts, stopping the thought in its tracks. *Smaller, lower. Smaller . . . Lower . . .*

I fumble in my mind for whatever thought just flitted past. *Hand it over, brain.*

Ellen's window, the peculiar feeling I had in her room . . .

Oh my God. I know what it is. Yes. Of course.

I know what it is, but I don't know what it means. *Perrine Ingrey. Malachy Dodd. Perrine and Malachy, in her bedroom, Ellen's bedroom . . .*

I think back over my conversation with Sarah Parsons and snag on a throwaway comment she made, one I laughed away at the time, thinking it trivial.

I have to read the rest of Ellen's story. Whatever it takes. And I need to talk to Sarah again.

Picking up the phone on the bedside table, I dial my own mobile phone number.

George answers on the fourth ring. "Um, hello, Justine's phone. George Donbavand speaking."

"George, it's me."

"Hello! How fantastic to hear from my . . . phone benefactor!"

I start to cry. "George, you don't have to say that. You don't have to keep paying me compliments. I need to ask you—"

"I mean it most sincerely, Justine. You're the first person who's ever called me. This is the first phone call I have ever received in my own right—not just a general family phone call, I mean."

"George, listen—do you know where we got our dog?"

"Figgy? Um . . . no. Don't *you* know?"

"Yes. I'm asking if you do."

"Right. No. Ellen said you turned up with him one day. London, I think she said. You went to London, and came back with a surprise dog."

"She never told you the name of the person I got him from, or the address?"

"No. Oh, but I remember now: she said you were driving and saw a house that you got obsessed with—"

"Did she say where? Which house?"

"No. Just a house in London. Why?"

"I'm trying to work out if there's any way your mother could have that information."

"I don't think so, no," says George.

Olwen, despite living in London herself, is part of my offline, post-London life. She might be the only person that Anne doesn't know I know. I've never followed her or communicated with her on Twitter, Facebook, LinkedIn. I remember asking my anonymous caller if she was Olwen, but I don't think I mentioned "Brawn."

There's a good chance Anne Donbavand knows neither Olwen's surname nor her address.

"Thanks, George."

"You're very welcome. Justine?"

"Yes?"

"Are you still in my house?"

"Yes."

"I'm outside yours, just about to knock on the door. I emailed Ellen from Lionel's boat. She didn't answer straightaway, so I emailed Alex—I found a message from him in your inbox and I replied to it. He said I could come over. It's weird and kind of symmetrical that we're at each other's houses, isn't it?"

"Yes. George, I have to go. Tell Alex I'm going to call him in about five or ten minutes, okay? It's important, so make sure he picks up the phone."

"I will see to it. Don't worry. Justine?"

"Yes?"

"There's an enormous hole in your garden."

"I know, George. I really need to go."

"No problem," he says cheerfully. "Maybe I'll see you later when you get home?"

"Um . . . yes, maybe. Bye."

I hang up, praying he used the word "home" because it's where I live, not because he wants to live there too from now on. Even if he does, I can't worry about it now—can't worry about anything beyond the immediate danger of Anne Donbavand murdering me and interring my body beneath a terrible poem. I must focus on keeping myself and my loved ones alive.

I pick up the phone again, then realize I don't know Olwen's number. I had it stored on my mobile. I dial directory inquiries. "Can you put me through to Brawn—B-R-A-W-N—house name Germander, number 8 Panama Row, London?"

"Checking that for you now," says the bored voice on the other end of the line. "I've got a Brawn at 8 Panama Row, initial O."

"That's the one. Put me through. Thanks."

Please be in, Olwen. Please, please.

"Hello?"

"Olwen, is that you?"

"Justine? Are you okay? Are you crying?"

"No." *Yes. With relief.*

"What's the matter? Is it Figgy?"

"No. No, he's fine. I can't explain now, but . . . Olwen, I know this is too much to ask, but can I come and stay with you—me and my family? I'd go to a hotel but I don't know how long it'd be for, and Alex and I are so stretched anyway with the mortgage—we'd run out of money in a few weeks." I'm babbling, and probably not making much sense, but I have to try and explain a bit or she'll think I'm unforgivably presumptuous. "I'd ask someone else— someone I haven't only just met—but everyone I know better than you, I can't go to because she's got their addresses. Yours is the only one she doesn't know. I need to be where she can't find me or I'll never be able to sleep again. You're the only one who isn't on the list."

"No problem at all," says Olwen. "You and Alex can have my bedroom and Ellen can have the spare. I'll move in with my wife for a bit."

"I . . . I didn't know you were married."

"Yes, to Maggie. It's okay—she only lives down the road. Hopefully us sharing a roof won't lead to divorce!"

Thank you, thank you. If I could only be there now, already . . .

"Justine? That was a joke about the divorce. It's fine. Get your people—including Figgy—together and come as soon as you can."

My people . . .

No. I'm crazy even thinking it. George can't come with us. He can't.

He's not my son-in-law. He's not my anything.

Chapter 13

Who, How, When and Why

Lisette knew her sister meant every word of the threat. She had failed to persuade Allisande. She would always fail. Allisande's eyes were full of hatred for her— more hatred than Lisette had ever seen there for Perrine, a three-times murderess.

Oh, Lisette understood it. It made sense, in a twisted way. It still broke her heart, though.

That night, Lisette packed a bag and ran away from home. She took the key from the glass-fronted cabinet and escaped by the back door. She went to the police and told them all she knew, then took herself far away. How she fared after that, and how she made her way in the world, is another story, but I will tell you this: she made a huge success of it. She worked hard to create a stellar career for herself and, once that was taken care of, she married a lovely man and had two wonderful children.

There was only one problem: Lisette had built her new life, with a new name, in a place hundreds of miles from Speedwell House. She missed Kingswear and the River Dart dreadfully. Not her family, or the house itself, or even Mimsie Careless. Lisette realized after years away that that spot in Devon where she had lived was a special place—one she pined for desperately.

And so eventually, after many years had passed, Lisette Ingrey (who by now had changed her name to protect herself and her family) moved back to the place where she had grown up. She took the precaution of living on the other side of the river from where she had lived before, hoping that this would be enough to ensure that she and Allisande never bumped into one another—though she didn't know if her sister and parents were still in the area. Did they still live at Speedwell House?

One thing Lisette did know: no one had ever been charged with the murder of Perrine. On local news, Lisette heard the occasional mention of how the killer of Perrine Ingrey was still at large.

Lisette was not surprised. Despite knowing for sure who had done it, she had been able to offer no absolute proof. The police, if they had interviewed Allisande, would have heard a very different story—no doubt Allisande would have pretended to see Lionel the boatman sneaking in and out of Speedwell House with his toolkit—and it would have been Lisette's word against her sister's.

And let's face it, everyone in Kingswear and its environs believed deep down that the death of Perrine Ingrey was a jolly good thing, and that included all the police.

Lisette suspected that her family would have moved out of the area, wanting to leave the terrible memories behind. After all, Bascom, Sorrel and Allisande had each other to rely on—they didn't need the River Dart and the sloping green hillsides on either side of it to nurture them emotionally and connect them to the bits of their past that were happy. (Don't think there were none, even amid the catalog of tragedy and violence that I have recounted.)

Lisette soon found out she was wrong. One day, she was eating a lobster salad at the Anchorstone Café in Dittisham, gazing out peacefully at the sparkling water of the river. When she'd finished eating, she asked for the bill, and when a folded piece of paper on a white saucer was placed on the table in front of her, she didn't think anything of it—until she opened it and saw her sister Allisande's instantly recognizable handwriting. This was no bill. The note read, "Leave Devon and never return, or I will kill you, your husband and your children." Lisette whirled around in her chair, but it was too late. Allisande was gone.

Lisette tore up the horrible note and left it in pieces in the saucer. She went inside the café and asked the woman behind the till if she had anyone working for her by the name of Allisande Ingrey. "Not working here, no," said the woman, "but do you know what? It's the strangest thing! She was in here only a moment ago. She ordered her usual—look, I'm actually preparing it now!—and she said she was going to grab a table on the terrace, but then I saw her taking off not two minutes ago! She's never done that before—ordered, then disappeared."

Lisette looked at the food the woman was preparing. It was two scones, both sliced neatly in half. Also on

the plate was a ceramic pot of cream and one of straw-
berry jam. Both pots were nearly empty. The café woman
had spread most of their contents onto the scones.

"I don't normally do this for customers," she said,
seeing Lisette staring, "but Allisande pays a little
extra in order not to have to do it herself."

Tears came to Lisette's eyes. This was typical Allisande, who, like Sorrel, always liked to make the
minimum effort. Neither of them would ever dream of
ordering lobster, for example, because of the hassle
of cracking the shell and pulling out tiny bits of
meat with a metal implement.

For the first time since she'd run away from Speedwell House, Lisette felt a strong tug of yearning for
her sister. (Imagine the pain of that, combined with
the fact that the very same sister has just renewed
her threat to kill you, in writing this time—it's
pretty horrendous, I think you'll agree?)

Lisette cleared her throat and asked, "Do you happen
to know if Allisande and her family still live in
Speedwell House?"

"Oh, no, they haven't lived there for a while,"
said the café woman. "Bascom and Sorrel now live in
a bungalow here in Dittisham, actually. It's just up
the hill, if you want to go and find them. Just keep
going up and up—you'll find them in Speedwell Cottage. Named after their former home, you see."

Lisette gasped. The thought of seeing her parents
after all these years . . . She was tempted, but decided she could not bear it. The whole experience
would be too painful.

"Allisande lives in London now, but she visits her parents every third weekend," said the woman. "She's been far better to them than that other sister, the one that ran off and abandoned them—I can't remember her name . . ."

"Lisette," said Lisette.

The woman leaned in and whispered, "According to Allisande—and please keep this to yourself, as I swore I wouldn't say a word—"

"Of course."

"Allisande says Lisette killed their younger sister, Perrine, then ran away to avoid being sent to jail."

Lisette was too shocked to speak. She had assumed her sister would frame the dispensable boatman, Lionel, but had never considered that she herself might be the one put in the frame. But of course, it made sense. How else could Allisande explain Lisette's sudden disappearance to Bascom and Sorrel? Oh, Lisette could imagine only too well the conversation:

Sorrel: "But where has she gone? And why? I can't bear to lose a second daughter!"

Bascom: "Neither can I! Aren't our lives ruined enough?"

Allisande: "She murdered Perrine, Mum and Dad. I saw her, while you two were in the kitchen serving up the breakfast. I saw her running out of the house with Perrine's body and the bits of bed."

Bascom and Sorrel would have protested vigorously. They would have said all the obvious things: someone would have seen her; she would have found Perrine's body too heavy to carry, being smaller and skinnier

than her sister despite being older; there was no time
for Lisette to have gotten to the jetty, reassembled
the bed, put Perrine in it and then gotten back to the
house before the meeting in the drawing room started.

Bascom and Sorrel Ingrey would have pointed all of
this out to Allisande, in Lisette's defense. But, when
Allisande kept insisting—as she undoubtedly did, more
and more desperately, as if she really believed it—
they would have eventually conceded that it was just
about possible. They would have considered the fact
that Lisette had run away without saying goodbye to
them, and they would have compared that to Allisande,
who was still there being a loving daughter. Having
weighed everything up, they would have decided to go
along with the lie that Lisette killed Perrine.

Lisette could even imagine her parents defending her
for this crime she hadn't committed. "She must have
done it to save us," Sorrel or Bascom would have said.
Perhaps they both said it. "She knew Perrine would
one day be released from prison, and then the killing
would start again. Lisette decided there was only one
way to stop that happening and protect us forever."

Allisande, of course, would have allowed her parents to impose this charitable interpretation upon
the made-up events. She wouldn't have challenged it,
because she believed in family loyalty. Family loyalty
means saying nice things about your family in public
while secretly issuing death threats.

Lisette was certain that Allisande hadn't mentioned
to Bascom and Sorrel that she'd threatened to kill
Lisette. The death threats were part of the truth,

and Allisande had chosen all those years ago to make the truth her enemy rather than her friend. In order for Bascom, Sorrel and Allisande to all live happily ever after together, the legend of family loyalty had to survive: Perrine was the only Ingrey who could be acknowledged as rotten to the core. Lisette, if she needed to be cast as a murderer, had to be a noble one who killed to protect Bascom, Sorrel and Allisande. Equally, if Allisande could not avoid pointing out (falsely) that Lisette was a killer, it was essential that she should do this in a noncritical way, praising and sympathizing with Lisette for the crime she had committed—making it as much of a good deed as possible.

Lisette was so, so glad she had run away when she did, and not only because it prevented her sister from setting fire to her in the night or something equally gruesome. She was glad no longer to be part of a family that had left the truth so far behind. Perrine's evil nature had ended up infecting all of the Ingreys apart from Lisette—and of course her husband and children, who know the truth and are totally on Lisette's side. It was Lisette's respect for the truth, and for proper justice, that led to Allisande regarding her as more dispensable than Lionel the boatman.

But what about you, who are reading this story? Do you respect the truth? I haven't told you what it is yet, have I? I could have done, quite easily, but then you would have taken it for granted. I don't want you to do that. I think you'll appreciate the truth more if you struggle for a while to work it out, and then

eventually succeed. The harder it is to come by, the
more you will value it when you get it. (This is why
mysteries are the best kind of stories: because you
only get the truth at the very end, when you're absolutely desperate, and that way of arranging things
makes you realize how scarce truth is, in stories and
in life, and that it's really all that matters.)

So let's see if you can solve the puzzle. Who killed
Perrine Ingrey—how, when and why? I have given you
every possible clue, so you should be able to work
it out.

15

---

read the last two paragraphs three times, then lay the pages on the floor. "Ellen, please."

"No. I let you read it. You said that was all you wanted."

"I didn't realize there'd be no ending!"

"Oh no you don't! Ha! Got there before you." One of Olwen's Bedlingtons has roused himself to come and see if what's been placed on the carpet is edible. Putting Ellen's story on a high shelf, she says, "There we go—out of harm's way." The dog barks an objection.

Alex, Ellen and I are still on probation. Olwen's dogs are happy to have Figgy back, but not so sure about the rest of us. I think they're worried about losing their majority status if too many humans turn up.

I am living the premonition I had all those months ago in a traffic jam on the North Circular. Germander, 8 Panama Row—a house I would not choose in a million years—is temporarily my home, and I don't mind its proximity to a six-lane road at all. The noise and the fumes don't bother me one bit. I'm so happy and grateful to be here, safely far away from Anne Donbavand, that I can't believe my luck.

It can't have been a premonition. There's no such thing. A

complete coincidence is more plausible. As for the strange, strong feeling I had when I first saw Olwen's house . . . it was the day I swapped my old life for a new one. I was probably more nervous than I realized. If Anne Donbavand can dream things up out of nowhere, perhaps I can too. Perhaps we all do it from time to time, and the mistake we make is falling for everything that crosses our minds that feels urgent and true.

"That's what real life is like," Ellen tells me. "Often there's no resolution."

"But in your story there is one," says Olwen. "You don't reveal it, but it's clear there's an answer."

"You've read it too?" Ellen looks surprised.

"Only the last bit. It caught my eye when I was at Maggie's printing it out for your mum. I liked the ending. It's a challenge to the reader."

"I don't want a challenge," I say. "I want to know who killed Perrine Ingrey, and—to quote your last chapter title—how, when and why?"

I never said that to read Ellen's story was all I wanted. It was one of my wants, the first one. Now I want other things.

"Why do you care who did it?" Ellen snaps. "What does it matter?"

How can I explain to her that, as a central character in Anne Donbavand's fiction, I need to understand my role as fully as possible? Maybe knowing who murdered made-up Perrine will make no difference to me—but until I have the answer, I can't be sure of that.

"I wonder if we should try and work it out, like the story tells us to," Olwen suggests. "If we get it right, Ellen might tip us the wink."

"Would you, El?" I ask.

"No." She chews the inside of her lip and looks down at her knees.

"Because George swore you to secrecy? Did he tell you that he and his family would be harmed if you told anyone at all? Even me and Dad?"

"No."

Olwen gives me a look that says, "Don't put words in her mouth. Let her speak."

I let the silence grow around us, hoping Alex doesn't pick this moment to come back. He's out with Maggie, doing the supermarket shop.

"I don't know who killed Perrine," Ellen says eventually. "Neither does George. The story's written as he told it to me. I've put in every detail I can remember, exactly as he said it. Most of it's word for word what his mum's told him, though George added a few comic touches for fun—like the Eminem rappy bit." Ellen smiles proudly. It's a sad smile. Unlike me, she isn't relieved to be far from the Donbavands. She misses being able to see George's window from hers.

"George doesn't know who murdered Perrine?" I snap. *For fuck's sake.* How can he not know?

Could Ellen be lying? She already feels guilty for "betraying" George by letting me read the story. Was that the compromise she made with her conscience: share the text but offer nothing beyond it; keep the family secret of her beloved fiancé Urban Ingrey?

A false secret is the worst kind of lie. *Swear you won't tell anyone this thing I'm telling you that isn't true—or else you'll soon find out I'm manipulating you. Swear you'll keep it to yourself and never check the facts with anyone else, especially not anyone more honest than me.*

Anne Donbavand invented a web of fake secrets to imprison her children and make them fear strangers. George decided he loved Ellen enough to stretch out that web and entangled her in it too. Now she's trapped with the Donbavands in their shared false knowledge of events that never took place, and I'm the stranger she fears confiding in.

"Whenever George asks his mum, she says he should be able to work it out," Ellen tells Olwen. She's given up on me as audience. I must look too angry. "She says the facts are all there for him to see. That's why my story ends the way it does."

I can't believe I'm hearing this.

"She won't tell George explicitly because that would put his life even more at risk than it is now, and she's always said that if he ever comes up with the answer, she'll refuse to confirm it."

"Well, then why tell the poor boy the story at all, for goodness' sake?" says Olwen.

"I wish she hadn't," Ellen says bitterly. "George hates knowing that all those horrific things happened and that he's related to them. Why did Anne have to tell him? I mean, she wanted to protect him and Fleur—I get that—but what kind of protection is that? 'Don't forget, children, there's someone out to get us all and there always will be, unless and until they succeed'?"

"Don't feel too sorry for George, Ellen," Olwen says. "His mother might be far from ideal, but he has the best and most loyal of allies: you."

Ellen looks slightly mollified. I wonder if she's told Olwen about her and George's marriage plans. For some reason, I suspect she might have, though Olwen hasn't said anything about it to me. Alex still doesn't know; he would certainly have mentioned it.

"Ellen, you know it's not true, don't you?" I say gently.

"What's not true?"

"The story you've written. I know George believes it because it's what his mother's told him, but . . . it's a lie from start to finish."

Ellen recoils. She shakes her head vigorously, as if to dislodge something. I wish I'd found a better, more tactful way to say it.

"But . . . no! How can it not be true, Mum? No one would make up something so elaborate! That would be, like, the craziest thing ever!"

"I think that's what Anne Donbavand is," I say. "No, actually— not crazy, but deeply and wickedly manipulative, disguised as crazy. Think about it, El. I can't believe you haven't Googled all the names—Perrine Ingrey, Lisette, Urban. I did, and I found nothing. No stories of murders, no Malachy Dodd death. No Ingreys ever living at Speedwell House . . ."

"That's because it was all hushed up! It was kept out of the papers, and never reached the internet. That's what George's mum told him."

"She's a pathological liar, El. I know which families have lived at Speedwell House in the last hundred years. I can show you a time-line, with no gaps. There are no Ingreys, and no families containing a murderer who was subsequently murdered."

I leave a gap for this information to sink in. Then I say, "George's family never changed their names. His dad was born Stephen Don-bavand. He's been called it all his life. Anne Offord—that was her maiden name—married him and became Anne Donbavand. I have paperwork from a private investigator to prove all this."

Ellen's eyes are all over the place as she struggles to take it in. "George said . . . he's got grandparents called Offord, but he says they're not blood relations. His mum told him they were her god-parents, and took over as parent figures once she was estranged from her biological family."

"I've seen Anne's birth certificate, thanks to this detective," I say. "Martin and Denise Offord are her biological parents."

"So . . . so . . ." Ellen is starting to look angry. "She just . . . I mean, she just *lied* about that whole story, all the . . . ins and outs of it? She created a whole other life and tragic past for herself and *she made her kids believe it?*"

"Yes. And let them think that they were under threat from someone who doesn't exist: Allisande Ingrey. When the only real threat to their well-being is Anne herself."

"But . . . but George *believes* it. Oh my God," Ellen whispers. "Why would anyone do that? Why?"

"I don't know," I tell her. Mad, crazy, loopy, insane . . . none of these words does justice to the enormity of what Anne has done.

"It has to be true," Ellen insists.

"No, El. It doesn't and it isn't. Why were George and Fleur called Urban and Garnet Ingrey when Ingrey was supposed to be their mother's maiden name? What about their father's surname? What happened to that?"

"Anne might be a feminist," says Olwen.

"More like a rampant narcissist," I say. "Her children—whom she regards as her property—had to have the same name as her in her fabrication. I think she views Stephen Donbavand as irrelevant—just a lackey."

"But all the details . . ." Ellen is still shaking her head. "I mean, is *any* of it true? I can't believe anyone would come up with all that, based on nothing."

"Anne's lies are based on at least one piece of very real pain," I say. "I had my suspicions when I was in her house—something occurred to me, but I needed to check with her sister Sarah to be sure. So I did. I also needed to read your story, El, and now I have. Now I'm sure."

"What?" asks Ellen. "Tell me."

"I will. First, though, I need to write Anne a letter."

"Why? If you're right and she's that big a liar, you should have nothing to do with her. What are you going to say?"

"I'm going to give her the chance to see sense and change her behavior. Don't tell me it won't work—I know that."

Do you? Or are you secretly hoping that you—the voice of pure, unbiased reason—will be able to get through to her and save the day?

"I'm doing it for my own sake as much as Anne's or anyone else's," I tell Ellen and Olwen. "Having heard and read so many lies, I'd like to see it written down: the truth. What I know. I need to know Anne's seen it—that she's read every word. After that, if she turns away from the chance of sanity for her family, that's up to her."

"And that's when you call Social Services and tell them she's keeping her son locked up on his own in the house day after day," says Olwen. "Though, as I've said, I'd do that right now."

"No," Ellen says flatly. "George would end up in care. That can't happen." She looks at me. "He wouldn't last five minutes, Mum. You know what people are like. Not all people, but lots," she qualifies.

I nod. It's as if we're two adults discussing a vulnerable child.

"If we're going to talk about knowing what people are like . . ." says Olwen. "Confronting a pathological liar doesn't work. Ever. Trust me, I've tried it." She sighs. "One day, if you're unlucky, I'll tell you my life story."

Pas devant les enfants.

"When challenged, all they do is make up more lies. 'Oh, you hired a detective?' Anne will say. 'Well, guess what? I hired him first and paid him to tell you the wrong thing and hide his true findings.' She'll lie and lie and lie—because you're not real to her, Justine. You're a pawn in her game. Everyone is. *She* isn't real in her own mind. That's how she can believe in a false identity for herself so easily. She has a tenuous, shaky, unsatisfying sense of self—all compulsive liars do. Generally, they've grown up in family structures that reward dishonesty and punish honesty: 'Yes, Dad, of course you're right about everything. You're a loving, caring family man, and not a violent alcoholic narcissist—of course.'" Olwen shakes her head. "That kind of family brainwashing's almost impossible to undo. I'd say your chance of persuading Anne Donbavand to pursue a more truthful path through life is almost nil."

"How do you know all this?" Ellen asks her. "About liars?"

"Apart from the aforementioned life story, you mean? I've trained myself: observation and analysis." Olwen manages to look humble as she says this. "People walk through my door, interested in a puppy from one of my litters? I've got roughly thirty seconds to size them up, decide if they're likely to be able to provide a good home. In those thirty seconds, I have to notice everything: Do they look at me or do they look past me? Do they speak to connect or to impress?"

"All right, so what do you suggest I do?" I ask her.

"About Anne?" Olwen shrugs. "Depends what you want to achieve."

"Apart from keeping my family safe, I want to help George and Fleur."

"Well, if I were you, I might try and call Anne's bluff. I might . . . I mean, obviously I haven't thought this through, but I might pretend to be Allisande Ingrey, as per Anne's fantasy, and see if that has any effect. How does a liar who's also a control freak react when someone else, a stranger, opens up her lie and climbs right in to pretend it's the truth? Suddenly she's got an uninvited coconspirator—what would she do then?"

My breath catches high in my throat. "Oh my God. Olwen, you're a genius."

"Mum, what?" Ellen sounds anxious. "I don't trust you when you get carried away."

"I've had a brilliant idea."

"But it was Olwen's idea."

"Part of it was and part of it wasn't," I mutter. "I'll do both: my plan and Olwen's."

"I don't have anything as solid as a plan," says Olwen. "Only a vague leaning in a particular direction. I'm probably wrong." She smiles. "Often wrong, but never in doubt—that's me!"

"I have a solid plan, thanks to you," I tell her. "It starts with me writing Anne a long letter. And then . . ." I run out of words. Too busy thinking. If I could work it out . . .

You never will. Neither will Ellen, neither will Alex. We are not magic.

"Ellen, would you mind if Olwen read your story?"

Ellen shrugs. "As long as I don't have to read it, ever again. It'd only make me feel stupid for believing it. There were things in it I thought were beyond weird when George told me. I thought, 'No way,' but they were just too strange to be made up. Knowing he was telling the truth—knowing he *believed* he was—made me believe it. Even the parts that I can totally see now are too insane to be real. George kept saying the Ben Lourenco story was unbelievable—and he's right, it is, it's *insane*—and I just thought . . . impossible things that shouldn't happen *do happen*."

"It's not your fault that you believed the story, El. Or George's. However hard it was and is to believe, it's close to impossible to believe any mother would lie to her son the way Anne has to George. You'll probably spend several months reflex-thinking, 'Surely it *can't* be a lie.' It still happens to me at least once a day."

If you'd asked me six months ago, I'd have said I was a suspicious, cynical misanthrope—especially after the Ben Lourenco business. Now I realize how trusting I am, without wanting or meaning to be, purely because the truth matters to me, and logic and reason matter just as much if not more. If you value verifiable facts and good sense, it's hard to conceive of someone as eager to avoid both as Anne Donbavand.

"Why do you want me to read Ellen's story?" Olwen asks me. "I'm happy to, but—"

"Because you get everything right. You've never given me bad advice. You gave me a dog I didn't want, and it's been completely life-enhancing. Turns out I want and need Figgy more than almost anything—we all do. The one part of this puzzle that I've already solved, I worked out thanks to you. And . . . I drove past your house and knew it would save me, and it did—here I am. It's my safe haven."

"Mum, you're embarrassing everyone." Ellen sighs.

I believe in you, Olwen, to a level that defies logic. You're my lucky charm. Something made Alex draw your house to my attention that day—something that knew I was going to need you.

"So you think I'll read Ellen's story and . . . what?" Olwen looks skeptical.

"You'll read it and you'll know who murdered Perrine Ingrey," I tell her. "That's what I'm hoping, anyway—because if it doesn't happen, my brilliant plan's a nonstarter. I'm relying on you, Olwen."

To: Anne Donbavand a.donbavand@exeter.ac.uk
From: Justine Merrison justine4PI@gmail.com

Dear Anne,

There's probably not much point in me writing you this letter. I'm hoping
you'll be curious enough to read it instead of deleting it immediately when
you see it's from me.

I know how interested you are in me and have been ever since I moved to
Speedwell House. You've got a thing about that house—it's the house you
pretend you grew up in. How dare I come along and live in it for real, right?
And then my daughter and your son started to develop a close friendship.
No wonder you targeted me for harrassment.

I know the story you've told your family about your life as Lisette Ingrey,
before you changed your name. I know you have files full of information
about me—all my friends and old work contacts that you've pulled from
Twitter, Facebook and LinkedIn—and I know you've chosen my coffin and
my gravestone inscription. I found the relevant files when I broke into your
house. (Yes, I smashed your living room window. Feel free to tell the police
if you want to.)

Usually when you pay that much attention to someone, part of you
hopes they will reciprocate, so here I am. I'm not sure if you'll be pleased or
displeased to learn that you've succeeded in making me as interested in you
as you are in me.

I would love to know if you genuinely believe that you were once called
Lisette Ingrey and that you grew up in Speedwell House, the eldest daughter
of Bascom and Sorrel Ingrey, with two sisters: Allisande the life-threatener

and Perrine the murderer. I'm not sure if you know on every level that none of this is true, and it's just a barefaced lie you've been telling your husband and children. Maybe you know deep down that it's not true, but you've persuaded most of your conscious mind to believe it anyway? The third possibility is that you believe the Ingrey story completely and are genuinely unaware that you invented it.

It's not true, Anne. You were born Anne Offord, eldest child of Martin and Denise Offord. You have one younger sister, Sarah. I've met her once and spoken to her twice.

Here are some of the things I've Googled since I started to take an interest in you: pathological lying, compulsive lying, pretending to come from a different family. You might suffer from something called mythomania or pseudologia fantastica, explained here: http://en.wikipedia.org/wiki /Pseudologia_fantastica. Anne, you need to seek urgent psychological help. Also, have you heard of Freud's "family romance" theory, about the delusion of belonging to a different family? Here's a link if not: http://www.answers .com/topic/family-romance.

I can't pretend to care about you, so don't let the advice I've just given you mislead you on that score. If you died in a ditch tomorrow, I wouldn't be sorry. Every time I think about what you're doing to your children, I feel the urge to beat the crap out of you. That's why I'm writing this letter—for Fleur and George's sake, not yours. They're the ones I want to help. You've told them their aunt was an evil triple murderer as well as a murder victim, without a care or a thought for how it might feel for Fleur and George to carry around this heavy burden of family guilt and harm. You have, additionally, made them believe that their other aunt would kill them, and you and Stephen, if she succeeded in tracking the four of you down. You have used this pretend danger to cripple Fleur and George's lives in the name of safety, and prevent them from having a normal childhood. Interestingly, George—while apparently having fallen for your lies about your and his family's history—doesn't seem remotely afraid of anyone outside of his family. He understandably seems to prefer strangers to his close relatives. He very evidently doesn't for a moment believe that I'm Allisande Ingrey, his psycho-murderous aunt. Did you not tell him that part, about you making me Allisande?

I think what you've done to your family is unforgivable. Or rather, it's only forgivable if you're crazy and not responsible for your actions, but when we met, I had the impression that you knew exactly what you were about. If you're sane, clever and in control, then your lies are evil.

Your name is not and never was Lisette Ingrey. It's important that you face up to that. And my name isn't Allisande Ingrey, nor was it, ever. My name is and always has been Justine Michelle Merrison. I grew up in Northenden, Manchester. I am not your sister who threatened to kill you if you didn't leave Devon, or if you told the truth about Perrine's murder—a murder that didn't happen, since Perrine is a figment of your imagination. And, just to avoid any ambiguity, Allisande/Sandie is also someone you invented. Speedwell House was never the home of anyone called Ingrey. The last two owners, before my husband and I bought it, were called Ainscough and Rutherford. Before that, the house belonged to the Deller family, having been passed down through the generations since 1765. No Ingreys. This has been checked and double-checked. (I hired a private detective—if you look at the email I'm sending this letter from, you'll see I'm writing to you from an address that begins "Justine4PI"—this isn't my normal email, it's an account I set up solely in order to correspond with a private investigator.)

Before I sat down to write this letter, I had a long telephone conversation with your mother, Denise Offord. She said she didn't see much of you these days, and sounded strangely unemotional about it. Also weirdly incurious. She wasn't eager to find out why I was interrogating her. It was as if I were asking about some glove or sock she'd mislaid in the late 1980s and not thought about since.

Maybe she's not particularly imaginative. From the Ingrey story you created, it appears that you're the opposite. I would guess that part of your reason for drifting away from your parents might have had something to do with this. They weren't on the same wavelength or intellectual level as you. But what about your sister, Sarah? When I met her, she seemed bright and interesting. I think you don't see much of her for a different reason. You're holding a grudge from childhood—against her and your parents.

The first time I spoke to Sarah, she said an interesting thing without realizing it. I asked her if she could think of anything in her and your childhood that might have turned you against her, or against Martin and Denise, and she couldn't think of anything. She described your family life as "building-society-advert dull." She said the most dramatic thing to happen was when she came down with what appeared to be some sort of respiratory illness, which later turned out to be an allergy: to the family dog.

I thought nothing of it at the time. It was only afterward that I put the pieces together. What would happen, I asked myself, if a child were allergic to the family pet? It's not the kind of allergy that's curable, and one can hardly evict the child from the family home. I also can't imagine that many families would force a child with such an allergy to continue to live with the dog in question.

The dog would obviously have to go. Where? To be put down? Or would a new home be found for it? In either scenario, how would the other child feel, the older of the two sisters, who wasn't allergic to dogs but who was nevertheless forced to say goodbye to her beloved pet?

I think she might blame her younger sister, while simultaneously knowing it wasn't her fault. I think she might fabricate a life story to substitute for her real one, in which her little sister was a cold-hearted killer.

But here's the interesting part: instead of two sisters in the fictional biography, there are three. Why?

I have a theory. You can tell me if I'm right.

After Perrine's murder, Lisette argues in favor of doing the right thing and telling the police the truth. She is shocked when Allisande suggests that perhaps they ought to kill Perrine. Even someone as awful as Perrine doesn't deserve to be murdered, Lisette believes. Allisande, meanwhile, would rather protect Perrine's killer and doesn't seem to give a toss about securing justice for her dead sister. Allisande ends up threatening Lisette's life more than once. And—though you might not include this detail in your version of the story, Anne—Lisette also goes on to threaten Allisande's life in return—by which I mean that you, Professor Anne Donbavand, plague me, Justine Merrison, with anonymous phone calls because you've decided I'm "Sandie" and we're sisters, and we're so at odds over the murder of Perrine that our once unbreakable bond is now in tatters. We are plotting one another's downfall. Well, you'll be glad to hear that I agree with that last part at least: we *are* plotting each other's downfall, but under our own names. It seems we don't need to be called Lisette and Allisande Ingrey in order to do battle.

I think you created Lisette and Allisande to represent two sides of you that were, and still are, at war: the one that hated your sister Sarah and wished her dead because if it weren't for her, the dog could have stayed, and the one that knew Sarah wasn't to blame and that she couldn't help having an allergy.

Was that where your hatred of your family started, with the loss of the pet you adored? Your dog was part of the family, and when your parents said he had to be given away I can imagine you thinking, "They pretend that we're a loving family, but what kind of loving family banishes its most defenseless member when he's done nothing wrong?" Maybe you thought that if you had been the one with the allergy, you'd have endured the runny nose and weepy eyes without complaint.

Does all this sound like the wildest of guesses? Did you notice that in the paragraph above this one, I referred to your dog as "he"? I began with guesswork and deduction, but as soon as I started to suspect what I now know to be true, I contacted your sister Sarah again and asked her for more details about the dog.

So now I know he was male. I also know his name, and what happened to him after he left the Offord family home. Happily, he was not put to sleep. He went to live with another family, didn't he? The Dodds.

His name was Malachy. He was a Sealyham terrier.

When you told Stephen, Fleur and George your elaborate fake life story, you missed out a crucial detail, didn't you? You didn't tell them that Malachy—the Malachy who was murdered by Perrine—was a dog. Why not? I know George doesn't know, because if he did, Ellen would know too, and she doesn't. She assumed Malachy was a boy, as I did for a long time.

I know that pets are forbidden in your house. Lachlan Fisher from Beaconwood told me Fleur wanted a cat and came to school crying one day because she'd been told she couldn't have one.

You lost a pet you loved, and now you can't bear to be around animals.

How did you feel when you attached the medallion with the threatening inscription to my dog's collar? Was that hard to do? You couldn't miss the opportunity, though, could you? You knew I'd panic at the thought of anything happening to my puppy because you'd experienced it as a child—wouldn't I do anything to keep him safe, including move far away from Devon and take my daughter away from your son, leaving him wholly in your clutches?

Did it make you feel better, scaring me in the same way that you were scared as a child? Did you feel powerful at the moment when you hooked the silver tag onto the metal ring?

I'm surprised Stephen and your children haven't yet guessed that Malachy Dodd was a dog. They must have heard the Ingrey story countless times. Frankly, I'm surprised I didn't cotton on much sooner. There were so many clues, but I only realized when I was inside your house, Anne. I found myself looking at a bedroom window and noticing how low off the ground it was compared to the windows in my house. That's when I knew there was something wrong with what I'd read about Malachy Dodd's murder.

I remembered the day I'd stood in Ellen's bedroom and had a sense of something nagging at the back of my mind, something I couldn't grasp hold of—an element of a half-formed thought that jarred. It had been no more than a tiny flicker across my brain, too quick for me to pin down.

Suddenly, sitting on your bed, Anne, and looking out through the window, I knew exactly what it was that had bothered me that day in Ellen's bedroom. Our new puppy was with us at the time—he was so little and helpless, and Ellen has a huge sash window in her room. I think my subconscious put those two things together, and in your bedroom—a different room, as I stared at a different window—it finally clicked. I knew what was wrong with the Malachy Dodd death story: it was the detail about it being impossible for Malachy to have fallen from the window accidentally because his center of gravity was too low. In other words, he was too short to fall out by mistake. But in which case, how could Perrine have been tall enough to eject him? Was there that much of a difference between their heights? The impression I had—admittedly, I might have been wrong—was of two children of roughly the same age.

A little later, after examining the story in more detail, I discovered that my suspicions were spot-on: Malachy was thirteen at the time of his murder, and Perrine was the same age. Yet she was tall enough, and with a sufficiently high center of gravity, not to throw Malachy or push him out of the very same window that he was too short to fall out of, but to drop him out?

I don't think it's a coincidence that the word "drop" was used in the version of the story that reached me.

If Perrine and Malachy were both thirteen-year-old human teenagers, there would not have been such a difference in their heights that one could have dropped the other out of a window.

Let's talk about the meaning of "drop." It's not synonymous with "push" or "shove" or "throw." If Perrine had thrown Malachy out of the window, she would have had first to pick him up and then to hurl his body out. Could a thirteen-year-old girl do that to a thirteen-year-old boy? I'm not sure. Maybe.

Pushing him out would have been easier: there's no picking-up requirement first—you simply stand behind and propel forward. But if Malachy wasn't tall enough to fall, I'm fairly sure that must mean he wasn't tall enough to be pushed either.

"Drop" implies that you first hold something, then let it go. Think about it using an egg as a test object. You can throw an egg out of a window without first holding the egg outside the window. Now think about dropping an egg out of a window. That suggests an outstretched arm protruding from the window, with the egg still held in the closed hand, and then . . . the hand drops the egg.

No thirteen-year-old girl could hold a thirteen-year-old boy outside a window in order to drop him a few seconds later, or even a second later. A small dog, on the other hand, a dog roughly the size of a Sealyham terrier, would present no problem. I think you use the word "drop" when you tell the story because you're picturing Perrine holding Malachy with both hands, her arms outside the window. I think you're imagining her looking him right in the eye, savoring that moment when there's nothing but her hands and her power between him and certain death. Do you torture yourself by acting out in your mind those seconds during which she might have decided to save him?

Is it a test for Stephen, Fleur and George? To see if they're as clever as you think they ought to be? Because you don't truly trust anyone, you test people constantly, setting yourself up as judge. You haven't told your husband and children that Malachy is a dog, but you've given them all the clues—including your careful use of the word "drop" whenever you tell them the story, and I bet you repeat it and discuss it often. They haven't guessed yet. Does that satisfy you or frustrate you? Do you think you're capable of having any interaction with another human being that isn't entirely manipulative?

It's not only the word "drop" that gives the game away. When everyone is invited to Speedwell House at the end of the story, the mother of Perrine's third victim, David Butcher, says to Malachy Dodd's "mother," "Will you pipe down? Do you know who my son was?" At first I thought, "Snooty elitist mother of Cambridge college organ scholar," but, really, what mother would say that to another woman in the exact same position as her, when they've both lost their sons? I don't believe anyone would, not even the snobbiest person in the world, and they certainly wouldn't follow it up with: "Are you even a tiny bit embarrassed about how much airtime you're taking up today?" (See, Anne? The oral tradition is alive and well. I have the whole story, as if from your mouth.)

It makes far more sense if Malachy is a Sealyham terrier, doesn't it: Mrs. Butcher thinking, "This is unbelievable! People have died, and she's playing the part of Chief Tragedy Queen when all she's lost is a bloody pooch!"? Because so many people don't understand, do they, that you can love a dog as much as you love a person?

Talking of love . . . there is more evidence in the Ingrey story to suggest Malachy is a dog. Lisette and Allisande loved Malachy, or so the story goes. Loved? Do teenage girls generally love teenage boys who are younger than them? Do they love teenage boys who are not relatives, or when no hint of romance or sexual attraction seems to be involved? Malachy made Perrine cry, though. This, I believe, is a direct reference to your real sister Sarah's allergy. Did Perrine have the same allergy, Anne?

In the story, Malachy's regular visits to the Ingrey house are "a compromise" between Bascom and Sorrel, your fake parents. In what way, though? Did one of them want him to come around regularly while the other didn't? I know the defining characteristic of Bascom and Sorrel as a couple is that they disagree about most things, but why would either of them not want Malachy to come around? From the rest of the story, there's nothing about either parent being against friendships for their daughters, or disapproving of visitors to the house—at least not before

the attempt on Perrine's life during the rounders match led to a complete
hunkering down.

There is, however, a reference to Sorrel wanting to fill the family home
with cute, furry pets, while Bascom is determined not to have even a goldfish
under his roof. Aha!—all of a sudden, this "compromise" makes perfect
sense. Malachy is the "pet compromise." He's not an actual pet, but, rather,
a regular animal visitor.

Because, let's face it, if he were a teenage boy of Perrine's age, would
he really be allowed to spend time with her up in her bedroom, with no one
else around? Especially by Bascom, who, we are told, would never have let
Malachy Dodd cross his threshold in an ideal world?

Let's pause for a second to reflect on the workmen you refer to as "the
bumcrackers"—those poor men who were forced to sleep on buses because
Bascom was so worried that they might molest his daughters: "One could
never tell," with strangers. Would that same Bascom Ingrey allow a teenage
boy to stroll on up to his youngest daughter's bedroom with impunity? I doubt
it. An elderly thirteen-year-old dog, on the other hand, would not pose the
same deflowering risk. Bascom expresses approval for Malachy at one
point in the story—why, then, does he not want him at Speedwell House?
Because, of course, Malachy is a dog and Bascom is one of those people
who doesn't want animals anywhere near him, however cute or well behaved
they might be.

So, what do you think of my evidence, Anne? I think it's pretty conclusive.
I think you should sit Stephen and the kids down and tell them, before I do:
"Malachy Dodd was a dog. My sister Perrine's first murder victim was
canine, not human. A Sealyham terrier." Or maybe you'd like to make him a
different breed in the story, maintain a bit of emotional distance? Remember,
though: choose a small breed, for dropping-out-of-the-window plausibility.

Then you can go on to explain to your husband and children that the
whole story is a lie. You can tell them about the real Malachy, the genuine
threat you believed your parents and sister posed to your well-being, even

if it was only emotional and involved no death threats. Did you cry and beg them to let your dog stay? Did they ignore you? Tell you to stop being so silly?

Describe to Stephen, George and Fleur whatever it was that you went through that made you believe it was safer to retreat into fantasy and avoid the facts altogether. Admit to George that the reason you can't stand the idea of his friendship with Ellen is because of your buried fear and repressed trauma from childhood. Admit that it has fuck all to do with Ellen being the daughter of Allisande Ingrey, your avenging sister.

Admit to your family that there is no rational reason for the four of you to batten down the hatches and hide, as if you're in danger of imminent attack. Explain to them that you aren't in danger, but that you can only feel happy and safe if you have total control of your children and can guarantee that they aren't subject to any influence apart from yours. Then tell them you know how screwed up that is, and promise to get help before you ruin all of their lives and what's left of yours.

George's name is George Donbavand, not Urban Ingrey. Fleur is Fleur Donbavand, not Garnet Ingrey. They have the right to know this. Why did you feel the need to give them secret names, secret identities? Do you believe no one can survive in the world if they are seen for who they truly are?

As you can hopefully see, I have become obsessed with you and your fake biography, Anne. You've made me part of it and I want a resolution. I'd like to know who murdered Perrine Ingrey. It's a tribute to your creative skills that, despite knowing she isn't real and never was, I still want to know who killed her and why.

Yours sincerely,
Justine Merrison

From: jmerrison71@gmail.com
To: ellencthatsme@gmail.com

Dear Ellen,

It's George here. I am missing you more than usual. I think it's because
I know you're not at home. Isn't that peculiar? When you're at Speedwell
House, I can at least see the building that contains you, even if I can't see
you. I hope you come back soon. I am devising a flashing-light code that
will allow us to communicate properly. It's quite complicated and will take
you a while to learn, but once you have, it will enable us to have proper
conversations.

All my love,
George xx

From: ellencthatsme@gmail.com
To: jmerrison71@gmail.com

You don't have to start every email with "Dear Ellen, It's George here"!!
I know it's you! Mum's switched over to a different email address now
anyway. Your code sounds amazing!! I'll learn it v v quickly. I can also write
it down and have a manual to refer to in case I get stuck (which I won't!!)
I can't WAIT to get back to Speedwell House. I'm basically living in a kennel
here. The dogs all stick their tongues into my cereal bowl while I'm trying to
have brekkie—so gross! I wish you could come and live here with us. Failing
that, I wish I could tell you where I am, but Mum says it's important I keep it
secret. You wouldn't ever tell anyone, would you?

Hugs and kisses and LOVE, Ellen xxxxxxxxxxxxxx

From: jmerrison71@gmail.com
To: ellencthatsme@gmail.com

I wouldn't dream of telling anyone your confidential location, of course, but
you still shouldn't tell me, much though I yearn to know. I would feel so much
happier if I just knew where you were, but I can't promise that my mother
won't find this phone. Call me a pessimist, but I suspect that one day she
will. This situation of being able to converse with you whenever I want to
(albeit by machine) is too good to be true, and my fourteen years on this
planet have drummed into me that things which are too good to be true don't
happen to me. Apart from meeting you, that is.

Dearest Ellen, don't tell me where you are because I would smash a
window and come and find you, and your mother is right: it wouldn't be safe.
My mother might find a way to get the information out of me. I wouldn't put it
past her to torture me (more than usual) and so it's better if I'm not in on the
secret. My only worry is how long this situation will go on for. I suppose it's
bearable for as long as we can email each other.

All my love,
George xx

From: ellencthatsme@gmail.com
To: jmerrison71@gmail.com

Don't worry, I think my mum's planning to tackle the situation so that we can
go back to our house—YAY! She keeps hinting she's had THE BEST idea, and
now she and the dog lady are having a whispery conversation in the garden!

xxxxxxxxxx

From: jmerrison71@gmail.com
To: ellencthatsme@gmail.com

That is heartening news. I have every confidence in your mother's brilliant
idea. After all, she had you!

All my love,
George xx

16

That's my best guess," Olwen concludes with a shrug. She throws a tennis ball for the dogs, using a plastic contraption that scoops it up off the floor so that she doesn't have to bend down. "I can't see who else could have murdered Perrine, but then everything I've said is based on the assumption that the story obeys its own internal logic. What if it doesn't?"

"I think it does," I say. "It might be a lie from start to finish, but it's the life history Anne's chosen for herself. She's effectively swept the facts aside, substituted this story, and said, 'This is who I am and what I've been through.' She'd want it to be good. Watertight. The solution you've come up with is the best one. It's the only one that works, and it's . . . well, if it were true it would be shocking, wouldn't it? For Lisette Ingrey, if she were real, it would be deeply traumatic."

"Yes, and if it's not true, it's certainly ingenious," says Olwen. "Though a little obvious, when there's no other possible resolution."

"Olwen, trust me, it's not obvious. I worked in TV drama for years. Thirty twists a day crossed my desk. I thought I'd seen them all, but I could have read that story fifty times and I wouldn't have gotten it."

"I reckon you would. All the clues are there, as Ellen points out in the final paragraph. She's a talented writer, your daughter. If you ask me, the most incredible thing about the story is that a fourteen-year-old wrote it."

"No. Anne Donbavand wrote it—in her badly warped mind if not on paper. George learned it by heart and passed it on to Ellen, who wrote it down." The tennis ball lands near my feet, dropped from a furry jaw. Before Olwen has a chance to scoop it up, I grab it and throw it so that it lands next to Figgy: pet nepotism in action. He wouldn't stand a chance of getting it otherwise, with all these bigger dogs around. He pounces on it and tears off to the bottom of the garden with a triumphant glint in his eye, happily unaware that he didn't win on merit. "I knew from the first sentence that story wasn't Ellen's," I say.

"And now we know who killed Perrine Ingrey, or we think we might—"

"We do."

"But how does that help you? The only real thing in the story's Malachy the dog, so what does it matter?"

"If I'm going to stand a chance against Anne, I need to understand her delusions. On my own terms, I'm always going to lose. She doesn't play by any rules I recognize. I need to play *her* game, and win. I think I can. I'm getting to understand her better."

"She's bonkers, Justine." Olwen flashes me a sympathetic look as if she fears I might be too. "What more is there to understand?"

"Some lies are purely functional," I say. "Like 'No, Dad, I haven't been smoking, honestly' or 'Yes, darling, of course I'm totally faithful.' They serve a practical purpose, but the teller knows they're not true. She doesn't need them to be true in order to survive psychologically. Other lies are fully fleshed-out fantasies, chosen as preferable to the truth. Anne Donbavand *wants* it to be true that she was Lisette Ingrey, that she went through all that horror as a child."

"Why would anyone want that?"

I sigh. "I could guess, but that's all it'd be: groundless speculation."

"No! I'm not throwing it again, Wenceslas. Enough! Run along, the lot of you."

"I think Anne feels victimized," I say. "Let down by her family— far more than any collection of autobiographical details can adequately explain. She's a clever woman. She knew she was wounded and probably didn't understand why. Maybe it was only the business with the dog, or maybe it was that and other things—other *ordinary* things. If you're unusually sensitive, it's possible to be destroyed by incidents that aren't at all spectacular or dramatic—it doesn't have to be full-on murder and horror to crush you."

"So she invented a murdered sister and another one intent on killing her as justification for the way she felt?" Olwen asks. "So that no one would deny her right to feel as bad as she did, or does?"

"I think so, yes. Would you risk describing your emotional pain if you thought everyone would say, 'Oh, come on, it's not as if you've had a hard life'? I wouldn't." *Didn't. Don't.* "Anne needed a story that'd make anyone who heard it step back and say, 'Wow. Poor you. How you must have suffered! Have *all* the sympathy and special treatment!' She created a new family to make up for the one that failed her so badly, and, again, her fantasy of being Lisette Ingrey pursued by the vengeful Allisande proves to be exactly what she needs. It enables her to imprison her children, effectively, and claim it's for their own protection. She's overwhelmingly invested in her lie."

"You think she's come to believe it?"

"If I had to guess? Yes and no. She knows it's not true by any consensus definition of truth. At the same time, she despises that way of defining things. Her story is *truer* than the reality. The *facts* of her life are untrue. So she doesn't feel as if she's lying. The story she's shared with her husband and children and no one else—her secret name, her unverifiable, unrecorded, unwitnessed life—that's the truth of who she is."

"I'm not sure I'm with you."

It's frustrating that I can't explain it properly. I know what I mean, but it's hard to convey to someone else. "You and I and most people—we accept that fact is fact. Anne's different. She's not going to allow herself to be limited by reality. If she can't alter it to suit her needs, she'd rather destroy everything. That's why I can write her persuasive letters from now until the end of time and I'll never get through to her. You couldn't either. There's only one person who maybe can."

"Who?"

I run through the logic of it in my mind one more time before I take the plunge.

"Allisande Ingrey. Her sister."

"But—"

"Allisande doesn't exist? I know. That doesn't mean no one can impersonate her. I couldn't do it—Anne wouldn't accept it coming from me, when I've been telling her over and over that I'm Justine and not Sandie—but someone else could try to be the sister she invented." I smile. "Someone with a tennis ball in one hand and a plastic . . . ball-throwing contraption in the other?"

Olwen laughs. "Forget it, Justine. I'm not pretending to be Allisande Ingrey. I know I suggested it, but a) I suggested *you* should do it, not me, and b) I wasn't being serious."

"It was a good idea."

"No. It really wasn't."

"Will you just—"

"No, Justine!"

"Olwen, there's no one else I can ask! It's just one email—maybe a phone call. You're right, it won't work. There's no way Anne'll go for it, but . . ." I lose heart before I reach the end of my pitch. "I don't know, maybe I'm as crazy as she is, but I think if Allisande removed the threat—maybe even apologized for it—that might help things. Imagine if Anne were to get an email purporting to be from Allisande, saying, 'Please can we meet and talk? I think I owe you a big apology.' She'd know it wasn't me; my strategy all along has been to deny I'm Sandie. And I've just emailed her a long letter in which I argue that facing up to the truth is the only way forward. So why would I suddenly change tack? So, a voice Anne doesn't recognize, claiming to be Sandie . . . she wouldn't think in a million years it might be me."

"Right, but equally she would know it can't be Allisande, who, after all, doesn't exist!"

"Maybe," I say. "But she'd love her to be real and contrite, wouldn't she? And if I'm right about her psychology, Anne believes Allisande *is* real, in the murky realm that facts can't touch. At the level of emotional truth, Allisande is very real to Anne—more so than her living, breathing relatives, probably. Either way, would Anne be able to resist an invitation to meet someone claiming to be her nonexistent sister?"

"Meet? I thought it was just an email I was sending. What would happen at this meeting? What would I say? My answer's still no, by the way. And to you, Good King Wenceslas—no more ball. I mean it."

"You'd tell Anne she was right all along. That you were young and frightened. You took your fear out on her and lost a beloved sister, when you should have supported her. Together, the two of you should have stood strong, like she wanted to, and gone to the police with the truth. However hard it was. You'd cry a bit, ideally, while saying all this."

"Cry?" Olwen tuts, as if crying is an activity she's long disapproved of.

"Yeah. Lisette needs tears and begging—lots of both. She stuck up for what was right and fair, and she was made to feel like a traitor and a pariah."

"Justine—"

"I know it's all bullshit, Olwen. I still think a hefty dollop of fake contrition in her fake world might make Anne less dangerous to us all in the real world."

"Even if I were willing, which I'm not . . . wouldn't Anne assume I was a friend of yours trying to trap her?"

"You're overlooking one crucial detail," I say.

"What's that?"

"You have dogs."

"So?"

"Allisande and Lisette both loved Malachy Dodd, remember? Isn't it plausible that, after Malachy's tragic death, Allisande would decide to be a dog breeder and kennel owner when she grew up?"

"Oh God!" Olwen covers her face with her hand. "I hate to say it, Justine, but I'm worried all this is turning you as loopy as her."

Something inside me hardens. This has to happen. I'll find someone else to play the part of Allisande Ingrey if I have to.

"People believe what they want to believe, Olwen—all over the world, every single day. They ignore logic and evidence and basic human decency and believe whatever makes their life more bearable in the immediate short term. Anne will believe in Contrite Sandie because she'll want to, desperately. It'll be her perfect fantasy fulfillment."

"Her fantasy, from what I can gather, is her killing Allisande before Allisande kills her," Olwen points out.

"At the moment, yes—because it hasn't occurred to her that her sister might grovel and admit that she, Anne-slash-Lisette, was right all along. I think she might go for that as an even more favorable outcome, and if she does, there'll be no more death threats— from anyone to anyone. Isn't it worth a try? What if all Anne needs is for someone—*anyone*—to take the time and trouble to apologize to her for everything she's been through—all the pain and misery that she didn't deserve. She might decide she doesn't need to kill me if she hears you say, 'I'm so sorry. You were as much a victim as Malachy Dodd, John Kirbyshire and David Butcher—a wholly innocent victim. Please tell me what I can do now to make it up to you, because there's nothing I wouldn't do to make this right.'"

Olwen sighs. "I understand the reasoning behind it, but . . . it won't work. I hate to sound defeatist, but it just won't."

"All right, fine," I say. "Let it not work. I'm asking you to try, not to guarantee success."

"What if Anne agrees to meet and turns up with a breadknife in her handbag? You're asking me to risk my life."

"If she agrees to meet you, we'll arrange it so that I'm there too. I'll make sure nothing happens to you. She wouldn't try to hurt you, Olwen. I'm the one she wants to harm, not you. Ellen and Alex can go to Maggie's so that they're out of the way. And Figgy, in case she recognizes him. You've got a house full of dogs that look a bit like Figgy—that could work in our favor."

"So she's coming here, is she? To my house? That's the plan?" Olwen closes her eyes. She knows that capitulation is not far away. It feels inevitable, to both of us. "How do my dogs work in our favor?" she asks.

I pick up a ball and throw it for Good King Wenceslas, who has been lingering hopefully near my feet.

"In her mind, Anne has made me Sandie," I say. "I think she's a proud woman—most people are who bury their own very real suffering and deny its existence—they'd find it too humiliating to admit to feeling the pain ordinary mortals feel. Anne's not going to admit she's wrong about the identity of her enemy-sister unless she sees a way to change tack without losing face. If I'm not Allisande but I turn out to be someone associated with Allisande—someone, perhaps, who got her dog from Allisande's kennel . . . Make sense?"

"Too much." Olwen sighs. "It's way too rational for Anne Donbavand. She exists in another stratosphere—the woman's completely loonytunes, Justine. We can't just open the door to her elaborate fantasy life and stroll in as if it's a . . . the local pub! It won't work."

"So you keep saying. Wouldn't you rather be able to say, 'It didn't work'? What possible comeback will I have then? That's the way to win the argument: prove me wrong."

Olwen makes a frustrated noise.

"I promise you, Olwen: I won't let her hurt you."

From: AllisandeIngrey@hotmail.com
To: a.donbavand@exeter.ac.uk

Lisette, it's me -- your sister, Sandie. I need to talk to you. Ideally, I'd like us to meet. I know this suggestion will be anathema to you. I know that for many years you have been afraid of me. But you have nothing to fear from me now. I want to make peace. This bad blood between us has gone on too long.

I would like to invite you to my home in London. Can you come soon? Can you come now -- or tomorrow? If you want to, you can bring someone with you, if you're worried I might harm you. Bring your husband. I would love to meet him. Bring your whole family if you wish.

In peace --
Allisande

From: a.donbavand@exeter.ac.uk
To: AllisandeIngrey@hotmail.com

Who is this?

From: AllisandeIngrey@hotmail.com
To: a.donbavand@exeter.ac.uk

I am your sister, Allisande Ingrey. Come to London tomorrow. Take the 1007 from Paignton. It arrives at London Paddington at 1338. I'll send a taxi to meet you and bring you to my house. There are things we need to talk about -- things we should have talked about long ago. It's my fault that we didn't and I wish to put that right. Please come, Lisette.

Sending you love and peace --
Allisande

From: AllisandeIngrey@hotmail.com
To: a.donbavand@exeter.ac.uk

Lisette, you haven't replied. May I assume you will be there tomorrow?

From: a.donbavand@exeter.ac.uk
To: AllisandeIngrey@hotmail.com

I'm not getting in your taxi. Tell me your address and I'll make my own way there.

From: Allisandelngrey@hotmail.com
To: a.donbavand@exeter.ac.uk

Sorry, I can't do that. I'm not putting my address in an email that you could show to anyone. Let's meet somewhere public. Why don't I meet you off the train? I'll wait on the arrival platform. We haven't seen each other for years, but I'm sure you'll recognize me. I have short spiky brown hair these days and I'll be wearing a green coat with a large brooch on it: a boat made out of pearls.

In peace --
Sandie

From: a.donbavand@exeter.ac.uk
To: Allisandelngrey@hotmail.com

I'll see you tomorrow.

From: Allisandelngrey@hotmail.com
To: a.donbavand@exeter.ac.uk

Thank you for agreeing to come, Lisette. This means so much to me. I promise you, you won't regret it.

Your loving sister Allisande

"Is that my bit done?" Olwen asks. "Can I go?"

"Yes. I won't be much longer. Half an hour after you, maximum."

We're in an internet café near Shepherd's Bush tube station. I chose somewhere random and far from Olwen's house. Just to be extra safe, I didn't want any communication to Anne's university address to come from a computer or device associated with Olwen. I can't let her end up in any kind of trouble for doing me a favor.

She stops halfway to the door. "Why did I need to write the emails?" she asks. "You could have done it. You told me what to say, pretty much."

"Author identification," I mutter, already busy with my next online task. In my former life as a slave to the TV industry, I made a drama about a forensic linguistic analyst who worked with the police in murder trials. His job was to identify who wrote what when it really mattered—did this murderer write that letter? As part of my research for the program, I spoke to a real forensic linguistic analyst, Professor Malcolm Coulthard from Aston University in Birmingham. He told me it's frighteningly easy to prove who wrote what if you have enough data to make comparisons.

Anne Donbavand has other correspondence from me. I don't want her hiring an expert to tell her I also wrote Allisande's emails. Olwen used words and phrases I'd never use, like "In peace" as a sign-off. And she uses a double-dash as punctuation—I've never seen anyone do that before.

"Justine?"

"What?"

"You don't honestly think Anne believes those emails are from Allisande, do you?"

I glance at the young Asian man behind the counter to check he's not taking too keen an interest in our conversation. I needn't have worried. He's texting someone, with a smirk on his face and busily jabbing fingers. Perhaps he too is pretending to be someone he isn't. Perhaps we all are: everyone in here—the people to my left and right and all along the row, staring at their screens, enjoying their private, insignificant deceits, or else trapped by them and wishing they could escape.

"Maybe she does, maybe she doesn't," I say. "She could be coming tomorrow because she's convinced or because she's curious."

"Or uncertain and confused," Olwen suggests.

"I hope she's confused as all fuck," I say. "If she is, she has only herself to blame. She's the one who turned messing with other people's heads into an Olympic sport and made me want to win the gold medal."

Olwen leans down and peers at the screen. "You've set up an email account in Anne's name. Why?"

"It's nothing to worry about," I tell her. "Leave it to me."

"I should get back to the dogs, I suppose."

"Yes. Go." I need to do this next part alone.

Once I'm sure Olwen's not coming back, I write an email to my former boss, Donna Lodge, with the subject heading "Private and Confidential." With forensic linguistics in mind, I alter my style as thoroughly as I can, using short, staccato sentences instead of my usual longer ones.

From: a.donbavand@gmail.com
To: Donna.Lodge@factotumproductions.co.uk

Dear Donna Lodge,

My name is Anne Donbavand. I'm a professor at the University of Exeter.
I'm also a friend of Justine Merrison. I think you used to work with her.
I urgently need to talk to you. It's about Justine. I'm afraid it's too sensitive
and confidential to put in an email. I can't risk sending this from my home
or work computer. I've asked a friend in London to send it from an internet
café. I'm in London tomorrow, as luck would have it. Could you meet me at
two o'clock? We'd need somewhere private where no one is likely to see us.

Also, we can't be overheard. I'm afraid I don't know London well. I'll leave the choice of venue up to you.

This is important. Indeed, it's urgent. I would very much appreciate it if you could meet me.

Very best wishes
Anne Donbavand

I press "send." Donna, who must hate me for walking out and leaving her in the lurch, won't be able to resist. If she has a meeting scheduled for two o'clock, she'll cancel it. She'll suggest meeting Anne at Pleasant's Café in St Gregory's Alley—it will be the first and most obvious "somewhere private" that springs to mind. We used to joke about it being the perfect place to plan a heinous crime. It's usually empty, being nowhere near trendy enough for the TV and media crowd, and there's no CCTV nearby.

Now there's evidence that Anne Donbavand made plans to come to London tomorrow—plans that had nothing to do with me—and I can forward the correspondence between Donna and "Anne" to Anne's university email account any time I like.

I don't feel guilty. Anne deserves everything I've done, and more. *Live by the lie, die by the lie.*

Not that anybody's going to die tomorrow. It's a turn of phrase.

From: jmerrison71@gmail.com
To: ellencthatsme@gmail.com

Dearest Ellen,

How I wish you were at home, at Speedwell House, so that I could come and visit you. My mother has gone to London at short notice, and I would have been able to hop on Lionel's boat and be with you in no time at all. But, alas, it is not to be. I am disappointed, but it's a useful disappointment, because it's made me realize that our light signal system has a drawback. I only found out this morning at breakfast that my mother intended to go to London (my dad found out at the same time, and looked as surprised as I was. Could Mater be up to something? Fingers crossed she elopes with another man and never comes back, though I can't think of anyone who would want her).

Where was I? Oh yes. Well, if disappearing at a moment's notice (with a preoccupied expression all over her face, I should add) is going to be a thing that Mater does from now on, I might have sudden opportunities to visit you that I won't know about the night before. How will I let you know that I'm on my way to see you? Do you check your emails in the morning at breakfast time? And what if you've already gone to school?

Do you have any ideas?

All my love forever,
George xx

From: ellencthatsme@gmail.com
To: jmerrison71@gmail.com

Just email me if you can come. I'll get it straightaway. Now that you can email me (yay!!) I'll obviously be checking my emails every few minutes. If I don't reply within half an hour, that means I'm at school. I mean, I assume Mum and Dad are planning to send me to one at some point in the near future??? I assume we will at SOME point go home? Maybe not?

At the moment it's like Mum and Dad have forgotten about my ENTIRE education. I woke up this morning and Dad whisked me out of the house for a day of shopping. He LOATHES shopping, AND he insisted on bringing Figgy with us, even though that means we can't both go into shops at the same time—one of us has to wait outside. I asked him if something was going on and he said no with his mouth all twisted in a funny way that only happens when he's keeping something secret. Parents!?!?!

Better go—Dad just moaned at me for being on my phone and ignoring him.

Love you NEVERENDINGLY,
E xxxxxxxxx

From: jmerrison71@gmail.com
To: ellencthatsme@gmail.com

Your parents are wonderful, dearest Ellen. I'm not sure you realize how fortunate you are in the parent department. Having said that, I agree that there is a marked lack of transparency in the older generation.

Your devoted George xx

17

'm waiting in Olwen's hall when the front door opens, as agreed. I hear the key slide out of the lock, then, "Go on, in you go." Olwen's voice, normally warm, contains no emotion.

Anne's royal blue coat is what I see first, then the blue and brown checked bag. Anything to put off looking at the face, but I have to see it eventually. Have to be brave. I inhale as much air as I can before meeting her eye.

She's here: Anne Donbavand. The only person I've ever been mortally afraid of. It's a shock to see that my plan has worked even to this small extent: getting her here. I expected and perhaps hoped that Olwen would return alone, with a shrug and a rueful "Sorry."

The worst shock is seeing Anne here, in my safe haven. That's how I think of Germander. It's not safe anymore, now that she's here. Never safe again. You can't wash a presence like Anne's out of a building. I want to cry, but it's the wrong time. I have a whole script to get through, an unwritten one, and I must remember every word.

"What's that?" Anne asks. She's looking at me, but I'm not what she means. The dogs, shut up in the living room, heard the door open and have started to bark.

"My Bedlington terriers. I told you I breed Bedlingtons."

"What are you doing here?" Anne asks me. Despite the question, she doesn't seem surprised to see me. I suppose when you agree to go home with a stranger pretending to be your invented sister, you prepare yourself for anything.

"Good question, Justine," says Olwen, who has learned her lines more thoroughly than I have. "What are you doing here? How did you get in?"

"Oh, I have my ways. I'm good at getting inside people's houses. Their houses and their heads. Anne'll tell you. Anne, this woman you're all pally with suddenly—she's not who she says she is, you know. She's only pretending to be your sister Allisande."

Anne turns to Olwen. "I don't want to see dogs," she says. "Can't you put them outside while I'm here?"

I walk to the living room door and pull it open. "These dogs?" I say as four of them run out into the hall.

Anne holds herself very still.

She's just a person. Look at her. She's not sure why she's here or what's about to happen. How can one person do so much harm and still look so ordinary, so vulnerable?

I remind myself of how Anne looked when she insulted Ellen's character: the sneer on her face. That was the same person. I don't feel sympathy for that woman who stood in my kitchen and said those things: none at all.

"Come on, Anne, you're not scared of dogs," I say. "Not puppies, anyway. If you were, you wouldn't have been able to get near enough to mine to put that nametag on him. Or did you make Stephen do that?"

"Justine, I'm going to have to ask you to leave," says Olwen. "Lisette and I need to talk."

"Ah, *Lisette*." I laugh. "Your big sister, I suppose?"

"Yes," says Olwen. Anne says nothing.

Come on, Professor. I'm the object of your hatred. You desperately want me to be defeated, so tell me I'm wrong. Tell me Olwen is your sister Allisande.

"You're as insane as Anne," I say to Olwen. "I wouldn't have believed it possible. The two of you are—sorry, dogs, no offense—barking mad."

"Justine got her dog from me," Olwen tells Anne.

"I'm so glad the subject of dogs has come up," I say. "Anne, did you get my letter, the one I emailed to you, about Malachy Dodd and how I worked out that he was probably a Sealyham terrier and definitely not a person? You didn't reply, but I think you got it."

"Lisette, don't listen to her," says Olwen. "Listen to me. I knew you'd find it hard to be in a house with dogs after Malachy's murder. I know it brings back awful memories, but I had to show you."

"Show me what?" Anne eyes the door. She wants to leave—she knows she ought to—but she can't. Olwen and I agreed: the condition for telling Anne anything at all was that she had to come here, to the house. Olwen promised not to talk to her at all in the car on the way. Silence until they reached Germander, apart from the basics of "My car's over here"—that was the deal.

So. If Anne wants to hear what Olwen has to say to her, she has to stay. If she goes, it's the end of the conversation forever—a conversation she'll never be able to have with anyone else.

A groveling apology from a nonexistent sister.

"Justine came to me because she wanted a dog," Olwen tells Anne. "I believe this is why you were so convinced she was Allisande—because of her connection to me. She'd been here, her dog's related to some of mine. I think you felt that connection, Lisette. You picked up on it."

"Does Allisande call you Lisette, Lisette?" I undercut Olwen's solemn tone with my own mocking one. "Or was it Lizzie, since you call her Sandie? Bit of a giveaway, isn't it, if she can't get your name right?"

"Sometimes Lisette and sometimes Lissy," says Olwen.

I roll my eyes. "How can you trust this woman?" I ask Anne. "You *know* she's pretending to be someone *who doesn't exist.*"

"Don't listen to her, Lisette. The bond between us is so strong, you felt it when you were around Justine—that's why, at first, you thought she was me."

"Except she never was 'around' me. But don't let that stop you. Let's all just make up lies all day long! I'm the reincarnation of Michael Jackson—hooray! Even though I was born long before he died. I'm the pope, you're St. Francis of Assisi!"

"You're not my sister," Anne says, looking at nobody. Her voice is dull; it could be disappointment, boredom or something quite different. I wonder who she is inside her head at this moment: Anne? Lisette? Both?

"I'm not your sister, and neither is the woman here who's pretending to be," I tell her. "Your sister's called Sarah Parsons and she lives in Totnes."

"Lisette, you know the truth when you hear it," says Olwen. "You know I'm your sister Allisande, don't you?"

"Anne, look at these dogs. Then think of my little puppy. That one over there's his mother. You can really see the family resemblance, can't you? Is there any such family resemblance between you and so-called Sandie over there? None whatsoever."

"That doesn't mean anything," says Olwen. "Not all siblings look alike."

"All right, then, if you're really her sister, tell her something about her childhood that only you and she would know. Something the two of you won't have told anybody else."

"Actually, that's why I invited Lisette here. Not that it's any of your business, Justine. We have unresolved issues from the past that we need to discuss. So, if you'd kindly leave . . ." Olwen gestures toward the door.

"Your shared past? The blood-soaked childhood of the Ingrey sisters?" I laugh. "I'm looking forward to hearing this. No, I'm not going anywhere, I'm afraid. Start talking. Convince me that you two are related and that your names were once Lisette and Allisande Ingrey."

"I'm not saying anything in front of you. It's a private matter."

"Oh, Anne doesn't mind, do you, Anne? If she'd wanted to keep her fantasies private, she'd have confined them to her imagination. How does it feel to see your lies walking around in front of you, Anne?"

It was my idea that I should keep calling her by her name—her real and only name. Part of me wants her to break down and scream, "I'm Lisette Ingrey!" That same part can't believe that she truly believes her own fiction, but also fears she might. I'd like it settled one way or the other.

"You can't accuse your fake sister here of lying, can you, Anne?" I say. "That would mean siding with me, which you can't bear to do."

"I'm not lying," says Olwen. "I am your sister Allisande—yes, I have a different name now—Olwen Brawn—but I'm still me. I invited you here to say I'm sorry, and I'll say it in front of Justine if I have to. I threatened and disowned you because I was frightened, after our father murdered our sister. I should have stood beside you. We could have stayed strong together, protected each other."

Anne's head jerks back, as if to avoid a blow.

"Oh, wait, wait." I giggle. "Bascom Ingrey murdered Perrine? That seems incredibly unlikely—within the terms of the story, I mean."

"He and my mother planned it together," says Olwen. "They're both murderers. But my father—*our* father, Lisette's and mine—was the one who did the deed."

For a moment, Anne's eyes are full of emotion. Shock and also . . . is she impressed that Olwen was clever enough to get it right? Or convinced, finally, that this is her estranged sister Allisande talking to her? Then it passes, and she's staring expressionlessly ahead again. It's strange watching her reactions like this. I feel like a scientist doing an experiment. She's different today from how she was in my kitchen. Then she was more herself. The Anne-Donbavand-ness of her burned stronger. Now she's like a hollow, person-shaped object. With her empty-tunnel eyes blank like this, it's almost as if there's no one inside the flesh-and-bone container.

"Lisette, tell Allisande that her theory of Perrine's murder makes no sense," I say. "Bascom and Sorrel Ingrey went to every conceivable length to protect Perrine from the local hordes who were determined to hang her from trees, etcetera etcetera. What I mean is: they *would* have gone to those lengths, if all of this weren't total and utter crap—but since we're pretending it's not . . . There's no way Bascom and Sorrel did it. If they wanted Perrine dead, why take her out of school after the attempt on her life? Why confine her to the house to keep her safe, and build gates and fences to protect her?"

"And your next question is going to be: Why hire the music teacher, David Butcher?" Olwen tells me.

"Yes. What's the answer?"

"Dad hired him because, when he and Mum had almost given up all hope of curing whatever was wrong inside Perrine's head, Dad had a brainwave. Music might do the trick, he thought. David Butcher, by instilling in Perrine a love of music, might save her soul."

"Okay, so why do *that*?" I pretend to get impatient. "Why try so hard to save your daughter's soul, and then suddenly decide to murder her?"

"Oh, there was nothing sudden about Mum and Dad's decision," says Olwen. "Was there, Lisette?"

Slowly, Anne starts to walk along the hall, toward the living room. She stops in the doorway, grips the doorframe with both her hands.

"Grab a chair, Anne," I say. "Make yourself comfortable for the rest of the story. Olwen, I think you'd better wait till she's sitting comfortably."

"She's right, Lisette—you ought to sit down. You look pale."

Anne takes three more steps. Then a pause, then another two. She perches on the edge of the nearest sofa. "I don't have to listen to either of you," she says, not sounding entirely sure.

"True," I agree. "You will, though." *Because Olwen's pretending to be the sister you so badly need to believe in. She's pretending to be sorry, to understand everything, to forgive everything. I'd take that deal if I were you—it's the best you're going to get.*

"You'll listen to Olwen because, even though we all know she's talking pure nonsense, she's right, isn't she?" I go on. "She's cracked the mystery. No one's ever done that before. No one's cared enough to try and work it out until now. Olwen, what did you mean when you said there was nothing sudden about Bascom and Sorrel's decision?"

Olwen sits down opposite Anne. She smiles at her. "Mum and Dad disagreed about nearly everything, didn't they, Lisette? They disagreed, and so they compromised. They took turns. Always. In everything. That was how they made family life work."

"Shut up," Anne mutters, her eyes darting left and right. "I don't know who you are."

She can't leave. She wants to, but she's stuck. Can't stop listening.

"I'm your sister Allisande. After Perrine killed Malachy Dodd,

Mum and Dad disagreed about what to do, didn't they? Do you re-member? Mum had no illusions. She knew she'd raised a monster—or given birth to one, depending on your views about nature and nurture. Perrine was a monster, plain and simple. Mum knew she'd kill again and again if no one stopped her. As someone who hated anything that wasn't easy and fun, Mum didn't want the unpleas-antness of Perrine's presence in all our lives to stretch out and take up years. She wanted it over with quickly, so that she could go back to enjoying herself."

"Are you saying Sorrel Ingrey wanted to kill Perrine?" I deliver my next line with what I hope is the right mixture of curiosity and disbelief.

"In the circumstances . . . yes, she did," says Olwen gravely. "She couldn't bear to have anything horrible or difficult anywhere near her—it was a childlike, almost pathological horror she had of any-thing that wasn't pleasurable. Perrine was her daughter, and for as long as she lived, Sorrel couldn't avoid close involvement with her. Sorrel, therefore, needed Perrine to stop existing. She dressed it up with altruism—pretended to Bascom that she wanted Perrine dead only so that she couldn't kill anybody else. But that wasn't her true motive."

"And Bascom Ingrey?" I ask. "What did he have to say about it? Anne, why don't you tell us?"

Silence from Anne. A small shake of the head.

"Dad passionately disagreed," says Olwen. "He said there was no such thing as an evil person and that anyone could be redeemed. He was horrified that Mum wanted to give up on Perrine without trying to change her, without giving her a chance. And so, as was their way in everything, they decided to take turns. To compromise."

"I see. That makes sense," I say. "So that's why they bickered about Bascom's method being tried first when it was Sorrel's turn.

He'd gone first last time they'd disagreed and had to take turns. She thought it was unfair that she had to go second yet again."

"Yes, but Dad argued, sensibly, that he *had* to try his way first— it simply wouldn't have worked the other way around," says Olwen. "You can't murder someone and then try to reform their character. No dead person has ever been persuaded to live a more virtuous life. Oh, Dad had moments of self-doubt—times when he thought Mum was bound to be right, and maybe they ought to just kill Perrine immediately and have done with it. But on those occasions, Mum didn't take advantage. She asked him if he was *sure* he wanted to end his turn prematurely. And of course he didn't—not really."

Did Anne nod her head? Did I imagine it?

"So, if this whole tale weren't pure invention, what's the explanation for the fact that Bascom and Sorrel Ingrey were never charged with Perrine's murder?" I ask.

"You've just said it yourself," says Olwen. "Bascom and Sorrel never fell under suspicion. Lisette here even went to the police with her story—with the truth—but they didn't take her seriously. She only went once, didn't you, Lissy? She was too scared of what I'd do to her to try very hard to convince anybody. Everyone local knew that Bascom and Sorrel had done everything they could, for two years, to save their daughter's life. Everyone, including the police, had witnessed their care and protection of Perrine, day after day. Why would you do that for so long, then suddenly change tack and murder the very person you've devoted all your time and energy to keeping alive?"

"Unless you're parents who can't agree and so are taking turns," I say. "Yes, I understand. Bascom and Sorrel made a deal: two years— or one year, or however long—of trying to reform Perrine, and if it didn't work . . ." With my hand, I make a slicing gesture across my neck.

"I wonder if Mum imposed a condition, in exchange for Dad going first yet again," Olwen says. "What do you think, Lisette? I mean, I can't prove it . . ."

"What condition?" asks Anne.

That sounded more like the Anne from my kitchen. I stiffen. I don't want her to find her voice; it's safer when she's tied up inside herself and can't get out.

Please God don't let this be a terrible mistake.

It will be okay. It will.

"The condition was that if, after two years or however long it was, Perrine wasn't a better, kinder person, Dad had to agree to be the one to kill her. Mum would have nothing to do with the actual . . . practical carrying out of the murder. Whereas if Dad had agreed to the killing of Perrine straightaway, Mum would have done the deed. Not that she wanted to, by any means," Olwen embellishes. "But she was willing to do it, in exchange for not having to prolong the agony of life with Perrine in the family."

Good detail. Nice work, Olwen. I am in a room with two accomplished storytellers.

"Anne?" I prompt. "Any views? Did it go down the way Sandie's describing?"

"Even after Perrine had killed two people—Jack Kirbyshire and David Butcher—Bascom was devastated to think of what he had to do to his own daughter," Olwen goes on. "He loved her. That's why he took the bed with him to the jetty. He disassembled it and reassembled it, so that he could tuck his youngest daughter up in bed after he'd killed her—so that it felt less like murder and more like saying goodnight."

"Anne." I click my fingers in the air to get her attention. "Just to remind you: Olwen's not your sister. She worked all this out based on what she's heard from Ellen, via me. Ellen heard it from George.

Olwen is not a member of your family. She's—no offense, Olwen—literally just a dog breeder who's nothing to do with you."

"You know that's not true, Lisette. We know the truth, don't we, you and I? The day that Mum unlocked the gates and invited everyone to Speedwell House, the day Perrine was supposed to be arrested and taken away . . . and by the way, why would Mum invite so many guests who would all need to be catered for? She *hated* making any kind of effort! She invited those people for one reason and one reason only: to be The Suspects. Not guests, not intruders, but murder suspects."

Olwen's good at this. More than once since she started, I've said silently to myself, *She's not Allisande. She's only pretending to be Allisande.*

"The morning The Suspects came around for breakfast, the morning Perrine was supposedly murdered—that wasn't when she was killed. No, it happened the night before! We knew it couldn't have happened while The Suspects were in the house, didn't we, Lisette? You and I sat in our chairs by the drawing-room window the whole time they were there. Dad brought us our breakfast there. We were the only ones who would have seen if anyone had left the house and grounds carrying our dead sister and pieces of her bed. And we saw, didn't we, that *no one did leave?*"

Anne is rubbing her left arm with the palm of her right hand. She seems nervous. *If I could only know what she was thinking . . .*

"We knew what it meant, that no one left," Olwen says gently. I wonder if she's starting to feel sorry for Anne. The idea makes me angry. "If Perrine and her bed weren't removed from the house that morning by one of our visitors, then they must have been removed during the night, and there were only two people who could have done that: Mum and Dad. We knew it was them in other ways too: after Perrine had murdered David Butcher and been locked in her room, Mum took supper up to her bedroom on a tray. Remember, Lisette?"

Anne shakes her head violently.

"Yes, you do. You also remember—I know you do—that on the morning that everybody was invited to the house to see Perrine arrested, no breakfast was taken up to Perrine's room. Think back to that day: Mum and Dad were in the kitchen, and so were we. Mum was preparing the breakfast buffet and told us to get out from under her feet. She said Dad would bring us our breakfast in the drawing room, which he did, but he never took up any breakfast to Perrine. Neither did Mum. I could hear her in the kitchen the whole time. Dad didn't go upstairs—we'd have seen and heard if he had. If Perrine had been alive upstairs, why wouldn't Mum have sent breakfast up to her like she'd taken supper up to her the night before?"

Anne's mouth is hanging open: a tunnel to the land of lies, everything inside it dark and dead.

"Sorrel didn't take breakfast up to Perrine because she knew she was dead by then," I say. "Dead, and tucked up in her bed on the jetty. Murdered during the night, by Bascom." It's comforting to tell the story. Silence would be worse.

I try not to think about how we're going to get Anne out of Olwen's house once this is finished. What if she won't go? What if she's not any kind of recognizable person anymore at the end of all this?

"I'm ashamed to say that I threatened Lisette," Olwen tells me. "I said that if she spoke out and incriminated our parents, I'd kill her. I was wrong to do that. I cast suspicion onto Lisette, made sure the police suspected her and believed she'd fled Devon to escape punishment. That was terribly wrong of me too. And . . ." Olwen lets out a jagged sigh. It's convincing.

She's still Olwen. Nice, trustworthy Olwen.

"What Mum and Dad did was terrible, Lissy. I've been trying

not to let myself believe that, all these years, but . . . Mum and Dad are old now. I don't know how long they'll be around, and once they've gone, you'll be my only family—my only sister. I don't want to be estranged from you for one day, hour, *second* longer than I already have been."

That line was my idea: *day, hour, second.* Olwen laughed when I first suggested it. Then she said, "If you insist. You're the one with the background in drama."

"Please forgive me, Lissy," she says now. "I'm so, so sorry for everything I've put you through." She stands and picks up the smallest of the three dogs in the room. What's this one called? Holly Bears the Crown, I think—Holly for short.

No. Don't give her a dog. This wasn't part of the plan. Olwen's improvising, and it feels dangerous. My stomach twists.

Slowly, Olwen walks over to Anne and places the Bedlington on her lap. "She's yours if you want her," she says. "A peace offering. Her name's Holly."

"Holly," Anne repeats in a toneless voice. Then she smiles. Something about her eyes has changed.

"No . . ." I start to say.

"Sweet little doggy," Anne whispers. She puts her hands around Holly's neck and squeezes. Olwen whimpers.

Anne's going to kill Holly unless I stop her.

I lunge across the room and grab her by the shoulders. Seconds later we're both on the floor, my head banging on the stone fire surround once, twice—a sharp corner nearly close enough to slice my eye. I twist my face away from the wide, wild eyes above me, the lips curled back in what I'd like to call a snarl, but it isn't. Anne's smiling. I can't stand to look. She thinks she's going to win, which means she thinks she's going to kill me.

Olwen howls. She sounds farther away than I need her to be.

I can't lose. No one can stop Anne apart from me. I growl and swing my body around. My elbow cracks against her head. Then I'm on top of her.

Where's Holly? Did Anne hurt her? Dogs are barking, circling us, but I can't tell if Holly's one of them. Olwen's screaming.

I wave my right arm around, trying to catch hold of something I can use as a weapon, and knock over the fire irons stand in the fireplace. There's a loud crash, and more barking.

Fire irons. That's good, that's what I need.

I grab something with my free arm. It might be a poker. I raise it as high as I can and bring it down. Over and over.

Anne's head. I must stop doing what I'm doing. *Must stop.* Before . . . no, not before it's too late. It's already too late. And I don't want to stop. I want to bring down the poker again and again, crack Anne's head open, see the gray sludge of brain where all the lies were stored, watch the blood seep out . . .

Finally, sickened by the mess, I stop.

Olwen is sobbing. Not screaming anymore.

This is not part of the story. Except now it is: a true part. It feels made up, though. Unreal.

Anne wanted to kill me. Not the person claiming to be her sister Allisande; not Olwen. *Me.* Now that she's dead, there's no possibility of finding out why.

It's not only the "why" that I'll never know, it's also the "who." Anne would have been my killer if I'd let her, but who, in her mind, would she have killed? When she flashed her bare-teeth grin at me and fantasized about ending my life, who was it she wanted dead? Justine Merrison? Allisande Ingrey? Mother of Ellen the son-thief; owner of Speedwell House?

I let the poker fall from my hand. "Is Holly okay?"

Olwen doesn't answer. I turn so that I can see her. She's nodding: yes. Holly is safe.

Thank God.

"It's over," I say. "They're both dead now: Anne Donbavand and Lisette Ingrey. They're gone."

To: Ellen Colley and family

Celebrate the Life, Cherish the Memories

Anne Donbavand

1969—2015

Wife of Stephen Donbavand

Mother of Fleur and George

Memorial Service: Church of Our Lady and English Martyrs,
Quoits Road, Dartmouth, Saturday, June 27, 2015, 2 p.m.

Celebrant: Rev Christine Ogden

RSVP: s.donbavand@exeter.ac.uk

18

"Mum, Mum! There they are." Ellen leans to her right, stretching her neck to point her head at the boys she wants me to notice. She doesn't want to look at them in case they detect her interest. "Declan and Sam. Which do you think is cuter?" We're in a crowded function room at Exeter University, surrounded by smartly dressed people eating spinach and ricotta pastry parcels and salmon vol-au-vents. I wonder if they're mostly the parents of George and Ellen's classmates. I find it hard to believe that Anne had friends, or even colleagues that didn't loathe her.

Stephen Donbavand is on the other side of the room, standing with his back to me. We haven't spoken or made eye contact since Ellen and I arrived. Now people are starting to leave. I can hear Stephen thanking them for coming—so much; it would have meant the world to Anne.

"Mum!"

"Sorry. Are they in your class, those boys?" I ask.

"Uh-huh. Sam and George are good friends. Declan, not so much. George thinks he's got no substance."

A lot has changed since Anne's death. Disappearance, I should say; her body has never been found—well, not much of it, anyway. George started back at Beaconwood almost immediately after she went missing, as did Fleur.

"George doesn't mind if I think his friends are cute," Ellen tells me. "He's not jealous at all. He knows it's just their looks I like. Every other boy is *so* boring to talk to compared to him. To be honest, I'm the jealous one, now that he's got other friends and they go around to his house and everything. I'm not the only person in his life anymore. But . . . that's a good thing, isn't it?"

"Yes," I say with a heavy heart. "Ellen—"

"Dad knows, by the way."

"What? Since when?"

"I told him this morning. Well, Anne gave the game away about the marriage part the day she climbed in through our window. But now I've told Dad George is gay—I've explained the whole situation." Ellen smiles. "You were too scared to tell him, weren't you? You always would have been."

I make a comedy face at her, hoping to be let off the hook. I'm too scared to tell Alex many important things. It must be the same for Olwen, with Maggie. I can't say for sure. Olwen and I haven't seen one another or spoken for nearly five months. Not since we took care of everything that needed to be taken care of. We agreed it was best to have no contact. I miss her nearly every day: the only person who knows. She feels the same about me; we're not in touch, but I sense it.

One day. One day, when enough time has passed, I'll ring her door-bell again. She'll invite me in; we'll talk like old friends.

"Mum? What's up? You look like you're about to cry."

"I'm fine. What did Dad say, when you told him about marrying George?"

"He said I should do whatever will make me happy."

"He's right. You should."

"You don't really think that. I can tell when you're lying."

Christ, I hope not.

I'm lying to my daughter. I know I'm lying, though, and I'm doing it so as not to hurt her, so that's okay. That's good. Except . . . I ought to tell her the truth.

"The thing is, El, it's just—" I break off and sigh as a woman in a floral dress knocks my elbow, spilling a bit of my elderflower cordial. "I'm not sure a wake is the best place to discuss this."

"It's not a *wake*." Ellen giggles. "Don't be such a relic, Mum. It's a party to celebrate—ugh! You know what I mean—celebrate, or whatever, Anne's life."

"I worry that you and George will get married and then he'll fall in love with someone else—romantic, sexual love—and leave you," I blurt out. "I worry that what he loves so passionately is normal family life, as exemplified by us." *Used to be, anyway.* "What if he only wants to marry you because . . ." For God's sake, what am I saying? This is too much truth, and I can't prove any of it anyway. What if I'm inventing problems?

Ellen isn't fazed by it. "Because he wants to be part of our family, were you going to say? Because we're happy and his family isn't, or wasn't?" She shrugs. "I don't care why he wants it, Mum. All I know is that, right now, he does. And so do I. Sure, we're only teenagers— we might change our minds. But think of it like this: in the old days, people often died when they were, like, twenty-five. Didn't stop them getting married at eighteen or twenty, did it, just because they knew it might not last forever?"

"No. I suppose not."

Ellen pats my arm as if I'm a doddery octogenarian who needs to be reassured about the modern world.

"Ellen, I need to ask you something. It's about your story."

She grimaces. "I want to forget about that, Mum."

"I know, and you can, but . . . you knew, didn't you? Who'd killed Perrine?"

"Yes. George and I worked it out. It had to be the parents: Bascom and Sorrel. Why didn't they give Perrine any breakfast that day if she was still alive as far as they knew? There was no mention of her getting any. And the turns thing. And how could Sorrel and Bascom have made a plan about what to do after David Butcher's murder when they'd only just found him dead? They must have been referring to the original 'taking turns' plan, made when they first took the girls out of school. And Sorrel talking to Perrine so harshly, accusing her of lying about the noose-tree thing. It was clear that she resented Perrine's existence."

Good. Great.

"So . . . you lied to me when I asked you who killed Perrine, at Olwen's house? You pretended you didn't have any idea?"

Ellen nods. "Sorry. George said we had to keep it secret from everyone or his mum would think he was a betrayer—the more people knew the whole story, the more danger for George and his family."

"It's okay. Just . . . do me a favor, Ellen: always know when you're lying, and why. Always keep a grip on the truth in your head. It's important. It's how you stay sane." Is she even listening to me? "Ellen?"

In a low voice, she says, "George says when the police found his mum's clothes in that alleyway in London they also found . . . brain matter. Is that true?"

I nod. "That's how they were able to issue a death certificate. What they found . . . she couldn't still be alive. It's impossible." A bundle of clothing and brain in a bag: easy to carry through London at night without arousing suspicion. Not so easy to do that with a whole human body. But Olwen and I agreed we had to do something to let Stephen, Fleur and George know that Anne wasn't coming back. It wouldn't have been fair to let them hope for her safe return. Or fear it.

Fleur Donbavand is leaning against the wall between two large windows, talking to Lesley Griffiths and another teacher from Beaconwood whose face I know but whose name I can't summon at the moment.

Today is the first time I've seen Fleur. She's tall and pale, with delicate features and mousy-brown hair in a plait. As she listens to Lesley, who is doing all the talking, she nods and side-eyes the wall next to her, as if hoping it will open and envelop her. She looks bored, then guilty, then embarrassed—like someone who has no idea how to react to her surroundings. The contrast between her and George, who, since we arrived, has been orating masterfully and loudly on the subject of grief to anyone who will listen, is marked.

"George is sad about his mum dying, you know," Ellen told me the other day.

"Of course he is," I said in a tight voice.

"Even though he really did hate her. He says it's weird—he'd never have thought he'd be sad."

Across the room, Lesley Griffiths gives Fleur a hug, and Fleur smiles and seems to relax. I feel guilty for asking Ops to investigate Lesley's background. I'll never tell anyone what he found out: that in her twenties, before she got married, Lesley was a journalist who plagiarized part of an article and lost her job at a reputable newspaper. She then trained to be a teacher and hasn't put a foot wrong since, as far as Ops could establish. Interestingly, the man who fired Lesley, Diarmid Griffiths, was the man she married four years later. They must have decided to give each other a second chance.

Some people deserve them. Some, not all.

"Justine. Ellen. I'm glad I caught you." Stephen Donbavand is at my side.

"We won't leave until it finishes," Ellen tells him. "I promised George we'd stay till the end, Mum."

Oh God. How long will that be?

"How are you, Justine?" Stephen asks me, as Ellen crosses the room to join her fiancé beside the buffet table.

What the fuck do you care?

"How am I? Fine. I ought to be asking you that question, I suppose."

"I'm doing well, in the circumstances."

"Fleur and George look well." Is this how I'd be speaking to him if I hadn't killed his wife? All I can do is hope that it is.

"They're enjoying being back at school," says Stephen.

"I can imagine. It's nice for them to have some friends. A normal life," I can't resist adding.

"Yes, it is."

Clever, Stephen. Can I call you Steve, now that you've dug a grave in my garden and I've caved your wife's head in? No need for formalities anymore. Very clever indeed. Benefit, and allow George and Fleur to benefit, from their new freedom, while never acknowledging the tyranny that preceded it. Way to have the best of both worlds. Fucking coward.

"It can't have been fun for you to have the police excavate your garden," he says.

"No. Well, they didn't find anything. We had the garden re-landscaped afterward."

"Why did you tell the police Anne's body was buried in your garden when it wasn't? I was told you insisted they dig up every square meter of your land, to check."

"I did. I had a hunch—it turned out to be wrong. I wanted to help try and find Anne, and . . . well, I suppose when someone digs a grave out of the earth immediately outside your front door, you can't help wondering if that someone plans to bury a body there." I smile at him. *Well, you did ask . . .*

Stephen bites his upper lip. "But the police never thought Anne died in Devon," he says. "You know what they found on her clothes."

Is he asking me a question? It sounded like a statement of fact. "Yes."

"They think Anne died in London, where she apparently went to meet one of your former colleagues—Donna Lodge—having sent an email from an internet café to make the arrangement. She never turned up for that meeting. It's funny—I know that can't be true, about the internet café. Anne was barely aware such places existed."

He looks hard at me. Says, "I didn't tell the police that. Don't worry."

My heart starts to pound. Is he saying what I think he's saying? *No. I don't want your help or protection. I'm not Anne.*

"I'm sorry for what you went through, Justine."

Sorry? I nearly laugh. It's so useless: a floppy, meaningless word coming from him, given everything he did and didn't do. "Apologize to your kids, not me," I manage to say. "I don't care how you feel."

"I'm also sorry my wife is dead. Missing presumed dead, but . . . well, I know she's dead, Justine. Beyond doubt."

And he knows who killed her. That's what his eyes are trying to tell me, that pointed look.

He says, "I'm sorry Anne's dead for her sake, you understand. All she'll miss out on . . . Well, and I suppose for my sake a little as well. Anne wasn't always . . . difficult. She could be very kind sometimes."

"I don't care, Stephen."

"No, I . . . I can see. Anyway . . . you mustn't worry," he tells me. *Anybody's ally.*

I don't want to be curious about him—I want not to think about him at all—but I can't help wondering if, in his own opinion, he stands for anything at all.

Feel ashamed, you bastard.

"The police won't dig up your garden again," he tells me. "They've already done so at your instigation and satisfied themselves that there's nothing there. Clever of you. They wouldn't dig up the same garden twice."

I nod. That was my reckoning precisely. Particularly since I insisted they check every inch of my land. I was so eager to help in the search for missing Professor Anne, the brilliant academic and devoted wife and mother.

The credit for my cleverness should, strictly speaking, go to Anne herself. I was less imaginative before she came into my life—considerably so. That's one benefit of knowing a pathological liar: first you marvel at their inventive brio, then you think, "I could do that too. What's stopping me?"

Anne gave me the burial-in-the-garden idea; Anne came up with the surprise solution to the Ingrey murder mystery—a mother and father who join forces first to protect their daughter from all harm and then, later, to kill her, because they have perfected the art of compromise. Who would ever guess that?

I rose to Anne's challenge and formulated an equally unguessable plan. I think I succeeded. Who would suspect me of burying a body—one missing most of its brain—in the very same garden I made the police dig up only a few days earlier to search for that same body? I insisted to every police officer who would listen that Anne must be buried in the grounds of Speedwell House, knowing full well that she wasn't—yet.

Was Stephen watching from one of our clusters of trees the night Olwen and I buried Anne's body? Or from his side of the river, with his binoculars trained on my house? I don't believe he guessed, so he must know.

"Look," he says, pointing.

I turn. Ellen and George are handing out the few remaining buffet snacks to their classmates, conferring about who's had how many so far and who's owed what.

"They must be the bossiest in their year," I say.

Why am I talking to him, and so politely? Because I think he could land me in prison if he chose to? Or because polite conversation is what's expected at memorial dos?

No one expects anybody, ever, to start yelling about evil. *Look, right there—evil! Wickedness, right here and now.* People would say you were mad if you did that. It would take up too much time, also. All of one's time, arguably. Better to brush it under the carpet, under the grass, under the tablecloth beneath the canapés.

"Either bossy or natural leaders, however you want to put it," I amend my previous statement to make it less critical.

"I want to put it this way: they're good kids," says Stephen. "In every way, good people."

"Yes. Yes, they are," I say. Is that supposed to be the happy ending to our story? He let his wife ruin people's lives and I killed her, but it's okay because we have wonderful children?

No one gets to write my story apart from me. Least of all Stephen Donbavand, ally of Anne for so many years.

I'll write it myself.

Once upon a time there was a woman called Justine Merrison. She tried so hard to do Nothing, but she failed. She ended up doing Something, a bigger Something than she'd ever done before: she killed a woman. Murdered? I don't know. Maybe. It wasn't self-defense, but there was an element of defense to the killing. I could tell you the full story, but I guarantee you wouldn't believe me, so I won't bother. Or maybe I'll tell you what happened but present it as fiction—you probably wouldn't believe me then, either. You might say, "You can't have made that up. Is there an element of truth to it?"

After causing the death of Anne Donbavand, Justine was either caught one day and locked up, or not—it's too soon to say. What I can tell you for certain is that she never regretted what she did, not for a fraction of a second.

She hopes to live happily ever after. She thinks that's what she deserves.

ACKNOWLEDGMENTS

I am hugely grateful to the following people: Peter Straus and Matthew Turner from Rogers, Coleridge and White; Carolyn Mays, Karen Geary, Lucy Hale, Becca Mundy, Abby Parsons, Jason Bartholomew, Anna Alexander, Valeria Huerta, Al Oliver, Jessica Killingley, Naomi Berwin and everyone else at Hodder—there are too many people to name all individually, but I'm extremely thankful to all of you for all your hard work on my books.

I'd also like to thank Dan, Phoebe, Guy and Brewster; Adele Geras, Chris Gribble, Emily Winslow; the inimitable Dan Mallory and all at William Morrow in America; all my wonderful international publishers who look after my books all over the world; Professor Malcolm Coulthard; and the real "Ops."

Speedwell House is loosely based on Greenway, Agatha Christie's holiday home in Devon, which I might never have come to know as well as I do if it weren't for Mathew and James Prichard—so an enormous thank-you to them, and to Agatha Christie for inspiring me since the age of twelve.

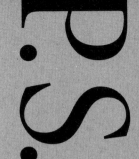

About the author

About the book

Read on . . .

Insights,
Interviews
& More . . .

Meet Sophie Hannah

Philippa Gedge

SOPHIE HANNAH is an internationally bestselling writer of psychological crime fiction, published in thirty-two languages and fifty-one territories. In 2014, with the blessing of Agatha Christie's family and estate, Sophie published a new Hercule Poirot novel, *The Monogram Murders,* which was a bestseller in more than fifteen countries. In September 2016, her second Poirot novel, *Closed Casket,* was published and became an instant *Sunday Times* top ten bestseller.

In 2013, Sophie's novel *The Carrier* won the Crime Thriller of the Year

Award at the Specsavers National Book Awards. Two of her crime novels, *The Point of Rescue* and *The Other Half Lives,* have been adapted for television and appeared on ITV1 under the series title *Case Sensitive* in 2011 and 2012.

Sophie has also published two short story collections and five collections of poetry—the fifth of which, *Pessimism for Beginners,* was short-listed for the 2007 T. S. Eliot Award. Her poetry is studied at GCSE, A-level, and degree level across the UK. From 1997 to 1999 she was Fellow Commoner in Creative Arts at Trinity College, Cambridge, and between 1999 and 2001 she was a fellow of Wolfson College, Oxford. She is forty-five and lives with her husband, children, and dog in Cambridge, where she is a Fellow Commoner at Lucy Cavendish College. ∾

Reading Group Guide

1. Is Justine a sympathetic character? How do you feel about her decision "to do nothing," and then take matters into her own hands at the end of the book? Do you see her as a good person?

2. There are at least two stories-within-stories in the novel. How do you think these stories intersect and work together?

3. Beaconwood is a very unusual school and its headmistress, Lesley Griffiths, has an unusual approach to education. How does this affect the characters and the plot?

4. Most of the characters in *A Game for All the Family* lie, some more than others. Can lies be justified? Do they make a character unsympathetic? What does the novel say or think about the various different kinds of lies?

5. Alex says that lies "can create facts. So can fictions." How is this reflected in the novel?

6. One character describes George's parents in the following way: "Nice, normal dad and unhappy neurotic mum." Do you agree with this assessment? How would you describe the Donbavands?

7. *A Game for All the Family* does not feature a series detective. Why do you think this is? Could it, nevertheless, be considered a detective novel?

8. How would you classify this novel? To which genre do you think it belongs?

9. Speedwall House was inspired by Agatha Christie's home, Greenway, which is referenced in the novel. Do you see Agatha Christie's influence at work in the novel?

10. Would you want to live in Speedwell House? Why, or why not?

11. What do you think about Justine"'s premonition at the beginning of the book, when she sees the house by the side of the busy road?

12. What right or duty do you think we all have to interfere in the lives of others, if we suspect those others of doing serious harm? How does this relate to the novel? ∾

Excerpt from
Woman with a Secret

MEN SEEKING WOMEN

IntimateLinks > uk > all personals

Reply: 22547652@indiv.intimatelinksUK.org
Posted: 2013-07-04, 16:17PM GMT

Looking for a Woman with a Secret

LOCATION: WHEREVER YOU ARE

Hello, females!

Are you looking on here because you're hoping to find something that stands out from all the dull one-line I-want-a-blow-job-in-my-hotel-room-type adverts? Well, look no further. I'm different and this is different.

I'm not seeking casual sex or a long-term relationship. I've had plenty of the first in my time, and I've got one of the second that I'm happy with. Actually, I'm not looking for anything sexual or romantic. So what am I doing on Intimate Links? Well, as I'm sure you're aware if you're clever (and I suspect that the woman I am looking for is very bright), there are different kinds of intimacy. There's taking off your clothes and getting dirty with an illicit stranger, there's deep and meaningful love-making with a soulmate . . . and then there's the sort of intimacy that involves two people sharing nothing more than a secret. An important secret that matters to both of them.

Perhaps these two people have never met, or perhaps they know each other but not very well. Either way, they can only establish a bond of common knowledge once the one who has the information has given it to the one who needs it. Think of the rush of relief you'd experience if you shared your burden after the agony of prolonged silence with the secret eating away at you . . . If you're the person I'm looking for, you'll be desperate to confide in someone.

That's where I come in. I'm your confidant, ready and eager to listen. Are you the keeper of the secret I'm waiting to be told?

Let's find out by asking a question that only the person I'm looking for would be able to answer. It will make no sense to anyone else. You'll have to bear with me. Before I get to the question part, I'll need to lay out the scenario.

Picture a room in a large Victorian house: a spacious, high-ceilinged first-floor bedroom that's used as a study. There are overstuffed built-in bookshelves in this room, a pale blue and brown jukebox with curved edges that has a vintage look about it and is much more beautiful than the kind you sometimes see in pubs, an armchair, a filing cabinet, a long desk with square wooden legs and a green glass top that has a laptop computer at its center. The computer is neither open nor closed. Its lid is at a forty-five-degree angle, as if someone has tried halfheartedly to push it shut but it hasn't gone all the way. The laptop is surrounded on all sides by cheap-looking pens, empty and half-empty coffee mugs, and scattered papers: handwritten notes, ideas jotted down. ▶

Excerpt from *Woman with a Secret*
(continued)

Pushed back from the desk is a standard
black office-style swivel chair, and lolling in
the chair, his head leaning to the left, is a
dead man. While alive, he was well known
and—though this might well have nothing to do
with anything—strikingly attractive in a stubbly,
cowboy-without-a-hat kind of way. If I were to
include his name in this account, I think most
people would have heard of him. Some of you
might shudder and say, "Oh, not that vile bigot!"
or, more lightheartedly, "Not that ridiculous
attention-seeker!" Others would think, "Oh, I *love*
him—he says all the things I'm too scared to say."
Our dead body is (was) somebody who inspired
strong feelings, you see. So strong that he got
himself murdered.

How was he killed? Well, this is the interesting
part. The murder process comprised several
stages. First, he was immobilized. His arms
were pulled behind the back of his chair and
taped together at the wrists. The same was
done to his ankles, which were taped together
around the pole of the chair's base, beneath
the seat. Then his murderer stood behind him
and brought a heavy object down on his head,
rendering him unconscious. The police found
this object on the floor beside the dead man's
desk: it was a metal kitchen-knife sharpener. It
didn't kill our well-known man (the pathologist
told the police after examining the body),
though it would have made an excellent murder-
by-bludgeoning weapon, being more than
heavy enough to do the job. However, it seems
that although the killer was happy to use the
knife sharpener to knock his victim out, he did
not wish to use it to murder him.

There was a knife in the room too, but it had not been used to stab the dead man. Instead, it was stuck to his face with packing tape. Specifically, it was stuck to his closed mouth, completely covering it. The tape—of which there was plenty—also completely covered the lower part of the murder victim's face, including his nose, causing him to suffocate to death. The knife's blade, flat against the dead man's mouth, was sharp. Forensics found evidence that it had been sharpened in the room, and detectives suspect that this happened after the victim was bound to the chair and unconscious.

Above the fireplace, on the wall between two bookshelf-filled alcoves, someone had written in big red capital letters "HE IS NO LESS DEAD." I imagine that the first police to arrive at the scene took one look at that and leaped to a mistaken conclusion: that the red words had been written in the victim's blood. Then, seconds later, they might have noticed a can of paint and a red-tipped brush on the floor and made a more informed guess that turned out to be correct: the words on the wall were written in paint. Dulux's Ruby Fountain 2, for anyone who is interested in the details and doesn't already know them.

Detectives examined the dead man's laptop, I assume. They would have found this surprisingly easy because the killer had red-painted "Riddy111111" on a blank sheet of white 8½" x 11" paper that was lying on the desk. This was the well-known man's password and would have led police straight to his email inbox. There they'd have found a new, unopened message from a correspondent by the name ▶

Excerpt from *Woman with a Secret*
(continued)

of No Less Dead, with an email address to match. There were no words in the message, only a photograph of someone standing in the room beside the unconscious, not-yet-deceased victim, wearing what looked like a protective suit from a Hollywood film about biological outbreaks—the sort that covers the head and body of the person wearing it. The killer's eyes would presumably have been visible if he or she hadn't taken care to turn away from the camera; as it was, the picture showed a completely unidentifiable person with one outstretched arm (for the taking of the photo), holding aloft a knife in his or her other hand, above the unconscious man's chest, in a way designed to suggest that a stabbing was imminent. The knife in the photograph was the same one (or identical to the one) that ended up taped to the murder victim's face, suffocating him rather than spilling his blood.

And now the question is coming up, so pay attention, ladies! (Actually, it's questions, plural.)

The murderer planned the crime in advance. It was about as premeditated as a killing can be. It involved bringing to the crime scene a knife, a knife sharpener, packing tape, red paint, a paintbrush and a biohazard suit. The killer obviously knew the deceased's computer password. How? There was no evidence of a break-in. Did her victim let her in? (I'm saying "her" because that's my hunch: that it was a woman. Maybe it was you?) Did the well-known man say to her, "Go on, then: bind me to my chair, knock me out and kill me"? That seems unlikely. Maybe the killer pretended it was some sort of erotic game, or maybe I'm only speculating along these lines because Intimate Links is the perfect place to do so— the online home of sexual game-players of all kinds.

The most puzzling question is this: why arrive at the victim's house with a knife and a knife sharpener when you have no intention of stabbing him? Why sharpen that knife at the crime scene if all you're going to do is tape it, flat, against his face? For that purpose, the knife would work just as effectively if its blade were blunt.

Or, looking at it another way . . . if you've got a newly sharpened knife, and you've covered your clothing to protect it from blood splashes, and if, coincidentally, you also want to write a strange message in big red letters on the wall, why *not* stab the guy and use his blood to write with? Because you particularly want to suffocate him? Then why not do it more straightforwardly, with, say, a plastic bag over his head, taped round his neck to make it airtight? Why use a knife at all?

For some reason, you wanted to kill this man with a sharp knife, but you didn't want to stab him. Why not? And the photograph you emailed— what's that about? What are you trying to communicate? Is it "Look, I could so easily have stabbed him, but I didn't"?

I realize I've slipped into using "you" when I talk about the murderer, rather than "she," or "he or she." I'm sorry. I'm not accusing you of killing ▶

Excerpt from *Woman with a Secret*
(continued)

anybody. Maybe you're not the murderer of the well-known man. You might be someone who wishes he were still alive, someone who loves him, or once did—a lover, a close friend. I'm really not sure. All I know is that you're reading this and you know the answers to the questions I'm asking. You desperately want to tell someone what you know.

I'm the person to trust with the information. I've taken a huge risk in sharing so many secrets, in the hope of eliciting a reply from you. So, please, contact me. I'm waiting, and I promise I won't judge you. Whatever you've done, you had your reasons. I am ready to listen and understand.

Looking forward to hearing from you soon.

C (for Confidant) x

- Location: Wherever You Are
- It's NOT OK to contact this poster with services or other commercial interests

Posted: 2013-07-04, 16:17PM GMT

CHAPTER 1

Monday, July 1, 2013

IT CAN'T BE HIM. All policemen wear high-visibility jackets these days. Lots must have sand-colored hair that's a little bit wavy. In a minute he'll turn around and I'll see his face and laugh at myself for panicking.

Don't turn around, unless you're someone else. Be someone else. Please.

I sit perfectly still, try not to notice the far-reaching reverberations of every heartbeat. There is too much distance trapped in me. Miles. I can't reach myself. A weird illusion grips me: that I am my heart and my car is my chest, and I'm shaking inside it.

Seconds must be passing. Not quickly enough. Time is stuck. I stare at the clock on my dashboard and wait for the minute to change. At last, 10:52 becomes 10:53 and I'm relieved, as if it could have gone either way.

Crazy.

He's still standing with his back to me. So many details are the same: his hair, his height, his build, the yellow jacket with "POLICE" printed on it . . . ▶

Excerpt from *Woman with a Secret* (continued)

If it's him, that means I must be doing something wrong, and I'm not. I'm definitely not. There's no reason for him to reappear in my life; it wouldn't be fair, when I'm trying so hard. Out of everyone sitting in their cars in this line of traffic, I must be among the most blameless, if I'm being judged on today's behavior alone: a mother driving to school to deliver her son's forgotten gym bag. I could have said, "Oh well, he'll just have to miss gym, or wear his school uniform," but I didn't. I knew Ethan would hate those two options equally, so I canceled my hair appointment and set off back to school, less than an hour after I'd gotten home from dropping the children off there. Willingly, because I care about my son's happiness.

Which means this has to be a different policeman up ahead. It can't be him. It was my guilt that drew him to me last time. Today, I'm innocent. I've been innocent for more than three weeks.

Drew him to you?

All right, I'm guilty of superstitious idiocy, but nothing else. If it's him, he's here on Elmhirst Road by chance—pure coincidence, just as it was last time we met. He's a police officer who works in Spilling; Elmhirst Road is in Spilling: his presence here, for reasons that have nothing to do with me, is entirely plausible.

Rationally, the argument stands up, but I'm not convinced.

Because you're a superstitious fool.

If it's him, that means I'm still guilty, deep down. If he sees me . . .

I can't let that happen. His eyes on me, even for a second, would act as a magnet, dragging the badness inside me up to the surface of my skin, making it spill out into the open; it would propel me back to where I was when he first found me: the land of the endangered.

I don't deserve that. I have been good for three weeks and four days. Even in the privacy of my mind, where any transgressions would be unprovable, I haven't slipped up. Once or twice my thoughts have almost broken free of my control, but I've been disciplined about slamming down the barriers.

Turn around, quick, before he does.

Can I risk it?

A minute ago, there were at least fifteen cars between mine and where he's standing on the pavement, a few hundred meters ahead. There are still about ten, at a rough guess. If one of the drivers in front of me would do a U-turn and go back the way they came, I'd do the same, but he's more likely to notice me if I'm the first to do it. He might recognize my car, remember the make and model—maybe even the license plate. Not that he's turned around yet, but he could be about to. *Any second now . . .*

He'd wonder why I was doubling back on myself. The traffic isn't at a standstill. True, we're crawling along, but it's unlikely to take me more than ten minutes to get past whatever's causing the delay. All I can see from my car is a female police officer in the road, standing up straight, then bobbing down out of sight; standing up again, bobbing down again. I think she must be saying something to the driver of each car that passes. There's another male officer too, on the pavement, talking to . . .

Not him. Talking to a man who, please God, isn't him.

Inhale. Long and deep.

I can't do it. The presence of the right words in my mind is not enough to drive away the panic, not when I'm breathing jagged and fast like this.

I wish I could work out what's going on up there. It's probably something dull and bureaucratic. Once before, I was stopped by fluorescent-jacketed police—three of them, like today—who were holding up traffic on the Rawndesley Road as part of a survey about driver behavior. I've forgotten what questions they asked me. They were boring, and felt pointless at the time. I remember thinking, My answers will be of no benefit to anyone, and answering politely anyway.

The car in front of mine moves forward at the exact same moment that the policeman with his back to me turns his head. I see him in profile, only for a second, but it's enough. I make a choking noise that no one hears but me. I'm embarrassed anyway.

It's him.

No choice, then. Driving past him is unthinkable—no way of avoiding being seen by him if his colleague stops my car to speak to me—so I'll have to turn around. I edge forward and swerve ▶

to the right, waiting for a gap in the oncoming traffic on the other side of the road so that I can escape. *Please.* I'll feel OK as soon as I'm traveling away from him and not toward him.

I edge out farther. Too far, over the white line, where there's no room for me. A blue Toyota beeps its horn as it flies past, the driver's open mouth an angry blur. The noise is long and drawn out: the sound of a long grudge, not a fleeting annoyance, though I'm not sure if I'm still hearing its echo or only remembering it. Shock drums a rhythmic beat through my body, rising up from my chest into my throat and neck, pulsing down to my stomach. It pounds in my ears, in the skin of my face; I can even feel it in my hair.

There's no way a noise like that car horn isn't going to make a policeman—any policeman—turn around and see what's going on.

It's OK. It's fine. Nothing to worry about. How likely is it that he'd remember my car registration? He'll see a silver Audi and think nothing of it. He must see them all the time.

I keep my head facing away from him, my eyes fixed on the other side of the road, willing a gap to appear. One second, two seconds, three . . .

Don't look. He'll be looking by now. No eye contact, that's what matters. As long as you don't see him seeing you . . .

At last, there's space for me to move out. I spin the car around and drive back along Elmhirst Road toward Spilling town center, seeing all the same things that I saw a few minutes ago, except in reverse order: the garden center, the Arts Barn, the house with the mint-green camper van parked outside it that looks like a Smeg fridge turned on its side, with wheels attached. These familiar objects and buildings seemed ordinary and unthreatening when I drove past them a few minutes ago. Now there's something unreal about them. They look staged. Complicit, as if they're playing a sinister game with me, one they know I'll lose.

Feeling hot and dizzy, I turn left into the library parking lot and take the first space I see: what Adam and I have always called "a golfer's space" because the symbol painted in white on the concrete looks more like a set of golf clubs than the stroller it's supposed to be.

I open the car door with numb fingers that feel as if they're only partly attached to my body and find myself gasping for air. I'm burning hot, dripping with sweat, and it has nothing to do with the weather.

Why do I still feel like this? I should have been able to leave the panic behind, on Elmhirst Road. With him.

Get a grip. Nothing bad has actually happened. Nothing at all has happened.

"You're not parking there, are you? I hope you're going to move."

I look up. A young woman with auburn hair and the shortest bangs I've ever seen is staring at me. I assume the question came from her, since there's no one else around. Explaining my situation to her is more than I can manage at the moment. I can form the words in my mind, but not in my mouth. *I'm not exactly parking. I just need to sit here for a while, until I'm safe to drive again. Then I'll go.*

I'm so caught up in the traumatic nothing that happened to me on Elmhirst Road that I only realize she's still there when she says, "That space is for mums and babies. You've not got a baby with you. Park somewhere else!"

"Sorry. I . . . I will. I'll move in a minute. Thanks."

I smile at her, grateful for the distraction, for a reminder that this is my world and I'm still in it: the world of real, niggly problems that have to be dealt with in the present.

"What's wrong with right now?" she says.

"I just . . . I'm not feeling . . ."

"You're in a space for mothers with babies! Are you too stupid to read signs?" Her aggression is excessive—mysteriously so. "Move! There's at least fifty other free spaces."

"And at least twenty-five of those are mother-and-child spaces," I say, looking at all the straight yellow lines on the concrete running parallel to my car, with nothing between them. "I'm not going to deprive anyone of a space if I sit here for another three minutes. I'm sorry, but I'm not feeling great."

"You don't know who's going to turn up in a minute," says my persecutor. "The spaces might all fill up." She pushes at her toothbrush-bristle bangs with her fingers. She seems to want to ▶

flick them to one side and hasn't worked out that they're too short to go anywhere; all they can do is lie flat on her head.

"Do you work at the library?" I ask her. I've never seen a Spilling librarian wearing stiletto-heeled crocodile-skin ankle boots before, but I suppose it's possible.

"No, but I'll go and get someone who does if you don't move."

What is she, then? A recreational protester whose chosen cause is the safeguarding of mother-and-child parking spaces for those who deserve them? She has no children with her, or any books, or a bag big enough to contain books. What's she doing here in the library parking lot?

Get the bitch, says the voice in my head that I mustn't listen to. *Bring her down.*

"Two questions for you," I say coolly. "Who the hell do you think you are, and who the hell are you?"

"It doesn't matter! What matters is, you're in the wrong space!"

"Read the sign," I tell her. To save her the trouble of turning around, I read it aloud to her, " 'These spaces are reserved for people with children.' That includes me. I have two children. I can show you photos. Or my C-section scar, if you'd prefer?"

"It *means* for people who've got children with them *in the car,* as you well know! Shall I go and get the library manager?"

"Fine by me." I'm starting to feel better, thanks to this woman. I'm enjoying myself. "She can tell us what she thinks the sign means, and I'll tell her what it says, and explain the difference. 'People with children' means 'parents.' Those with offspring, progeny, descendants: the nonchildless. There's nothing in the wording of that sign that specifies where the children need to be, geographically, at this precise moment. If it said, 'This space is reserved for people who have their kids with them *right here and now in this library parking lot,*' I could see a justification for moving. Since it doesn't . . ." I shrug.

"Right," Short Bangs snaps at me. "You wait there!"

"What, in the parking space you're so keen for me to vacate?" I call after her as she stomps toward the library. "You want me to stay in it now?"

She makes an obscene finger gesture over her shoulder.

I'd like to wait and argue with the librarian—all the librarians, if possible—but the return of my normal everyday self has brought with it the memory of why I left the house: to deliver Ethan's gym bag to school. I should get on with it; I know he'll worry until he has it in his hands.

Reluctantly, I slam my car door shut, pull out of the library parking lot and head for the Silsford Road. I can get to the school via Upper Heckencott, I think. It's a ridiculously long-winded way of getting there, involving skinny, winding lanes that you have to reverse back along for about a mile if you meet a car coming in the opposite direction, but you generally don't. And it's the only route I can think of that doesn't involve driving down Elmhirst Road.

I check my watch: 11:10 A.M. I pull my phone out of my bag, call the school, ask them to tell Ethan not to worry and that I'm on my way. All of this I do while driving, knowing I shouldn't, hoping I'll get away with it. I wonder if it's possible, simultaneously, to be a good mother and a bad person: someone who enjoys picking fights with strangers in parking lots, who lies, who gets into trouble with the police and nearly ruins her life and the life of her family, who thinks, Fuck you, every time anyone points out what the rules are and that she's breaking them.

I blow a long sigh out of the open window, as if I'm blowing out smoke. Ethan deserves a mother with no secrets, a mother who can drive to school without needing to hide from anyone. ▶

Excerpt from *Woman with a Secret*
(*continued*)

Instead, he has me. Soon he'll have his gym bag too.

It could be worse for him. I'm determined to make it better, to make myself better.

Three weeks and four days. A verbal scrap with a self-righteous idiot doesn't count as a lapse, I decide, at the same time as I tell myself that I mustn't let it happen again—that I must be more humble in future, even if provoked. Less combative, more . . . ordinary. Like the other school mums. Though less dull than them, I hope. Never the sort of person who would say, "A home isn't a home without a dog," or, "I don't know why I bother going to the gym—forty minutes on the treadmill and what do I do as soon as I get home? Raid the biscuit tin!"

As safe and honorable as those women, but more exciting. Is that possible?

I like to have it both ways; that's my whole problem, in a nutshell. ❧